Few Are Chosen
K'Barthan Trilogy: Part 1

Few Are Chosen was awarded 3rd place in the Teen category of the Wishing Shelf Independent Book Awards, 2011.

This book has also been awarded the Awesome Indies Seal of Approval, which means it's endorsed as an excellent read by a group of qualified, publishing industry professionals.

Here are some things other readers and reviewers have said about Few Are Chosen:

"Recommended, especially to fans of fantasy, but also to those who might usually avoid it" - http://bcfreviews.wordpress.com

"I found I was turning pages as fast as I could... there wasn't a single character that didn't engage me in some way" – http://gracekrispy.blogspot.com

"Once I got used to the tone and style of the dialogue, I really began to appreciate The Pan's self-depreciating humour and sharp wit, and how his cowardly nature allows him to look at events with a more detached view, enabling him to make rational, intelligent observations.

"Filled with a host of brilliant characters from various wonderfully weird races, none of the different personalities introduced fail to fascinate." – http://www.thebookbag.co.uk

"The Pan of Hamgee is one of my favourite characters of all time" – http://www.awesomeindies.net

The writing was clever, witty, wickedly good in places and the story kept me turning (clicking?) page after page when I should have gone to bed! The Pan is a wonderful character and one I look forward to reading more about. – http://www.amazon.co.uk – Ignite, top 500 reviewer

Few Are Chosen

K'Barthan Trilogy: Part 1

M T McGuire

HAMGEE
UNIVERSITY PRESS

First published in 2010 by
Hamgee University Press,
www.Hamgee.co.uk
This edition November, 2014

ISBN-978-1-907809-00-2

Written by M T McGuire
Designed and set by M T McGuire with advice from Robert Attwood
Published by Hamgee University Press
Cover design by A Trouble Halved
This copy printed by Lightning Source UK Ltd, Milton Keynes

M T McGuire is 46 years old but still checks inside unfamiliar wardrobes for a gateway to Narnia. Boringly, she's not found any.

For
Sharon Henson and Hamdi al-Menshawy
who left the party way too early.
Gone but never forgotten.

Thank you for buying this book.
If you enjoyed it you can keep up with
news of the author online by
visiting www.hamgee.co.uk

You can also sign up for the
M T McGuire mailing list by
e-mailing list@hamgee.co.uk
or buy Few Are Chosen merchandise at
www.zazzle.co.uk/drawnbyhand*

Chapter 1

For the first time in months, The Pan of Hamgee was about to spend a night indoors. Not any old indoors, either; this was a luxury apartment, in a luxury area. The Planes was the swankiest place to live in the entire city: central, near the financial quarter and full of the loaded gentry. Outside, a gale battered the trees and flung hailstones against the windows. Inside, The Pan relaxed a little further into the easy chair and smiled to himself, enjoying the rare sensation of being somewhere pleasant.

"Oh yes. The Hamgeean has finally arrived," he murmured drowsily. Yeh. Let's face it, it was about time.

The flat was warm, and as long as he was very, very careful to discharge his caretaking duties correctly, it was his for the duration. All he had to do was live there, keep the place clean and not break anything. The not breaking anything part worried him, but in theory, the rest should be easy. Surely he could cope with that.

He stretched and tipped his hat lower over his face. His eyes felt heavy and, as he let them close, he enjoyed the soft firelight and then, the feeling of drowsiness and warmth as he dozed. Such a luxury: he hadn't let his guard drop like this in months.

"Firelight ..." he thought and yawned. He had a small inkling there was something wrong but he was looking forward to his first night in a bed for two months and he was too tired to care.

The flames leapt and crackled, warming his feet, but the worrying feeling continued to nag him. An orange glow flickered across the walls and filled the room with an eerie light.

It was also filling the room with smoke.

"Pants!" shouted The Pan, leaping to his feet.

What had he done?

"No no no no noooo." All in all, it would have been a lovely fire if it wasn't for one small technicality. It was in the middle of the carpet.

By The Prophet, this was serious. He was supposed to be looking after the flat not wrecking it!

He stood looking about him, raking his hands through his hair as he tried to think. What had possessed him to leave the candle on the table? Idiot!

Despite his fear, part of him couldn't help being fascinated, in a dangerously detached manner, at the speed with which the flames were taking hold. Please don't let the rug be valuable.

No time to panic, stay calm. Breathe ... good. It was only one carpet. So long as nothing else got damaged, the flat's owner, Big Merv, would probably spare his life. What to do? Easy, smother the flames. Quickly, he folded the edges of the rug over the top of its burning centre, but he merely succeeded in igniting them, too.

By The Prophet's hair! What now? He cast about him with mounting panic. The window. He would carry it over there and hurl it out. No wait; it might melt and stick to him, charring his arms to a crisp or, worse, it might stick to the wall and set the whole building ablaze. Burning Big Merv's carpet was bad enough, torching his entire block was another matter entirely.

Right. There was only one thing for it. He would have to sacrifice his supper. Sole and chips would be fine on its own. He could live without the peas.

The Pan scuttled into the kitchen where the peas bubbled merrily away on the stove. It was a pity to waste them – he liked peas – but it was quicker than running a bowl of water, and he could put some more on once he'd put the fire out. The peas were easily replaced. The Pan, on the other hand, was not. However, he had a small chance of surviving another week if he could put out the flames NOW before they did any more damage.

He had already learned how well Big Merv's pans conducted heat, even the parts which weren't supposed to, so he put on the oven glove, grabbed the handle and went back into the sitting room. It was even smokier in there now. His eyes stung and he coughed as he blundered through the acrid fumes towards the fierce glow of the fire.

He tried to hold his breath and think of the moment when he'd doused the blaze with the water from the peas and the danger was past. He held the pan out and poured the contents deliberately onto the centre of the flames.

There was a sound. A loud sound. "Whump!"

Ah. That was wrong. A gust of boiling air lifted him bodily from the floor and hurled him into the kitchen.

Very wrong. He looked at the pan in his hand. He'd used the chips.

2

How could he be such a monumental cretin?

Trying not to cry, he shut the door and put on the extractor fan. There was nothing he could do about the sitting room now. It was better to keep the flames in there, stay where he was and try to save the rest of the flat. Which reminded him: he called the fire brigade. As he explained his predicament, another worrying thought occurred to him. He'd set fire to the carpet and then, instead of putting it out, he'd poured a couple of pints of boiling cooking oil over it. Big Merv was bound to think it he'd done it on purpose; nobody normal could be that stupid.

The Pan realised his future wasn't looking bleak, so much as short. Big Merv would kill him, horribly, most likely. He didn't want to die young, especially now, when he'd almost got it together.

Oh well. Back to life on the run.

"Trust me to screw it up," he said aloud.

Such a simple, straightforward assignment, and he had blundered on day one. He glanced at his watch. Where was the fire brigade, for Arnold's sake? His nerves couldn't stand waiting around for much longer. He had to be gone before Big Merv arrived.

He glanced out of the window. No sign yet.

"Come on ..."

How could one stupid wisecrack to a Grongolian police officer have brought him to this? How he wished he'd kept his giant gob closed. He'd be back in Hamgee or at university by now and his family – well, OK, he would probably never have managed to patch things up with his dad – his family would have been dysfunctional at best but at least he would have had one.

He'd messed it up again, but wallowing in self-pity wasn't going to help. Being sacked from Big Merv's organisation was terminal. The fire brigade would have to sort this out alone. He grabbed his hat and hurriedly put on his cloak. It was time to run away. He noticed that the grill was still on and without really thinking what he was doing, checked the sole.

"Done to perfection," he told himself and then put on his best mumsy voice. "This is the last meal you'll have for a few days so you'd better eat it." He called this self-parenting. In the absence of any real parents, he sometimes tried to imagine what they might have said, and say it for them. The accent didn't sound remotely like his mother but it made her imagined utterances that bit more believable.

"Yes," he agreed with himself – he did a much better impression of his father. "You'll need all the energy you can get."

3

He couldn't normally afford to eat a luxury item like sole, but he'd wanted to cook something healthy that morning so he'd got up very early in order to steal it fresh from the fish market.

"Yeh. It would be a pity to waste this after going to all that time and effort. I had to run for ages before that fishmonger gave up the chase."

Another sigh. He was too old to do this any more. Children had imaginary friends although, as an orphan, he supposed an imaginary family wasn't so strange.

"Except that you're nearly twenty-one now, a little old for imaginary anything, aren't you?"

Yes. Of course he was. Never mind. This was wasting time.

He scooped the fish onto a plate, drained the peas, turned off the stove and, glancing out at the driving rain, placed a second plate over the top of it. It would be a shame if it got waterlogged. A quick rummage in Big Merv's fridge and he found a plastic squeezy lemon. He would have preferred a real one but it would do. He stole it, along with a knife and fork, and grabbed his keys. Pausing by the mirrored oven door to give his reflection the bird – what a brain-dead twerk – he ran into the hall, plates in hand.

The fire brigade would turn up before long and so would Big Merv. They could take care of everything. If he played his cards right he would be on the other side of the world by that time, living under an assumed name. He left the door on the latch, so the fire brigade could get in if they arrived first, and ran outside.

A crowd was gathering.

"Not good," he muttered.

He ducked behind a parked burger van which was setting up, like some evil-smelling vulture in reverse, to churn out food for the spectators, and ran across the road through the sheeting rain. He had gone a couple of hundred yards before he dared turn round. One of the windows of the flat blew out. Flames poured into the night air, licking hungrily at the side of the building and the dry wooden sills of the windows on the floor above.

"Please no. Please not the whole block." He raked his free hand through his hair.

The Pan didn't make a habit of retrospection. Dwelling on the past didn't change anything, and he had enough to regret without continually reminding himself of each and every single thing he'd stuffed up. He turned his back on the carnage and walked away, into an uncertain future.

Chapter 2

Not far away, in the cellar of the Parrot and Screwdriver, an esteemed local hostelry which also happened to be The Pan of Hamgee's local, dark things were afoot. This was mainly because, despite the fact the cellar was thoroughly insulated to hide their current nefarious activity, the first of the pub's landladies, Gladys Parker, wouldn't let the second, Ada Maddox, turn on the lights.

"My eyes isn't what they was. If it ain't dark I won't see proper."

Every now and again there was a loud thump against the door and a harsh avian voice shouted, "Arse!"

Ada's pet parrot, Humbert, had belonged to her uncle. He was a sailor and Humbert swore like one. Such a delicate experiment was no place for a domestic pet, especially not one of Humbert's disposition. However, the reason for his exclusion was a complicated concept for a parrot to grasp, especially a parrot like Humbert when he didn't want to be where Ada wasn't.

In the dim gleam of a guttering candle the two old ladies were setting up something that looked like a gyroscope, only not. It was cobbled together from bits of a fully functioning original (which had met with an accident), a Biro, an old saucer and some of the red elastic bands the postman always left on the step.

"Are you sure this will work, dear?" asked Ada, her voice full of concern.

"Yer. Trev went down the Business Side and found some longer elastic bands." Ada wore a blank expression. "'S bigger parcels in business and more post," Gladys explained. "It'll wind longer, so's it'll get up more speed and run longer." She was busy with a small wooden propeller that had a hook in it, twisting it round and round. One end of the larger elastic band under discussion was attached to the hook; the other was attached to the central spindle of the wobbly home-made contraption. As Gladys wound the elastic band, Ada held the machine steady with one hand, while in her other hand was a tuning fork.

Finally, Gladys stopped twisting the elastic band.

"Are you ready, dear?" Ada asked.

"Yer. What's yer note?"

"G."

Gladys sniffed. "Should be an A."

"I know dear, but there's only one note's difference. I'm sure I can find an A."

"I hopes so. Does you have the jar?"

Ada checked that the jar of Gladys' homemade chutney was within reach, towards the edge of the only clear surface available for them to set up their apparatus; the lid of the freezer.

"I do."

A curt nod. "Hmph. You knows what'll happen to the chutney if we done it."

"Yes dear," said Ada, who was aware, or at least partly aware of what would happen to the chutney – partly, but not wholly – on the grounds that while she knew the chutney would disappear, neither she nor Gladys had a clue where it would actually go.

"I is going to count three."

"Right-ho, dear."

"THREE!" shouted Gladys, letting go of the propeller. Everything happened very quickly. By some miracle of science, the wobbly gyroscope began to spin with remarkable stability. Dim bolts of electrical charge flickered between the machine and the chutney jar. They gave off a green glow, while the machine itself hummed; a low bass hum. Ada bashed the tuning fork on the table, put it to her ear and sang:

"Laaaaa!"

Gladys grabbed a thing which looked a little like an upholstery needle and stuck it into the green flecks; moving it towards the jar. The note emanating from the machine changed. As the elastic band wound down, there was just time for the green flecks to turn blue before it ceased to spin.

The old ladies waited in silence. The chutney stayed where it was.

"Oh dear! I was so sure we had it that time," said Ada. Gladys and Ada had been paying regular visits to the cellar to work on their project for some time. They planned to make contraband equipment with which they could establish an escape programme for the blacklisted; a ticket to a new identity and a new life. A one-way ticket, of course, because they couldn't come back, but then, why would they want to? Where they were going, there was no blacklist and nobody was vermin. OK so some of them weren't exactly going to blend in, but there were other ex-K'Barthan residents waiting for them, ready to help. The original scheme had gone swimmingly for two years, until Ada had dropped a vital piece of equipment and Gladys' son Trev had trodden on it. With the last few years' purges, and the establishment by the government of a New Moral Order, the need for this sorely missed social service was more urgent than ever. The old ladies sought to re-establish it fast, without being discovered by the wrong people; the state or the Resistance, for instance.

Gladys and Ada would donate their services to the organisation they belonged to – the Underground – and anyone the old ladies considered worthy, who needed to be somewhere else; because they were allowed a little discretion. People like that nice lad with the hat, The Pan of Hamgee. He was a dear boy – so well brought up and polite, so considerate of his peers, so kind to domestic pets, and so clearly blacklisted by the state. How he was still alive, neither could imagine.

In the face of substantial failure, Gladys and Ada were on the brink of giving up on their plan and informing their colleagues in the Underground that they had failed; that the organisation must make do with only very occasionally transporting its people or qualifying others (nice young men, with hats, who were kind to parrots, for example) to safety, by using a far more dangerous means, one of the few – and therefore, eminently traceable – pieces of equipment designed for the purpose. It could be done without discovery, but the fugitives could only be transported in small numbers, by people with enough special training. No, not people, a person – Sir Robin Get, the last of the great Nimmists, the last hope of the nation – special training aside, nobody else seemed to be able to do it, nobody who was alive any more, anyway.

Sir Robin was, as Trev would put it, 'knocking on a bit' and Gladys and Ada were keen to get their disposable transport system up and running before he, or they 'pegged out' (Trev again). It had taken some hours to get the machine going, and several apparently successful attempts to set up the chutney jar had turned out to be failures, when, for all the hopeful signs, the chutney remained stubbornly in position. This latest attempt was no exception.

"That were the note." Gladys scratched her head. "We isn't doin' this wrong. I is sure."

The two regarded the jar thoughtfully. Always a chutney jar and always full, because that was the only thing in the Parrot and Screwdriver that gave a suitable reading for conversion – on Gladys and Ada's somewhat hit-and-miss machine, at any rate. Ada shook her head sadly.

"Oh dear. I don't understand it. Why won't it go?"

Gladys shrugged.

"'S gotta be an expla—expla—reason."

Ada picked up the jar and turned it over. Nope. Nothing. The chutney remained stolidly where it was, except the jar was different. She held it in front of the candle.

"Has it changed shape a little?" In the dim light it was difficult to be sure but, it seemed to have acquired a waist. No. Surely not. She handed it to Gladys who tried to take the lid off. It wouldn't turn.

"'S stuck." Gladys banged it on the side of the freezer and removed it without further trouble. She stuck her finger in the contents and licked it.

"'S not done the chutney no harm," she said, proffering the jar to her friend with a definite here's-the-bright-side ring to her tone. Ada stuck her finger in and tasted some. A fine kick there – a little more than usual, perhaps – or was that simply down to age?

"I think it might be a tad richer than before," she said.

Gladys put the jar down and they both looked at it for a moment.

"I is not surprised. We has been working on this jar a long time an' given it time for ageing. It's good for ageing, my pickle."

"So what are we doing wrong?"

Gladys sucked a breath in through her teeth. "I dunno. It's something blindin' obvious I reckons. Or we is missing a step."

There was a noise, small but growing louder and louder. Like the sound the water used to make running out of the bathtub upstairs in Ada and Gladys' flat, before Trev and his mate Stan the Plumber had ripped out the old stuff and replaced it with something better – a noise like soapy water gurgling and screeching through ancient, decrepit pipes. And a pop.

"Ooo!" said Ada.

"Yer," said Gladys.

The chutney had disappeared.

Something in Ada's mind floated to the surface, something from a science lesson at school all those years ago, about vacuums. Of course it had disappeared. It would probably have disappeared a long time before

8

now, she thought, if only they had taken off the lid.

"Should we try another?" she asked her friend.

Gladys looked grudgingly at the jars of chutney stacked behind them. Ada could sympathise. One jar was bad, but two ...

"Hmph. 'S a criminal waste of chutney." There was a long pause while Ada waited in understanding silence. "Yer, OK."

They repeated the process and breathlessly Ada watched as Gladys unscrewed the lid of the jar. Once again, the chutney disappeared. Gladys chuckled.

"Lorks! I reckons we is back in business!"

"You know, dear, I do believe we are!"

They looked across the dimly lit table at one another, a whole world opening up before them. This was no longer the end; it was the beginning: a new K'Barth; in waiting; in exile. The whole national ethos; religion, moral viewpoint, lifestyle, outlook and way of thinking – all of it could be preserved. And no-one had to die any more, or at least, not everyone.

Gladys folded her arms and gave a brief, satisfied nod.

"Good," she said.

Chapter 3

Twenty-four hours had passed since the fire, and to his great surprise The Pan was still at large. Perhaps his lack of status helped. Blacklisted, or otherwise, he could hardly be classed as a rebel, and was only a very small cog in the city's criminal machinery. Perhaps Big Merv had better things to be doing with his time.

No. Unlikely. Big Merv was a Swamp Thing. Swamp Things were the only creatures that could punch as hard as Grongles, but since they had led an uprising a few years before The Pan was born, there weren't many of them left. They were slow to anger, but once riled they were passionate and uncompromising, and even slower to forgive.

Nobody in their right mind would mess with a Swamp Thing, not even a mild-mannered one, and Big Merv wasn't the least mild-mannered. He didn't like people upsetting him, and torching his flat would make him about as upset as it was possible to be. Flat-sitting for The Big Thing, as they called him, was a weighty responsibility – almost as weighty as the lead they'd tie to The Pan's feet when they caught up with him, before they chucked him in the river.

He stood in the familiar surroundings of Turnadot Street, surveying the ramshackle – but spotlessly clean – facade of the Parrot and Screwdriver. In so far as The Pan had a home any more, it was here, and if he had any family these days it was the pub's proprietors, Ada, Gladys and Gladys' son, Trev.

It was an emotional moment and The Pan was there for several minutes, trying to remember every nuance of the stonework, every crooked window, so that he would always be able to picture it in his mind's eye, even if he never set eyes on it again.

What to do now?

He shrugged. There was nowhere to run. Big Merv had contacts everywhere. Sure, he could stay ahead of his pursuers for a while, but where would he go? Even if he escaped the confines of the city, they'd be bound to track him down sooner or later, if the Grongles didn't beat them to it. He had been blacklisted for four years and he was tired of running away. It was time to say farewell.

"Mmm," said The Pan to no-one in particular, "one last beer."

As he opened the door of the smoky saloon bar, he smiled. Ada was there, as usual, dressed in her standard attire: a maroon satin tent-like dress, seemingly constructed from several large parachutes, with similarly extensive swathes of maroon chiffon over the top. The Pan supposed there were legs under there somewhere but if there were, he'd never seen them. She glided, as if on air-ride suspension, with only the square toes of her buff Queen Mum-style court shoes ever visible. Ada was the Parrot's PR front. She appeared to be mistress of all she surveyed, but it was her sidekick, Gladys, who brewed the Parrot's famous own brand beer and was the one in charge.

Gladys was about five foot two with fluffy white hair. She habitually dressed in woolly tights and something made out of green and beige textured Terylene that could once, before many hard winters and boil washes, have been a dress. It went down to her knees and her spindly bow legs started at its edges, even though her ankles met in the middle. Her shoes were 'comfortable' – that is, lace-ups with a little circle of leather at the end of each lace. There was speculation as to whether the toe-caps were steel, but nobody dared provoke her enough to find out. The tights contained numerous wrinkles in each ankle and naturally, neither article was quite the right colour green to go with the other. This tout ensemble was topped with a very moth-eaten red cardigan, spattered liberally with a selection of authentic-looking brown stains. Even for a woman of her advanced years, her face was wrinkled. When she saw The Pan she grinned, revealing a set of teeth which, like Ada's, were all her own.

Together with Gladys' Trev, the two old ladies lived in a flat over the pub. Occasionally, when their mood or their finances required it, they would take in a lodger. There was no-one staying there right now and The Pan had been receiving clear signals that if he could scrape the cash together for the smallest peppercorn rent, the guest room was his for the duration.

Too late for that now. All the more reason to bid his friends a polite goodbye.

He was doing the right thing. It'd be a good double bluff too. Big Merv would expect him to take off, so the smartest course of action, for the next few days, at least, was to stay put and use the time to formulate a decent escape plan. Prospects of that were bleak but he had to try.

His stomach growled. He hadn't eaten anything since the sole he was cooking when he started the fire. Yes, that was a point. As a regular, Gladys and Ada occasionally gave him a round of sandwiches on the house.

Well, it was worth a go.

Chapter 4

Neither of the Parrot's septuagenarian landladies flinched when The Pan took his usual seat at the bar and – having taken off his cloak and hat and put them carefully on the seat beside him – produced one of those plastic squeezy lemons from his pocket and set it on a beer mat in front of him. Most of their customers were, at best, eccentric, but keeping the tone of the establishment low kept the Grongles and therefore the Resistance out, and that made for a quiet life. Ada and Gladys didn't like violence. If they had been forced to choose between either of the two warring parties they'd have plumped for the Grongles rather than the Resistance. At least you knew where you were with them, and while you had to give both sides drinks on the house, the Grongles, unlike the Resistance, were teetotal – much cheaper to entertain.

Both the Grongles and the Resistance had a habit of 'asking' for help, usually with information. You couldn't say no to either and live, but you could passively resist the Grongles until they got bored and went away, or you could deliberately misinform them, sure in the knowledge that they'd never double check, and that justice was on your side.

The Resistance were harder to deal with. They behaved almost as badly as the Grongles, and expected Gladys and Ada to betray their customers in the exact same way. They were the kind of zealots who checked up on people though, so Gladys and Ada had to research each set of circumstances thoroughly before they could misinform the Resistance in a realistic and credible way. This made the old ladies uncomfortable. Misleading the Grongles was a thoroughly laudable and commendable thing to do while, technically, misleading the Resistance was betraying their country – even if it was to save some poor innocent's neck.

Gladys and Ada didn't like betraying their country but they didn't like getting people killed either, so they contented themselves with entertaining the dregs of society. You knew where you were with the dregs of society, and they didn't go murdering each other in public and bleeding all over the Parrot's nice clean floors at the drop of a hat. They kept their affairs private and they didn't ask any awkward questions about Gladys and Ada's business either.

Ada served The Pan that evening.

"What will it be, dear?"

"I'll have a beer, please."

"Anything else, dear?"

While Ada pulled a pint, he consulted the contents of his wallet. Hmm, could he run to a packet of crisps? Yes, if he made the second pint a half.

"I'll have a packet of crisps as well."

"Would you like any particular flavour?"

Ah, the joy of simple decisions.

"Salt and vinegar."

Surrounded by the relative normality of the pub he began to feel better. It was easy to pretend the accident in Big Merv's flat hadn't happened and delude himself that there was safety in a crowd. Big Merv's henchmen could hardly barge in and kidnap him in front of everyone. Gladys and Ada wouldn't stand for that.

There was a sudden light pressure on his shoulder.

"Bum!" said a harsh, parroty voice in his ear.

Ah yes. Humbert. The eponymous Parrot that went with the Screwdriver. The Pan had forgotten about him when he ordered his packet of crisps.

"Hello, parrot."

Humbert belonged to Ada and was almost bald but – by some inexplicable victory of will power over the laws of aviation – still able to fly. The Pan, like all Ada's regulars, was wary of him and with good reason. If he had one feather left on each wing he would still have managed to get airborne somehow, The Pan reflected dourly, in order to relieve himself on people's heads. Though a parrot, he was every inch a gannet and zoned in on the plastic rustling sound as The Pan opened his bag of crisps. Humbert wouldn't leave The Pan alone now: not until he'd had his share.

The Pan fished out the biggest crisp and put it on a beer mat where Humbert slubbered and pecked at it voraciously.

"That's your lot, parrot, so make it last," he warned him. After a whole day and night without eating The Pan wasn't in the mood for sharing. However, going hungry was one thing; being hungry and covered in the kind of guano Humbert produced was a different, far more unpleasant, proposition. The parrot operated a peculiar brand of psychology and The Pan had long since learned the first rule of the pub – be kind to Ada's infernal pet and it wouldn't poo on your head. If he was very kind, it might even leave him alone completely.

"Wipe my conkers!" shouted Humbert.

"Mmm," said The Pan, raising one eyebrow at it. The parrot put its head on one side and stared back at him. Would it make a lunge for the other crisps? Gladys put some sandwiches in front of another customer. It squawked delightedly and started to sidle down the bar towards him, taking the mangled crisp with it.

Good.

Right. What next? Now that he was no longer working for Big Merv, The Pan had no way of earning money and therefore, no means to pay for food – or anything else for that matter. He was desperate, but not to the extent that he'd volunteer for the Resistance. He wondered if it was worth asking Gladys and Ada if they'd give him a job and let him work for food.

No. It would put them in danger because it would annoy Big Merv. He glanced over at Ada who was busy serving a hulking great bloke with a beard.

****

Unaware as she was of the rules of psychology, The Pan's touching display of affection towards her pet warmed what Ada called the 'cockles of her heart'.

What a nice young man, she thought. So thoughtful and considerate. Ada liked people who were kind to parrots, even if they were shady criminal people who'd nick anything that wasn't nailed down. Come to think of it, most of the Parrot and Screwdriver's regular clientele behaved like that. But the others were always aggressive and defensive when she challenged them, The Pan would merely tell her he wasn't a talented thief before apologising and handing back whatever he'd stolen.

Ada watched him from the other end of the bar as he ate his crisps. She had always assumed he wasn't entirely human. Hamgee was a rum place – she wouldn't have been surprised if there wasn't a touch of goblin in him somewhere. But he was so nice, polite, attractive even – in his own ordinary way – he had smiley eyes, a sense of humour, and a kindly disposition. He was smart. It was such a shame. He'd have made some lass a lovely husband.

Pity he was blacklisted, or at least, she suspected he was. It might be just a rumour or even an attempt on his part to hype himself up as an iron man who was best not trifled with. If he was a GBI – a Government Blacklisted Individual – he'd been alive an extraordinarily long time, because the state classed them as vermin. Those on the blacklist seldom made it past a couple of months, and he'd been a regular customer at the Parrot for at least a year.

She watched him patting his pockets one by one and wondered whether he was going to pull his usual stunt of pretending he had mislaid his non-existent cash.

He continued the ritual until it was clear he'd patted every available pocket and found them wanting. It turned out he was looking for the squeezy lemon which he finally noticed on the bar in front of him and placed back in his pocket.

She smiled when he caught her eye and held up his empty glass.

Chapter 5

As far as The Pan was concerned, formulating a viable escape plan was proving difficult, as in his heart of hearts he knew there wasn't one. Even so, he wasn't ready to give up yet and decided to try stimulating his brain with more alcohol. He ordered another drink, but this time a half, given his meagre funds. He smiled as Ada selected a glass and filled it from the special undiluted pump reserved for the Parrot's regular customers.

"Here you are, dear," she said, "will there be anything else?"

He shook his head and poured the beer into his empty pint glass.

"Some more crisps?" she asked. He would have given anything for another packet of crisps, but unfortunately, the one thing he didn't have was money.

"No thanks, I'll stick to liquid food." He felt at home here with Gladys, Ada and Their Trev. He liked them. They were kind and uncomplicated and they didn't ask questions. He caught sight of his face in the mirror behind the bar. No scars as yet. After working for Big Merv's organisation that was a surprise; he'd expected somebody to cut his head open sooner or later. He looked for any signs of fire damage. Hair? Check. Dark and tousled, it was standing up or out, depending whereabouts on his head it was situated. Nothing to do with the fire that one, it always looked like that. He liked his hair. He kept the sides and back shorter and the result was a spiky look, only naturally, without gel.

Eyebrows? Singed slightly. A smut on one cheek but otherwise, no apparent damage. As faces went, The Pan's wasn't bad: reasonable bone structure, straight nose – not too large – decent skin, expressive, attractive rather than out-and-out good looking, OK though.

Pity about the person behind it, who was a complete idiot. His assessing gaze turned into a glare of contempt. It wasn't so much that he was unhappy with his personality; he just wished it belonged to somebody else.

For what felt like the millionth time, he unzipped the mental baggage at the back of his mind and had a good rummage through it. Why couldn't he be less of a wazzock, on speaking terms with his father – not that there was anything he could do about that now – and good at something useful? Then he wouldn't be a GBI and he could have applied for a real job, instead of working for Big Merv as a minor minion in the city's biggest organised crime cartel.

He stopped looking at his reflection and turned his attention to his beer for a moment.

Further down the bar, Ada clucked about like a mother hen – a faded debutante in swathes of maroon chiffon, but a mother hen, nonetheless. She seemed convinced he needed somebody to look after him. When she next ducked through the door behind her, into the Holy of Holies where they kept the spare cutlery and did the washing up, Gladys glanced quickly in his direction and then followed her. They stood and spoke to one another privately for several minutes, but made the mistake of standing in front of the open door. He watched them carefully. His lip-reading skills were poor, but he could still work out the general gist of their conversation.

Chapter 6

"Don't you go wasting yer sympathy on that one, Ada Maddox," said Gladys, "it's incredible he's still alive. He won't be for much longer, that's for sure. Ain't you heard?"

"What, dear?" asked Ada, putting down her tray and heading back into the crowded bar.

"Big Merv's flats," said Gladys, following her out into the bar and back into the Holy of Holies again, with a second tray, like some wizened harbinger of doom. "The whole lot was consumed in a huge conflag—conflag—fire."

"I know. Wasn't it terrible?"

"Yer. You know who were s'posed to be looking after 'em?" She jerked her head in The Pan's direction.

"Was he?" Ada gazed over at the topic of their conversation, who was staring longingly at the crisp Humbert was still eating.

"Yer," said Gladys and without actually making any sound, mouthed the words, "set it on fire with the chip pan, by mistake."

"Oh bless him."

"Yer. If he ain't dead now he will be afore the week's out. You mark my words." Gladys patted the side of her nose with one finger and did her mouthing trick again. "He is a walking corpse."

They exchanged glances, acknowledging a shared thought, which Ada eventually put into words.

"Surely ...?" Ada began but Gladys shook her head. "We are going to help him, aren't we?" said Ada with a meaningful glance downwards at the floor, underneath which lay the cellar and their dark secret.

"Ner," said Gladys, letting her guard slip and allowing some emotion to creep into her voice. "Not if we don't want to get done in by Big Merv. 'S too dangerous."

They sighed in unison.

"He's only a boy, really," said Ada.

"Yer," said Gladys. "'S not right. 'S a crying shame." And she went off to wash some glasses.

****

19

The Pan reflected that news travels too fast in K'Barth.

Presently, Gladys and Ada re-appeared from the Holy of Holies. Gladys carried a large plate of cheese and pickle sandwiches, the bread sliced doorstep thick, which she handed solemnly to her friend. Ada handed them, with equal solemnity, to The Pan. Gladys hovered behind her. The pickle was Gladys' secret recipe and famous for its virulent heat. A small teaspoonful could reduce grown men to tears. The Pan was also famous, among the clientele of the Parrot, for his ability to eat it in large quantities without medical assistance. Ada supposed it was only to be expected. He was from Hamgee, after all, and they were odd down there – they ate squid, even the tentacles.

"Leftovers, dear," Ada said, even though he could see they were freshly made. "Waste not, want not. Be a pet and finish them up will you?"

"Yer," said Gladys. "'S my pickle."

"A gentleman ordered these an hour ago but when he tried them he found the flavour of the pickle a little overbearing," said Ada.

"Ah. I see, you mean, he couldn't make the cut?" asked The Pan.

"Yer, so you has to eat 'em," said Gladys wagging her finger at him. "An' don't you go leaving them crusts."

"No," said Ada. "We won't like it if you leave the crusts."

"Would I do such a thing?" He adopted a mock-serious expression and picked up the first sandwich. The bread was still warm and he was so hungry it was all he could do not to drool or stuff the entire thing into his mouth at once.

"Yer, you would," said Gladys, "you'd sell yer own grandmother an' all."

The Pan raised one eyebrow. It had taken him years of practice in front of the bathroom mirror to learn and it was one of the few things he considered he did well.

"Only if the price was right," he said pointedly, taking his first bite of sandwich from the crust side. Gladys clearly viewed this with approval even though it meant most of the filling spilled out the other way, onto the bar.

"Do you have a grandmother?" began Ada, bending the limits of protocol. These days, you didn't ask people about their relatives, not when the state tended to arrest them in the middle of the night and mislay them by the morning.

"I'm afraid I've already sold her," he said, taking another bite of sandwich. He was distressed to notice that neither of the old ladies laughed. They must genuinely want to know. He managed to look Ada in the eye for a couple of milliseconds. He didn't have much family – well he did, but they were officially Missing in Police Custody. In other words, they were in a labour camp somewhere, the salt mines, the ketchup farms or, most likely, dead. He gave the humorous approach one more try.

"Actually, I sold all my relations," he said.

"Don't be so crass, dear," retorted Ada.

"Yer," said Gladys.

"Mmm ..." He squinted at them thoughtfully and then turned his attention to the beer in his glass. He swilled it this way and that. "You really want to know, don't you?" He glanced fleetingly up at them again.

They nodded.

"Why?"

There was an uncomfortable silence between the three of them but the old ladies continued to watch him expectantly.

"Alright," he said slowly, "my guess is you're wondering where to send my personal effects, should I have the misfortune to run into Big Merv." Ada went puce with embarrassment.

"Put it like this, if they're still alive (and I hope they are) they'll be working very hard," a questioning glance from the old ladies, "they'll have joined the farming or mining communities."

Had the penny dropped?

No.

Arnold in the Skies, was he going to have to spell this out?

"You know, farming tomatoes or mining salt – as employees of the state, on a strictly non-voluntary basis."

Ah, now they'd caught up.

"There's no forwarding address," he added, "and if I were you, I wouldn't get involved."

The old ladies' expressions were a combination of embarrassment and sympathy that made him downright uncomfortable. He couldn't think of anything to say. They withdrew in tactful silence, leaving him alone with his thoughts.

Then somebody put a heavy hand on The Pan's shoulder.

Chapter 7

"Gotcha you little toerag."

Yikes! It was Frank the Knife (no relation to Mac) one of Big Merv's gang.

"Erk," said The Pan, putting his hand in his pocket.

He took a deep breath and his panic subsided. He might be a wazzock but he was smarter than Frank and when it came to running away he was world class.

Big Merv had often remarked on The Pan's mysterious ability to escape from the most dogged of pursuers and usually quipped about 'rear-view mirrors' or 'eyes in the back of his head'. Big Merv didn't know that The Pan literally did have eyes in the back of his head. They had grown, overnight, four years previously, when he was sixteen. He remembered it vividly because it had coincided with one of the Grongles' purges.

The Grongolian hordes had invaded K'Barth, imprisoned the Architrave – the K'Barthan ruler – and seized power years before The Pan was born, though officially the country had operated as an affiliated principality rather than a fully annexed state. This particular 'purge' was aimed at ending the K'Barthans' repeated attempts to establish home rule; or at least, a version of home rule which was different from that which the Grongles dictated. Anyone K'Barthan in a position of power was invited to 'retire' gracefully and those who didn't were tried for treason and imprisoned or executed. The religious leaders disappeared in one way or another. Even the ones toeing the Grongolian party line, who had merely been watched and harassed until then, were imprisoned. The High Priest, who fiercely resisted any attempts to force his retirement, was killed in his snurd in a freak 'accident' – although everyone thought that his demise was engineered by the Grongolian security forces. Then, as life began to settle down again, the Grongles finally got round to actually chopping off the Architrave's head.

He was probably the worst Architrave ever, little more than a puppet, but even so, he was K'Barth's spiritual and temporal leader, ordained by Arnold the Holy Prophet and chosen by the priests. Putting him to death was a special kind of sacrilege. It should have been a step too far, but most K'Barthans preferred to stay alive and stay silent rather than complain and end up ... well ... like the Architrave. And anyway, with all the indigenous leaders gone, who in K'Barth would be brave or stupid enough to start a rebellion?

As far as The Pan was concerned, growing an extra pair of eyes had merely been the culmination of a vexing fortnight. At the time he had assumed it was all part of growing up and being Hamgeean. Naturally, he was far too reticent to discuss the puberty thing with his family and before they had a chance to notice of their own accord, the Grongles had come and carted them away. Being able to see in two directions at once had given him vertigo to start with, but after a while he'd grown used to it and stopped giving it a second thought. By the time he'd got over his embarrassment he had realised he was unique. No-one noticed the extra eyes under his hair, but to be doubly sure he often wore a hat. He didn't want anyone to discover his secret in case he was branded a freak, or worse, in case it meant something.

"You're coming with me," Frank told him sternly. "Any funny business and you're history, got it?"

It was hard for The Pan to play it cool as, in his pocket, his fingers closed round the reassuring form of Big Merv's plastic, squeezy lemon.

Was it upright?

Yes.

Good. He flipped open the lid with his thumb and waited for the right moment. To annoy people like Frank the Knife went against every fibre of The Pan's being. He was a major coward, top scorer on the yellow-o-meter every time. However, the only thing that outweighed The Pan's cowardice was his overriding desire not to die – not yet at any rate. If he went with Frank, he would wind up at the bottom of the river

"OK. Let's go. An' I'm warning you. NO funny business," said Frank.

"Yep." He took a deep breath. It was now or never – and it wouldn't be funny.

In one swift movement he yanked the lemon from his pocket and squeezed the contents over his shoulder. A jet of acidic juice hit Frank the Knife in the eye, causing him to bellow in pain and put one hand up to his face. The Pan felt his grip loosen, wriggled free and ran for the door.

****

23

"Oi!" shouted Smasher Harry, as the door caught him full in the face and The Pan leapt over his sprawling form and fled. He was supposed to be lying in wait outside to catch The Pan if he tried to escape.

"Stop him!" shouted Frank as they watched him accelerating up the street.

Smasher Harry whistled. "That kid can run."

"Yeh," said Frank. "Pity he's such a jerk. We could use him."

"Oi!" shouted Harry again, half-heartedly.

"Stop him!" shouted Frank into the silence.

"He stole my wallet," added Harry with a flash of inspiration. His voice echoed along the empty street, but the only answer was the sound of The Pan's receding footsteps. Never mind, they'd catch up with him before long. Finding the slippery little wretch wasn't so hard – it was nabbing him that was tricky.

Frank's leather trench coat creaked as he shrugged his shoulders.

"Pint?" he asked, holding the door open.

"Yer, don't mind if I do. It's a damp old night," said Harry. He'd been standing out in the rain for ten minutes and he was soaked, despite the new mac he was wearing. He wished he'd worn his leather coat like Frank's, but he'd seen the mac and felt like a change. He would have to find the hawker he bought it from and smash his face in. It was supposed to be waterproof. However, clearly this was only true if the water and the mac were in different countries. There was Frank, dry and snug and here was he, sodden. Git.

In the distance there was a strangled yelp and a noise. *Shadadadumph,* it went. Frank and Harry stopped and turned round. They had thumped enough people to know the sound of an unconscious body hitting the pavement when they heard it.

"You think the security forces have got him?" asked Frank sheepishly. Neither he nor Harry had any time for The Pan; they thought Big Merv should have dumped him in the river ages ago. All the same, being dumped in the river by the security forces was a different matter entirely. The Pan was a criminal like them; they were of one kind, they were family. Sure it was a psychotic, dysfunctional family and its members would die rather than spend time together – actually, they would die *if* they spent time together – but they were a family, nonetheless.

"Dunno," said Harry.

The two of them waited to see what would happen. At the far end of the narrow street a figure appeared, silhouetted against the glare cast by the one and only street light. They watched it approach.

It was about six foot three and built like a truck, or at the least, like someone who worked out a lot – in this case, judging by the size of it, probably all day – only, unusually for the muscle-bound, it had a neck. Its extensive physique was partly concealed by the kind of expensive made-to-measure pinstriped suit which accentuated the contrast between the broad – very broad – shoulders and the slimmer waist. The result made it seem big and imposing without looking lumpy. Punching it would be like hitting an anvil, pointless and painful. On its feet it wore leather boots with zips at the side, and over the top of its suit, the ubiquitous leather trench coat like Frank's, though these items, too, were clearly handmade. It wore a trilby hat because it had a pair of antennae which, even in K'Barth, was too memorable an attribute for a member of the underworld to sport openly. It didn't have any hair, except for its eyelashes and eyebrows; it was orange and clammy-looking and clearly in the mood to thump someone. It was Harry and Frank's boss, Big Merv. The antennae and clammy skin were usual attributes for a Swamp Thing, the orange colouring was not. Swamp Things are green, but this is not something the wise mentioned to Big Merv, since he was unusually sensitive about the fact. Harry and Frank couldn't help noticing the bulky object he was carrying slung over one shoulder.

Chapter 8

"Arnold's Y-fronts! Can't I trust you bungling idiots to do anything on yer own?" growled Big Merv the minute he was close enough to Frank and Harry to be heard. "You great pair of spanners."

He dropped The Pan on the ground in front of them and turned him onto his back with one foot. Big Merv had punched him hard and he was already showing the first signs of what was going to be a spectacularly black eye.

"Well?" he demanded. "What d'he do, thump you and make a run for it?"

Frank cleared his throat.

"Nah," he said emphatically. "He squirted lemon juice in my eye and made a run for it, while Harry was out here dozing instead of actin' back up."

"I weren't. It were dark and he's bleedin' quick."

Big Merv nodded and prodded The Pan's limp form with his other foot. There was no reaction. He was still out cold.

"He's not so bleedin' quick now is he? Arnold above! What did I do to deserve a pair of spanners like you two?" Frank and Harry shifted mutely from one foot to another. "Well?" asked Big Merv. "What you waiting for, the police? Pick him up and let's get moving."

"OK boss," said Frank. "Go on then," he said, nudging Harry who, grumbling and muttering, yanked their captive up by the arms and slung him over one shoulder. He was heavy, for a wimp, and Harry was annoyed; he was gasping for a drink. Now they'd have to take this unconscious wazzock back to the warehouse. Never mind, maybe they would get to chuck him in the river this time. Harry liked chucking people in the river; it was a rare treat.

****

Big Merv took off his hat and wiped his forehead with a handkerchief. His antennae wiggled in annoyance. Frank and Harry irritated him to distraction. It hadn't always been like that. Back in the good old days, he, Frank, Harry and their driver Hal, had been bank robbers together. Their gang, the Mervinettes, had stuck exclusively to branches of Grongolian banks and came to enjoy the status of folk heroes. When it came to bank robberies you couldn't get more solid or reliable than Frank and Harry, but in these lean times, when bank robbery was no longer an option, he found they had depressingly little upstairs when it came to the niceties of organising organised crime.

"Where d'you park?"

Harry nodded to a nearby alley where the pristine paintwork of Big Merv's midnight blue MK II snurd caught the light.

"Right," he said. "Let's go." And he strode off down the street.

Chapter 9

In Ning Dang Po, the capital city of K'Barth, later on that same drizzly night, a group of shadowy figures huddled on a quay by the river Dang. If you'd noticed them, you might have thought trouble was afoot and on this particular evening, you wouldn't have been wrong.

The Pan of Hamgee stood shivering in the rain, trying not to contemplate his future. He looked up at the sky. The moon was obscured by low clouds from which a thin miasma of pathetic rain fell. It plopped steadily into the Dang and pattered on the umbrellas held by Big Merv, Frank the Knife and Smasher Harry. The Pan waited miserably in their midst trying not to think about the pins and needles in his feet and heaviness of his dripping clothes. He raised his bound hands and slicked his soaking hair from his face, wishing he'd remembered his hat when he'd fled from the Parrot and Screwdriver.

The silent warehouses of the docks towered into the night sky, refining the darkness and hemming him in. In a couple of hours this area would be bustling with people: dockers, office workers, forklift truck drivers, accountants, shipbuilders and sailors, all safe in their allotted roles within society.

They had jobs, families and at the end of each day, homes to go to. He could see them in his mind's eye, acting out their daily routine in the bright sunlight while he, an invisible outsider, rotted in the harbour below them. He tried to think positively but the mental image of his drowned corpse kept returning to haunt him.

"Shall I cut 'im?" asked Frank.

Arnold The Prophet – wasn't the concrete enough?

"Nah. Not yet," said Big Merv glaring at his prisoner with menacing intent.

The Pan of Hamgee tried to meet his eyes in a devil-may-care sort of fashion but he was shivering too much. He told himself that this was because he was soaked to the skin, not because he was absolutely petrified and definitely not because he was standing on the edge of a harbour, up to his knees in a box of quickly drying, quick-drying cement with the prospect of a short, vertical swim in the River Dang.

"You're a GBI," lectured Big Merv, "without me you'd survive a couple of weeks at the outside. You're nothing, d'you hear me? NOTHING. I take you off the streets, give you a job and a roof over your 'ead and how do you repay me?"

That was the trouble with upsetting underworld legends such as Big Merv, they got so wound up. The Pan stood silently in the concrete and watched his life flash across the backs of his closed eyelids. It took a depressingly short time. He had achieved so little. Now he was going to disappear swiftly, anonymously and without trace. No-one would mourn his passing. It was no good panicking, he told himself; death was a universal truth which could not be avoided. He failed to convince himself, and carried on with the trembling.

"Merv, please, can we talk about this?" he whimpered.

"'S nothing to talk about you insignificant little tart. And don't call him 'Merv' call him 'Sir'," shouted Smasher Harry, as he whacked The Pan across the backs of his knees with a pickaxe handle. His legs buckled and he sank backwards but Frank the Knife caught him by the scruff of the neck and yanked him upright. Big Merv held up one hand and Smasher Harry, pickaxe handle raised for a second swipe, waited.

"'Arry's right, what's to talk about, you little squirt?" he demanded. But, The Pan reasoned to himself, Big Merv must be prepared to talk or he wouldn't have stopped Smasher Harry from hitting him a second time.

There must have been a reason why Ning Dang Po's biggest underworld boss would take him under his wing. Big Merv had collared him trying to steal his wallet and instead of thumping the living daylights out of him, he'd offered him a job. Since he caught The Pan in the act, it was doubtful he appreciated his pickpocketing skills. It dawned on him that if he could only work out what Big Merv had seen in him, preferably within the next thirty seconds, he might be able to talk his way out of this. Otherwise he'd be too dead to care.

"Do you understand what you've done?" Big Merv asked him. "I owned five blocks of flats in this city and now, thanks to you, you snivelling little twonk, it's four."

"It was an accident—" began The Pan.

"Yeh?"

"YES. Please, you have to believe me. It was a mistake. The candle fell on the carpet. I tried to put it out but I couldn't see ... the smoke ... I threw the chips on it instead of the peas. I'll pay for the damage."

"How much?" The Pan cleared his throat. "Yeh. Thought so," said Big Merv without giving him time to answer. His eyes flickered sideways at Smasher Harry and the pickaxe handle made contact with a dull thud.

"Please—ooof! I can't pay you yet Mer—yowch!—Sir. I don't have any cash. I'm not solvent, but I promise I will pay you, soon," The Pan gibbered. "I mean it—I swear I will pay you the instant I get a job."

Big Merv raised his hand again and once more, Smasher Harry stopped. There was a short silence during which, The Pan assumed, he was appraising the chances of a Government Blacklisted Individual finding gainful employment. Not likely to happen. He would have to wait a long time for his money.

"Don't listen to him," sneered Frank the Knife who, doubtless didn't want all the efforts he had expended constructing a nice wooden box – dovetail joints those corners were – and mixing the concrete, to come to nothing.

"No, please do listen to me," begged The Pan, "try to see me as an investment. You let me go and when I'm a high-flying multi-million-earning businessman, I'll pay you back a hundred-fold. There's no point in killing me now. You won't even get the price of this box."

He glanced downwards at Frank's handiwork. You could make a tidy profit if you made it a lid, painted it and sold it on in the market but Frank was a henchman, not a craftsman, and putting his talents to legal use wouldn't occur to him.

"I have nothing worth selling," The Pan added with a shrug, "except my wheels." And the only reason he still had those was because he had been living in them for several months now. "They're all I have left." He put his hand in his pocket, which was difficult when it was so tightly tied to the other one, and pulled out a keyring with a bunch of keys on it. "Here ... take them," he said, miserably holding it aloft.

"You can keep 'em." That figured. Merv already owned a dark blue MK II snurd. It was the best of the best, the stuff of folklore when The Pan was a kid. Big Merv wasn't going to want a new set of wheels, especially not The Pan's. Dumb to offer. The silence lengthened and no-one said anything. Beside him, Frank and Harry waited, mutely, for orders. Big Merv stood looking at him, his antennae waving to and fro. Did that mean ...? Yep.

Thinking. Definitely. But was that good news? Maybe. He seemed to be weighing the situation carefully.

Chapter 10

Big Merv was indeed thinking, and his thoughts went like this.
Staff had a short shelf-life in the world of organised crime, and by rights
The Pan of Hamgee's should have been shorter than most. So, what Big
Merv couldn't understand was how somebody so perennially cack-handed
continued to evade capture. It had to be a rare talent; the burning question
was, could he use it? Deep in the dark recesses of his brain a tiny light came
on and the germ of an idea began to form.

The Pan was a smart cookie.

Too smart.

It was a waste to chuck a mind like that in the river – he was only a lad
and all – but you had to make sacrifices these days. It was hard enough
keeping one step ahead of the government without employing the kind of
person you constantly needed to outwit. Best drop the little toerag in the
Dang and get home. He tried to put the memories from his mind of the
glory days, before the Resistance had got a real hold, when he, Frank, Harry
and their driver, Hal, had been proper, respectable criminals and had earned
an honest living from bank robberies.

Chapter 11

Things were looking bleak for The Pan.

"Spare my life, please," he begged.

"No," said Big Merv, "you've had your chance and you blew it. Do you know how much your little caper has cost me?"

"I told you. It was a mistake. If it takes the rest of my life I'll pay you back."

"Then you'll have to pay up quick, you ain't got much life left."

"Please, you can't do this. You're honourable. You're a Swamp Thing." An abrupt silence fell.

"I'm what?" asked Big Merv quietly.

"You're a ..."

What The Pan had wanted to say was that Big Merv, as a Swamp Thing, belonged to a species which, as well as having a reputation for being brave and honourable, was somewhat depleted in numbers and was also regarded as unsophisticated and looked down upon in some metropolitan circles. And he wanted to tell Big Merv that as a Hamgeean, even a human one, so was he. Then there was Big Merv's colour. Swamp Things are bright green and clammy, with antennae and eyes that match their skin – felt tip green. Big Merv, though born of Swamp Thing parents and bestowed with green eyes, slime and antennae was, by some accident of genetics, orange instead of green. His unique complexion made many Swamp Things look down on him, too. An outcast, among a nation of outcasts. There had to be some common ground with a blacklisted Hamgeean even if it was only small.

Right now though, Big Merv was angry and his look suggested that one more word and he would wave Frank and Harry to one side and chuck The Pan in the Dang himself. Perhaps playing the species card wouldn't be very clever at this point.

"Please, you know I didn't mean to do it. I promise I won't let you down again, you know you can trust me. Give me one more chance!"

"No, if I let you go, you'll disappear before I can say 'short swim' which, you little git, is what you're about to have." He turned his back and began to walk away. That's the trouble with telling the truth, The Pan thought bitterly;

if it's too ludicrous people think you're taking the mickey. He felt his face turning a shade whiter.

"No, wait!" he wailed at Big Merv's receding form. "You can't, it hasn't hardened, I might escape." Smasher Harry and Frank the Knife lifted up the box and began to edge towards the side of the quay. "Merv! Please! Don't leave me! I can get you the money. I can get you the money!" he screamed. Merv turned and nodded at his colleagues who put the box down.

"Tell me how and make it quick, you plank," he said.

The Pan wiped what could have been rain or cold sweat (he wasn't sure) from his face with shaking hands. He was keenly aware he would only get one shot at this and he didn't want to mess it up.

"Don't you miss the times when you used to rob, you know, banks and things?"

Big Merv glared at him. This was brazen cheek and therefore, risky. What The Pan didn't know was that it was exactly how to get to Big Merv, which was why he was on the brink of losing his temper. The time had been when people were born knowing the name of Big Merv, and The Pan was one of them. The Big Thing and his gang had been the most famous bank robbers in K'Barth. Not that there was a shred of proof it was them, of course, but they denied it with a special type of gangster irony which was almost more believable than a straight admission. For Merv, being a loan shark and running protection rackets wasn't the same. It was like suddenly having to play the part of King John when you had been Robin Hood. Being a bank robber was dangerous, thrilling and more to the point, glamorous. Everyone wanted to hear the details afterwards – particularly, stunningly attractive females (but with gratifyingly relaxed morals about inter-species liaisons) who wouldn't ordinarily have looked at a green Swamp Thing twice, let alone an orange one.

Big Merv ached to return to the excitement and champagne lifestyle of his old existence. He hated the Grongles, hated the Resistance, but most of all, at this moment, he hated The Pan of Hamgee for highlighting his situation.

"Robbing the banks ain't the problem," sighed Merv.

The gang would still be in business if the Resistance hadn't nicked every decent getaway driver in K'Barth. Neither Merv, Frank nor Harry could handle a getaway vehicle well enough for robbery. Since the Grongolian hordes had set up a police state, the underworld had felt the squeeze like everyone else – especially in the market for contract killers or escape men. The Resistance snaffled them all, and if you trained one up, the Resistance snaffled him too.

"It ain't like old times," he said and Frank and Harry nodded.

"Nah," they said.

Once, a quick shoot-out would have taught the Resistance not to steal the talent from someone else's patch. Now, they were not an organisation Big Merv was equipped to confront. Those in the Resistance were hard, well-trained, fanatically devoted to their cause and best avoided by anyone who valued their life or their kneecaps.

Chapter 12

The Pan realised he had touched a raw nerve when Big Merv grabbed him by the collar, pulling him as close as his cemented ankles would allow, and glared into his eyes.

"You wanna know if I miss robbing banks?" he snarled, "whadda you think?" His breathing was shallow and his blood pressure almost visibly rising.

"Mmm. I think," The Pan swallowed hard, "that you probably do." He wondered if he should have played the species card after all. The way the conversation was going right now, it might have been safer.

"Yeh? Well you're wrong. I've outgrown all that," said Big Merv, but to The Pan the words sounded hollow. "I extort money, it's safer and I can guarantee my returns. And, officially, sonny, I ain't ever robbed no-one."

The Pan pressed on, "I understand and I appreciate what you say about extortion, but wouldn't robbing ..."

The bright green eyes burned with pent-up anger which was firmly directed at him. Ah. He started again.

"What I'm trying to say is, wouldn't ... not robbing banks—the way you used to—be more profitable?" Yes. That was better. "Wouldn't you get more cash for less expenditure? Then there's the status," said The Pan, warming to his theme. "It's no life for a criminal of your stature, standing on the edge of a nasty wet river at all hours of the day and night," he glanced upwards at the steadily descending drizzle, "and in all weathers, tipping people in. You'll probably catch pneumonia."

Big Merv let go of him and The Pan watched him carefully. His antennae tied themselves into a reef knot – a sign of intense concentration. Good. They drooped forwards a little, still knotted and untied themselves as he spoke.

"'S not the water, I like a bit of rain. Reminds me of home," he said wistfully. "'S always warm in the swamp though." The antennae waved back and forth. He looked cold and miserable and ready to concede that The Pan was right. There was silence.

Please, please, Arnold let him give me a chance, thought The Pan. Big

Merv's antennae continued to knot and unknot themselves.

"Fair enough, son," he said eventually. "I reckon you've proved you're smart. So ... if you've got somethin' to say, 's about time you said it."

The Pan took a deep breath.

"OK. Not to imply that you ever did, or would but ... what if you wanted to start robbing banks again?" Merv raised his arm. "Please, don't hit me, yet." To his relief, Big Merv demurred. "Look, purely hypothetically—"

"Hypo what?"

"I mean, just for the sake of argument," said The Pan swiftly, "say you wanted to rob a bank. What's to stop you?"

"Don't gimme that cobblers." Big Merv grabbed him by the collar again and put his face so close their noses were almost touching, "You know why, you tart. The same reason no-one else does." His antennae straightened themselves, pointing upwards – a bad sign. He was losing patience. Time to hurry this up.

"I would guess you need a getaway driver," said The Pan, surprising himself with the calmness of his voice.

"'S right."

"So why not me? I can drive. Spare my life now and I'll drive for the next five years; for free." He was painfully aware that his fear was making him speak faster and faster, that 'free' was not going to work and that rather than five years he had meant to say two. "Alright, not quite free, but all it will cost you is the rent on a room for me," he gabbled. "And a small allowance for food. You'll recoup the cost of the flats in weeks."

Having made his case, The Pan shut his eyes and waited for the icy embrace of the river.

It didn't come. Big Merv didn't snatch the pickaxe handle from Harry and hit him either. He merely relinquished his grip on his collar, looked him up and down and scratched his head.

A deathly hush fell.

Only the hissing of the rain as it landed in the harbour broke the silence. The Pan prayed that Merv was thinking about what he had said rather than how loud a splash he could make by throwing a Hamgeean and a box of cement into a river. The moment seemed to stretch to interminable minutes, while nobody spoke. In the face of Big Merv's continuing silence The Pan feared that his time had, in all probability, come. There was a *splot* as he tried to kneel in the semi-hardened concrete.

36

"Please don't kill me," he begged wringing his tied hands, "please ..." He wondered whether he should go the whole hog and kiss Big Merv's shoes.

"Will you shut up, you toerag, I'm thinking," shouted Merv. "You might be a great wuss, but against my better judgement, I like your idea."

The Pan had hoped he might. Big Merv was ambitious, and being able to carry out successful bank robberies would boost his organisation's prestige as well as its coffers, giving it a powerful advantage over its competitors. Who knew, once he had accrued enough funds, he might even gain an edge over the Resistance.

"If we're gonna do this you can't tell no-one. Your identity as my driver will be your deepest, darkest secret."

The Pan nodded.

"Has to be that way, mate. To protect you from outside influences. It would be a pity if you grassed me up, now, wouldn't it?" A horrible sinister edge to the voice there which made The Pan shudder but at the same time, a suggestion Big Merv might be about to take the bait. If this was going to work, Big Merv would want his getaway driver to be somebody insignificant, and Arnold above, The Pan knew he fitted the bill.

It would also be handy if the driver was somebody who owed Big Merv and who could therefore be controlled.

The Pan knew he ticked that box, too.

In a nutshell, from Big Merv's point of view, the driver would have to be the kind of person nobody would suspect, somebody, well ... a bit spineless and irrelevant, frankly.

Excellent. Another box ticked, then.

The Pan was under no illusions about his personality, he'd always been a coward. But he knew he could drive, and being a getaway man was little more than glorified running. It wasn't the most attractive career option but it had to be better than the concrete alternative.

No worries about appearing genuine; he was trembling so much it was obvious he was scared. But now there was something in his heart besides the fear – hope. As long as his driving measured up to Big Merv's expectations, he might yet live to see another day. By the Holy Prophet, please let that be so.

"You're a class one tool-bit but you're bright and you're devilish hard to catch," said Merv with a brief glower in Frank and Harry's direction. "'S

37

down to whether you can handle a snurd like Hal, an' I'm gonna see if you can. You said you had wheels?"

The Pan nodded again.

"Good coz yer not goin' near mine. You've just bought yerself half an hour. Get him outta there." There was a squelch as Frank and Harry pulled The Pan out of the thickening concrete and unceremoniously dumped him on his feet, both of which had gone to sleep. Before he had a chance to fall over, Big Merv grabbed him by the lapels. "You're going to take us for a little drive," he said. "You'd better be able to back this up. Any monkey business and you'll go the same way in a few hours, only we'll make sure you suffer first, d'you get my drift?"

"Oh yes. Thank you," said The Pan as another attack of shivering came on. He coughed experimentally and, while Frank untied him, tried to ascertain if he had caught his death of cold or whether the shivering was merely due to abject fear.

Chapter 13

With freezing hands The Pan fumbled with his keyring. 'Snurd,' it said on it.

There was a button, which he pressed and after a few minutes a sound similar to a light aircraft engine drifted across the water. A small dot appeared in the dawn sky. Snurds do look like cars and they are used for getting around but that's where the similarity ends. They run on water for a start (the engine splits off the H2 and discards the O). In addition, this one had a revolving number plate, a submarine conversion option, machine guns behind its lights, wings and a number of other handy bolt-on extras. The wings and submarine conversion option were normal; the machine guns were legal so long as they only fired blanks (they didn't, but The Pan had never used them); the dodgy part was the revolving number plate, which had saved his life several times so far.

"Don't tell me a two-bit piece of plankton like you has a snurd with a homing button?" exclaimed Big Merv.

"Er, yes." He was proud of his snurd. It was running well; it was in good condition considering the price he paid, and it had been a bargain.

"Is this it?" asked Smasher Harry in disgust, as it dipped low over a row of derelict buildings opposite and landed in front of them. It was small, two-tone in shades of light and dark silver, and somewhere, in another version of the universe, it was a variant of a late nineteen sixties Lotus Elan. In K'Barth it was merely a Snurd SE2. "You're having us on. You can't outrun the Grongle police in that!"

"Yes I can," said The Pan as it folded its wings away. He hoped it hadn't heard. For a supposedly inanimate object it was surprisingly sensitive and easily upset.

"Don't make me laugh. It's a hairdresser's snurd. You won't last two minutes in it," said Frank.

"I'm a full-on GBI and I've lasted four years so far," replied The Pan smugly. "Surviving a police chase isn't about straight-line speed, it's about manoeuvrability and cornering," he winked, "and a bit of low cunning."

"Alright, don't push it, son," said Big Merv, "I hear you, you're a survivor. But I weren't born yesterday so I know that no-one lasts four years on the blacklist."

"I have," said The Pan.

"Lying little smecker," Frank muttered, while in all likelihood, Smasher Harry only allowed this piece of insubordination to go unpunished because he'd been forced to hand his pickaxe handle to Frank when Big Merv had handed him the second umbrella. Big Merv looked The Pan up and down.

"Yeh? I don't think so," he jabbed a finger at Harry and Frank. "You two, wait here. This ain't gonna take long. With any luck I'll be back soon enough for us to finish 'im off before it sets."

The snurd obligingly opened its doors and sank significantly as Big Merv climbed sullenly inside. His nickname did him justice; there wasn't much room once he had made himself comfortable and The Pan squeezed into the driver's seat as best he could.

"Where to?" he asked.

"Home for some dry togs," ordered Merv, "I'll show you. An' you can do it on the road, none of this airborne cobblers. We're not drawing attention to ourselves. Once I'm set, we'll go to a nice outta the way spot I know and you can show me what you're made of."

The Pan nodded, pressed the starter, and they bunny-hopped away into the night.

****

"I said we shoulda dumped him in the river," muttered Harry as he and Frank watched from under their umbrellas.

****

"Stop!" shouted Big Merv.

"No. No," begged The Pan. "Please, it hasn't warmed up yet." He hadn't warmed up yet either.

"Alright. Drive, you scab."

The Pan could tell Big Merv was uncomfortable – The Big Thing was famed for his dislike of travelling – but it seemed he'd also decided to give him a second chance and everybody knew that once Big Merv made a decision, he liked to bide his time while he saw it through.

It was early morning by this time, and following Merv's directions, The Pan drove through the gradually building rush-hour traffic without mishap

40

to the centre of the city. As they stopped at a set of traffic lights a police vehicle pulled up alongside them.

Not ideal at all.

"Don't look at them, keep your eyes on the road ahead," he said.

"What?" asked Merv menacingly.

Arnold's pants! He'd just said that out loud, hadn't he?

"Sorry, talking to myself."

"You'd better be you little squirt, coz no-one orders me around."

Sensing the hostile stares from the snurd next to him, The Pan kept his eyes glued fixedly to the lights in front but it was to no avail. Out of the corner of his eye he could see the Grongles in the patrol snurd talking earnestly to each other and breaking off occasionally to stare out of the window at him. He knew what that meant, they were running a check through their on-board computer. They must have seen him on a poster somewhere and recognised him.

Big Merv might be a bank robber but as a high-status gangster he would have bribed the right people and cultivated the right contacts to ensure his record remained spotlessly clean, even of the most innocuous traffic offence. On the other hand, The Pan's criminal record, or at least, the list of enquiries with which the police required his help, was long enough to dwarf War and Peace. It was all petty crime, usually stealing essential items like food, clothes, toothpaste or soap but unfortunately, that made no difference and what with being on the blacklist and still at large, the police wanted him quite badly. The officer in the passenger seat climbed out of his vehicle and walked over to the SE2.

"Oh marvellous," muttered The Pan, "here we go."

"Shut it, you spigot," growled Merv as the officer leaned down and knocked on the window.

Oh, didn't life suck?

With a resigned sigh, The Pan wound it down. Well, it wasn't as if things could get any worse.

Chapter 14

With his most contrite expression in place, The Pan looked up at the being towering over him which, like all Grongles, was green and about six foot six. It had red eyes, too, except that instead of round pupils they had slits in, like a cat's. In the hope of getting into his good books, The Pan addressed him in halting Grongolian. He thought he was going to be sick.

"Good morning, officer, how can I be of service?"

"I have reason to believe this snurd is stolen."

Oh dear. The Pan stared up at him. He felt his mouth drop open and closed it again.

"No, I paid for it myself."

Were it possible, the Grongle's attitude became even more hostile. Ah yes, he had dared to contradict the word of the law and he'd forgotten the 'Sir'. Bad start, that.

"When?" asked the Grongle.

"Five years ago," said The Pan. The Grongle laughed humourlessly.

"But your name was added to the government blacklist four years ago. Everything you own belongs to the state, including goods you purchased before you were allocated with your current status. You may have paid double for this heap of junk for all I care, but it doesn't change the law. This snurd is government property and your failure to surrender it to the proper authorities is theft."

The Pan wanted to argue but when he opened his mouth to speak, what actually came out was a small squeaking noise that sounded like a mouse being strangled.

"What was that, vermin?"

"Er ... nothing, officer, sir," replied The Pan, smiling ingratiatingly while trying, as subtly as possible, to engage first gear.

"Put your hands where I can see them."

To try and impress the officer The Pan clasped both hands round the wheel and looked up in his most innocent manner. The Grongle gave the impression he had never seen anyone so seedy. Probably true.

The Pan failed to disguise the way his gaze slid leftwards to check the colour of the traffic lights or his dismay when he noted they were still green, which in K'Barth is at the top and means stop.

"You have been brawling," said the Grongle, noticing the black eye Big Merv had given him. "Fighting is forbidden amongst natives."

"N-no ..." stammered The Pan, "I haven't been fighting, I walked into a door."

"Get out of the vehicle, please," said the Grongle, who had that special knack of making the word 'please' sound ruder than outright abuse. He leant down and stared past The Pan, into the passenger seat. Big Merv stared back. "Both of you," he added. He straightened up, returned to the squad snurd and leaned through the window to speak to his colleague.

The Pan glanced, nervously, at K'Barth's most celebrated ex-bank robber sitting next to him.

"Do what he says," glowered Big Merv. "The river'll still be there when he's finished." He nodded in the Grongle's direction and smiled unpleasantly. "If he don't take care of you first, I will."

"Do you really think that's a good idea?" asked The Pan. Big Merv fixed him with a steely glare causing him to wilt, visibly.

"What's the alternative?"

"I could drive off, um, fast."

"You think you're gonna get out of this?"

"Yes."

Merv guffawed mirthlessly at him.

"Yeh? Now that I would like to see."

"Just say the word." The Pan couldn't keep the smugness out of his voice. This was one of the few things he knew he could do.

Merv shook his head. "Don't make me laugh."

Very seriously The Pan said: "That wasn't my intention."

For all his cynicism, Merv must have noticed how confident The Pan was. Not only confident but calm. All the more striking in one whose default was a state of barely controlled panic.

"You're very cocky all of a sudden," he said, "you're either very good or very stupid. My vote's with stupid."

"You heard him. Four years," said The Pan. "I've been four years on the blacklist and I'm not dead. How d'you think I did that? Come to think of it, how many other people do you know who can say they've been blacklisted for four years?"

A shrug.

"'S a few."

"Really? Name one." Sarcasm? Probably going a bit far. The Pan glanced at the policeman. He seemed to be coming to the end of his conversation. No. Probably not going far enough. He had to hurry this up.

"You're too insignificant for 'em to care."

"Then how come I'm significant enough to blacklist?"

A pause, another shrug.

"OK. 'S a fair point."

For all his outward calm The Pan was close to panic. Big Merv was taking too long to make up his mind. Time to lay it on with a trowel, then.

The Grongle was still talking with his colleague in the patrol vehicle. Good. This would only take a moment. He took a deep breath.

"Listen, you can see I'm not popular with our rulers, but the thing is, after tonight you won't be either. If we hang about much longer they'll find out all about you and blacklist you too.

"Even if your record comes up clean, they'll do it because you're here with me. They'll take everything you own and then they'll put everyone you care for on the blacklist and if they don't kill them, they'll take everything they own, too. You spared my life and now, maybe, if we act fast enough, I can save yours. They haven't had a good look at you yet so they won't have confirmed your ID. It's me they're discussing. I've done this before, remember? Except that without you here I'd be running already. So, do we stay or go? It's your call, Big Merv, sir, but you have to make it, now."

The Grongle returned and leaned into the window again.

"Did I not ask you to get out of the vehicle?"

"Yes," said The Pan except it was more of a croak. Damn. He hated the way fear did that.

"Then I suggest you would be wise to do as you are told." A pause. "In your own time, K'Barthan scum." He reached for his gun.

Chapter 15

The Pan was allergic to guns, especially when they were being pointed at him, and he wasn't going to let anything, not even his fear of Big Merv, expose him to one. He took his foot off the clutch and burned away through the green light. As he saw the wall of traffic approaching from their left he swung the snurd violently round to the right and sped off up the street.

"What are you doing?" shouted Big Merv as a fleet of police snurds appeared from nowhere and began to pursue them. "We'll end up in the salt mines! Pull over!" But it was too late. Any capacity in The Pan for objective thought had been clouded by a single aim, escape. A road block loomed up ahead. It was approaching rapidly.

"Will you pull over NOW you little squirt?" shouted Merv who was approaching fury at escape velocity. The Pan ignored him and pressed a switch underneath the dash. It slid away, revealing the optional extras. He regarded the shiny buttons in front of him. There were a few seconds of awe-struck silence in the snurd. Big Merv knew a deluxe model when he saw one, however manky. What he didn't know, of course, was that most of the buttons were for show and not, strictly speaking, connected to anything.

Praying that his temperamental vehicle's wings would unfold, The Pan plumped for aviator mode. There was a whirring sound and a clunk as the mechanism engaged followed by a short whine, and silence.

Half wings.

Arnold's toe jam! This was going to be close. The pursuit vehicles would catch them in seconds.

He slammed on the brakes and pulled a hammer from under the seat.

"Would you ...?" he asked as the snurd's bonnet dipped and their speed slowed to a crawl.

Merv snatched it from him, wound down the window and hit the outside of the passenger door with a smack.

More whirring, a second clunk and the wings fully extended.

Phew.

"Metamorphosis is complete," said a husky female voice, in case they hadn't noticed the transformation. The Pan smiled to himself as they speeded up again. The on-board computer had what he considered to be the ultimate in sexy female voices; it was one of the things that had attracted him to this particular vehicle in the first place.

"Thank you," he told the snurd.

"What are you doing, you tool-bit?" shouted Big Merv. "It's a machine. It ain't alive."

"Sometimes I'm not so sure. Better to be safe than sorry, no?"

"No. You insane twonk! An' I dunno why you're even botherin' to get this rust bucket airborne. They're gonna blow us to pieces. Arnold! I wish I'd never agreed to this."

"A bit late now."

"Why, you cheeky little—"

Merv was thrown backwards into his seat as the snurd accelerated sharply towards the roadblock. Seconds before ploughing into the first police vehicle, The Pan pulled the wheel towards him, they left the ground and disappeared over the houses.

"Stop him!" came shouts from below and yet more police took off in hot pursuit.

"There are ..." he stopped to count them, "fifteen police snurds behind us," shouted Big Merv in incandescent rage. "Do something or I'll kill you."

"If you kill me, you'll die," replied The Pan, "so I suggest you shut up, sit tight and enjoy the ride."

Blimey! Where had that come from? Even the most favoured of Big Merv's henchmen wouldn't have dared to speak to him like that. The Pan had surprised himself, but chases like this were about the only times he felt anything approaching confidence. When it came to running away he was sure of his talent, calm and in control.

Yep. He wasn't going to be fazed by a little thing like telling the toughest, most short-tempered gangland boss in Ning Dang Po to shut up – not until afterwards, anyway. He'd clearly surprised Big Merv, too. So much so that he did as he was told.

As they flew out over the city the streets began to change from the wide, tree-lined avenues of the West End to the narrow winding streets of the East.

Ah yes, the Goojan Quarter, the oldest and most closely packed part of town and the escapee's paradise. The Pan put the snurd into a dive. As they flew, sideways, down one of its many three foot wide streets there was a loud clunk as one of the Grongle drivers misjudged the width of his vehicle and piloted it at high speed into the side of a grade one listed building. The Pan accelerated and they sped off. Big Merv had one hand over his eyes while the other, white knuckled, gripped the dash.

"Here. Take this," said The Pan opening the glove compartment and pulling out a plastic bag.

"Arnold's Y-fronts! Keep your hands on the wheel," shouted Big Merv, but to The Pan's amazement he also thanked him.

Twenty minutes later, after a series of stomach-churning evasive manoeuvres which had caused the other fourteen Grongle snurds to fly into walls, trees, bridges and in one memorable instance, the funnel of an ocean-going liner, there were a lot of dazed Grongolian policemen in Ning Dang Po and no sign of the silver snurd they had been chasing.

The Pan could see Frank and Harry waiting as he landed the SE2 gently on the quayside. He switched off the ignition, climbed, trembling, out of the driver's door, jumped over the bonnet and held the passenger door open for Big Merv. If it hadn't been an inanimate object the casual observer might have sworn that The Pan had only reached the other side of the snurd in one piece because it had ducked. He opened the passenger door with a flourish. Frank and Harry watched him expressionlessly, but gave him the impression that, in their view, his new-found confidence didn't bode well.

Big Merv climbed out. He hadn't used the plastic bag but he was pale and obviously feeling very queasy. During the escape, he had told The Pan that Hal had never driven like that, but since Hal would never have escaped from such a scenario, he would allow a bit of leeway. He staggered away from the snurd and perched himself on a nearby bollard. He was sweating and his legs were shaky.

"Never, in all my born days, have I been chauffeured like that," he said.

"You alright guv?" asked Frank.

"Yeh," he put one hand on Harry's shoulder. "You ain't gonna believe what just happened boys." He shook his head, "Arnold! I wouldn't believe it myself if I hadn't seen it with me own eyes."

"Do we waste 'im then?" asked Frank.

"You gotta be kidding. That snivelling, conniving, little nerk," he waved a hand in The Pan's general direction, "he's only gone and outrun fifteen police snurds from a standin' start."

There was a respectful silence. As a feat, it was unheard of. Neither Hal nor the other seasoned pros driving for the Resistance had ever done that. Big Merv chuckled to himself. "By The Prophet's pants, that was a gas! I'd laugh if I didn't feel so blummin' sick."

"Do we chuck him in the river, then?" asked Harry.

"No," said Big Merv emphatically (much to The Pan's relief), "we're sitting on a gold mine here boys. We're going back to our roots," he rubbed his hands together, "we're gonna rob banks. We'll need the MK II fitted with tinted glass."

"Uh?" said Harry, "how?"

"Go to Snurd and get 'em to effin' fit it, that's how."

"Nah, I meant how're we gonna rob banks?"

"Yeh," said Frank, "'s like you're thinkin' he's gonna drive."

"He is," beamed Merv, nodding in The Pan's direction, "Hal didn't 'ave nothin'on him."

A long silence fell while The Pan watched Harry and Frank stare from Big Merv to him and back, several times, in pained disbelief, clearly wondering how he could have achieved such a radical shift in outlook.

"But Hal were a good bloke," said Harry.

"Yeh," said Frank, "we liked Hal."

"And you'll like 'im," said Merv. An order, definitely.

"I get it," said Harry nervously, "you're joshing us, right?"

"No," said Big Merv firmly, "we rob, he drives."

"But he torched an entire block," said Frank.

"An' you can't trust him. He said he's been on the blacklist for four years," said Harry. "That's a lie for starters, innit? The whole world knows yer usual GBI makes three months at the outside."

"Yeh 'cept that bloke wot did a year," Frank chipped in, "an' that was only coz he was in the nuthouse for 'alf of it."

"He ain't lyin'," said Big Merv, "the Grongle who stopped us confirmed it."

"But he's yellower than a bowl of custard," said Frank.

"Too right, mate," said Merv proudly, "that's why he's so damn good."

"What about the concrete—" began Harry, with a mournful look at the box in which The Pan had originally been standing.

"Are you listening to me?" asked Big Merv, "I said we rob, he drives and if you don't like it, you can chuck yourselves in the effing river – or perhaps you'd like me to do it?"

Big Merv's tone of voice had acquired a dangerous edge and, huddled under their respective umbrellas, Frank and Harry ceased to put up any more argument. As The Pan watched them, they shifted uncomfortably from one foot to another and nodded.

"Yes Boss," they said.

"I want him and the MK II at my place tomorrow afternoon two o'clock sharp, with those tinted windows in place. Got it?"

"Yes Boss."

"Good," said Big Merv. The Pan couldn't help noticing that it was hardly tomorrow so much as today. The sun was up, rush hour was in full swing and the first dockers had already arrived at work. In half an hour or so the quay would be bustling with activity.

"I know what you're thinking," Big Merv wagged his finger at him, "you can run but we'll find you and next time I won't be so willing to listen." He jerked his thumb in the general direction of the river. "D'you get me?"

The Pan glanced down at the dried lumps of concrete sticking to his boots and trousers; he wasn't going through that again. Not at any price. He nodded.

"Well? Cat got your tongue? I said, d'you get me?"

"Mmm," said The Pan, hoping it would be enough. He was still shocked at the rapid turnaround in his fortunes.

"Good." Big Merv turned his attention back to Frank and Harry, "You've already seen 'e's a slippery little bleeder. Don't, I repeat, DON'T let him out of your sight."

"No Boss," they said.

When the other two made to go, Big Merv hesitated and The Pan hung back. All he wanted to do was give the whole lot of them the slip and run away, preferably to somewhere where he could have a hot bath.

"On second thoughts. He'll only go and escape," said Big Merv. "You," he pointed imperiously at The Pan, "come with me. I need a lift home."

"Yes Boss," said The Pan, hoping it was the right thing. He realised, with a shock, that he had finally found himself a job.

Chapter 16

Far away in a different, parallel version of the universe, Ruth Cochrane was sitting in the dark, underground. The train she was on was also sitting in the dark. It hadn't gone anywhere. Not for nearly an hour. Oh, the joys of living in London during a bombing campaign.

There was always a bombing campaign. Periodically the nutters behind the carnage changed, but the end result was the same. An outrage and some dead people followed by months of security alerts and delays on the tubes, as everyone became extra vigilant. Being extra vigilant entailed reporting every mildly suspicious-looking package to the police and of course, an increase in the numbers of suspicious-looking packages, mainly due to the removal of all the bins from the tube stations. Most security alerts centred around a half-eaten burger and an empty plastic cup in a paper bag.

It was boiling, too, of course. The carriages reached the same volcanic temperatures year round, but for Ruth, there was the added torture that because it was winter on the surface she was wearing a heavy woollen coat. She looked through her reflection in the glass at the darkness beyond. Against the black, dust-caked bricks of the side of the tunnel hung a series of cables. One was new, covered in shiny purple plastic. By the end of the year it would be furred up with black stuff like all the others. Still no movement. It was funny how the bombs tended to go off, and only abandoned lunches and misplaced briefcases were defused. Well ... no, that wasn't funny. First day. New job. Late in. Late out. Brilliant.

Never mind, there was a recession, and being an arts graduate, Ruth was lucky to have found a permanent job at all, let alone one which paid more than the minimum wage.

Nobody would have offered her the kind of work she sought without relevant experience and of course, without a job, experience was thin on the ground. For all her years of highbrow learning, she'd given up on a traineeship and taken a secretarial course. She feared she'd make a poor secretary – she was bad at taking orders – but a girl must eat. A girl must leave home at some point after leaving university, too. So there it was, a secretarial course, followed by a few months of shaky employment at a company belonging to a friend of her father's, and now she'd found a plum job; as a secretary, yes, but in arts PR. Alongside her secretarial duties, they were happy to train her as an executive. So, by giving up on her career she'd achieved the exact start she wanted. Result!

She turned her attention from the wall outside to her fellow passengers. The carriage was packed and about three seats along from hers she noticed an old man standing in the aisle. He sighed, wearily. A bunch of shopping bags were squished into the spaces around his knees. The usual turn-your-arms-out-sideways supermarket type of bags. There wasn't room to put them down and she bet his fingers had gone to sleep ages ago. He smiled at her – a twinkly smile – and winked, which was a little surprising. Perhaps? Yes, she really should.

"Excuse me," she said.

He ignored her, along with everyone else.

"Excuse me," she said again, a little louder. He and the five passengers jammed into the small space between the two of them all turned their heads towards her with questioning expressions. She ensured she'd made eye contact; it would be a pity if she ended up inadvertently offering her place to one of the others. "Would you like my seat?"

The rest of them shifted irritably. One tutted. Gits, thought Ruth. "At least let me take some of those bags."

The old man had white hair, bushy eyebrows, a hooked nose and as he flashed her another twinkly smile, a gold tooth caught the light.

"My, my! How very kind. But I doubt there's room to squeeze by."

"Oh no, it's fine," said the passenger who had tutted initially – a quintessentially London volte face. Most city dwellers wore a veneer of grumpiness but knew how to behave when pushed.

With a good deal of commotion the old boy shuffled sideways past the others and sat down. Almost immediately the train started with a jolt and Ruth nearly fell into his lap. She felt a little better, though. Late home, boiling, packed train but at least she'd done somebody a kindness.

The tube gradually emptied and surfaced in the suburbs. She was surprised when the old boy got off at Kilburn, too. He didn't look the type, too well-heeled. He had lots of bags and they had to be pretty heavy. What the heck? Lucy, her flat mate, was out so it wasn't as if being late home would make a difference. She ran and caught him up.

"Do you have to take those far?" she asked.

Not as it turned out. Amazingly, considering she'd never seen him before, the old man lived at the bottom of her street, in a two-bedroom ground floor flat in a red brick Victorian villa – much like her own. Except that it was his flat, of course, while hers was rented. He'd told her his name was Robin Get, 'like Stan, only without the z'.

"Stan who?"

"Saxophone player," he said.

"Oh yes, of course."

Who? She thought. And Robin Get? He had to be joking.

The old man, Robin Get, had offered Ruth a cup of tea and she'd felt churlish saying no so she'd stayed. She'd discovered he was retired – obvious – and that he had only recently moved into his flat – surprising. Ruth had always assumed people came to rest where they were when they were aged about 50 and stayed there. Perhaps he had downsized. He was also not Mr Get but Sir, Sir Robin Get.

"Who was that?" asked Lucy, her flatmate when she finally got in.

"Who?"

"You walked past the window with an old guy about an hour ago."

"I thought you were coming home late."

"I did." Oh yes. Ruth had forgotten about being stuck in the tunnel for an hour.

"He's one of our neighbours," she began to giggle, "you'll never guess what he's called."

"Ivor Biggun?"

"Ha, ha. Nearly as good. Robin Get. Sir Robin Get, no less. Do you think he's a retired banker? That would be funny."

"Not if he's living round here."

"No."

After that, both Ruth and Lucy kept bumping into the old man and took him under their wing. One or other of them – usually Ruth – would see him most days, on the way home from work, carry his shopping and – more often than not – accept his offer of a cup of tea.

"He's your boyfriend," Lucy told her one day.

They both chortled with laughter.

"Yeh right. He's about five hundred years old."

"I reckon he fancies you though."

"Cobblers!" said Ruth. Privately, she worried he might – presumably old people have amorous intentions too, and it's just the young who assume they don't. Who knew what went on in the secret world of the elderly? Hmm. Who wanted to? "I bet he fancies you, he's just using me to get to you."

"Shut up!" said Lucy. They giggled. Ruth thought Sir Robin would be a better bet than Lucy's current boyfriend whom she considered unspeakable, but forbore to say anything.

The old boy was harmless enough, she and Lucy decided, and remarkably switched on for someone of such advanced age. So they fell into a routine of looking out for him, checking he was OK, and in his own way, he, too, was doing the same for them.

Chapter 17

The Pan settled into his new job and rented the spare room above the bar in the Parrot and Screwdriver. The months passed and became a year.

Finding something he was good at suited The Pan. However, he would have preferred to pursue a legitimate career, as a chauffeur perhaps – or even better, a racing driver. He was beginning to enjoy the glamour of being talked about and yet, when he heard people lauding his exploits, it was frustrating not to be able to own up to them – especially to some of the girls. If only he drove a racing snurd, everyone would know it was him.

He was the one member of the anonymous Mervinettes who actually was anonymous. Everyone knew the identities of the other three, even if there was no evidence. Like any sensible crime lord Big Merv had a clean record and a series of watertight alibis, as did Harry and Frank. They denied any involvement in the sudden spate of robberies when asked. But everyone believed the Mervinettes were back in business because the snurd was a MK II and because, without openly admitting what they'd been doing, Harry, Frank and Big Merv let them.

Everybody was talking about the gang and speculating as to how Big Merv had managed to find a driver that good ahead of the Resistance.

The Pan would hardly have dared admit to himself, let alone to any of the other Mervinettes, that escaping from the best the Grongolian security forces could throw against him had been quite easy. He'd been interviewed about it by the Free K'Barthan Broadcasting Corporation, the unofficial, underground news provider for anyone in K'Barth who was sick of the Grongolian stations. Not as the driver, of course, even anonymously that would be suicide, but pretending to be a passer-by.

"What's your theory as to the Mervinettes' miraculous ability to escape?" the reporter had asked him.

"It's hardly miraculous, is it? They're being chased by drones following orders," he'd said, "and don't forget, each one of them is driving a set of Grongolian wheels, that is, just about the worst ever made, while the Mervinettes are in the best snurd money can buy! If the police want to actually catch our boys maybe they should send some smarter guards and give them snurds, then they might get somewhere."

The bloke had given him a disdainful look and told him he was disrespecting the Mervinettes, being uncharitable about their driver's skills, and unpatriotic.

That was the point when The Pan knew, for certain, he'd been an idiot. And too cocky by half.

He felt guilty about it now, even if it was true. The longer they sent drones the better. He shouldn't go telling them how to catch him, even in the underground press.

The police would never be issued snurds, though, so he was probably safe there. And the MK II was in a league of its own. The Pan was beginning to believe he might survive his five year tenure and live to do something else.

In fact, the Resistance was far more likely to catch him, as it was offering a bigger reward for him than the Grongles were for Big Merv, a fact which had initially caused tension in the gang.

Most anxious not to join the Resistance at any cost, The Pan had procured a disguise. When he went to collect the MK II from Merv's lock-up before each robbery he sprayed his hair and eyebrows white, donned a flat cap and tweed suit and stuck on a false moustache. To complete the picture he wore aviator sunglasses with brown tinted lenses which faded to clear at the bottom, and when his finances and Big Merv allowed he would puff on a fat cigar as he drove (though, after the robbery he was often compelled to hand the cigar over to Harry or Frank to finish off).

It was a pleasant enough routine. The robberies usually took place on a Wednesday afternoon every month or so – for the difficult ones, the planning process might take longer. That gave The Pan plenty of time to study the target bank, make maps and visit the site to familiarise himself with the surrounding area. The rest of the time was spent reading up on the latest gadgets for the MK II and liaising with the mechanics at Snurd to ensure it was properly prepared for its coming ordeal. He wore his disguise for all of these tasks but was especially careful at Snurd, having been there as himself, about his own wheels. With a vehicle as conspicuous as the MK II he didn't want to run the risk of anyone there making a connection.

Despite the relative ease with which they were escaping, there was usually damage to be patched up after each robbery before the next job. Big Merv was fastidious to the point of mania about his snurd and liked it to be at its best whenever it appeared in public.

When the robberies took place, The Pan was never allowed to touch the loot (Harry and Frank would have smashed his face in if he had) but anything left in the snurd afterwards was considered fair game.

"Help yerself, mate. Driver's perks," was how Big Merv had put it.

The Pan felt no guilt at keeping the dropped booty. Why should he, when it was all Grongolian? Big Merv was a better PR man than to upset the populace by stealing from K'Barthan-owned banks. It also helped that K'Barthan banks were legally obliged to pay lower interest rates on savings and charge higher interest on borrowing than Grongolian banks. Nobody liked that. Of course, Grongles were the only life forms who could open an account at a Grongolian bank. As Big Merv had said:

"If they wanted us to leave 'em alone they should've played fair, shouldn't they?" And The Pan agreed.

After each robbery he would check carefully under the seats. So far, he had acquired two gold rings, a diamond earring and a gold sovereign. Not much, but a start. He kept it carefully in a secret compartment behind one of the barrels in the cellar of the Parrot and Screwdriver. He planned to sell something soon to pay Gerry – the best mechanic at Snurd.

In The Pan's eyes Gerry was a bit of a prodigy, despite his lowly position as Work Experience Creature. Lucky that, since he was the only one whose services The Pan could afford to procure.

Gerry had agreed to restore the SE2 in his spare time, for a small fee, to the same standard as the MK II. It was to be his apprenticeship piece. The Pan wasn't going to be a Mervinette forever and if his identity was discovered he was going to need a premium-quality escape vehicle of his own, as there was no hope of 'borrowing' the MK II.

He wasn't a patient man and waiting until the restoration process was complete was taking all his self-control. Not that he had any choice, Gerry was doing him a great kindness taking it on. The Pan therefore drove the MK II as crazily as he could after each robbery to maximise the amount of loot which fell out of the bags. Not for his own sake, of course, but for Gerry's.

Chapter 18

One Wednesday afternoon, as the antics of the Mervinettes were beginning to become a little less newsworthy, they robbed not a Grongolian but a K'Barthan bank. Low interest rates aside, many well-to-do Grongles in the city had taken note of the Mervinettes' tactics and started to use the safety deposit facilities at K'Barthan banks for their belongings. At this particular bank, Big Merv had a man on the inside who knew which boxes belonged to whom and so, in a breathtaking PR coup, they removed every single Grongolian box and left the K'Barthan ones untouched. Having shaken off their pursuers relatively quickly, they were on their way to their secret hideout.

Behind the safety of the MK II's tinted windows Merv, Frank and Harry reviewed the day's haul as they drove. Most of it was gold and jewellery.

"Whatsis?" said Harry as he went through the bag he'd removed from one of the final boxes, "I thought you said this was all Grongle stuff?"

"Yeh. Should be," said Big Merv.

"Don't look like it to me." Harry passed it over to the front seat where Big Merv – who was a delicate traveller at the best of times, let alone when The Pan was driving – always sat. Big Merv rummaged around in the bag. Out of the corner of his eye The Pan watched his boss remove the items one by one. There was a small screw-top jar labelled 'prunes' in old lady copper plate handwriting, a metal thing not unlike a gyroscope and a small leather pouch which Merv didn't even bother to open.

"Nah, load of junk," he said. "Here, driver's perks," he told The Pan, "you have it."

The Pan reasoned that while it appeared to be old junk, it must be worth something to somebody or it wouldn't have been put into a safety deposit box, so he accepted Merv's uncharacteristic gift with alacrity. He became certain of its worth when he returned the snurd to Merv's lock-up on his own and had the opportunity to examine the contents of the bag more closely.

The pouch, which Merv had left unopened, contained a small leather case and a large signet ring. The ring was gold and inset with a huge ruby. It was old, truly old. It should have been in a museum. The gold was that special shade of yellow that says, 'I am more ancient than anything you will ever see, let alone be able to afford'. The Pan knew it must be worth more than enough to complete the restoration of his snurd and probably enough to pay for a small house on top. He wouldn't get that for it, of course – there is a ceiling on the worth of even the most precious stolen goods – but it would still fetch enough to finish the snurd.

For a moment he was tempted to keep it. It was big enough to be a bloke's ring – too big for The Pan – but despite its huge size it felt surprisingly natural to slip it onto his finger. He stuck his hand out and examined it thoughtfully.

Had it? Yes. It had shrunk to fit.

Interesting.

He spread his fingers apart and turned his hand upside down but the ring stayed where it was.

Weird ... and cool.

"Looking good," he said aloud. Yes. Jewellery, on a Hamgean man – not likely and yet, it suited. It was as if it belonged to him already, it felt so ... what was the word? Natural yes, that was it. Natural.

Yeh, right, to a man who had never worn jewellery in his life? One who came from a nation of men with a macho thing about adornment. No, he decided, he had standards to keep. Hamgean men were not comfortable with wearing jewellery – not even wedding rings. Anyway, a ruby that large was too striking and too unequivocally stolen to wear for some years.

"Pity," he said.

The leather case contained the strangest item of all. It was a sewing kit. There were some needles, a pair of scissors, a thimble and three bobbins, each of which held saffron thread of varying shades. Either Big Merv's contact had made a mistake and this box was the property of a priest or it was looted from the High Temple by one of the Grongles. He put the items back in the bag, along with a gold sovereign he found under the carpet in the back of the MK II. Then he locked all the doors, took its tailor-made dust sheet out of the boot and went round to the bonnet.

"I don't like this," The Pan said aloud.

The thought that he might have taken part in a theft from a priest made him feel uneasy. He was old fashioned like that. K'Barth had never had an official state religion as such, but the religious elders commanded more than respect – awe. They elected the national leader using, The Pan shrugged ... yeh, weird stuff and a dash of hocus-pocus.

It wasn't so much that religion and politics weren't mixed, more that religion was so ingrained in everyone that nobody noticed and, of course, it made politics easy.

The proper K'Barthan ruler, the Architrave, was neither a politician, nor a religious leader, nor born of a ruling dynasty. The Architrave was simply a person who had the right physical signs and there was only ever one at a time. Anyone, or any species, could be Architrave, from the richest person in the world, to a street urchin, Swamp Thing to Hamgeean.

The single religion, Nimmism, took its name from its founding prophet, Arnold of Nim. Everyone could believe in the eternal – and let's face it, blindingly obvious – truths of Arnold The Prophet, because it was easy. The single, central commandment of Arnold of Nim was that people should be decent to one another. There were eight books of prophecies and another seven books of handy hints on how to be decent to one another, but everyone knew that was all optional stuff.

"Do the decent thing and you are in the clover," as The Pan's dad had often put it.

The High Temple was in Ning Dang Po and good Nimmists were supposed to visit once a year, but since every town had a temple of its own, not everyone did. Worship comprised turning up for a service every once in a while, singing a few rousing songs, eating a large meal and going home full of wine and bonhomie. Most people liked it. The Nimmists priests were kindly men and women who were often excellent company and provided quality food and drink in suitable abundance. All they asked in return was a few pence in the collection tin and a pretence of listening while they tried to persuade their audience to treat each other with kindness.

For The Pan, as for many others, it had seemed a thoroughly sociable habit, especially when you didn't have to join. Openly practising Nimmism nowadays bore the penalty of beheading. Then again, there were so few distinguishing features (apart from the saffron coloured robes worn by the priests) that it was difficult to identify a Nimmist. You couldn't go to the temple any more, of course, but otherwise it was perfectly possible to be ardently religious and go around being fanatically decent to people without anyone noticing.

The Pan finished draping the dust sheet over the bonnet and unrolled it gradually along the roof to the back of the snurd. He took time and care.

He had never quite understood why the Grongles had sacked the High Temple and beheaded all the religious leaders, but assumed it was because they never had got the hang of being decent to each other, let alone others. Perhaps they thought that without a religion, the K'Barthans would cease to notice how horrible the Grongles were or start being equally horrible themselves. Whatever the reason, nothing much had changed; most people in K'Barth were still Nimmists; they just had to forego the songs and eat the meals in smaller groups at each other's houses.

He smiled to himself. Yeh. Passive non-cooperation, that was the K'Barthan way, unless you were a member of the Resistance. Every psychotic nutter in the country had joined them.

With the dust sheet in position he walked round, straightening the edges until he was satisfied that the MK II was suitably cocooned.

"One day ... one day ... I will have a real life. You are my passport out of here," he told it, patting its roof. "Sleep tight."

He shook his head in disbelief. What a spanner. Talking to a snurd and it wasn't even his.

"I talk to the trees and they put me away," he sang to himself as he turned out the lights. Remembering he was in disguise and that he had to walk as if he was suffering from mild arthritis, he stepped out into the street and closed and locked the door.

Chapter 19

The Pan left the lock-up, edged carefully along in the shadows to the end of the street and set off on his usual route home.

****

"That him?" asked a voice in the darkness, once it was convinced he was safely out of earshot.

"Yup?"

"That old duffer?"

"Yup."

"You've gotta be kidding. Denarghi must be out of his mind. What now then? Do we follow him?"

"Yup."

"Alright, then. You go first."

Two dark figures slipped out of their hiding place and set off in the direction The Pan had taken. Their quarry moved with surprising speed for an old man and by the time he reached the end of the street he was so far ahead they had to run a little way to catch up. They didn't want him getting away again. Denarghi had made it very plain how important it was that they followed this old gimmer home, tonight, and found out where he lived.

Chapter 20

Not far away.
    In another part of the city.

A darkened room.

On a desk, in the pool of light thrown by a single spotlight, a small machine sits spinning. It looks a little like one of those toy gyroscopes, only not. It is very similar to the one The Pan is carrying home.

A pair of hands clad in black suede gloves – with the rings on the outside – perform a complicated set of movements over the spinning dial. The needle flips from one end to the other and stops.

Somebody breathes out. Slowly. And then laughs. A soft, malevolent laugh which has nothing to do with anything being funny.

"A little more information and then ..." says a quiet voice. Yes. "Someone's life is about to become seriously unpleasant. How unfortunate for them."

Chapter 21

As usual, The Pan feared he was being followed and a quick glance at the road behind him confirmed that yes, he was, for the second consecutive night. He hefted the sack over his shoulder, and thanking The Prophet for equipping him with his handy set of extra eyes, prepared to take the scenic route. He doubled back a couple of times until he was sure he had lost the two burly gentlemen who had been shadowing him, then he went back to the Parrot. He entered the usual way, by going down a side alley, climbing up a drain pipe and wriggling in through the landing window. Even The Pan would have admitted this behaviour was a trifle paranoid, but it did save him having to explain why an elderly gentleman in a tweed suit arrived at the Parrot and went upstairs and a shifty young man wearing dark blue canvas jeans and a loud purple and green paisley shirt came down again.

Having to take such a meandering detour made him late and having to wash the white dye out of his hair and eyebrows made him later. Gladys and Ada were annoyed. The Pan cooked his own meals, but they always made supper for him on Wednesdays because on that day he routinely returned from 'work' a couple of hours after his accustomed time. Gladys and Ada knew The Pan worked for Big Merv but not, officially, what he actually did. Unofficially, however, they had a shrewd idea. If his habit of departing for work, in disguise, via a drainpipe, instead of using the door like anyone else hadn't given them a few clues, the fact his rent was discreetly paid, in cash, by one of Big Merv's henchmen probably had. Gladys berated him for missing her meticulously prepared evening meal by explaining, in graphic detail, just how good it had been. She was an excellent cook so he had no trouble believing her. She usually made fish pie on Wednesdays and he almost wished he'd been a little less wary about returning home unobserved.

"You ain't got no consideration for others," she told him, "breezing in here at all times of the day an' night. Serves you right if you gets yerself killed." All of them were aware that she didn't mean it.

"I'm sorry," he said humbly.

"So you should be, young man," said Ada tersely, "couldn't you have called and said you were going to be late?"

"Not really, no," he said, thinking of the size of the two men who'd followed him and what might have happened if he'd allowed them to catch up by stopping to make a phone call. Doubtless Smasher Harry, Frank the Knife or Big Merv would have made short work of the pair of them but The Pan knew his limitations. His talents lay in running away.

"Why not?" demanded Ada. "We worry."

"You shouldn't," he said, "I'm well protected."

"Yer?" Gladys' voice was full of disbelief, "how come?"

"I meant that I work for Big Merv."

"That was Gladys' point, dear," said Ada.

"But it means there is nothing to worry about, tonight I was just ..." he held his hands out, palms upwards and shrugged in a characteristically Hamgean fashion. The Pan, like all Hamgeans did a lot of his talking with his hands. "I was held up. You know I often work after hours and I can look after myself, not that I need to, Big Merv takes care of my safety."

"That's why we worry, dear," said Ada.

"Well that's why you shouldn't," he forced a confident smile. "I've been GBI since I was sixteen years old; five whole years, give or take a day or two. I'm not going to die for a while."

Gladys frowned at him in a way that suggested she didn't buy his attempt at being upbeat. He didn't bother to argue because he didn't buy it either. Once he'd moved into the Parrot's spare room, Gladys, Ada and Their Trev had quickly become his substitute family, but he had no illusions about his situation. He was blacklisted, immersed in the world of organised crime, and the one Grongle he had chosen to annoy, albeit a mere sergeant at the time, had since been promoted at astral speed and was now in a position to make life very dangerous for him. He was already living on borrowed time.

"We didn't eat your supper," said Ada, clearly satisfied that he was suitably contrite for being late.

"Ner," said Gladys, "it would have served you right if we had, mind."

"Exactly," said Ada, "but we kept it hot."

"Yer. It's in the oven. I done it special. It weren't fish pie neither. It were calamaries." Gladys pronounced the word very carefully as if it might bite.

"Squid?" asked The Pan, his eyes lighting up. Like all Hamgeeans, he was particularly fond of squid.

"Yer," said Gladys as she hefted a plate out of the oven and dumped it on the kitchen table, "'S disgusting! Eating the tentacles an' all. I dunno how you does it."

"It's very tasty and nutritious," he said, grinning, "you should try one. Here," he proffered a fork full of sucker-ridden tendrils at her and in absence of a positive reaction, ate them himself. By The Prophet it was good. "Done to perfection, are you sure you won't try one?"

"Very," said Ada.

"Suit yourself," he said, waving the fork, "all the more for me." He had a distinct impression Gladys and Ada wanted to speak to him about something else. Normally, at this point, they would head back to the bar. This evening they hovered uncertainly. Ada eventually broke the silence.

"You do realise, don't you, dear, that if you ever get into any trouble, we have contacts, Gladys and I?"

The Pan couldn't stop himself from doing a double take. He froze, knife and fork poised over his plate and as he stared at her, felt the colour drain from his face, not that there was much there. He seemed to have become paler recently. Lack of light, he presumed, from all the makeup he was having to wear.

"I hope you're not in the Resistance," he said coolly.

"Not the one you're thinking of, dear," she said.

Surely they hadn't betrayed him, he trusted them, he always had, and he knew he had good instincts. No-one behind him. He listened. Nothing but the usual burble of voices from the bar downstairs. He was ready to run if he had to but it would be a pity to leave that squid.

"Mmm," he put his knife and fork down, "then what are you talking about?" He made eye contact. It wasn't something he did often which was why, by doing so the right way, he could make people feel extremely awkward. Not awkward enough to tell him the truth, though, even if Ada blushed and looked away first.

"Nothing," she told him breezily. Yeh, right. He raised a quizzical eyebrow at her.

"Nothing?"

"Eat yer squid," said Gladys in exasperation, "Ada and I has to get back to the bar; Trev's on 'is own."

The Pan was puzzled. Whatever it was she had wanted to say, she'd chickened out. He had been so wrapped up in concealing his own secrets it had never occurred to him that Ada and Gladys might have any. They didn't strike him as the secretive type. Clearly, he'd misjudged them. Somehow, he would have to find out more.

Chapter 22

The next morning dawned bright and clear. The Pan donned his Mervinette disguise and sold the ring. Then he returned home to the Parrot to change – entering the usual way, up the drain pipe. Disguise jettisoned, he left, dressed as himself and took the money to Gerry the Work Experience

Creature at Snurd and they spent the morning discussing the finishing touches to be made to his own set of wheels. He returned to the Parrot at lunch time with a bunch of flowers he'd stolen for Gladys and Ada and went to his room.

He had slept little the previous night, but he had done a lot of thinking, partly about his enigmatic conversation with Ada and partly about the things he had been given by Big Merv. He opened the bag Harry had removed from the last safety deposit box and spread the contents across his bed. It was odd stuff. He opened the sewing kit. First he examined the scissors. The Pan knew good craftsmanship when he saw it. This was the best, which was only to be expected if his theory as to the previous owner's identity was correct. The Nimmists were never ones to stint when it came to commissioning works of art. In many respects the Nimmists were never ones to stint full stop. Perhaps that was where the K'Barthans had earned their reputation of being happy-go-lucky. The scissors were gold, intricately patterned and too distinctive to be sellable. On to the needles and bobbins then. The needles were newer, ordinary and therefore worth very little, the bobbins were as problematic as the scissors and the thimble ... the thimble. He held it up to the light and turned it over and over in his hands.

"Oh man," he said and whistled.

It had a border depicting tiny scenes that he recognised from his brief Nimmist education as episodes from the life of Arnold, The Prophet. It was beautiful, exquisite and would be even more impossible to sell than the scissors. He could have it melted down he supposed ... no he couldn't. Had he finished his education, he'd planned, against his father's wishes, to go to Art School. He would starve before he trashed anything so beautifully made.

"This is a serious piece of kit," he told himself.

Oooh. There was something stuffed into it. Interesting.

A piece of paper. He took it out and unfolded it. It was old and yellowed and covered in mathematical symbols. Adding up had never been The Pan's forte, let alone reading equations, and he wished he'd paid more attention in his maths classes at school. There were geometric drawings, too and he wondered what they were all for.

He folded up the paper but when he came to put it back in the thimble he noticed something very strange. A faint glow appeared to be coming from inside. He turned it over, puzzled. The top was made of the same gold as the sides but when he held it open-end up there was a small dot of light in the bottom as if he was looking towards the end of a tunnel. He held it up to his eye and almost dropped it in astonishment.

He could see through it, but the view was not his room. Instead he saw the sea bathed in sunlight, gulls circling and small ships dancing on the waves. The picture was so bewitchingly realistic he could almost feel the wind on his face. It made him intensely homesick. He thought about the seaside in Hamgee, about the bar where he and his brother had gone to hang around and chat up girls. He thought about his sister, who had usually spent her time warning the other girls about her brothers while allowing their friends to chat her up. She was the middle one of the three, his older brother was a regular Casanova. The Pan was not. There had been girlfriends but nothing like the numbers who had flocked around his big brother.

It wasn't that girls weren't attracted to him initially – the difficulties usually began when he spoke.

The Pan wanted a girl he could really talk to but most seemed to find his jokes offensive and anything more than small talk off-putting – and what with all the trouble he got into at school, they tended to regard him as a dangerous freak. He had hoped the problem would go away when he became an adult, but being blacklisted, he'd never had the chance to test the theory.

"It would probably help if you managed to grow up and actually become an adult," he told himself in his Virtual Father's voice.

"I am an adult."

"I was talking about mental maturity."

"OK, you have me there."

He didn't have the energy for a row with his Virtual Father right now and turned his mind to remembering happier days. As he did so, the view

68

through the thimble changed. When he thought about the bar he'd visited in his youth he saw it as he imagined it might be currently and when he thought about his other childhood haunts they also appeared as if in the present, bathed in warm evening sunlight.

"Hmm, showing me what I want to see are you? In that case ..."

He thought about his family but no matter how vividly he tried to imagine his parents or his brother and sister, the thimble produced nothing but a misty grey blur. Perhaps they were dead, or maybe it had been so long since he'd seen them that his subconscious mind – or whatever was feeding the images he could see in the bottom of the thimble – had forgotten what they looked like.

It was time for the pubs to open, so he experimented with a more immediate subject, the saloon bar of the Parrot and Screwdriver. To his surprise, in his thimble's faintly fish-eye view, none of the regular early evening clientele were there, only a group of Grongles. The inside of the thimble had seemed to be showing his dreams, it must be showing his fears now. He shoved the bag, the thimble and the rest of the strange items it contained in the bottom of the wardrobe and went downstairs.

Seven Grongles looked up sharply as a shifty young man in blue canvas jeans and a loud green and purple paisley silk shirt walked into the deserted bar. Apart from the Grongles it was empty, all other customers having wisely made their excuses and left. Even Humbert, Ada's foul-mouthed parrot, had been sensible enough to shut up. Any conversation the Grongles had been making died on their lips at the appearance of The Pan. For his part he was in shock. Grongles hardly ever came into the Parrot. He was suddenly afraid it might be all his fault and that while playing with the thimble he had inadvertently imagined them there.

"Ah," he said.

Chapter 23

The Grongles eyed The Pan coldly.

Here was a tricky dilemma. He was already in the room and to leave would look pointed and might cause them offence. Offending Grongles was never shrewd, especially if you were a government blacklisted person and you were trying not to draw attention to yourself.

However, staying would be foolish if the Grongles had decided they would like to spend their evening alone. He hesitated, trying to glance round the bar with an air of affected nonchalance. Humbert took off.

"Arnold's air biscuits!" he shouted, flying over to The Pan and sitting on his shoulder.

Oh great.

"Thanks Humbert. Now they'll think you belong to me," he said quietly.

Never mind. Too late now, he was going to have to order himself a drink, neck it and leave as quickly as possible.

"Evening gentlemen," he said casually and walked over to the bar. The only sound to break the silence was the clatter of his elastic-sided pointy boots as they made contact with the stone flagged floor. He was painfully conscious of the fact he was not in disguise as a tweedy old man but was appearing as himself, The Pan of Hamgee, in all his GBI glory.

"Alright mate?" asked Trev, giving him a reassuring wink. "What'll it be?"

Something fortifying, if only to help dull the pain of the parrot claws digging into his shoulder. Humbert was scared, too, and hanging on with surprising strength.

"A large brandy, please," squeaked The Pan, "a very large one."

Trev poured him a triple on the house and he stood at the bar, with his back to the Grongles, using his pair of extra eyes to watch them closely. He tried not to start shaking too obviously as one of them came and stood next to him. He recognised the voice at once when the Grongle said, "Good evening to you, vermin." It was the patrol Grongle who'd stopped The Pan and Big Merv when they were taking the test drive in his snurd.

"Good evening, sir," said The Pan.

Oh dear. It seemed the Grongle had recognised him and wanted to chat.

"Do I know you?" he asked. Bad that he had recognised The Pan but good that it appeared he couldn't remember where from.

"I don't think so, sir." By The Prophet's snot this was unlucky.

"No. I do know you."

"Begging your pardon," said The Pan, only too aware that he was about to contradict something larger and more prone to violence than he was, "but I don't believe we've had the pleasure." He held out his hand. "How do you do?"

The Grongle made no attempt to shake his hand and stared at him blankly.

"Your accent," he said, "are you Hamgeean?"

"No, no," said The Pan swiftly, "can't stand southerners. No sophistication. Do you know they eat squid? Even the tentacles? Disgusting they are."

The Grongle nodded.

"I used to be stationed in Hamgee. Personally, I like a bit of squid myself," he said, "as, I suspect, do you."

"Ner, not me, mate," said The Pan imitating the way Trev spoke, "I'm a pie and chips man meself."

"If that's so, vermin, I'm sure you won't mind my checking," retorted the Grongle, taking a static-powered hand-held computer from his pocket. Like most Grongles, his military-style haircut meant he couldn't charge his computer the usual way, by rubbing it in his hair. Instead, he rubbed it on a special patch of fur sewn onto his tunic for just this eventuality. He locked eyes with The Pan and stared at him while he powered up his electronic gizmo. It beeped to indicate it was charged and he flipped open the screen.

"Let us see, Hamgeean, five nine, early 20s, dark hair, blue eyes, shifty ..." he said typing rapidly at the tiny keyboard with his thumbs. "Status: GBI – your continued existence is treason," he glanced at The Pan. "No matter," he continued, closing his computer with an abrupt snap. "We are not here on your account. Two days ago a robbery took place in the city."

Didn't it just. The Pan adopted his most innocent expression.

"Really?" he asked. "How interesting."

"Some worthless artefacts were stolen which were of great sentimental value to the new Protector of Ning Dang Po, Lord Vernon."

71

The Pan could see, via his reflection in the mirror behind the bar, that he had lost any hint of colour.

"L—Lord Vernon," he stammered. "I thought the name of our auspicious Protector was Mergatroid."

"Protector Mergatroid met with an unfortunate accident."

"Ah," squeaked The Pan, nodding sagely. The Protector must have been in Lord Vernon's way, he reflected. People who got in Lord Vernon's way tended to meet with 'unfortunate accidents', except for The Pan who'd merely been blacklisted. Lord Vernon had only been Sergeant Vernon then, of course.

The Pan had been standing looking in a shop window in his home town when some hapless unfortunate came running down the street towards him, closely pursued by Sergeant Vernon.

It had been one of those side-stepping incidents. The fugitive sped past and The Pan had been momentarily distracted by the fact he was old and yet moving very fast for a man of that age. Then he had realised Sergeant Vernon was chasing the man and that he was standing directly in his path. Most anxious to avoid contact with any Grongle, most of all one with a reputation like Sergeant Vernon's, The Pan had stepped smartly to the left. So did Sergeant Vernon. The Pan had stepped quickly to the right and so had Sergeant Vernon. The Pan had made one final effort to avoid a collision, by stepping back to the left again but Sergeant Vernon had done the same thing and they had collided. The fleeing felon had escaped and Sergeant Vernon had got to his knees with lightning speed, clamped his hands round The Pan's throat and begun to squeeze hard. Sergeant Vernon wore black suede gloves, even in the height of summer, with a selection of rings on the outside.

"You are obstructing justice," he had said.

Unfortunately, although The Pan was a perennial coward, he never knew when to shut up.

"I don't think I am."

"Oh really?" said Sergeant Vernon, increasing the pressure on The Pan's neck, "how so?"

"Because I'd have to obstruct the Just to do that. You don't qualify."

In reply, Sergeant Vernon had squeezed his neck so hard he couldn't breathe. He remembered little else other than feeling the increasing pressure on his windpipe and listening to the voice of his father, which seemed to be coming from a long way away, pleading for his son's life.

The bruises had taken weeks to go down and his father had spent the subsequent evening lecturing him about the differences between being brave and being an idiot. The Pan would have plenty of opportunity to be brave when he became a man, he was told, always assuming, of course that he could avoid being an idiot long enough to allow himself to become one. Hardly a day passed, now, when he didn't wish he could wind back the clock, repeat the experience and this time, keep his big mouth shut.

Unlike every other Grongle in the world, Sergeant Vernon had grey eyes, and instead of slits they had circular pupils like a human. Something about those human eyes in a Grongle face, the tone of grey, the absence of any warmth or humanity, gave Sergeant Vernon a powerful stare – almost hypnotic.

The Pan shivered as he remembered how the sergeant had leaned towards him, subjecting him to the full power of his ice-eyed glare. He remembered how he had stared back into those eyes and felt as if they were drawing something out of him, in a very evil way; his essence, his being, his soul.

"Who are you?" Sergeant Vernon had asked and instead of making something up, The Pan, half-mesmerised and unable to stop himself, had told him his real name.

"As I was explaining to you, vermin," the Grongle at the bar continued, bringing The Pan's thoughts abruptly back to the present, "Lord Vernon wishes to have his belongings returned. One item has been discovered. A ruby ring. It was sold yesterday morning by an elderly man who has been seen in this establishment on several occasions. Bring him to me and I may forget to tell Lord Protector Vernon I have found The Pan of Hamgee. Think about it. You know where I am if you would like to talk." He went back to the table and sat down, leaving The Pan shaking and fearful at the bar.

Chapter 24

Lord Vernon. It couldn't be anyone else running the country could it? Oh no, it had to be him and it had to be his stuff sitting in a bag upstairs. Typical. While The Pan had to admit he'd had several lucky escapes over the years, he felt that on the whole, his luck sucked. Almost as mightily as his life, he thought miserably.

"Wossup?"

"Nothing you need to know about." Trev adopted a hurt expression. "Seriously, don't get involved."

Before Trev could utter a reply, one of the Grongles shouted: "You there! Barman! Another drink."

There was a slight kerfuffle as Ada and Gladys appeared from the Holy of Holies behind the bar and by-passed Trev.

"Just coming," called Ada cheerily, waving a full pitcher of orange juice in the air. Ada hurried over to the table with Gladys in hot pursuit and poured each of the Grongles a full glass.

"May I propose a toast, dears?" she asked them.

"If you must," said the patrol Grongle who'd recognised The Pan, gracelessly.

"To the people in charge," she said, and The Pan had a distinct impression that rather than the Grongles, she was referring to somebody else. "Cheers!"

"To us," said the Grongles, the irony of Ada's statement passing, unnoticed, over their heads as everyone downed their glasses.

There was a moment's silence and then, as one, they keeled over unconscious. Well, that answered a lot of questions. Gladys and Ada were clearly working against the government, but presumably not with the officially designated organisation. The Pan wondered whether they were part of a different, less well-known group or operating alone. Ada turned to him and smiled.

"Now that's what I call resistance," she said proudly.

"Yer," Gladys chipped in, "none of yer letting guns off an' bleedin' all over the place."

"Exactly," said Ada, "subtlety is our hallmark."

"If you call poisoning Grongles in groups of seven subtle," said The Pan drily, although his sense of relief was overwhelming and try as he might, he couldn't wipe the huge grin he was wearing off his face. "Who's going to clear that lot up?" he asked, "you can't just leave them there—although, I suppose I might be able to help." He wondered if he could call on the expertise of Frank or Harry in this situation or whether he'd have to busk it, relying on the snippets he'd picked up from their conversations about the art of what was known, in the trade, as 'cleaning' and 'waste disposal'.

"No need for your assistance, dear, they'll clear themselves up," said Ada.

"How?" asked The Pan. "You've poisoned them," he held his arms out sideways and then let them drop to his sides again. "They're dead."

"They ain't. We hasn't poisoned 'em!" exclaimed Gladys.

"Then how did you do it?" asked The Pan with interest, "whatever you did, it's strikingly effective."

Gladys tapped the side of her nose conspiratorially with one finger.

"Calvados," she said, "can't take their liquor. 'S only a few drops in it."

"Exactly," said Ada. "They won't remember a thing when they wake up. Which reminds me, they'll come round before long and when they do you should be upstairs, now run along." She picked up the brandy glass he had left on the bar and shooed him towards the door.

"Should I pack?" asked The Pan. "I mean, won't they ...?"

"No dear, if you leave the room now they won't remember they ever found you." The Pan allowed himself to be shoved unwillingly into the hall and stopped. Left to his own devices he'd have liked to have examined the Grongles' wallets or at the very least, relieved the one who had spoken to him of his static-powered hand-held computer.

"What about ... um well ... that personal organiser ... the search history, won't I ...?"

"Oh no dear, he'll never know he found you if we get Trev to clear the cache."

"You know, a bit of kit like that would come in handy, can I ...?"

Ada gasped.

"Stealing from an unconscious drunkard! Surely you have better morals than to take advantage of the socially disadvantaged?"

"Well, actually, no. I don't. That's why I'm still alive. Anyway, they're not drunkards are they, they're Grongles and aren't I the socially disadvantaged one? More to the point it's not self-inflicted—you knocked them out." Ada's expression was stern. "Oh go on ..." Her expression changed from stern to frosty. "Their small change then?"

"No! Honestly, dear, I'm shocked. That would be quite immoral."

Arnold's pants! Foiled! The Pan wondered if he should try another tack. Hmm, probably not. There was a certain tone of 'no' which, when used by either old lady, brooked no argument.

"Do hurry up, dear," Ada said. "It doesn't work so well the second time. I'll let you know when they're gone."

"Mmm," said The Pan thoughtfully, "perhaps then we should all have a chat."

"All in good time. Here," she shoved the half-finished glass of brandy into his hand, "you might want this. Now git." She pushed him towards the stairs, retreated back into the bar and slammed the door.

The Pan didn't need to be asked a third time. He did as he was told.

Chapter 25

Nothing was quite the same for The Pan after the Grongles visited the Parrot. So far, apart from the first terror-stricken night on the edge of the River Dang, being a Mervinette had felt like taking part in a light-hearted prank. Now the danger of the situation had begun to sink in. Especially once he realised the significance of the articles the gang had stolen. If the safety deposit box from which Big Merv had taken them really belonged to Lord Vernon he would be very annoyed; and if Lord Vernon was annoyed with them, the Mervinettes would be dead within the week.

When it was time to drive for the next robbery, The Pan's altered perception of his situation had begun to play on his nerves. He drove the MK II through the bustling city with a great sense of foreboding. It wasn't necessarily the prospect of another getaway which was filling him with such dread, it was the culmination of various events.

First, there were the two bulky gentlemen who had tried to follow him home and kept popping out of the woodwork whenever he went out dressed in Mervinette mode. It was easy enough to shake them off but it took him hours to go anywhere these days, because every route was scenic.

Second, there were the endless precautions he had to take to avoid being recognised by the Grongles, and the fact he had to spend most of his time disguised as an old man, when what he really wanted to be doing was going out and partying and ... well ... dating.

Third, he had no real friends because his GBI status and his secret Mervinetting activities meant that anyone he got close to would be highly likely to die, or worse, betray him. He was on nodding terms with most of the regulars at the Parrot, but there was nobody he could confide in, not even Gladys and Ada who were the closest thing he had to a family. The Pan wasn't the type to thrive on solitude. He tried to tell himself that in a few years it wouldn't matter, that he'd have done enough getaway driving to have repaid Big Merv for his block of flats tenfold, that he'd be rich enough to buy himself a new identity, join the real world and live a normal life. In the meantime, though, he feared he might go a bit too la-la for a life of normality before he got there.

He glanced at the formidable hulk sitting next to him. He was being a fool if he thought he'd ever escape. Big Merv was addicted to robbing banks. Unless the Resistance stopped monopolising all the getaway drivers he'd always find some way to force The Pan to continue his work. The only hope of escape was if the Grongles gave up on world domination and went back to Grongolia. Then the Resistance would just be another cartel and they wouldn't need all those drivers.

Some hope.

The Pan was tired and fed up and beginning to wonder if he could be bothered to pursue his twilight existence for another four years when the outcome was so unlikely to be in his favour. He kept asking himself if the type of future for which he was destined would be worth it. Unfortunately, his answer to this question was normally negative. That was what scared him more than anything. If he stopped caring about dying, the chances were, he would.

He slowed the MK II as they came to a pedestrian crossing and waved an attractive young woman across the road. Big Merv indicated his disapproval by shifting impatiently in his seat and drumming his fingers on the doorside arm rest. The Pan sighed and Big Merv gave him a sideways look.

"What's your problem, today, you tart?" he asked.

"Nothing," said The Pan.

"Nothing," said Merv flatly, "it had better be, because if there is something you should tell us, you'd better say it now. Nobody keeps secrets in my organisation."

By The Prophet. Did he know?

"I'm not keeping any secrets," said The Pan wearily. He thought about the strange objects hidden in the bottom of his wardrobe back at the Parrot, or more to the point, their reputed owner. If what the Grongles in the Parrot had said was true, he had a bag of things belonging to Lord Vernon in the cupboard in his rented room. The mere thought made beads of cold sweat appear on his forehead. Lord Vernon, himself, owned the stuff they had stolen. That was definitely something he should tell Big Merv but he also knew how Big Merv would react and he didn't think his nerves would take another evening stood in a box of concrete on the edge of the river Dang.

"What's up then?" said Big Merv, "you're sweating like a pig."

"I don't feel very well," said The Pan. It wasn't strictly a lie, although the nausea he felt was due to fear rather than ill health.

"Yeh. You look crap an' all. Whatever you've got, you'd better not give it to me or there'll be trouble."

"I'll be very careful not to," said The Pan making a great show of breathing in the other direction.

The robbery went without a hitch, despite all The Pan's fears, and the Grongolian police were even dopier and easier to shake off than usual. Maybe that was what aroused his suspicions. Glancing behind him he thought he caught sight of another snurd cutting swiftly through the traffic. It might be somebody in a hurry, he told himself. There was no reason for anyone to be following them, they had thrown off all their pursuers, but The Pan wanted to be sure. They were travelling through one of the newer parts of the city, which was built in a grid formation, so he turned swiftly down a side road and zigzagged onto a parallel street.

Behind him, in the distance, was a glint of light as a distant snurd pulled out of a similar side street and continued to follow them. It was black, with the same anonymous dark tinted windows as the MK II. The Pan pressed the button labelled 'wings', waited while the MK II transmogrified itself into aviator mode and took off. Almost a mile back, half concealed by the traffic in between them, he could make out the shape of the other snurd taking off, too. He increased his speed, flipped up another side street and landed again. He pressed the button to retract the MK II's wings and continued on his way. Behind him the other snurd mirrored his manoeuvre.

"The robbery's over. What are you doing?" demanded Big Merv.

"Trying to spill himself some loot," said Frank. The Pan sighed. He was used to Frank's digs. The two of them didn't get along. In fact he suspected that, left to his own devices, nothing would please Frank more than cutting his throat.

"We're being followed," he said.

Frank turned round in his seat and surveyed the road behind.

"I don't see nothing," he said.

"That's why you rob and I drive," muttered The Pan.

"What did you say? You little piece of—"

"Shut it!" warned Big Merv.

Frank and Harry fastened their seat belts – any chance of a chase and they knew the drill. They craned their heads through the back windows. The Pan waited while Big Merv scrutinised the view in his wing mirror. He was glad that his boss was suspicious, not to mention cautious, enough to check.

"What's it look like?"

"Black, low slung, fast. It's not a shape I'm familiar with."

"Nah," said Big Merv. "Me neither. Tinted windows though, like ours. If it ain't another gang, it must be Grongolian. Either way, I reckon it's bad news. Lose it."

Far away in another dimension of space and time the pursuing snurd was a 1955 Mercedes prototype, the Uhlenhaut, with gull-wing doors.

The MK II morphed back into aviator mode and doubled its speed in two stomach-lurching seconds, as The Pan floored the accelerator. He flew upwards, skimming the rooftops of the adjacent buildings and down into the next street in the opposite direction. Slowing up he checked his surroundings carefully.

Nothing there.

Surely it wasn't going to be this easy?

No.

The Pan shuddered. He hadn't lied to Big Merv, the shape of the black snurd was unfamiliar, but it did fit with rumours he had heard. The kinds of tales no getaway man would want to dwell on. Stories of desperate flights, of the finest drivers relentlessly pursued through the darkness of the night and downed in a boiling fireball. Stories of an invincible shape, a legend, a ghost, a mechanical banshee that came screaming out of nowhere to do its lethal work and disappeared as quickly. It was called the Interceptor and nobody was sure it existed but then hardly anyone who'd seen it had lived to describe their experience – certainly none of the people who had been chased. If the anonymous black snurd was the Interceptor, The Pan realised he and his colleagues were as good as dead and there was nothing he could do about it.

He decelerated to normal speed, landed among the rest of the terrestrial traffic and carried on as if he and the Mervinettes were a group of normal people going about their business.

They had gone almost a mile and there was still no sign of their pursuer.

"Have you got rid of it?" asked Big Merv.

Whoever was driving that black snurd had been very subtle and The Pan suspected it was still out there. He took his hands off the wheel to make a 'search me' gesture.

"I don't know," he said. "It's not like the others. He knows what he's doing."

They were driving along one of the main thoroughfares of the city and as usual, it was busy. The Pan was sick with nerves. If anything happened, the presence of other traffic gave him little room to manoeuvre and although he could remain inconspicuous more easily with other snurds around him, so could his pursuer. He turned into a side road and pulled onto a narrower, less frequented street one block over that ran parallel to the one they had been on.

They were going in the wrong direction and he would need to turn around, but he wanted to be doubly sure they had lost their tail before he did. Although he could see nothing, he had an instinctive belief they were still being followed. He had learned to trust his instincts but as yet for his fellow Mervinettes – especially Frank and Harry – trust was still a work in progress. They were getting restless; he was going to have to turn round soon or they were going to get irritated and Big Merv was going to vent his irritation on him the only way he knew how – physically. Big Merv never hit him hard, but he still didn't want to get thumped. If anyone was behind them he would have to draw them into the open by going so fast they had to concentrate on keeping up rather than concealing themselves. He accelerated, and as he did so the black snurd pulled out of a side ailey ahead of them, turned towards them and stopped in the middle of the street. The Pan screeched to a halt, engaging reverse. As the MK II's backing lights came on, a flotilla of police snurds pulled out from side roads and garages up and down the street, behind him, about forty of them.

"Arnold!" said Big Merv. "It's a trap."

"Mmm," said The Pan, selecting first gear.

Chapter 26

Inside the immaculate cockpit of the black snurd all was calm. The Interceptor was a prototype, a secret piece of Grongolian hardware, commissioned and built for the military. It had been in testing for over a year and when it eventually went into production a less sophisticated version would be used by the security forces. Higher spec models would be used by ministers, government officials and upper echelon ruling party members.

However, none of the production models – even the most lavish – would achieve the levels of sophistication present in this one.

Despite the chaos going on outside, little could be heard inside but the gentle thrumming of the engine and the breathing of the occupant. His suede-clad hands squeezed the steering wheel. As usual, he was wearing rings on the outside of his gloves. The jewels caught the light. The most recent acquisition, a huge, red ruby, particularly pleased him. He held his hand up and moved it this way and that. Centuries old, it glowed in the soft light, feeling heavy with the weight of tradition. He smiled to himself.

"First this ring and now the Mervinettes." He breathed a sigh of something approaching ecstasy and waved the hand with the ruby on it casually. "Two life goals in one week."

And then he laughed. A quiet, malicious laugh – with a touch of smugness – because nobody outran the Interceptor. A pair of cold, grey eyes stared through the windscreen at the MK II in the road ahead. No need for sunglasses to hide that distinctive colour in here. The blackened glass assured anonymity.

"Do you know me?" he asked them. "No. But soon you will learn who I am."

Chapter 27

Back in the MK II The Pan was so afraid that he was having to divert all his energies to not throwing up. The sensation of prickly heat hadn't gone away. Now he was certain the black snurd ahead of them was the Interceptor and for some loopy reason he had a very horrible suspicion that Lord Vernon himself was at the wheel. Whoever it was, he was clever. Maybe that was why. It was going to take more than driving skill or an unusual ability to see forwards and backwards at the same time to outrun this one; it was going to take intelligence; intelligence he was not a hundred per cent certain he possessed. It would also depend, a lot, on whether or not the snurd in his path was as lavishly equipped as the MK II. From the look of it, he feared it might be.

"You little scrote! You've set us up!" shouted Frank, and Big Merv glared at The Pan.

"Well? Is that what's got into you? Have you been disloyal to me?" His voice had an ominous tone and The Pan realised, with horror, that he was close to believing Frank.

"No, no, I promise," he whimpered.

"If you have, we're going to be paying a visit to the river later," Big Merv continued, "it'll be just like old times."

"N-no," stammered The Pan. "This isn't about us. It's something we stole."

"Have you been keeping information from me?" asked Big Merv.

The engine of the black snurd revved and with his foot on the clutch The Pan revved the MK II back.

"Yes," said The Pan distractedly before realising the gravity of his admission, "I mean no," he corrected himself quickly, "not on purpose." He turned to his boss who was glaring at him. The antennae were moving but only just, and they were standing up straight, which meant Big Merv was on the brink of blind rage. The Pan glanced down the street at the black snurd, which was still revving its engine aggressively and at the same time, sneaked a look behind at the ranks of police snurds blocking his retreat. This was not a good time for Big Merv to lose his rag, The Pan needed him to be able to listen, answer questions and more to the point think. Better make the explanation fast.

"Remember that stuff you gave me? The junk?"

"Yeh," said Merv, "we remember."

"It might have belonged to Lord Vernon," said The Pan. He said it quickly in order to lessen the impact.

"What?" bellowed Big Merv.

"Some Grongles came to the Parrot and they said it belonged to—"

"I heard you the first time, you twonk," shouted Big Merv. "Why in Arnold's name didn't you tell me?"

"I didn't think it mattered," lied The Pan, who'd spent several wakeful nights wondering how on earth he could bring the subject up and had chickened out.

"You're not here to think, I THINK, you drive. Anything, ANYTHING you hear, you tell me, right?"

"Yes," squeaked The Pan. The snurd ahead of them revved its engine again and he glanced nervously about him, checking his escape options.

"Can you get us out of this?" asked Big Merv.

"I don't know," said The Pan. He could feel himself going white, he was shivering with fright, cold sweat running down the side of his face. A big part of his job was appearing to be in control, in this instance it was vital. It would be testing enough coping with the chase, let alone if the gang lost their confidence and he had to contend with any backseat driving. He smiled, with what he hoped was a devil-may-care demeanour, rather than the rictus grimace that would more truly reflect the way he felt. "I'll give it my best shot."

"You'd better," said Big Merv, "an' if you don't, they won't catch you alive because I'll kill you myself. You get me?"

"Oh yes," muttered The Pan, "I get you."

He checked the MK II was still in gear and pressed the accelerator pedal as far down as it would go. As he did so, the driver of the black snurd in front of them did the same thing and they hurtled towards each other. The two snurds were on a collision course. The Pan moved the MK II left and the Interceptor moved right. He swung the MK II back to the right and the Interceptor moved left.

"What are you doing you great plank?" shouted Big Merv. "I said get us out, not take him out."

"Yes, that's what I'm trying to do. Unfortunately, he's trying to hit us."

It was Lord Vernon against him, it had to be. It was a replay of that whole sidestepping incident again, only on wheels. He abandoned any effort to avoid contact, selected aviator mode and carried on accelerating. The Interceptor was yards away now but The Pan was going fast enough to take off. Both snurds left the ground at the same time. As The Pan saw the front of his opponent's vehicle looming ahead, he moved the MK II sharply upwards and as the other snurd followed, he yanked the wheel downwards. The underside of the Interceptor filled the windscreen, blotting out the light, and there was a bump as it, too, moved lower and clipped the roof of Big Merv's snurd. The MK II hit the ground with a massive crash and bounced into the air.

"Mind my suspension you pillock!" shouted Big Merv angrily as they accelerated upwards.

"If you don't shut up the suspension's going to be the least of your worries," said The Pan, who was beginning to feel more in control, and therefore at liberty to be lippy, "this is going to be difficult enough."

The police snurds didn't follow, they were pursued solely by the black snurd and The Pan could only view this as a bad sign. It was the first piece of Grongolian technology he had seen which measured up to the MK II, more than measured up. The Pan couldn't match the acceleration of the Interceptor and after ten minutes it was as close as ever. After fifteen minutes it tried to ram them and it was only by jinking sharply to the right that The Pan was able to avoid contact. Instead of passing them and cutting them off, it hung back waiting for an opportunity to repeat the manoeuvre. Big Merv was scared and reacted the only way he knew how, by hiding his fear behind a facade of anger. The Pan could forgive him that – nobody was perfect – and on the few occasions it happened, he saw it as a bond, a tiny patch of common ground in the vast desert between them.

"I thought you could drive," Big Merv growled.

"I can and you know it," The Pan raised his hands and shrugged, "unfortunately, so can he."

"Keep your hands on the wheel you great pranny!"

"Then, keep your hair on," muttered The Pan, "you trust me to do this, remember?"

"Don't get arsey with me you wimp, just get us out of this," shouted Big Merv, "NOW!"

The Interceptor fired a snurd-to-snurd missile. The Pan wove in and out of lamp posts, buildings, chimneys and trees with the missile in hot pursuit until, finally, he managed to corner so sharply it continued onwards and exploded harmlessly against the side of a nearby office block. Having failed to obliterate its quarry the Interceptor reappeared and made another attempt to ram them. At last The Pan could see a way out, but it wasn't one Big Merv was going to like.

"I think I can lose him," he said, "but the MK II—"

"Just do it," shouted Big Merv, "and for Arnold's sake get a move on before you make me throw up, you spotty little Herbert. I have some pride, unlike you, so don't make me humiliate myself in front of the boys here because if I do, YOU will be valeting this vehicle from top to bottom. Got it?"

"Merv," began The Pan, wearily, oops too wearily, "sir," he added quickly, "you know my aim here is to keep us alive, not to make you ill. Concentrate on looking straight ahead, or the view out of the window or something. If it's that bad, there's always a plastic bag in the glove compartment."

Ahead of them was the financial district of Ning Dang Po, complete with skyscrapers. The Pan, hotly pursued by the Interceptor, skimmed over the parapet of the Quaarl Futures Building. He flew low over the roof garden full of resting traders in a selection of bizarre striped and coloured blazers, who scattered in all directions, flattening themselves to the green plastic lawn. As the MK II swooped over them and reached the parapet on the other side, The Pan yanked at the wheel. The bonnet dipped and the front bumper clipped the stonework with a loud thud. The impact flipped the MK II upside down and immediately, The Pan accelerated. As Big Merv's snurd had somersaulted its back bumper had hit the bottom of the Interceptor and thrown it forward causing the driver to lose control for a few precious seconds. Not long, but enough time for The Pan to fly away as fast as he could. After a minute or two he realised he was still flying upside down.

He righted the MK II and descended swiftly into the nearby Goojan Quarter where the streets were narrow and the houses close enough together to mask a snurd from the air. By the time their mystery pursuer had regained control and turned round the MK II had disappeared from sight.

Chapter 28

Nobody with a sense of self-preservation would have wanted to be inside the black snurd at this point. Lord Vernon wasn't used to being beaten at anything. He did not intend to get used to it.

He believed in honing and channelling his anger, but in this instance it almost overcame him and with a bellow of rage, he smashed his fist into the middle of the steering wheel.

They had escaped – eluded the Interceptor, the pinnacle of Grongolian military invention, a vehicle so far in advance of any other that such an outcome should have been impossible. Watching the Mervinettes outrunning the missile was a severe inconvenience, but a piece of creative driving like the one he had just seen was intolerable. He breathed deeply until he could finally bring his temper under control.

No matter. It would be a novelty to contend with a worthy opponent – keep his mind sharp and focussed – and of course, he would succeed in the end.

"You may run but I will find you," he whispered as he flew back and forth searching for the MK II, "I will hunt you down and when I do ..."

The Mervinettes were becoming a thorn in his side and their antics were bad for morale but there are always consolations to any setback. In this case, the more they angered him, the more pleasurable the anticipation of his revenge became. And he would have his revenge because no-one can run forever, and the handful of people who had escaped his clutches before had not only been exceptional but, more to the point, they had not been trying to evade him in groups of four.

No, escape for the Mervinettes would be impossible.

Lord Vernon was nothing if not tenacious. He would bide his time; sooner or later he would catch these upstarts and when that happened he would ensure they endured an end of unimaginable pain for their impertinence; especially the driver.

Chapter 29

The Mervinettes sat in stunned silence as The Pan drove them back to the lock-up. Big Merv's snurd was his pride and joy and The Pan suspected he would be unhappy about the scratches the wall had left on its paintwork. But at the same time, they were all still alive and his partners in crime, even Frank, were clearly too jubilant at not being dead to care. They were also impressed, and The Pan couldn't help feeling a little pleased with himself.

It felt good to be more talented at something than anybody else – except, perhaps, the driver of that black snurd. If The Pan's suspicions were correct and it was Lord Vernon, he wasn't going to let them get away again. To outrun the Interceptor once was close to a miracle – nobody had ever done it before – but Big Merv's MK II would need some radical improvements if The Pan stood any chance of escaping a second time. He made a mental note to talk to the boys at Snurd about equipping the MK II with a missile protection system when they checked it out the following day.

Big Merv did something unprecedented that night. In front of Frank and Harry, he gave The Pan a share of the loot. It wasn't a quarter but it was enough to show his appreciation. The Pan realised it signalled acceptance, that he was considered to be a fully fledged Mervinette, by the leader of the gang, at least. He packed away the MK II with extra special care. Up to a point, snurds are indestructible. The polymorphic metal had reverted to its original shape, but the paintwork was badly damaged and would need to be re-sprayed and re-polished. However, considering how close they had come to being blown out of the sky, the damage was minor. When he finished tidying away he put out the lights. Remembering his anonymous pursuers from the previous week he decided to leave the loot where it was. He could always collect it in the morning, if he lived that long. He was deep in thought as he padlocked the door of the lock-up and he didn't notice when somebody said, "Pssst," from the shadows behind him.

"Oi! You! You deaf or something?"

The Pan froze. It was a southern voice, with an accent similar to his own but it didn't speak the Hamgeean way. His heart lurched as he realised where it came from. The Resistance had finally found him. Slowly, so as not to provoke any untoward reaction, he turned round. At first, he didn't see anybody.

"In front of you, right here," said the voice irritably and The Pan, seeing no-one at his specific height, diverted his gaze downwards in the direction of his tatty, elastic-sided pointy boots. Standing in front of him was a Blurpon. This was bad news.

Blurpons are about three feet tall, red and furry. Their facial features and ears are cat-like, but they have hands as opposed to paws. And only one leg. Being uni-pedal doesn't hinder them, of course; they can hop about fifteen feet and are known for three things: their extreme ferocity, the ease with which they are offended and their excellence at laundering. Naturally, it was the first two items on this list which were worrying The Pan, and not their unsurpassed skills with cotton bed linen. The worst thing you can do to a Blurpon, despite the way it looks, is tell it it's cute. Being beaten up by a gang of Blurpons is like having a load of giant furry tennis balls fired at you from a cannon and The Pan was painfully aware that to enter into a conversation with a Blurpon was to enter a minefield of potentially fatal faux pas. He doffed his flat cap, hoping his elderly gent's disguise would bear up under professional scrutiny and spoke.

"Hello young man," he said without thinking and in his best wobbly septuagenarian voice added, "what can I do for you?" He hoped Blurpons had rules about thumping old people, and that the one addressing him wasn't going to be offended by being called a 'young man'.

"Just a question, old man," replied the other evenly. As his eyes became accustomed to the darkness of the street The Pan noticed his inquisitor was not alone. The two burly gentlemen who had tried unsuccessfully to follow him home before were standing either side of him. Each held something across his chest which, in the dim light, looked horribly like a sawn-off shotgun.

"Certainly, certainly," said The Pan, who was now scared enough not to have to concentrate on putting the wobble into his old man's voice, "fire away." He stopped and cleared his throat, glancing nervously at the guns in the hands of the Blurpon's assistants. "Er, I mean do go on, by all means."

"Is this your lock-up?" asked the Blurpon.

"No."

"Who does it belong to?" asked the Blurpon.

Oh great. They were only on the second question and already he couldn't think of a plausible answer.

"You said there was only one question," he piped reedily, "that's two."

With a flurry of activity the Blurpon leapt at him. One minute it was on the ground, the next it had its foot on his chest and was leaning outwards, putting its full weight on his tie. Small it might have been, but it was heavy. It held both ends of the tie, one in each hand and when it was sure it had The Pan's full attention it released the tension on the wide end. He felt his collar tightening round his neck and fervently wished he'd gone for the less classy clip-on option.

"On this occasion, I will overlook your impertinence, but I will only do so once," said the Blurpon. "Who does this lock-up belong to?" The Pan shrugged in what he hoped was an arthritic fashion but it was difficult with four stones of Blurpon hanging round his neck.

"I dunno," he said, which was all he could think of. He felt his tie tighten further. "He never told me his name, he just pays me to pick up the snurd and come back here," he gabbled, praying the Blurpon hadn't seen him returning with the other three Mervinettes. "I swear I don't know any more than that," he added, letting his fear do the talking. The Blurpon held a business card in front of his nose. The Pan hoped it wouldn't knock off his fake moustache.

"Then the next time your boss calls you, my friend," it said, in a tone of voice which indicated it was using the word 'friend' advisedly, "you and I will go collect the snurd together." He tucked the card into The Pan's breast pocket, patted it, jumped back to the ground and melted into the shadows. So the Resistance had got to him, which was bad, but they didn't know what he really did, or they'd have kidnapped him then and there, which was good. All he had to do now was arrange for the character he was currently disguised as to 'die' and think of another one. It would take some time and he might have to pick up the MK II disguised as himself the next week. The episode didn't put him in a good mood, especially when he examined the name on the card.

'HM Denarghi XVII, Ruler of the Blurpon Nation' it said. Blurpon nation aside, Denarghi was also the leader of the Resistance. Naturally, there was no address, simply a mobile phone number. Trust him to have a mobile phone when they were banned for all non-Grongle life forms. Flash git. No, The Pan's brain corrected itself, flash psychotic git.

Great.

The Pan changed his mind about his share of the loot. It seemed a waste to leave it overnight when he would probably be dead before he had the chance to collect it. He unlocked the lock-up, wrapped the jewellery Big Merv had given him in newspaper to minimise any tell-tale clinking noises it might make and put it in a plastic bag. He patted the cotton-wrapped bonnet of the MK II, took one final look around, locked up, and taking extra special care to avoid being followed, set out for the Parrot.

Chapter 30

High above the battlements of the Security Headquarters was a suite of palatial rooms that had originally belonged to the Architrave. Not any more. Lord Vernon gazed out of the glass wall of his office across the city of Ning Dang Po. These quarters had been his from the rank of colonel upwards. He regarded his luxury rooms as a testament to his destiny, that is, to be supreme ruler. Other people regarded them as testament of how scared everyone was of him.

The Mervinettes might have evaded him temporarily but everything else was proceeding according to plan. Indeed, he was surprised at how easy it had been to remove Lord Mergatroid and assume control. No bloody coup and public beheading, of course; instead a private stabbing. Much neater, swifter and more effective. From Lord Vernon's point of view, more enjoyable, too. Few things compared with the sensation of power he felt when he ended a life. Lord Mergatroid had been dead three weeks and it was only now that the people were beginning to realise what had happened and who had taken control. The longer Lord Vernon was in power before the news leaked out, the harder it would be to remove him. Not that anyone would dare. Not anymore. There was nobody left – or at most a handful and they were in hiding.

He smiled and indulged himself in a moment's self-congratulation, before strolling back to his desk. Laid out across the blotter was a selection of items he had recovered from the religious men and women he had imprisoned over the years. He was not religious, but he was a great believer in the maxim 'know your enemy', and since the pre-invasion K'Barthan State had been run on religious principles, he ensured that his knowledge of Nimmism was greater than most. He had heard the stories about the magical powers of the elders: inner knowledge, mind reading, matter transference et al and had investigated them fully.

"Every legend contains a grain of truth," he said, quoting the fifth book of Arnold. He often quoted The Prophet, the irony of doing so amused him. He had discovered that the technicalities of Nimmism, far from legend, were straightforward science. Advanced science, imaginative science, secret science, possibly even great science, but science, nonetheless. Not magic.

He picked up a small machine which looked like a gyroscope, only not, and spun the wheel. Blue sparks flew off it as he set it on a stand and watched the dial.

Yes. Finally. There it was. A name. A woman. A place. The Chosen One.

Someone must have selected her, which meant that somewhere out there was a Candidate – again, Lord Vernon's gaze was drawn to the lights of the city, glinting among the roofs.

Did any others know about her? He thought of his enemies, the last handful of religious elders. Possibly. It mattered little. What could they do? Nothing more than he could. There was no-one left with the knowledge and all the books were destroyed or – he glanced up at the book cases – inaccessible to them. Yes. She was unattainable for now, but he was confident that if his studies continued according to plan, he would soon be able to rectify that. When he did, he would reach her first. Once she was in his power, the Candidate could not help but reveal himself.

He set the machine in motion again and took his own reading. His score had risen to an eight. High enough, in the circumstances. Soon it would be time.

She would choose him. And if she didn't ... He had never balked at taking the things he wanted and he would make no exception now.

Chapter 31

As The Pan walked home, checking intermittently for any shadowy pursuers, he tried to rationalise his situation. The Resistance had finally caught up with him. He would have to tell Big Merv, but after his performance when pitted against the Interceptor, the prospect of giving his boss bad news held less fear. Perhaps there was now a chance Big Merv would demur from thumping The Pan if he said something controversial.

Gladys and Ada's behaviour, on the other hand, worried him. They couldn't be working for the Resistance. They couldn't be working for the Grongles either, because had they done so, they wouldn't have dealt with the ones in the Parrot's bar. They would have stood by and let The Pan be dragged off to prison. That left Big Merv, which was highly unlikely, or another criminal organisation. Or could they belong to another Resistance organisation, a less violent Resistance of which The Pan knew nothing? He was too preoccupied, as he climbed up the drain pipe in the alley behind the Parrot, to notice anything untoward. The excess adrenaline in his system after the afternoon's drive, coupled with his run-in with Denarghi, had left him jelly-legged, and twice in the course of what was usually a straightforward climb, he nearly lost his footing. He was relieved to reach the window sill and throw his bag of loot through the opening. He heard the reassuring thump as it hit the landing carpet. As he was about to climb in, the window was flung open as wide as it would go and an elderly man stuck his head out.

"Ah! There you are, my boy," he said proffering a gnarled fist, "can I give you a hand?"

The Pan was so shocked by the old man's sudden appearance that he slipped and fell straight backwards into the alley below. He landed, with a surprisingly quiet rustle, on the pile of black plastic bin bags Gladys and Ada had put out for the dustmen. It smelled like the bottom of a parrot's cage and what with Ada's diligence in cleaning out Humbert's living quarters every day, much of it probably had been. The bags had split and most of their insides were now on The Pan's outside, including something damp and vile-smelling which had landed across his nose.

"Good grief," he heard the old man above exclaim, "are you hurt?"

The Pan groaned and tried to move amid a crescendo of black plastic rustling accompanied by the plink, plink of empty beer bottles and food tins as they scattered about him in all directions. The Pan glared upwards. He'd never seen the old boy in the window before but something about him was strangely familiar.

"Are you there?" asked the old man.

"No," said The Pan tetchily, "at least, I hope I'll wake up in a moment and discover I'm not." He finally managed to scramble to his feet.

"Coo-ee, dear!" trilled the disembodied voice of Ada from above and The Pan breathed a sigh of relief. Yes, he had just fallen from a second storey window and was covered in evil-smelling refuse, but at least the old man, whoever he was, was merely a friend of Ada's and not a Grongolian informant or a Resistance spy. In light of the day he'd had so far that had to be a plus.

"Are you concussed?" he heard Ada ask.

"No," said The Pan. "But I wish I was. The smell ..." He gingerly peeled whatever it was off his nose and held it at arm's length between his thumb and first finger. It was a piece of semi-decayed fish skin. "Eugh!" he said, flinging it away in disgust. He could hear the old boy chuckling to himself.

"This isn't funny," he said tersely. He scrutinised the visage of the old man above him, framed in the light from the hall window, and classed him as essentially harmless – irritating, but harmless.

"Aren't you going to come inside?" the old man asked.

"Not while you're there," said The Pan. "Ada, can't you tell him to go away?"

"Oh no, he's a dear old friend of Gladys' and mine. We go way back," said Ada. "Now hurry inside so I can introduce you properly."

"He's certainly very old," muttered The Pan, who by this time was on his hands and knees, searching the rubble for his false moustache. He finally found it, covered in something yellow and slimy, which looked like egg yolk but smelled far worse. Unfortunately, it was an essential part of his disguise, and what's more the old man had seen him wearing it. He could hardly reappear at the window without it. He wiped it on his sleeve and stuck it back. "I would have thought a man of your advanced years would have had more consideration than to scare the living daylights out of a man

95

of my advanced years," he said, trying not to breathe though his nose; the moustache smelt truly terrible.

"You aren't my age," said the old man.

"Yes I am," snapped The Pan.

"You don't climb a drain pipe like a man my age."

"I doubt you've seen many men our age climb a drain pipe," said The Pan, "how can you tell without a point of reference?"

"That's exactly my argument. Men my age don't climb drain pipes. By the time a man has reached my advanced age he's been around long enough to know better. He'll use the door like everyone else, or at the very least, a ladder."

"You could have given me a heart attack," said The Pan.

"Your moustache has fallen off again, dear," said Ada, and the old man started another bout of chuckling.

The Pan folded his arms and glared upwards.

"Don't take it to heart, my boy. As disguises go, yours is capital, absolutely capital. Now, do get a move on. Time is of the essence and you and I must talk."

Says who? The Pan thought. "Not until I've had a bath," he said, "and anyway, how do I know I can trust you?"

"Ada will vouch for me,"

"Ada would vouch for me," said The Pan, "that hardly commends her powers of judgement."

"I understand you're upset, dear, but it's perfectly safe," said Ada. There was an awkward pause. Something bounced off his shoulder and flapped against the wall. It was a rope. The Pan glanced up and raised one eyebrow, as cynically as he could at the pair of them, before beginning, a second time, the climb to the landing window.

Chapter 32

It was late. Lord Vernon had not slept. In his apartment, he sat in the armchair which afforded him the best view over Ning Dang Po. His plans were proceeding reasonably well. He was master of all he surveyed, and one day soon he would be master of Grongolia. His strategy for world domination was foolproof. He would bestride the planet like a colossus and every living thing would pay homage to him. He smiled. That would be most enjoyable. He would crush all resistance, destroy anyone who stood in his path. It would be ... delicious.

His reverie was disturbed by a knock at the door. He stood up, strode across the room and flung it open. He liked catching those beneath him – which in K'Barth was everyone – off their guard.

"Lord Protector," said a flustered officer.

Lord Vernon noticed, with disdain, that he was a member of the Imperial Guard. They were separate from the army, which in K'Barth was commanded by Lord Vernon himself, and they were usually tasked with the protection of things or people. They were fiercely loyal to the state and the High Leader who had sent them to K'Barth – ostensibly to guard Lord Vernon, but, privately, he suspected they were there to watch him. He did not trust or require them. Indeed, he considered them an inconvenience and an insult, foisted on him by his fearful superior. Lord Vernon made sure they were kept busy with a string of pointless and demoralising tasks well beneath their skill set and station.

"Yes," he said softly. He wasn't wearing his sunglasses. That was good. He liked the way his deformity scared others and only wore them to ensure the impact was all the more shocking when he chose to remove them. He looked into the officer's face and saw his fear. "What do you want?"

"I am with the detachment conducting excavations on your behalf at the High Temple," the officer said, holding out a bag. "I believe these may be the items you seek."

These. Yet the bag contained one box.

"Wait." Lord Vernon took it from him and closed the door. As he emptied the contents onto his desk he tried to suppress his excitement. The bag contained a small leather box that, in turn, contained three ornate thimbles: one of copper, one of bronze and one of platinum, with empty spaces for two more.

"As I expected," he said softly, "gold and silver are missing."

The K'Barthans had run their state on democratic lines, but the final say rested with the Architrave. To advise him – or her – were three high-ranking officials, chosen by the Parliament; the Council of Three. Each of these three had a thimble-shaped portal; one of silver, one of platinum and one of copper, while the Architrave's was made of gold. The last portal, a bronze one, was lent to high ranking officials when it was deemed necessary, for a special assignment, or a dangerous one.

"Three portals." These were the source of the rumours about Nimmism – a portal could be used to move instantly from one place to another. It could be used to watch others, unobserved – but apart from himself, was there anybody left with knowledge of such things? No, not anymore. Not now the K'Barthans had been cleansed of their leaders. Now, anyone owning a functioning portal would be ... indomitable.

The gold thimble was, supposedly, lost forever, long since according to police records, and the final Architrave had substantiated this. Questioned under the influence of Truth Serum, shortly before his summary trial and execution, he had confessed to losing it and being too embarrassed to tell anyone. Hardly surprising. He was vacuous and vain, and conveniently, from the Grongolian point of view, possibly the most useless Architrave ever. Even so, Lord Vernon, ever thorough, was conducting his own search to substantiate these claims.

The silver one had plunged into a ravine with the High Priest – and his snurd – four or five years previously. Lord Vernon had several squads of Grongles searching the wreckage, but from the molten state of the vehicle it was looking more and more unlikely that a piece of silver would survive.

These three were the last known portals – for now. He was optimistic that the boffins in his laboratories would be able to reverse engineer them and create a bespoke – and superior, naturally – Grongolian version.

"Remarkable." He had been waiting for this moment, expecting it to come soon, but not quite this quickly. He took the platinum thimble from its place and turned it over in his hands. It was a work of art, finely crafted with scenes from the life of The Prophet. He laughed, a manic evil guffaw. A laugh like that wasn't a luxury he allowed himself often, but on this occasion, he couldn't help himself.

Lord Vernon left the box on the desk and returned to the officer outside the door. A colonel, he noticed, one he didn't recognise. Unsurprising, as a staunch army Grongle, Lord Vernon ensured he had as little as possible to do with the Imperial Guard.

"You are new here, Colonel?" The red eyes returned his stare with equanimity. He had clearly prepared himself for eye contact, the second time. He was plucky, this one.

"Yessir, just posted here."

"Where were you before?"

"I commanded the garrison guarding the Bank of Grongolia, sir."

"Interesting. Your name, Colonel?"

"Moteurs, sir."

"The items you have so kindly given me. Are they what I think they are?"

"I believe so, sir."

"Yet you doubt."

"It is difficult to tell."

"Because ...?"

"Because they are not currently functioning, sir."

"No matter, that can be rectified."

"I'm not so certain, sir." Contradiction? That was close to insubordinate. Perhaps it was time to show Moteurs who was in charge.

"Why, exactly?" asked Lord Vernon, with all the menace and sneering disdain that he could muster – which was quite a lot.

Colonel Moteurs began to sweat. Good.

"I believe two are damaged beyond repair, sir," he said. "But I am told the platinum one might be revived with the help of a priest ..." an awkward pause, but entirely natural, since it was largely due to Lord Vernon that priests were such a rarity these days, "should there be one left in the cells."

"A priest will not be required. Do not be taken in by these savages and their religious hype. This is not ju-ju, Colonel, it is science. Intelligent, advanced science but nothing more. Do you understand me?"

"Yessir."

Another glare of sneering disdain.

"I assume you did not come by these artefacts at the High Temple."

"No, sir."

"Naturally. Where did you find them?"

A long, long, pause. The officer was choosing his words carefully. Lord Vernon watched and waited.

"I cannot tell you, sir," said Colonel Moteurs, eventually.

"I'm so sorry, I seem to have misheard you," said Lord Vernon glibly, "I am almost sure I heard you say could not tell me."

"I'm afraid I did, sir. My sources are secretive and they trust me. I would not wish to compromise the safety of a reliable informant."

Lord Vernon made no effort to keep the menace out of his voice when he said, "Do you imply that telling me who your sources are would compromise their safety?"

"Nossir."

"Then what do you imply, exactly? Think carefully before you answer. Remember that if I choose to, I can make you tell me in a manner which may be ..." he waved his hand casually as he sought for an appropriate word, "disagreeable to you."

The Colonel glanced up and down the corridor.

"Your Gracious Exaltedness," he said, using the Lord Protector's full title, "there is no such implication, but we do not know who might be listening. This person is blacklisted—he should be shot on sight—but he has information which could be of use to us; information about the few enemies of the state who remain. At the beginning he agreed to work for me in exchange for his life, but I have convinced him I am dissatisfied with those in power at home and here, and that I am working to promote a new Grongolian order. He now trusts me implicitly because he believes I am using these as part of a ruse to trick you." Lord Vernon was impressed. Colonel Moteurs was now sweating profusely but his voice was steady and throughout his speech he maintained eye contact without flinching or turning away. To increase the Colonel's discomfort, he waited before answering.

"Then, perhaps, it is your lucky day, Major General Moteurs."

"Thank you, Your Most Gracious Exaltedness," said the new Major General Moteurs with a bow.

Lord Vernon paused. Yes. Why not? Moteurs was brave enough to look him in the eye, brave enough to contradict him.

"General Moteurs," he said, "let us skip to plain General. I like to keep things uncomplicated." The General's face darkened in a green blush. He'd just been promoted four ranks at once.

"How can I ever thank you, Your Gracious Exaltedness?"

"With your loyalty, General." And how that would cost him. Lord Vernon looked the General up and down and was tempted to smile.

Everybody has a price – even a Grongle courageous enough to contradict him, like this one.

"I may ask a small favour of you one day." He waved one arm in a dismissive it'll-be-tiny gesture. Ah, if only the newly promoted General knew, he would spurn his freshly-won rank and head back to the Bank of Grongolia. "For now, that is all. You may go."

The General bowed.

"Thank you, sir."

Lord Vernon shut the door. He loved playing with the lives of those who served him.

He took a leather-bound tome from the bookcases which comprised most of one wall of his office. Officially, all Nimmist books had been burned. However, unofficially, Lord Vernon had ensured those which were important or useful to him had escaped incineration. He leafed through the well-thumbed pages and then read for a few minutes with rapt concentration.

Still reading, he walked back to the desk, opened a secret drawer and removed a box of implements. He selected a small plinth of greenish metal and stood it in the middle of the desk blotter. After a brief consultation of the book he took a black Biro and drew a circle round the plinth and placed the platinum thimble on it. He walked over to the safe and removed a small machine which looked like one of those toy gyroscopes, only not, wound it up with a key, placed it on the table and moved the small release lever to set it spinning. It wobbled less and less as it gained speed, until it stood steady on its single spindle, humming quietly. Small flecks of crimson lightning crackled between the spinning plate and thimble.

"Interesting."

He consulted the book again. Yes, a good sign. He took a deep breath. Was it really going to be this easy? Riffling through the implements in the box he selected a long thin piece of metal, somewhere between an upholsterer's needle and a screwdriver in appearance. He placed the tip gently into the lightning and listened as it began to hum. When he moved it towards the thimble the tone rose in pitch and when he moved it back towards the spinning machine the tone dropped.

"Excellent," he said softly.

With his free hand he took a tuning fork from the box. He rapped it on the edge of the desk, held it to his ear for a moment and then rapped it on the edge of the desk again, this time standing it on its end on the wood. It gave off a single note – A.

He moved the metal implement through the crimson lightning until the humming sound it made was also an A. Surely reactivating the portal would require more than this.

Leaving the gyroscopic machine spinning, he placed the thimble carefully on the blotter, put the stand, the metal implement and the tuning fork back, and returned the box to the secret drawer. He breathed deeply, composing himself for a moment or two before picking up the thimble and holding it up. In the bottom, clearly visible, a tiny dot of light.

"So, General Moteurs, my mysterious friend," he said quietly, "I do not think it is broken now."

So easy. A piece of breathtakingly complicated quantum mechanics, made simple for the types of academic, religious men and women who liked their science straightforward and user-friendly.

Clearly The Prophet had never foreseen this, or he and his followers would have guarded his secrets more carefully.

Yes. The old order was ending and a new world was about to begin. His search was over. He had prepared for this. Everything was ready. Now, for a few moments, at least, he would have access to the Chosen One.

He went back to the safe and took out a bottle of pills. The machine on his desk was still spinning but the red lightning had turned to blue, its usual colour. He placed the thimble closer and consulted his book once again, before performing a complicated set of hand movements above both items. The machine pinged.

"Like taking sweets from a child."

He turned his attention to the pills. He couldn't enter the Chosen One's world without making certain physiological changes.

He poured himself a glass of water, opened the bottle, took one of the pills and sat back with the book. An hour, the boffin in his laboratories had told him. It had better be, or this was the last potion he would live to concoct. Lord Vernon put the book down and pulled out a large hunting knife. He twirled it absent-mindedly from one gloved hand to another. After a short while he stopped playing with the knife and glanced at his wrist watch. Twenty minutes. He held up the polished blade and looked at his reflection. Yes, the green flesh was changing colour. He smiled and adjusted his cravat.

"Excellent," he said again. The pills had worked. The boffin who made them would live to see another day. Which reminded him. He opened the secret drawer and took the other two thimbles from the box, rewound the gyroscope-like machine and repeated the process of resetting them too. He put the copper one back in the box, checked the bronze one was functioning and then strode to the door.

"Guards," he shouted into the corridor.

There was the sound of running footsteps, and a short, stocky corporal skidded to a halt in front of him and saluted.

"Yessir?" Staying in the shadows so the corporal wouldn't notice his altered skin colour, Lord Vernon handed him the bronze thimble.

"Take this down to the labs. I want them to reverse engineer it by ..." he paused for thought, "this time tomorrow. If they fail, I want a good reason why, and the precise date by which they will have succeeded, or I will be compelled to kill each and every last one of them."

"Yessir."

"Slowly."

"Yessir."

"Now get out of my sight. I am busy."

The corporal turned and ran.

Lord Vernon slammed the door and returned to his desk, breathing hard with excitement. He was about to gain access to the one person who would deliver the last of his enemies into his power and destroy all meaningful resistance to his rule, forever. He paused to savour the sensation.

It was good.

He picked up the thimble and consulted the book a third time. Again, more hand movements. As his anticipation built he breathed a little faster. He closed his eyes for a moment, concentrating, held it up to his eye and looked in.

There. Far away, in a parallel universe, talking with another.

Visible, audible, but more importantly, accessible – for a few precious minutes. He'd expected her to be asleep. The fact she was not made it even more interesting.

"At last, I have you, Chosen One."

One final, quick check of his reflection in the knife. Yes, he was no longer green, and though paler than human flesh, his skin would pass, especially in darkness. It was time.

He put the thimble on his finger and disappeared into thin air.

Chapter 33

Once he had taken a lengthy bath The Pan secreted his first ever official earnings as a Mervinette in the back of the cupboard in his room. He took out the other bag, the one with Lord Vernon's worthless but nonetheless, 'sentimentally valued' artefacts inside it, and put it on the bed. He sat down beside it with a heavy sigh.

"This stuff is red hot," he said to himself.

These artefacts were either very valuable or very important. Their presence in a safety deposit box showed that. Sentimental didn't feature as Lord Vernon hadn't a sentimental molecule in him. The Pan was beginning to wish he'd never sold the ring.

He paced back and forth as he tried to think his situation through. The voice of reason told him the best thing he could do was chuck the rest of the things in the river Dang at the earliest available opportunity.

"No way!" he said aloud, for emphasis.

Anyway, since he'd already sold the ring, the smartest thing to do would be to hang on to the other artefacts; at least then, if his secret was discovered, he might be able to return the bag and its contents to Lord Vernon in exchange for his life. His encounter with Denarghi, coupled with the Grongles' visit to the Parrot, was a compelling reason to save every bargaining chip, no matter how small, that he might use to save his skin.

There was another reason, too. The thimble. He couldn't explain his relationship with the thimble. It wasn't his, he had never seen it before and yet, like the ring, nothing had ever felt so perfectly his own. It was as if it wanted to belong to him and he felt so guilty about selling the ring that it made him feel almost protective over it.

He carried it around with him wherever he went. When he had a spare moment he would take it out and imagine something he missed, usually his home. Then he would hold the open end up to his eye and peer in. Whatever he had thought about would appear in the bottom. It was as if he was looking through a telescope at images projected from within his mind. Anywhere he visualised, even the street outside, would appear in glorious Technicolor. A few hours after he had discovered this, The Pan had put it to his eye without thinking about anything in particular, and had seen a girl.

"What a babe," he'd said. She had dark brown eyes and mousey hair which was almost as flyaway and unmanageable as his own. She wasn't beautiful in the conventional sense, but somehow she was, to him. He had watched her talking animatedly to a friend, laughing and smiling. She was lively and attractive, she looked fun, and good company, and he was instantly besotted. Ever since then, he'd spent a lot of time looking at this girl, whoever she was, even though he felt voyeuristic and creepy watching her. He shouldn't be doing it but he was becoming addicted.

"Just a tiny peek," he told himself as he stopped pacing and took out the thimble.

There she was. Ada would have called her 'big-boned', but she had a good figure. He usually went for leggy blondes and well ... this girl wasn't leggy or blonde. And she wore glasses.

Watching her now, he was beginning to suspect she lived on another planet. Wherever she lived it was certainly different from K'Barth. Perhaps she did, knowing his attraction to the unattainable, that would explain why he was so taken with her.

"Where are you?" he asked her. He put the thimble down for a moment. He was being an idiot. He wasn't in love with her. They'd never met and the thimble wasn't wired for sound, so he hadn't even heard her speak.

"Get a grip," he muttered, "she's a figment of your imagination."

And a voice behind him said:

"She's as real as you or I."

To say The Pan was surprised was an understatement. He leapt in shock across the room. His knees felt all wobbly, so he leant his back against the wall for support and stood facing the doorway. The voice belonged to the old man who had surprised him, earlier, by suddenly appearing at the window. Now he was standing nonchalantly by the door.

"I'm so sorry, did I startle you?" he asked.

As if he didn't realise.

"Er," squeaked The Pan as his knees gave way and he slid to the floor, "a tad."

One of the luxuries of having eyes in the back of your head is that no-one can ever creep up on you. The Pan stared at the old man, wondering how long he had managed to stand there, in what should have been full view, without being seen. Something was definitely wrong.

"Don't be afraid," said the old boy, equably.

"Don't be afraid," repeated The Pan, as he sat hunched ignominiously against the wall, "that's rich."

Nobody had crept up on him unobserved since his extra eyes had appeared. It didn't happen. In his panic he wondered if they had disappeared without his realising. He ran his hands cautiously though the hair on the back of his head and inadvertently stuck his finger in one of the eyes in question, painfully proving its continued existence.

The old man wore a quizzical expression, with a hint of a smile.

"You'd better not be laughing at me," said The Pan acidly as he stood up and fixed him with what he hoped was a level, fearless and withering gaze.

He seemed harmless enough. He was wearing sandals, yellow socks and mustard-coloured cord trousers worn bare on the knees and, The Pan assumed, although he couldn't see from where he was standing, the bottom. He sported one of those cream 'country' checked shirts usually worn with a flat cap, a waxed cotton jacket and a golden retriever, but instead of the waxed jacket he wore a tweed one – similar to the one in The Pan's own elderly gent's disguise. The entire ensemble was coloured in coordinating shades of brown and yellow. He was clearly a Nimmist, probably a retired priest. Uninvited, he sat down on the bed. The Pan glared at him. There was something very humiliating about being outwitted by a septuagenarian.

"Have you the faintest, smallest notion how badly you scared me?" he asked. "I hope you realise that if I was as old as I've been pretending to be I'd have died of shock, for all you know I might be about to—I might have a weak heart."

"Yes," said the old man sagely, "but you don't do you? In fact, considering the life you lead your health appears to be surprisingly robust. It must be Gladys' cooking." He beamed, displaying a gold tooth, and The Pan couldn't help noticing that he bore a strong likeness to Gladys' son Trev.

"What do you mean the life I lead?" he asked nervously. "I'm a very sober and upright citizen."

The old man laughed, the gold tooth catching the light again as he smiled.

"Why of course you are—very sober, very upright and—very blacklisted."

Uh oh! How did the old git know that? Time to lie through his teeth, then.

"I'm not blacklisted."

"No, no, of course not," said the old man wryly as he fished a small hand-held computer out of his inside jacket pocket. The Pan recognised it at once. It belonged to the Grongle who had questioned him in the saloon bar of the Parrot. He felt cheated. If he'd known Gladys and Ada were going to steal it, he'd have got in first. The old man powered it up by rubbing it in his hair.

"Hmm ..." he said glancing over the top of its minute screen at The Pan. "About five foot nine are you?" The Pan nodded dumbly. "Yes," said the old man to nobody in particular as he tapped away at the keyboard. "Early 20s, dark hair, dark eyes—blue?" He squinted down his nose at The Pan. "Yes," he said again, "blue. Shifty looking. Well, well, well. You've earned yourself a triple star." The Pan was intrigued. Until now, he had associated stars with restaurants. "Your very existence is treason," said the old man, "if you're recognised, you can be shot on sight."

"Mmm," said The Pan cagily, "luckily I don't have a very memorable face."

The old man grinned.

"Perhaps not, but you must have upset somebody enough to remember you. Blacklisting is a rather stiff punishment for 'obstructing the course of justice', I would have thought."

Was that all it said? The Pan raised one eyebrow.

"Maybe it depends which piece of justice you happen to be obstructing."

As he remembered the events that had led to his being blacklisted, he was unable to suppress an involuntary shudder. It didn't escape the old man's notice.

"What did you really do?" he asked.

"Nothing much. I got under the wrong Grongle's feet." He didn't want to think about it, let alone talk about it.

"My, my, we are enigmatic, aren't we?" said the old man and The Pan glared at him. "All part and parcel of your bank robbery activities is it—this cloak and dagger stuff?"

Despite his best efforts, The Pan felt his eyes widen and, he suspected he was going white. He closed his eyes and put his head in his hands.

"I'm not a bank robber," he said.

"No," said the old man, "as I am well aware. Big Merv masterminds all that. How did he put it now? Ah yes, that's right: he thinks, you drive."

There was a long, uncomfortable silence while The Pan wondered how on earth the old boy had known what Big Merv had said earlier.

"You shouldn't know things like that."

"I know many things I am not supposed to."

"Not about me," retorted The Pan, "I haven't a clue what you're talking about."

"Haven't you?" The old man smiled indulgently, showing his gold tooth again. "Then why are you so peaky all of a sudden? No facial colour?" he began to chuckle, "or is that fabled weak heart of yours playing up?"

The Pan failed, spectacularly, to see the funny side. He didn't like being cornered.

"This is no joke," he snapped, "you're quoting a conversation which took place among four people, alone, and you weren't one of them. Who blabbed, Frank? Harry? Or is this some kind of test from Big Merv?"

The old man seemed disappointed.

"Nobody 'blabbed' as you put it. Don't be afraid. Your secret is quite safe with me."

"Oh thank you. Why yes, of course. But if some coffin dodger I've never seen before can walk calmly in off the street and display such in-depth knowledge of my life history and ..." he moved one arm expansively, "and quote private conversations it should have been physically impossible for him to hear, how many thousand others can do the same thing? You're not the only one, are you?"

"As a matter of fact, I'll wager I am," said the old man. "I'm not your average 'coffin dodger'." His tone of voice bore the supreme confidence of a man not only used to being obeyed but who spent his life a couple of steps ahead of everyone else. It reminded The Pan of his father.

"Listening is simple enough, but it is a skill. You can trust me," the old boy continued, but The Pan shook his head.

"No I can't. That's the point. I can't trust anybody and I don't. How d'you think I've stayed alive all these years?"

"Whether or not you choose to is your business, but you can trust me," said the old man gently.

The Pan had a plan. He might not be able to outwit this septuagenarian but he was confident he could outrun him. "You come here and scare the living daylights out of me ... twice," he waved his arms theatrically to divert the old man's attention from the fact that he was edging towards the door. "I live here. This room is all I have. It's my home." The old man didn't appear to notice what he was doing. "The least you could do was knock before you came in, you're accusing me of being a public enemy and you appear to know more about my life than I do." A few more feet and he'd be able to make a run for it while the old boy was busy worrying about calming him down.

"Oh, now don't be upset," began the old man.

"Can you blame me?"

"Not entirely."

The Pan was trying to gauge the distance between himself and the open door. When he started to move, the old man was bound to stick his leg out and try to trip him. He would have to dive and roll into the corridor. The bag containing the remaining artefacts from Lord Vernon's safety deposit box had fallen under the bed but on the side nearest the door. If he timed his move right he would be able to grab it as he rolled past and be up and running before his elderly adversary knew what had happened. He dived, rolled, successfully grabbed the bag but then hit something solid with a thump, and stopped dead.

Chapter 34

The Pan realised he was lying on his back, mostly upside down, half unrolled, with his legs in the air. He had rolled into the door, which the old man had kicked closed.

"Alright. You win," he said. The old man bent down and took the bag from his hand.

"Thank you. I promise, you are the last person on Earth I would wish to harm. Here, let me help you." The old boy held out his hand and helped The Pan to his feet. "I didn't think I'd catch you! You are quick off the mark."

"So are you," a shrug, "credit where it's due."

"Ah! Yes, but I have an unfair advantage," said the old man and The Pan raised an eyebrow at him, "I was able to anticipate your actions, you see. I have been watching you for some time, so I have begun to learn a little about your methods."

"No you haven't," said The Pan. Oh! If only he could believe that, but the old man was different, confident, smart, authoritative and well-informed. "Trust me, if you'd been watching me, I'd have seen you."

"Oh, I don't know about that," said the old man breezily, "we Nimmists have a knack of blending in." The Pan raised the other eyebrow. "Furthermore," the old man continued, "there are many ways of watching somebody, not all of them necessitating the observer's physical presence."

"Naturally," said The Pan drily. He wondered what the old boy's cryptic statement might mean. There were rumours about the higher echelon secret orders of Ninja Nimmists, which told of super-human abilities such as seeing through solid matter, time or enemies, and reading minds. There was even a colourful tale about matter transference. Most sensible people discounted rumours like these as tall stories. Now The Pan was beginning to wonder. If the old man had read his mind, it would explain how he knew the contents of a private conversation. His style of dress was understated for a holy man, but there was a chance he might be a Nimmist priest and he had managed to stand in full view of The Pan's extra eyes without being seen. He'd have to be seriously gifted at 'blending in' to be able to do that, especially since it was unlikely he realised his quarry could see backwards just as well as he could see forwards.

"Hmm," said the old man, looking him up and down, "do sit down," and he gestured to the only alternative to the bed, a battered armchair. The Pan did as he was told. "I'm sorry if I frightened you. I did come here for a good reason."

"I'm sure you did."

"Yes," said the old man slowly, "if my reports are correct I believe you have come by a ring."

The Pan rolled his eyes, why did it have to be the ring, the only thing he'd already sold?

"Mmm," he said, "I did have a ring but ..." He glanced helplessly around the room in search of inspiration. "Alright, I admit it, I sold it and if what I heard the other night is correct, I think Lord Vernon has already found it. But then, you know that don't you?" The old man nodded and sighed heavily.

"Perhaps – but I wanted to confirm. It's a great pity if it is true."

"Well, I'm afraid it is," said The Pan coldly.

"Yes. How much do you know about Nimmism?"

The Pan sighed. He'd had a good old-fashioned Nimmist education but he'd wasted much of it. In theory he should have been better versed than most of his peer group, but in practice he wasn't confident how much he could remember. He cleared his throat.

"Not much," he said.

"No," said the old man. They lapsed into silence and The Pan waited to see what the old boy would do. The interview must have been going differently to the way he'd expected because he seemed to be wondering where to start. He took several deep breaths, as if he were about to speak and then said nothing.

"That ring, was it important?" asked The Pan. The old man narrowed his eyes slightly.

"Oh yes," he said.

"I met a Grongle the other night, who said it came from Lord Vernon's safety deposit box," said The Pan.

"That would be wishful thinking on Lord Vernon's part. He is no fool, he knows its worth. If the ring had been in his possession, he would have been wearing it for some years and he would have become Lord Protector Vernon a long time ago."

The Pan was beginning to have that all too familiar feeling that he was in over his head.

"Does that mean he's wearing it now?"

"Oh yes," said the old man sadly.

"Look, for what it's worth, I'm sorry. I needed the money and the ring was the only thing I could sell."

"Weren't you tempted to keep it, to wear it yourself?"

The Pan smiled.

"Very," he said, "but having 'I'm a Mervinette, please arrest me now' tattooed on my forehead would have been less dangerous and more subtle."

"And the other items? How tempted are you to keep those?"

"It," said The Pan turning the thimble over and over in his hands, "it, there was only one other item."

The old man shook his head, smiling and held up the bag.

"What about these?"

The Pan shrugged.

"Now, if you'd managed to use that," he pointed at the thimble, "for a slightly more constructive purpose than ogling a girl, you'd realise how I know."

The Pan blushed. "You're beginning to sound like my father," he said.

"I'm beginning to understand what the poor man was up against," retorted the old man. The Pan glared at him. "I'm sorry, I haven't handled this well at all. You see, I have been watching you for so long that I feel I know you. May I start again?"

That was a bolt from the blue. The Pan thought a moment. He nodded.

"Jolly good! Would you like a brandy to calm your nerves?" The old man went on, "I may even have some of Gladys' home-made Calvados if you're interested?"

Now that sounded better. Unless it was poisoned of course – then again, Gladys' home-made Calvados was probably strong enough to neutralise most toxins.

"Alright," said The Pan cautiously. The old man beamed at him again.

"Marvellous! Now then. Watch this, you might learn something." He produced a thimble from his pocket. It was similar to the one The Pan had but it was silver instead of gold. He held it in his hand, closed his eyes and

112

concentrated for a few short seconds. Then he held it up to his eye and squinted into the bottom. "Capital," he said, "that should do." He held the thimble in his left hand and put the first finger of his right hand into it.

The Pan was surprised how deep it was – the old man's entire hand seemed to have disappeared. Come to think of it, it had, along with most of his arm. He watched in awe. There was a sucking noise, like the sound made by the bath emptying in premises equipped with some of K'Barth's earlier attempts at plumbing, followed by the sound of bottles clinking together. Finally, there was a subdued pop and the old man's arm reappeared, along with a bottle labelled 'Calvados' in Gladys' copperplate, old-lady handwriting. He placed it carefully on the floor and beamed at The Pan.

"Isn't it amazing what you can do if you couple a little imagination with the wonders of quantum mechanics? Now, I like to use the right glass for my drinks. Would you be able to find me a couple of brandy balloons from somewhere?"

There were proper brandy glasses behind the bar downstairs, The Pan remembered. He stood up. To his annoyance, the old man glanced at the gold thimble in his hand and tutted.

"You're not going to walk all the way downstairs, are you?"

"That was my plan, since the brandy glasses are behind the bar."

"There are other ways," said the old man nodding at the thimble in his hand.

"You want me to do what you just did?" asked The Pan incredulously.

"Is there a problem?"

The Pan gazed speechlessly at him.

"You're not afraid are you?" said the old man with a hint of mock incredulity which The Pan didn't appreciate.

"Of course I'm afraid," he retorted, "what d'you think I am? An idiot?" The old man smiled at The Pan in a way that made it perfectly obvious that he did, indeed, think he was an idiot.

"Fine, I'll give it a go." He glanced at the thimble in his hand and wondered what might go wrong and whether or not it would kill him. The old man was watching him intently. "Seriously, what do I do?"

"You've already had a demonstration. Let's see if you can fathom it out shall we?" replied the old man. "It isn't so difficult."

"Is this a test?"

"Perhaps."

"I see," said The Pan slowly. "What if I get it wrong? Will I die?"

The old boy chortled.

"Don't be so ridiculous. Of course not!" He waved The Pan forwards. "Go on! Nothing ventured, nothing won. Try."

Giving the old boy a withering look, The Pan sat back in his chair for a minute to think. He had to figure out how his thimble worked. Although he had been given a graphic demonstration, combining 'a little imagination with the wonders of quantum mechanics' wasn't the most articulate set of instructions he'd ever heard. He held the thimble in front of him and imagined the shelf behind the bar where the brandy glasses lived. Then he put it close to his eye and glanced inside.

In the fish-eye view through the bottom he saw the exact scene he had imagined complete with brandy glasses and not the girl. Trying to hide his disappointment, he put the thimble gingerly on his finger. There was the same sucking noise he'd heard before and his whole hand disappeared. It was like putting his arm into a turbo-charged vacuum cleaner. The force pulling him in was incredibly strong and it was all he could do not to be sucked in after it. He felt something wooden. The shelf? Maybe. Very cautiously he groped his way forward until his fingers rested on something glass-shaped. Once he'd located the stem, he hooked one finger round it and felt for another one. He found it quickly. Good. Two. There was a chink as he pulled them towards him.

"Mmm," he said. There was something in the way. There was only one thing for it, he was going to have to look. He shut his eyes, took a deep breath and leaned through the thimble, as if he was leaning into a cupboard. He could feel the change in air temperature and opened his eyes. Yes, he was behind the bar and yes, seeing somebody's right arm, shoulder and head – minus any other body parts – hovering in mid air in front of the glasses shelf had had a remarkably silencing effect on the bar's occupants. The only two people who didn't appear to notice were Gladys and Ada. The Pan coughed nervously.

"Sorry," he said waving the glasses. "Just ... just ... er ... just ..." still waving the glasses about he smiled apologetically, "bye," he said. He leaned backwards and the sucking noise grew louder while the strength of the force pulling him back began to increase. He shut his eyes – he didn't want to see what happened when he passed through the thimble. The reappearance of the familiar surroundings of his room was accompanied by the same

114

popping sound he'd heard when the old man removed the bottle from the silver thimble.

"Well done, my boy!" he said, "well done, indeed." He took the glasses The Pan held out, which were clinking together as his hand shook. "It takes some people years of concerted effort and training to do what you've just done."

"I thought you said it wasn't difficult."

"I lied. I wanted to see what you are capable of. Quite a lot, it turns out. That was most impressive, my boy, most impressive."

"You flatter me," said The Pan, but he was unaccountably pleased to have exceeded the old man's expectations. He watched the old boy open the bottle and carefully pour equal amounts into each glass. He handed one to The Pan, who was shaking all over now and had never needed a strong drink so much in his life. However, he was still cautious enough to sniff it carefully and wait for the old man to drink some of his before taking a very small sip. He swirled it around his glass and sniffed it again. Yep, it seemed to be fine. He counted to thirty, but there were no ill effects so he decided it wasn't drugged and began to relax.

Chapter 35

The Pan had no idea who the old man was, but it was clear he had not yet divulged the true purpose of his visit. It was now obvious he'd known what had happened to the ring, and his enquiries about it were merely an excuse to introduce himself, or make his displeasure known. Then there was that neat trick with the thimble; there'd been no need to give up a secret like that unless he was going to ask The Pan for a favour in return, a big favour. His enigmatic visitor seemed harmless enough, sitting on the bed sipping his drink, but The Pan suspected he was a man of principle who was brave enough to risk getting into trouble with the authorities for his beliefs. The Pan had great admiration for brave people, but he was in enough trouble with authority as it was, without going looking for more. He took another sip of brandy and waited.

"There is something else you could do for us," the old man said eventually.

'Us' The Pan noted. It seemed the old man was part of an organisation; he was afraid it would be the Resistance.

"Who's 'us'?" he asked. "More to the point, who are you?"

The old man paused.

"You're really not very well-informed, are you?"

"I've never met you before in my life so, unsurprisingly, no."

"Haven't Gladys and Ada said anything?" The Pan remembered the strange conversation he'd had with them after the Grongles had visited the Parrot, all those cryptic hints about other ways to resist and that they had contacts if he was in trouble. He could imagine that the old man was one of the very few people who might conceivably be able to get The Pan out of trouble in the right situation.

"Not in so many words."

"Perhaps I should start from the beginning."

"It might help," said The Pan. "I'm not an idiot, but the kind of intuition you're expecting is beyond most people. It would be a big ask from a magician, let alone an everyday petty thief like me."

"You're not an everyday petty thief though, are you?" No smile, but a definite twinkle.

"Maybe not—but doing my job is a simple case of common sense."

"Don't sell yourself short—there's talent involved. You're the best getaway man in K'Barth and you're the only man alive who has ever outrun the Interceptor. That, alone, is extraordinary. Even I know it takes more than common sense. You've got something, my boy, anyone can see that."

"Thank you. You flatter me," The Pan smiled, "I get very frightened. Perhaps that gives me an unfair advantage. After all, cowards are good at running away."

"Are you a Nimmist?" asked the old man.

"Isn't everyone?"

"No, and you haven't answered my question."

"I've never really thought about it but I suppose I am," said The Pan.

"Do you remember much about the Looking?"

"The search for the new Architrave?" He shrugged, "I was—"

"No, of course you don't," the other interrupted him. "Before your time. You probably weren't even born before they made it illegal."

"I don't know if it was legal at the time, I was only a kid, but I do remember something I think."

The old man seemed surprised.

"Do you?"

"I believe so. I think my father was involved, although I can't be sure, he was very cagey about his university stuff, so I never found out exactly. I was only about eight and none of us were supposed to know what was going on."

"Did they ever interview you?"

"Not really. If they did, then not in the normal way." The Pan remembered his chagrin when his father wouldn't allow him to meet the holy woman who'd come to question the other kids in his year. They hadn't been told it was the Looking, of course, although many of their parents suspected it. Officially, they were being interviewed by members of staff from Ning Dang Po University as part of a scheme to sponsor the education of gifted children from poorer backgrounds. "Dad asked me some strange questions, over the course of a week—maybe longer—and there was some odd stuff left lying around the house for a while. I kept getting told off for playing with it."

The old man smiled.

"Did you play with it much?"

"Arnold yes! I couldn't leave it alone. Red rag to a bull. I'd been told not to touch it and you know how it is ..." he stopped. "Looking back on it now, I reckon that was the point when things started to go wrong."

The Pan thought of the sun-drenched carefree days of his childhood. His father had been his idol at that point, before their relationship deteriorated. He was a lecturer in Random Mathematics at the University of Hamgee. It was a distinguished post and he was an equally distinguished scholar, which may have explained why, in later years, his youngest son's academic ineptitude and generally wayward behaviour had become such a bone of contention between them.

"Yes," said the old man thoughtfully, "your father was involved," he paused, "somehow." The word hung in the air. The Pan surmised the old man knew more about his father than he did but then, that wasn't difficult. "However," he continued, "that is another story. What is your understanding of the Looking?"

"They talk to everyone between the ages of eight and ten until they find somebody with the right criteria who gives the right answers to their questions—it's a secret and only the senior priests know the answers. Then they take the kid to the High Priest and the Architrave and show him a load of stuff that has always belonged to the Architraves and the clincher is whether or not he recognises any of it or knows what it's all for."

"That's roughly what happens," said the old man. "There's a thread, an inspiration if you like, which is passed on from generation to generation. The Architraves are not the same soul, but theirs are interrelated. There are physical signs—characteristics borne by all of them—and prophecies, too."

The Pan grinned, his courage fortified by the generous measure of Calvados settling on his empty stomach.

"I'd heard the prophecies were part of the problem," he said, "I heard Arnold of Nim liked to cover his options and nobody ever had a clue what he meant."

"Then you have heard wrong," said the old man. "What do you understand by the term Reality Theory?"

The Pan stared at the old boy blankly. This conversation was entering uncharted waters and he was rapidly approaching his maximum depth.

"Er ..." he struggled, "I think it's the idea that small actions can have consequences which spread out, like the ripples in a pool, so they get bigger and bigger, so by, say, walking to the right of a lamp post instead of the left I can cause a series of unspecified small changes in space and time which could eventually add up to something big and cataclysmic."

"Very good," said the old man. "So if a man made prophecies forty generations ago, which were to be accurate today, he had to account for people like you walking the wrong side of lamp posts."

"Er, I suppose he did."

"Indeed. So predicting anything happening as far into his future as we are now would take remarkable skill."

"Mmm," said The Pan, beginning to see how Arnold of Nim's prophetic abilities might be viewed in a new light, "perhaps."

"Most certainly. You are right in that the Holy Prophet did give us options, but only because of the nature of reality. Do you know much Reality Theory?"

The Pan cleared his throat.

"Yes," he began before deciding that on this occasion, honesty was the best policy, "well actually, no."

"Did you not pay any attention in school?" asked the old man, a hint of desperation creeping into his voice.

The Pan shrugged. This was like being questioned by a teacher – he was twelve, in trouble and being told off by the headmaster again. He could feel a blush rising.

"Not as much as I should have done," he said, "but even if I had, I wouldn't have got to study the Philosophy of Reality. I never made it as far as the sixth form."

The old man smiled benignly.

"No," he said, "no, of course not. I'm sorry. Talking to you, it's easy to forget," another sly compliment, The Pan noticed. "Well, it's quite straightforward. Reality Theory is like this: let's say, for argument's sake, that you decide to walk past that lamp post on the left-hand side. Somewhere in another version of space and time another you is walking to the right."

"What about the real one?" asked The Pan, "the one who isn't looking where he is going and walks into the lamp post."

"This is a metaphorical situation," said the old man cheerfully, "let's keep it simple shall we? What would you say if I told you that for each time we make a choice, we create another universe where another version of ourselves, in another dimension of space and time is making a different decision?"

"I'd ask you to show me the one with no Grongles in it and I'd move there."

"This is no laughing matter."

"Do you see me laughing?"

The old man smiled sadly.

"No," he paused. "Well?"

The Pan held his hands up for a moment and let them drop to his sides.

"It sounds plausible enough to me," he said slowly.

"It is. Now, if The Prophet is to predict the events of tomorrow, he must be sure of the outcome of this small act of yours. Not only must he first identify which decision will be made by the version of you living in this dimension, but he must also decide what effects your decision will cause. Ninety-nine point nine per cent of these small decisions don't significantly alter our future, and time will continue upon its predestined framework. However, the other fraction of the percentage will sculpt a new destiny for us all. They are seemingly small things but nonetheless key factors which will shift our tomorrow. When he made his prophecies Arnold had to account for each one of those tiny events which was likely to occur between his then and our now, and identify which would affect our future and which would not."

"Ah," said The Pan who was beginning to appreciate how this could get complicated. "So what you're saying is, in theory by doing something as simple as walking to the left or right of a lamp post, I could change the entire future of this planet to one which didn't involve Grongles."

"You can't write them out of existence but you could cause some effect, some sea change in their make-up, which might alter the nature of their role in the world."

"Or a terminal illness in Lord Vernon?" suggested The Pan.

"Even if it were known how to bring that about, to do so would not be ethical," said the old man.

"Shame," said The Pan before he could shut himself up. He shouldn't have said that in front of someone who might well be a priest. "This hasn't happened already has it? I mean, is that how they got to us?"

"A very pertinent question. One we have no way of answering."

"Well, surely it's reasonably straightforward to make things better.

Wouldn't you just find out when an important event is due to take place and make sure it causes the Grongles to want to go home?"

"Not as such. That would be too specific. We are only permitted to alter destiny for the better and in a way that will not adversely affect other realities."

But they were still able, and allowed, to alter it. Arnold in the Skies!

"There will not be an event of that nature in this dimension of space and time for some years."

"Can't you manufacture one artificially?" asked The Pan.

"Indeed—but it is far from easy," said the old man. "And it can only be attempted with access to certain pieces of equipment." He held up the bag and shook it so the objects inside chinked together. "Unfortunately, while you have inadvertently unearthed a substantial portion of the things we need, we don't have everything."

"You don't?" asked The Pan, who was beginning to have a horrible idea where this conversation might be heading.

"No and it is unlikely we will ever find the things we need," said the old man.

"So no changing space-time then?"

"Since we are unable to do so safely, no. At least, not unless we absolutely have to."

"Is there an alternative option?"

"Oh yes. Many of the artefacts you have discovered are used in the Looking, the process of searching for a new Candidate for the position of Architrave. They may help us, since, alas, no Candidate was agreed upon when the Looking was last conducted."

"Is that usual?"

"No."

"I see. Well, I dunno if it's any help but one of the few things I remember about the last search was thinking my father didn't like the way it was being done. He didn't mention he was involved in the Looking but he used to talk about how this country needed a Candidate to get rid of the Grongles. He used to say there *had* to be one, if only the people searching were able to check the right places. There was nothing concrete, nothing disloyal—Dad was good like that—just hints. The way he spoke, I always thought the problem was that they couldn't look where they needed to, but he was never the same after that time and now I think maybe he fell out with them because they refused to look where he wanted them to."

"Your father didn't suffer fools gladly, or take the word 'no' well," said the old man with a smile, "he could be a little abrasive with his colleagues at times if he didn't get his way."

"Yes, well, he was the same at home after that."

The old man seemed thoughtful for a moment.

"He was under a great deal of strain, more than you can imagine."

"I'm sure he was and, rest assured, he shared it generously," said The Pan, and regretted it immediately.

"He was a man trying to do what was right for his people." The old man's tone was unruffled, and yet The Pan could tell he was angry. "It may not have made him a perfect parent, but he would have known that and it would have cut him to the quick."

The Pan couldn't meet the old man's eyes anymore, so he bowed his head and examined the carpet around his feet.

"In your heart of hearts, my boy, I believe you understand that."

Yes, The Pan realised, he did. "I'm sorry, ignore me, I'm bitter and twisted," he said.

The old man smiled kindly, "And almost as hard on yourself as he was. But he may have been right about the Looking. The old Architrave was beheaded before his time, so it may be that the new Candidate was then too young to be identified; he might not even have been born at that stage. Their arrival in itself will be a significant enough event to alter our reality without damage to others. It would be a tiny shift but it would suffice to make the Grongles change or go home. However, our problem is this: even if the Candidate is of age, or alive, all the signs would be unlikely to manifest themselves until the hour at which the Architrave's death would naturally have taken place. The Architrave was only fifty when the Grongles murdered him, and it may be another ten or fifteen years before his natural time. Even if we were able to conduct the Looking again we would simply end up with the same problem. It would be impossible to determine, with absolute certainty, whether or not our choice was the Candidate, until all the signs were present."

"Isn't there a shortcut? Forty generations is a long time, there must have been the odd blip with the Looking. You can't make me believe we've managed hundreds of years of smooth government without some kind of contingency plan for when it goes wrong. It would have been chaos."

"Indeed and for that exact reason there is one vital artefact which would allow us to establish the Candidate's credentials beyond reasonable doubt. Unfortunately, despite your friends' fine efforts locating these," he gestured with the bag of loot again, "we don't yet have it."

'Yet' – another worrying word. He paused, and The Pan waited.

"There is a further difficulty. In situations where no Candidate exists, it is possible, with the right knowledge and equipment, to set up a fake, to make an ordinary individual able to pass enough of the physical and spiritual tests to be made Architrave, even though he is not the true Candidate. As you might imagine, it is difficult to disprove the candidacy once it has been accepted by the people, no matter who the individual might be or how strong the evidence against him. As matters stand now, the true Candidate would be no more credible than such a fake."

"But how can you fake a Candidate? I thought there were signs. That hasn't happened before has it?" asked The Pan. He was confused. Surely if there had been any false Candidates he'd have been taught about it in history?

"Only once, several centuries ago in a similar situation to our own; when the Architrave died young and no Candidate was found. That time, the false Candidate was on the side of good and under the authority of the elders. She was carefully chosen and she merely stepped into the role to assure continuity. Eventually, the Looking succeeded, the true Candidate was found and the succession assured. It was then that the special equipment we seek was designed; to ensure such a vacuum never occurred again and that the Looking could never be what you term 'chaos'."

"So why not set up an interim, a fake Candidate like that?" said The Pan.

"Because there are already two false Candidates and there is nothing like being, as the sales people put it 'first to market' in situations like this. It is too late for us to catch up unless we can find the real McCoy, and while I have my own theories as to who that might be, without the artefact I refer to, it would take time and resources to confirm my view—time and resources we don't have. The forerunner, for the Candidacy, at present, is Lord Vernon.

Chapter 36

"Are you sure?" asked The Pan. "If Lord Vernon was setting himself up to be the Candidate, I'd have thought the Grongles would have announced it – or at least be preparing the ground. There's no sign of that."

"Oh, it'll take him a month or two but he has been researching, learning and preparing for years and he has already begun the process. If he succeeds, the people will believe he is destined to rule K'Barth and all effective resistance will cease." The Pan tried not to look nonplussed but he knew it wasn't working. He could almost feel the old man's frustration at having to spell out every little thing.

"Let me explain. Nobody likes being ruled by the Grongles do they?"

"Of course not," The Pan agreed. He checked himself, "Well, thinking about it, that's not one hundred per cent true, some people are sort of enjoying it. I mean, Denarghi wouldn't be much without it, would he? And there are the black marketeers—what will they do if things are stable and there isn't a black market?"

"Exactly," said the old man, "and then there are the people. They will get used to buying illegal goods, they will get used to the status quo and before you know it, they will start accepting it. They have learned the dos and don'ts, know how it all works, and unless they are being directly persecuted, they will begin to get comfortable. They will start thinking that life isn't so bad if they keep their heads down and don't get involved. The Grongles run an ordered, if not strictly free, society and when people ignore the problems, whether through apathy or self-preservation, they start to see the benefits in keeping things the way they are."

"The trains run on time," said The Pan drily, "Arnold knows they never used to. Is that the type of thing you're talking about?"

"Indeed, a simple case of investment, efficient maintenance and intelligent route scheduling. Nothing we couldn't have achieved on our own. Strange how the Grongles are given credit for that, don't you think?"

"You mean, people only have so much fight in them before they give up and accept things the way they are?"

"Yes and no. We are adaptable, which is usually an asset but it also means we get used to things very quickly. So, if an injustice goes on for long enough, it becomes normal and people are blinded to it. In this regime people disappear every day without trial, but that doesn't make it just, even if it has become normal."

"Mmm. I see your point but aren't you up against nature on this one?" asked The Pan.

"No," said the old man firmly.

"Really? I mean, won't people believe whatever they want to believe, regardless? They don't need Lord Vernon's help to start thinking like that, it's their fundamental make-up. For most people, day-to-day living is broadly similar, whoever is in charge. All they want is a quiet life, so when things are bad or dangerous, they keep their heads down. They know what will happen to their families and the people they love if they make too much noise, so they say, 'I'll take care of the little island round me and keep that right. I'll start small.' They never admit the real reason; that it's too scary and too dangerous to think big. No-one will resist the Grongles unless there's somebody braver and stronger for them all to stand behind, and there isn't."

"And there you have it, proof positive that by planning to set himself up as a false Candidate Lord Vernon is already beginning to affect space and time, himself."

"Not necessarily, I'm known to be sceptical. What about the other false Candidate?"

"I believe the Resistance are attempting to set up one of their own, but they are not being as clever about it as Lord Vernon."

A stark choice then. When it came to the nitty-gritty of bog-standard existence, there wouldn't be much difference between those two. Despite their directly opposing ideologies, their stances on things like free speech and democracy were surprisingly similar.

"I don't mean to be discouraging, but that's not much of a choice—civil liberty isn't a big issue with the Resistance any more than it is with Lord Vernon."

"We may be able to influence the Resistance."

That was a bit optimistic. The Pan felt his eyes rolling before he could stop himself.

"I take it you've never met any of them," he said tartly. "They're exactly the same as the Grongles only better brainwashed and more efficient. You'd have more luck trying to herd cats than influence the Resistance."

"Do you argue the toss with everyone like this?"

"Yes," said The Pan. "Look. I don't mean to be rude, but neither of the false options appeals does it? I'd have thought with the skills you have you'd be better off running yourself, or finding your missing bit of stuff and validating the real one. You can't bank on manipulating people, it never works and in the short time you've been here, even I have seen enough to realise you are way too smart to make a plan that stupid—unless you're working with a committee? You're not though, are you?"

There was an uncomfortable pause.

"The pressing issue, now, is to stop Lord Vernon."

Not a totally straight answer; no reference to The Pan's actual query. In other words, no reference to the real plan. He had to admire the old man's courage, though. A few nutters tried every now and again, but nobody stopped Lord Vernon.

"What if Lord Vernon doesn't want to be stopped?" he said.

"There are many ways to resist," said the old boy, smiling. "Perhaps, it is more a case of delay than out and out opposition. However, we do need to lay our hands on our 'missing bit of stuff' as you call it and ensure it is kept from Lord Vernon's clutches. When the true Candidate is identified beyond argument, then no matter how carefully he has prepared himself, Lord Vernon will fail."

"A lot of people believe there won't be another Candidate."

"Once again, your view merely proves my point. Lord Vernon's work has already begun, the hearts and minds of the people are turning. Yes, the thread is weak now, but if we are able to validate the Candidate it will never be broken."

The Pan sighed.

"I wish I could share your optimism."

"You don't believe me, do you?" said the old man. The Pan shook his head, it was more complicated than that. He knew the old man believed what he was saying and deep down he knew that he wanted to believe it, too. He would almost stake his life that everything he'd been told was true, but whether those truths related to one another in the way the old man had presented them was a different question. He guessed not.

"It isn't that your theory doesn't appeal, more that you've chosen the world's most cynical person to expound it to." He smiled; that wasn't a lie, but he hadn't said whether or not he believed the old man, either. He could be evasive, too. "I gave up hoping for a miracle a long time ago." The Pan knew he hadn't given up, he simply couldn't afford himself the luxury of hoping for anything anymore. "I'm sorry, that came out wrong," he said,

"I'm not quite so self-pitying, but I'd like to think I'm a realist. Reading between the lines, it sounds like you have found the Candidate, and stalling Lord Vernon is important because they're only four and you have to wait for them to grow up."

The old man chuckled.

"You are right, in a way. The Candidate is actually about your age but has a lot of growing up to do."

"Ha! I knew it! You have found him."

The old man steepled his hands and gave The Pan a long, appraising stare.

"Yes," he said slowly, without breaking eye contact. "I think I have."

The Pan looked away quickly; it was good to find out he was right but he didn't want to go any further and risk getting involved. He feared he'd given something of himself away.

"Well if you have, he's ..." He stopped. "Is it a he?"

"Yes, it's a he."

"Right, well, he's not going to be around long. People who oppose Lord Vernon have a short shelf life."

The old man's gold tooth flashed as he smiled again.

"Not everyone. One person stubbornly refuses to lie down and die," he said, giving The Pan a knowing wink.

"You mean me?" The old man nodded. "Oh no! I didn't oppose him, I merely got in his way once. These days, I do my best to keep out of it."

"Exactly, and you are highly successful. In his eyes, you are nothing, he should be able to wipe you out at a stroke, but try as he might, he can't. It makes your existence all the greater an outrage. It rankles his pride. It's that which fuels his hatred." The old boy seemed almost proud of him and though wary, The Pan couldn't help but feel pleased. "Then—although he doesn't know—you are also a member of that other thorn in his side, the Mervinettes. He can't catch them either and it must be down to you—that's why you are the best man for the job."

For what job? The Pan ran his hands through his hair. He didn't like the direction the conversation was taking. There'd been an undercurrent all along and at some point soon the old man was going to ask him for help. He was not a joiner-in-er, never had been, and he wasn't about to start now.

"It all started when Lord Vernon and I had an accidental collision and I'm not sure avoidance and opposition are quite the same," he said. "If you're talking about opposition, I'm definitely *not* the man for the job. I don't do bravery."

"You don't have to be brave, all I'm talking about is doing what you do already," said the old man. "The final artefact is safe, for now, in the only place the Grongles would never look; but if Lord Vernon finds out where it is, which I believe is highly likely, he will seize it. I cannot allow that to happen, I must ratify the Candidate and unite all the resisting factions behind him. Unless I can do that we will remain divided, the Grongles will rule forever and civilisation will come to an end. We have to get to it before Lord Vernon does and the only way we can do that is to arrange a bank heist."

It figured. It so figured. The Pan knew he would be asked for a favour. No. He doubted Big Merv would rob to order.

"There are four of us and I don't decide which jobs we do. I'm the getaway man, that's all."

"Big Merv listens to you."

"Not in the conventional sense. He trusts my escape instincts; that's not the same as trusting me. As for the other two—"

"All I am asking is a small favour; that when you are planning your next robbery, you mention the job in passing."

The Pan thought for a moment.

"Look, I can't guarantee anything, but because you're a friend of Gladys and Ada, I'll ask. Which bank and which branch?"

"The Grongles have no idea it's there and it's the last place they'd look. The unfortunate thing is, what with the Grongles being the way they are, it's also the last place we can look—it's in the Bank of Grongolia."

There was a loud spluttering noise as The Pan choked on his Calvados. The old man walked over to him and patted him on the back. By the time he had finished he was seeing stars.

"Do you mean *the* Bank of Grongolia, on their home continent, in their capital city?" asked The Pan when he was finally able to speak.

It was more than secure; non-Grongles weren't allowed in.

"Of course," said the old man, "where else? I told you it was safe."

"No," said The Pan flatly, "it would be suicide."

"If anyone can achieve this, it's you and the Mervinettes," said the old man.

"No chance." The old man showed such disappointment that The Pan felt almost hard-hearted practising what was, after all, only common sense.

"Look," he held his hands out, palms upwards in his stock 'c'est la vie' gesture. "I don't mean to be difficult but you have to understand there is no way in a million years that I can commit any bank robbery without Big Merv, Frank and Harry, and there is absolutely no way in the lifetime of this entire universe that any sane being—and I like to count both myself and my colleagues as sane, here—would attempt robbery of the Bank of Grongolia. It's—It's—" The Pan waved one hand expansively, "only an *idiot* would attempt it."

"Exactly. So they'd never expect it," said the old man.

"No, you don't understand. It wouldn't work," said The Pan. "Not only would we fail, we would all die. What good would that do? Anyway," he held up the thimble, "what about this? If you can just reach into your cellar through one of these and pull out a bottle of Gladys' Calvados, what's to stop you reaching into the vaults of the Bank of Grongolia and doing your own dirty work?"

"Life is never quite that straightforward, my boy," said the old man solemnly. "Were I to try, even with a portal as powerful as that," he gestured to the thimble in The Pan's hand, "I could not reach everywhere I wished—many places are inaccessible even to me. The Bank of Grongolia is one of them."

"Well there's a coincidence," retorted The Pan, "the Bank of Grongolia isn't accessible to me, either—small world isn't it?"

"It would be a brave and noble action."

"Maybe, but I told you before, I'm not brave or noble."

The old man fixed him with another penetrating stare.

"I believe you are," he said quietly.

The Pan shook his head. He felt awkward and embarrassed and he knew he was blushing.

"You have me all wrong," he said sadly.

"Yet in time, I am confident you will prove me right," said the old man. "You don't have to commit yourself to anything at this stage. I'm merely asking you to speak to Big Merv and persuade him to talk to me."

Despite his disbelief The Pan couldn't help smiling. The old boy was certainly persistent.

"You're barking mad aren't you? Or is it simply that you don't know Big Merv? He's a Swamp Thing and as if that isn't enough, he's orange instead of green; can you imagine the size of the chip on his shoulder? If you thought the average Swamp Thing was sensitive about his appearance, try

129

meeting Big Merv! He makes Denarghi and his Resistance cronies look laid back—he makes Grongles look shy and retiring."

"They are brave and honourable creatures, though."

"There you go again always expecting the best in people," The Pan sighed. "You realise he'll never agree to it don't you? He'll probably kill me for even suggesting something this dumb."

"Killing you would be a dreadful waste of his prize asset," said the old man. "Would you rather I hired somebody else to work with you—the Resistance, for instance? You seem to know all about them and I'm sure Denarghi would be happy to assist us. I expect I could arrange for them to liaise with you, direct, if I gave them your address."

Unbelievable. The unspeakable, low-down, cheek!

"Are you blackmailing me?" asked The Pan. The old man said nothing.

The conversation had taken an unreal turn in the last few minutes and he was finding it difficult to appreciate what was being said. It was as if he was watching it happen to somebody else. Part of him, the sensible bit, was telling him he should be angry with the old man but another more reckless aspect of his personality was thinking what the heck, everyone has to die sometime, right? He was tired of running away, perhaps it was time he got himself shot and put an end to it. Anyway, there was no such thing as a one hundred per cent probability. The Pan knew that the Mervinettes were the only ones who could do this job. In theory, if they agreed, they could ask the old man for a lot of money. It meant he could, possibly, ask for an introduction fee on top. Somewhere, in some version of space and time, the robbery had to succeed. If it did, and The Pan was right, the Mervinettes would all be rich beyond their wildest dreams. He would be able to buy himself a new identity and live a normal life. Perhaps it wasn't such a bad idea to gamble everything on one world-beating heist.

"You are blackmailing me, aren't you?" he said again, just to check.

"I'm afraid so."

"I knew it. I don't suppose I get a chance to say no, do I?"

"I'm afraid I can't afford to give you that option."

The Pan nodded.

"How could I tell you were going to say something like that?" It was amazing what a levelling effect a police state had on the most upright of citizens. He was supposed to be the criminal here, so it was surprising to have the moral high ground over an old boy who was clearly a senior holy man.

"You're a Nimmist and I'd stake my life you're a lot higher up the tree than priest—yet you're blackmailing me into certain death," he said. "Isn't that a little unethical?"

"Yes it is, but in the light of what's at stake, I think I can bend the rules. If you do this thing, the entire civilised world will thank you. If you turn your back on us now, within two years there may not be any civilisation left. Grongolian world domination—is that what you want?"

"Er, isn't that what we already have?"

"No, not yet."

"Seriously. Why me? What have I done to deserve this?"

"You are ... important."

The Pan stared at him. There was more to this than his visitor was letting on, that much was obvious.

"Important," he repeated, "don't think flattery will change my mind." It might, of course, but he didn't want to show it. "Why am I important?"

"You'll know soon enough—here's a clue though, it's to do with your refusal to give up and be captured. They can't catch you unless you let them," said the old man.

"No. They *can* catch me. They haven't succeeded yet, that's all. Anyway, if I'm so important wouldn't you be wiser to keep me alive?"

"If you are the man I think you are, you'll keep yourself alive," said the old man. The Pan sighed, the poor old boy had clearly lost his grip on reality.

"I'm not indestructible you know," he leaned forward on his chair. "Look. There's something you need to understand about me and it's this: I'm a coward. Brave people get clobbered because they go sticking their necks out, looking for trouble. I'm not lucky or alive because I'm brave and clever, I'm alive because I'm too scared to end up dead." How could he explain this in a way that would make the old man understand? "Do you not see the difference? When trouble comes, I run the other way. I'm not here because I stand and fight, I'm here because I run."

"And when there's nowhere left to run to?" asked the old man.

"There's always somewhere," said The Pan with far more conviction than he felt.

"No-one can run forever. Not even you. One day, soon, you will have no choice but to stand and fight your corner."

"Oh no! Absolutely not. I don't do fisticuffs."

"I'm not talking about physical violence. I'm talking about being who you are, sticking up for yourself, for once, and for what you believe in."

"Again, I think you are confusing me with a man of courage and principle. Don't let my suave exterior fool you," said The Pan.

"You don't fool me for a minute, my boy and be advised, your 'exterior' is far from suave."

The Pan laughed, bitterly.

"I am aware of that. I was being sarcastic."

"You'll be paid handsomely for your trouble."

"Mmm. Every man has his price. The question is, can you afford me?" A round of Gladys' cheese and pickle sandwiches would have bought him, but the old man wasn't to know and he wasn't about to let on.

"How about the installation of all known optional extras on your own, personal snurd?"

"I've already taken care of that."

"Of course yes. The proceeds from the sale of the ring worn by forty generations of Architraves, a potent symbol of power, now in the hands of the charlatan who wishes to seize it."

"Quite." The Pan raised one eyebrow, "No need to rub it in—you want my help, after all. If you want me to be nice to you, you have to be nice to me."

"Don't get antsy with me," said the old man. "We both know you have no choice in this matter." His tone of voice was stern, but his eyes were smiling again. "Alright then, how about the installation of all available optional extras on your snurd, including those which are not common knowledge?"

Wow! That sounded brilliant! Better play it cool though. The Pan folded his arms and tried to appear belligerent. "And a new identity?" added the old boy, hopefully.

Ah. It seemed he was susceptible to guilt. That was handy.

"Now you're talking. And ...?"

The old man looked taken aback.

"I told you I was very expensive," said The Pan, "and don't forget, I have a lot of persuading to do. My colleagues will take a great deal of convincing."

"Don't worry, we'll make it worth their while." There was that worrying word 'we' again.

"How worth their while?" asked The Pan, glancing down at the bag of loot the old man had taken from him earlier and eyeing him knowingly.

"Not *that* worth their while," the old man smiled, "but you can keep the thimble if you wish."

There was a result.

"Thank you," said The Pan, trying to appear calm and unconcerned and failing, dismally, to hide his delight.

"On one condition," said the old man, "try to use it for something a little more constructive than—"

"I know," said The Pan, "ogling a girl.

"Exactly." He stood up and, to The Pan's disappointment, he remembered to pick up the bag of loot. "Well, I must be going now," he said, "let me know how you get on with Big Merv."

"Er, yes," said The Pan hesitantly. If Big Merv reacted the way he thought, he doubted he'd be alive to tell the old man anything. "Is there a time scale on this ludicrous mission?"

The old man thought for a moment.

"Well now, I understand you will have to pick your moment, but we need to move quickly. Is three months long enough?"

"Three months is fine," said The Pan gratefully. From the way the old man had been talking he'd been expecting a deadline of three days. Clearly the Nimmists had a more relaxed approach to time scales than anyone else. "If I manage to put this idea to Big Merv and survive, how will I contact you? I mean, I don't know where you live."

"No," said the old man, "I know where you live, though, don't I?" He winked, "I'll see you around."

The Pan stood up and made to escort him downstairs to the front door.

"No, no my boy, don't worry. I'll let myself out," he said, and was gone.

Chapter 37

London. Late at night. Or should that be, early in the morning? Ruth Cochrane was not asleep, or in bed. She was walking home and as she did so, she was having an attack of paranoia.

Yes, she told herself, it was paranoia, but even so, she was beginning to think she was being followed. As she listened to wind rustling the leaves in the trees, she thought she heard something else: footsteps. Well, this was a city and other people would be making their way home, even at this time of night. Except ... She stopped and pretended to fiddle with the heel of her shoe. It meant she could bend down and give the road behind her a thorough check while, at the same time, being ready to leap up and sprint away if she saw anything scary.

The footsteps behind her stopped. She checked the road. Nope. Nothing.

Casting her mind back over the day's events she tried to decide in her own mind whether or not she was imagining things. The day had started well. Recession apart, her company had bagged a new account, a massive one. They wanted an executive to work on it, reporting to Ruth's two favourite colleagues, and now she had completed four of her six months' training they wanted Ruth to be that executive. Wahoo! She'd finally made it off the bottom rung. They were promoting her, giving her a pay rise and most importantly, the MD was advertising for a new secretary. She'd been walking on air all day and then, as if that wasn't good enough, she had been out for a great night, a friend's birthday dinner followed by a trip to a comedy club.

It was way past midnight when the show finished but because the moon was as bright and clear as the street lights, Ruth had decided to walk home. It was only two miles or so, twenty or thirty minutes if that, mostly through respectable, well-lit neighbourhoods and half of it would be with a friend of the friend who lived in Bayswater, anyway. She would have bet any money that when she and the other girl set out, there was no-one in pursuit. They walked part of the way home together and after they'd parted company she realised she was too late for the tube and still too far away from the stop to make a run for the hourly night bus. She turned left into Little Venice. She'd slowed, admiring the big houses and generally enjoying the fact that she lived in such a huge metropolis. Yep, he must have picked her up somewhere there.

She walked on a little way, until she could hear the footsteps start up again before stopping a second time. Once again, they stopped when she did.

More than a coincidence then? Maybe and that was grim.

OK. One last try. She walked on, the footsteps walked on.

Hmm, an echo? Possibly. She tried tap dancing a yard or two but the accompanying footsteps continued their measured, one, two.

Or maybe not.

As she reached the end of the road and turned the corner she ran fast along the next street. It was a long row of three-storey terraced houses with small, walled gardens in front, many of which were bounded by privet hedges.

Hoorah! Somewhere to hide, thought the irresponsible, frivolous part of Ruth which treated existence as a glorified spy movie.

Running as fast as she could but at the same time trying to make no sound so her shadowy pursuer, if there was one, wouldn't realise what she was doing, she decided to try to reach one of the hedged-in gardens and hide there, before the person making the footsteps got as far as turning the corner.

Not the first one. That's exactly where he'll look, she thought as she made to duck through the nearest entrance. She ran on to the third enclosed garden and nipped in through the open gate. It was a completely mad thing to do, she knew. Behind the hedge was a pair of bins.

That was a stroke of luck.

She ran over and found that, a little way behind them, there was a hole in the foliage that allowed her to creep right inside the hedge.

Even better.

She crept in, pulled one of the bins towards her to help hide the gap at the bottom of the privet and waited.

A few moments and there it was.

Footsteps. Running.

They stopped. She could hear somebody in the road, the other side of the hedge, walking backwards and forwards as if looking for something. Please no. He, it had to be a he, didn't appear to be out of breath even though he'd just sprinted up the street – he was obviously marathon-runner fit – only bigger, a lot bigger than a long-distance runner. As she watched the dark shape moving to and fro she shuddered and the hedge rustled a little. He stopped, stood absolutely still and ... yes ... sniffed the air.

Lord no! That was too creepy. He was after her and he was also, clearly, a member of the serial killers' guild. Normal people don't use scent to track others, come to think of it, normal people don't tend to track others, anyway. Good plan to hide behind the bins, then. He moved out of sight but she could feel he was still there and then, yes, she knew it. He'd come into the garden. He stole silently over to the dustbins and lifted the lids, he even peered between them, but in the dark didn't notice the gap in the hedge. Luckily the glaring, tell-tale patch of damp concrete that would show the second bin to be recently moved was obscured by shadows.

He paused, as if in thought, before taking something from his pocket and rubbing it on the front of his coat. He was wearing a long, dark trench coat, probably black or blue, open, with brass buttons which glinted as they caught the light. Underneath he wore a jacket made from a similar material but it had a stand-up collar, like a military uniform and was fastened with a single button in the middle – she could see a contrasting white V shape it made against the stock or cravat – too many ruffles for a shirt – which he was wearing with it. His belt had a holster hanging on it, complete with gun, she assumed, and it was one of those military-style belts with a strap that goes diagonally across the chest with ... yes. He was wearing a sword. His trousers had a stripe of different-coloured material down the outsides and with them he wore knee-high boots in a matte black material; suede? A dress uniform? A disguise for a sci-fi convention? He didn't have a hat, but was wearing a pair of dark glasses – please dark glasses and not night vision glasses – and in a cruel and unpleasant way, he was extremely good looking. He was also wearing gloves, with rings on the outside. Except for that bit, his getup was as if she'd dreamed up Mr Darcy's dark alter ego or Evil Adam Ant and he'd come alive.

Nice touch, My Brain, throwing the handsome thing in there. Had somebody spiked her drink? Silently, he crouched down.

No. These events were real.

He pointed the object at the hedge and, ah yes. It was a torch. Ruth did the hardest thing she had ever done in her life. Hoping he wouldn't train the beam down and see the gap she had squeezed through or the soggy black circle showing where she'd moved one of the bins, she took her glasses off and closed her eyes. Slowly, as quietly as she could, she moved the hand clutching her spectacles behind her back. He must be looking for a reflection. If she kept the specs out of sight and her eyes closed he wouldn't find it.

Every part of her screamed "RUUUUUUN." But her only chance, she knew, was to wait where she was.

"Come to me. I know you are there," he whispered as he shone the torch back and forth across the hedge. His voice had a hypnotic quality and without thinking she almost did as she was told. But she managed to keep still and sat, frozen, trying to subdue her breathing, not to mention her trembling. The darkness behind her eyelids changed colour as the beam of his torch played over her face. It was taking all her self-control not to look.

Please let the hedge be thick enough to hide her.

The beam of the torch stopped moving and he laughed quietly. A laugh conspicuously lacking in mirth or human warmth. A laugh so utterly evil Ruth felt a shiver run down her spine.

"Now I have you," he said and the little hairs on the back of her neck stood up. His voice this time was soft, malevolent and very, very scary. She suppressed another involuntary shudder.

A sudden flurry, and with a loud scream a cat leapt from the bushes beside her and ran past him into the street. He breathed out with a hiss, straightened up to his full and considerable height and turned the torch off. While she willed him to go, he stood there and tapped it thoughtfully against the palm of his hand.

"You will not evade me forever, Chosen One. I will find you," he told the darkness quietly.

She watched from her hiding place as he turned on his heel and strode out into the street. She stayed where she was long after his footsteps receded into the night and waited another half an hour before daring to creep out of the hedge.

"No further chances to be taken, tonight, Ms Ruth Cochrane," she said to herself and headed straight back to the Edgware Road and the night bus, which was arriving as she reached the stop. Wow! Had that taken a whole hour? She consulted her watch. Yes.

So. Had somebody spiked her drink?

No, but oh how she wished they had.

Chapter 38

The old man's visit had left The Pan somewhat at a loss. He would have to be cautious about raising a delicate matter like a robbery at the Bank of Grongolia with Big Merv – pick a suitable place and time when he was in a benevolent enough mood not to get angry at the idea, but not such good spirits that he'd agree to it. He had hardly slept. Instead he had spent most of the night pacing backwards and forwards across his room trying to think of a way to broach the subject of taking on a suicide mission with Ning Dang Po's premier gangland boss.

What if Big Merv was mad enough to agree? There was the Interceptor to contend with now. It was faster and slicker than the MK II and The Pan would have to use his brain, as well as his driving ability to redress the balance. He didn't trust his brain, and given the choice would have preferred to stick with his driving ability. He was a better driver than his pursuer – he was a better driver than most people – but even though it had every state-of-the-art upgrade available the MK II was outclassed, and he feared that sooner or later, he was going to be outwitted.

He would have liked to believe the whole escapade with the old man had been a dream. He could have convinced himself were it not for the thimble, or more to the point, the girl in the thimble.

The Pan had never been one to do things by halves, but he realised that even by his standards his regard for her was somewhat full-on. He was smitten with a capital S and it had happened very quickly. If he had dared he would have leaned through the portal – the way he had when he had collected the brandy glasses from the bar at the Parrot for the old man – and spoken to her. Several times he had thought about trying to climb through it completely. However, he realised that the sight of a seedy young man appearing out of thin air to the accompaniment of sounds associated with ancient plumbing would scare her off for life. Especially taking into account the fact that he knew nothing of her civilisation and try as he might, he was unable to imagine anywhere in this New World unless she was present. Even if he did think of a way to materialise in front of her without her noticing, he would have to wait until he was well versed enough in the manners and customs of her world to blend in, otherwise, he was afraid that, in his ignorance, he would make some unmentionable social gaffe and blow any chances of romance clean out of the water. He didn't know where, or even when, she lived and his only link with her surroundings was her. The thimble worked on imagination and without her there, he didn't know what to imagine. All he could do was wait and hope that by watching her go about the mundane tasks of her day, he would learn enough about her world to join her in a more discreet manner. From what little he had seen thus far, wherever it was she lived, there were no Grongles and no Resistance. He became obsessed with finding out about her surroundings. If he could only discover enough about how life worked on her planet maybe, one day, he could step through the thimble to reach her, leave his troubles behind forever, and start afresh.

Then again, maybe not. Even if she was anything more than a figment of his imagination – the old man had said she was real but The Pan didn't entirely trust him – he was nowhere near expert enough on the workings of her world to leave his own, not until he could materialise somewhere alone. In the meantime he was supposed to persuade Big Merv and his fellow Mervinettes to sign a suicide pact with the old man and agree to take on the most ludicrously insane bank heist ever. His quest for information about the girl's world had gained a new urgency.

The Pan had always considered himself to be a man of action. When something bad happened he could be very decisive, and run away at once. Only this time the number of places left to run to was dwindling. He felt trapped. His world was contracting. No matter where he fled, he would soon meet with the Resistance, the old man, Big Merv or the Grongles. His only option was to pick the least grim of four unattractive choices: to work for the old man. When he finally lay down to rest, he couldn't stop his mind racing.

A new day eventually dawned. The Mervinettes would be meeting for a debrief of the previous day's robbery and to plan the next one. Presumably, if the old man knew what Big Merv had said to him about thinking and driving, he would also have known about today's debrief. It was only beginning to get light but The Pan had given up hope of sleeping and stood in front of the bathroom mirror scrutinising his complexion.

"You look terrible."

The word 'bags' didn't do justice to the dark rings under his eyes, they went right round, panda style; suitcases perhaps, or full container ships. He was paler, too and already regretting the way he'd spent the night. The Virtual Parents stepped in.

"Nothing is so important it should get in the way of a good night's sleep," he said in the voice of his Virtual Mother.

"Your Mother's right," he chipped in, doing the voice of Virtual Father. "If you must live by the few wits you have then you should at least rest them properly."

"Yeh, yeh. I know," he told them wearily, and plastered his face with shaving soap. He had been a bad son, always in trouble at school, never revising for his exams and always late with his course work. It wasn't much good beating himself up about it – he could hardly do anything to repair the damage now, but he blushed at the thought of the shame he'd brought on his family. He watched his face darken in the mirror. His blushes were very odd, these days and he seemed to go more blue than red. He wondered if he was anaemic and should see a doctor. Perhaps his heart was as weak as he'd been pretending it to be.

"No. Don't be an idiot. You're just stressed."

He dabbled the end of the razor in the water. Behind its beard of shaving cream, his reflection stared back at him expectantly. He liked talking to himself. It made his thought processes seem more real and definite.

"You're going to have to sort this out. You can't drive the Mervinettes to Grongolia and back; you'll die," he said, jabbing the razor authoritatively at his mirror image.

"I know," it said, "but how?" He raised his eyebrows, watching as the reflection mirrored his movements.

"Good question ..." With a sigh he started to shave one side of his face. It did look a strange colour. Perhaps a visit to the doctor wasn't such a bad idea.

"No. You can't afford it," he muttered continuing to shave as he spoke. He wasn't concentrating and cut himself. He swore, and bleeding copiously all the while, he reached for a tissue which he dipped in the water and stuck over the cut. The flow of blood soon slowed and he reached down for the razor. In the dim light the smears of blood on his fingertips appeared darker than usual.

"Hmm," he said, holding his hands closer to the neon tube above the mirror. Yes, the blood was darker, much darker than it should be. He looked up at his reflection again and leaned forward, giving his face the type of close inspection usually reserved for checking spots. The blood on the tissue was wrong. It wasn't red at all, but a dark purple, as if somebody had added blue ink to it. He looked down at his hands again. They were purple, too.

"Smecking Arnold," he whispered, clutching at the basin for support, "I'm cracking up." No, he wasn't cracking up; it was stress, that was all, a warning. He would be able to tell Big Merv about the old man in a couple of hours and then everything would be alright. He turned the light out and carried on shaving. The bathroom only had one tiny window which was fitted with frosted glass. In the stygian gloom he couldn't see what he was doing and cut himself again. At least he couldn't see what colour the blood was this time.

Chapter 39

In the cold light of morning, Ruth felt able to view her stalking experience with detachment. The scary stranger had called her 'Chosen One' and she was adamant that in order to be 'Chosen' the 'One' in question would know. So; chances of it happening again? Not high.

However, her view of the experience, itself, didn't improve. It was the sniffing thing. Was that human? Not strictly. It was amazing how the ideas behind the vintage horror movies she watched had come into their own after her experience. Ruth marvelled at the way the flimsiest of plots and cheapest of special effects could return to haunt an imaginative person with the right kind of giant, sniffing, evil-voiced-bloke-shaped catalyst (with a static powered torch.) Half-heartedly, she had reported her experience to the police. The weary-looking sergeant obviously believed she was barking mad because she didn't write a single thing down throughout the whole interview. Ruth had to concede that if she'd heard the events described by somebody else she'd have thought so, too.

Later that evening, she went over her story again with her flatmate.

"Let me get this straight," Lucy was a great deal more sympathetic than the police sergeant. "You were followed home by a bloke."

"Yes," said Ruth, "only not home, I noticed him and hid."

"Good plan. Could happen to anyone."

"Exactly! That's not what I'm worried about, the bit I'm worried about is—"

"That he tried to find you?"

"Well, surprisingly, no, not really. He was trying to find someone but he didn't seem to know who and I'm pretty sure it wasn't actually me."

"So you're not expecting him to pop up again?"

"No. Not if I think about it practically—or at least I might see him again but I doubt he'll be looking for me. No, I was scared because of—"

"The sniffing thing."

"Yes and although I'm sure it was a mistake, the way he called me 'Chosen One' was so horrible and I can't help thinking—"

"Ruth, he called the person he thought was hiding in that hedge 'Chosen One'. We both agree that doesn't necessarily mean you."

The relief. Like hitting a wall but in a good way. Thank you, thank you, Lucy.

"That's exactly what I thought—" she began.

"—but you're still worried?" Lucy had a habit of finishing others' sentences. It annoyed a lot of people, but since she usually guessed what Ruth was about to say correctly, Ruth didn't mind.

"A little."

Less so, now – the mere fact that her sensible flatmate's take on the 'Chosen' question was the same has her own made it easier to dismiss. That and her fervent desire for it not to be true. She clutched at another straw. "I thought it might be Nigel playing a prank." Nigel, Lucy's vile, odious and obscenely rich boyfriend; Nigel who'd made a pass at Ruth and gone out of his way to be unpleasant to her and cause trouble from the very minute she turned him down; Nigel, the love of Lucy's life, the bane of hers.

"I know he can be a bit of a twit but I can't believe Nigel would do anything that stupid," said Lucy.

"No. Me neither," said Ruth.

A half truth. In her view Nigel was easily mean enough to rig an experience like the previous evening's but in this particular instance, she didn't believe he had. She had no idea who the man with the torch might have been but she knew he was far too convincingly menacing for it to be an act. Her pursuer might behave in other ways when he was mixing in society but Ruth reckoned what she'd seen was evil. She shuddered. A level of evil Nigel could never hope to aspire to, no matter how hard he tried.

Chapter 40

The Pan was wearing a new disguise when he left the Parrot – he was now a distinguished member of Ning Dang Po's business community. After the old man's departure he had gone to Gladys and Ada and explained, indirectly, about the Resistance. He had skirted delicately around the subject of why they were looking for him, but after the Grongles' visit to the Parrot the previous week he suspected his landladies already knew. They had a selection of clothing left by long-departed lodgers, among which was a pinstripe suit. It smelled of mothballs but it was tailor made, albeit for somebody else, with a bright blue lining. The pinstripe was blue, too, instead of white. Its previous occupant had been roughly the same size and shape as The Pan so it fitted reasonably well. They'd also found an aluminium briefcase to go with it. What he hadn't told them, of course, was that he was hoping this new disguise would fool not only the Resistance but also their friend, the old man.

Ada said he looked a veritable eminence grise – whatever that was – while Gladys assured him he looked like a company director and warned him against the dangers of 'sticking out like a sore thumb' and being mugged on his way home, since Turnadot Street, where the Parrot and Screwdriver was situated, was a notoriously insalubrious quarter of the city.

The two Resistance heavies from the previous night were waiting for him outside the Parrot but failed to penetrate his new disguise. Perhaps the confident upright, middle-aged walk helped, or the change of moustache and hair colouring from white to a darker grey. The Pan nodded at them.

"Morning, gentlemen," he said, his mood lightning as he walked away, still unrecognised and more to the point, unmolested. By the time he'd arrived at Big Merv's place he felt positively buoyant.

Big Merv owned a nightclub called 'The Big Thing'. True to gangland form, the door was staffed by large gentlemen whose necks were wider than the tops of their heads, and inside, a bevy of scantily clad ladies strolled, sat or sometimes danced provocatively about the place, looking 'decorative'. The Big Thing was the equivalent of a sixteen-year-old's really cool bedroom – only for older gentlemen. 'Look at my pad with my stolen road signs, my fantastic spangly decor, sound to light system, home brew under the bed, up-to-the-minute gaming console and cool posters,' has been supplanted by; 'Don't look at my stolen goods, look at my pad with my fantastic spangly ladies, sound to light system and fruit machines. Then drink some of my exotic cocktails and forget you saw anything, anyway, except the ladies, of course, because I'd like you to come and spend some more money here, again.'

The ladies – and Big Merv – were well protected, not only by the no-neck bouncers but also by a complicated set of security protocols. For The Pan, these centred around the amount of grovelling required to persuade whatever Neanderthal was on duty to actually allow him in. A small square peep hole in the middle of the door opened abruptly in reply to his knock. Framed in the square were two eyes, the beginnings of a broken nose and possibly a hairline, although it was difficult to tell because it was all shaved off.

"Yes?" said a deep bass voice.

"Mr Rogers to see Mr Big," said The Pan, noticing to his dismay that this morning's doorman was a newbie.

"Mr Rogers is an old man, you're not. Now hop it," came the reply.

Ah yes, the new disguise. There was a protocol for this, The Pan remembered.

"Sorry, I forgot. Please tell Mr Big that Mr Rogers has moved away and that Mr Marchant, his replacement, is here to see him."

"Mr Big isn't expecting anyone this morning." The steel peephole slid shut. No change from usual then. Why he had to ritually humiliate himself like this every time he couldn't begin to fathom. He could imagine the conversation as one peanut-head handed over to another and briefed them on intimidating him. Not that he needed intimidating of course; he was a coward after all and you can't scare somebody who is already frightened. Never mind. He knocked a second time and once again the small steel window slid back.

"I told you—" the gorilla behind it started.

"I'm Mr Rogers," said a voice, "I do, indeed, have to move away and this is, indeed, my replacement, Mr Marchant." The Pan had seen who it was behind him, but something made him turn round anyway. "Your dedication to your job is commendable," the old man was telling the doorman. "I will make sure I inform Mr Big of your diligence when we see him."

There was a long silence while the bouncer appeared to be concentrating.

"He means he's going to tell Big Merv that you work hard and are thorough," said The Pan, and noticing the bouncer's continuing blank expression, added, "he'll tell the Big Man you're good at your job."

"Uh-huh," said the bouncer slowly. The Pan took advantage of the few minutes it would take for him to grasp the new situation and open the door, and rounded on the old man.

"What in the name of all that's holy are you doing here?" He knew, positively knew he hadn't been followed. Not on foot anyway. Perhaps the old man had contacts who could follow him over the roofs.

"Strengthening your resolve."

"Railroading me more like! You said we had three months!"

"We do—three months to plan, not three months to bring the subject up. These things take time to arrange."

"If we had three years to plan this heist it would still be death on a stick," said The Pan. "Anyway," he added, thinking about the scantily clad ladies inside the building, "this is no place for the likes of you!"

"I think it's rather nice—I like a pretty lady."

"Now you're taking the mick. How in Arnold's name did you find me?"

"I'd have thought that would have been abundantly clear. You know, for a bright lad you are remarkably slow on the uptake."

The general gist was insulting but The Pan noted 'bright lad' was a compliment.

"Oh, thank you." He flashed a sarcastic smile. As if the Resistance and the uniqueness of eyes in the back of his head weren't enough to contend with, he had spent the entire night awake – developing mauve blood in the process – and now this. Putting this ludicrous heist to Big Merv was scary enough, without having to worry about being needled by some annoying old giffer into the bargain.

Despite being a 'bright lad' The Pan knew he wasn't as bright as the old man, mainly because of the old boy's tendency to treat him like an imbecile. It wasn't out of spite or unpleasantness, it was merely the habitual condescension of a person used to living in a world where everyone else was several orders of magnitude less shrewd than him. He treated The Pan the way his father had – and there was another man who was several orders of magnitude cleverer than most of his colleagues. The old man clearly thought The Pan was bright – which was flattering – but the wrong kind of smart – which was not – and worse, not smart enough.

The most galling thing was that even though the old man was cocky, irritating, creative with the truth and happened to be blackmailing and railroading him into certain death, The Pan couldn't help liking him. It was like dealing with an older, wiser smarter version of himself, or at least, the bits he liked. Even so, Big Merv's reaction was going to be a picture when the two of them walked into his office together.

"Why haven't you slept?" the old boy went on, "you look terrible!"

Arnold's hair! He knew how to be annoying alright. The Pan shut all four eyes and counted to ten.

"I'd have thought that would have been abundantly clear! You know, for a bright man, you really are slow on the uptake," he said mimicking the old man's earlier statement. "Guess what," he went on. "I would have liked to have got some sleep last night. I was very tired but I couldn't drop off. I can't think why but I seemed to be worried about something!"

The old man took a deep breath, and was about to make a lengthy reply when the door opened.

"Mr Big will see you now," said the bouncer.

"Mr Big is aware that both of us are here to see him, isn't he?" said The Pan.

The bouncer nodded. Phew, that was a relief then, he'd get thumped over the lunacy of the plan but at least he would only be surprising Big Merv once, not twice – or was that twice, not thrice? The Pan thanked him and they made their way inside.

The Big Ms, Merv's 'decorative, erotic dance troupe' stopped practising and moved, giggling, to one side of the sprung maple dance floor. Big Merv called them 'the girls', but The Pan reckoned most of them were on the shady side of forty.

"Morning, ladies. Don't mind us," said the old man as they made their way to the other side of the room where the stairs to Big Merv's office were. "I say!" he added in one of those stage whispers that is actually louder than talking at normal volume, "some of them are almost my age."

"Shut up. They'll hear you," snapped The Pan, and he followed, shaking his head and muttering.

As they walked into Big Merv's office, the first thing he noticed was the set of plans laid out on the table. The title across the top sheet was written in Grongolian, not that he needed it translated, of course, he could already guess what the plans were. Once again, he felt strangely detached, as if he were sitting on the outside of his life, merely watching as it slid out of control. How could he have been taken in by that congenial air of innocence? How could he, the best getaway man in K'Barth, allow himself to be so completely stitched up by this old giffer? How could he have not realised that the blighted old codger was bound to go and put the idea to The Big Thing, himself?

Chapter 41

"You took your time, you little scrote," Big Merv told The Pan, his antennae waving in irritation, "your friend here wants us to undertake the most daring bank heist ever!" The Pan noted, gloomily, how his eyes were shining. Doubtless the old man's moronic idea appealed to his vanity. Big Merv had a dangerous bent towards flashiness and ostentation.

"He's not my friend," said The Pan shortly, "and it's a suicide mission."

"Oh dear." The sense of innocent hurt and confusion emanating from the old man was touching and in The Pan's view, completely unscrupulous. "As I understood it, you had a different view when we spoke the other day."

"Yeh," said Big Merv. He jerked his thumb in the old man's direction, "He says you told him you'd walk the driving."

"No," said The Pan patiently, "I never said I'd drive and I told him it was a suicide mission too."

"But you agreed to do it," said the old man feebly. The Pan shook his head, speechless. The cheek of the old get!

"No, I agreed to talk to Big Merv, which is what I came here to do today," said The Pan flatly. Big Merv was glaring at him. It was a weighing-up kind of glare, as in amount of concrete required and size of box. "Merv—sir—you're not serious are you?" he finally managed to gasp, "you don't actually believe robbing the Bank of Grongolia, in Grongolia, itself, would ever be a piece of cake?"

Everyone turned to the old man. His face was the picture of septuagenarian innocence. The Pan, on the other hand, wore an expression of controlled panic. He knew what would be happening. Big Merv would be realising that he had seen that expression before, on the faces of people who were saying 'I would never grass on you' a few hours after doing so.

"Maybe," said Big Merv. "I hear you was boasting down the pub."

"And you believe that?" asked The Pan. "Are you mad?"

"He can tell me things only you, me and the boys here were witness to. He can talk about them like he was there."

"He did that to me too," retorted The Pan. "It doesn't mean he was. It isn't real. Look at him!" He gestured to the old man who was wearing even more yellow than on the previous occasion they'd met, "He's a Nimmist! You've heard the rumours, he's reading your mind or something."

All three Mervinettes simultaneously turned their heads and stared at The Pan, their leather coats creaking in unison.

"He's reading your mind," growled Big Merv, "not mine."

"It doesn't matter whose mind it is does it? It's not normal and it gives him an unfair advantage!"

The silence in the room was absolute and the air heavy with unspoken accusations. The other three Mervinettes were like that – but The Pan could see he had got them thinking. There were all those rumours about the Secret Order of the Most Holy Ninja Nimmists, after all.

"Arnold above! Please, listen to me for a moment. I know I'm an idiot, I know I'm a liar but I never, NEVER boasted to him in the pub. I've been blacklisted for five whole years now, and you of all people know that if I was really that crass I'd have been dead on day two."

"Hmph." A curt nod. Big Merv began to look thoughtful instead of angry. His antennae tied themselves in a knot and The Pan wondered if he was beginning to get through to him, at last. Maybe he should just tell the truth and throw himself on Big Merv's protection. Yes, that's what he'd do.

"Please, you have to believe me. I don't know how he found me but this is some kind of upper echelon Nimmist mind game. He knows where I live and if I don't help him make you go to Grongolia and rob the state bank he's going to give my address to the Resistance."

Big Merv folded his arms and gave the old man a long appraising stare. The Pan had been a member of the gang long enough to know that, although Big Merv was scary, with his size and temperament, he could spot the difference between honesty and lies and he would listen to people if he thought they were telling the truth.

"That right?" Big Merv asked the old man quietly, checking for a reaction.

"I'm afraid it is," the old boy was embarrassed, positively sheepish, which, in The Pan's view, was a good thing. But he was also calm and relaxed and patently unafraid, while Big Merv was beginning to give off an aura of barely controlled rage.

"That makes things different," said Big Merv, "first I don't take kindly to blackmail, see? Second, I can believe you're a Nimmist, you'd have to be to go poncing about in that lot without getting arrested, an' that would make you pure as the driven snow wouldn't it? Right? But you lied to me and now

150

I find out you've been blackmailing one of my prize assets. Nimmist or not, mister, I have a problem with that. It's not a trustworthy way to behave. What if I change my mind? What if I decide this job's too dangerous and that I'm going to protect my asset—I repeat, MY asset—by dumping you in the river?"

"My dear chap," said the old man, "first of all, I can see you are a Thing of honour and principle! As such we both know you don't have it in you to murder a man of the cloth. And second, as I am sure you will appreciate, unless I were very unwise I would never have come here uninsured, would I?"

Big Merv was thoughtful.

"Maybe, but you're gonna have to be very well insured to get out of this one, mate."

"I believe I am. I have proof—concrete proof, you understand—that you commit bank robberies," replied the old boy, evenly, as he handed over a brown envelope, "I imagine you wouldn't want it to fall into the wrong hands and of course, it goes without saying, this is not the only copy."

The Pan watched Big Merv open the envelope and shuffle through the papers and photographs it contained. For all his frustration and panic, he had to admit that, behind the amiable elderly buffer facade, the old boy was a razor-sharp, not to mention ruthless, operator. He felt a twinge of envy. He knew he could never be that cool-headed.

"I'm sorry it has to be this way," said the old man as he took another envelope from the inside pocket of his coat. Was that genuine regret in his voice, The Pan wondered? No. Not after what he'd just done. It had to be acting. "I see you have already made a start; a man on the inside has furnished me with some information which could be of use: guard rotas, security codes, camera locations and the like." He held it out.

"How do I know if I can trust you?" asked Big Merv.

"You don't," said the old man, true to form, "but I don't think you have much choice do you? For what it's worth, we understand your services won't come cheap. Name your price."

There it was again, thought The Pan. 'We.'

"I don't want yer money," snapped Big Merv. He spoke calmly but he was shaking with suppressed rage.

"Then shall we make it one million?"

"One million what?" growled Big Merv. The Pan could see he was still livid because his antennae stuck straight up from the top of his head.

"Well now, since they are a little more stable than K'Barthan Zloty, I suggest Grongolian dollars. Would one million Grongolian dollars be sufficient?" asked the old man.

Big Merv said nothing.

"Each?"

Arnold's Y-fronts! One million Grongolian dollars. That was almost more money than The Pan could imagine.

Big Merv nodded.

"Alright, we'll do it," he said sullenly, "we'll do this robbery for four million Grongolian." He swung round and glared at The Pan: "And as for you," he strode over to him, shouting, "you stupid, snivelling—" Without warning, he punched him in the face. The Pan saw the fist approaching his nose but didn't have time to duck before it hit home. The impact tumbled him backwards over a chair and the pain erupted like a firework. He hit the floor, sprawled on his back and clamped his hand over his face, rolling onto all fours. Big Merv stepped smartly round the chair and pulled him to his feet.

"That's for getting us into this!"

The Pan had had enough.

"Now who's the stupid one?" he said nasally as he clamped his handkerchief to his bleeding nose, "thumping the assets you're supposed to be protecting." Big Merv let go of him.

"I'm sorry, mate. I was out of order, but I couldn't bring myself to punch that old relic," he said, glaring at the old man. It hadn't been a hard punch; The Pan's nose was already beginning to stop bleeding, and although it was bruised and swollen it didn't feel broken. He peeked gingerly at the contents of his handkerchief. It was blue. Not red, not purple, but pure blue. Biro ink. He contained Biro ink. He had to be cracking up, there was no way this could be real.

"That don't look right," said Harry, leaning over him.

"Nope. It's fine, absolutely fine. Just a trick of the light," said The Pan, screwing his handkerchief into a ball and stuffing it swiftly into his pocket. Arnold in the Skies! Harry thought it was odd, too! That meant he wasn't cracking up which, though reassuring, didn't do much to offset the alternative, that his blood was now blue, instead of red. He must be very ill. He wondered if it was terminal. Undoubtedly. Then again, it would hardly

152

make a difference would it? He felt his nose carefully and glowered at the old man.

He was glad to see that an experience of violence, first hand, had finally ruffled the old boy's air of calm. For a moment he stared at The Pan as if he was Lord Vernon, himself, before excusing himself and leaving rapidly. Good! Now that he'd witnessed how much damage it could cause, perhaps he'd think twice before he blackmailed anyone else!

Chapter 42

The lights of the city twinkled across the dawn sky and, as Lord Vernon watched them, went out, one by one.

The Chosen One had evaded him – which was trying – but his enemies had also failed to locate her, so, using the platinum thimble, he had transported some of General Moteurs' most reliable troops, with a plentiful supply of his research department's de-greening pills, to keep an eye on her. He had put other operatives in place undercover in her world to access every scrap of computerised information about her; they had been through her credit card bills, her medical records, everything. The surveillance team had instructions to abduct her, if required, to keep her from 'unsuitable influences'.

However, it was more of an insurance policy than an expediency. He had confirmed that only he knew of her existence and her whereabouts. She was safe enough where she was for now. In the meantime, he would turn his attention to the Mervinettes.

He had gained some useful information from General Moteurs' contact and would learn more when he mastered the use of the thimble. Much of the close surveillance work had been done by a very small team which he had led himself, General Moteurs acting as deputy. It had taken patience and application, but now the quality of the data he was gathering was better than he had dared hope. He gazed thoughtfully at the thimble in his palm.

According to the General's secret source, the gang intended to undertake a bespoke job and steal an artefact used in the Looking. General Moteurs' man had suggested this might be the one definitive item which would confirm, for sure, the identity of the true Candidate. It wasn't an item Lord Vernon wanted to see in the public domain.

So he would let them find it for him and then ...

He smiled maliciously. Simple, he would destroy the artefact and nobody could disprove his Candidature. Nothing would stand in the way of his becoming Architrave. Afterwards, of course, he would destroy the Mervinettes. He thought about their driver, an unlikely character; older, possibly even retired by the looks of the surveillance photographs General Moteurs had provided. Well-heeled, too. Lord Vernon had expected someone with reactions that quick to be young and most likely, desperate. No matter. They were all doomed.

And as for the Chosen One ... He licked his lips.

"You will not escape me either," he said aloud.

Oh yes, he had plans for her, such plans. He couldn't wait to meet her. It was going to be luscious. He breathed deeply, closing his eyes for a moment to savour his anticipation, and raised the thimble to his eye.

Chapter 43

Ruth got on with her new promotion and her new life, but like a small wrinkle that won't iron out, her disquiet stayed. It was only natural after such a stressful experience, Lucy reassured her. She didn't tell anyone else, as her family and friends would only worry. She nearly told Sir Robin Get, but she didn't, despite the fact he was very easy to talk to. He didn't judge, either. He simply listened and offered advice from time to time. Although neither of them would admit it, both Ruth and Lucy had begun to regard him as extended family. She wondered if she should have spoken to him, since for all Lucy's assurance that she would forget about her experience in time, Ruth didn't.

Three months on and she was having little success conquering her fear, although she was beginning to get used to living with it. One bright, frosty morning, a rare occasion dawned when she and Lucy were leaving for work at the same time. Since they used the same tube line this was always a pleasure. It meant they could gossip all the way in – well, almost. Ruth got off at Farringdon but Lucy carried on to Aldgate. As they headed for the tube, two tall men rounded the corner at the end of their quiet residential street. Ruth stopped abruptly.

"What's up?" asked Lucy breaking off, mid flow, from a story of Nigel's exploits with the wine list at a top London restaurant.

"Those guys," said Ruth, starting to walk again. They crossed the road, while up ahead the two tall men slowed and turned their heads in unison, eyes-right style, to look over at the two girls. They stayed where they were, on the other side of the street and carried on walking.

"See what they're wearing!" whispered Lucy as they passed. It was pure sci-fi. Dark grey leather tunics with, no? Really? Yes, swords and what appeared to be guns, slung from their belts. Woollen trousers, also in dark grey, with a red stripe down the sides and jackboots. Similar but not the same as the man who'd followed Ruth into that garden. How did they manage a getup like that on a London street without being arrested? Then again, people probably thought they were on their way to a sci-fi convention, that new romanticism had made a return or the like.

"Coo," said Lucy, "is one of them your man?"

"No. Not nearly as sinister, but they're the same."

"Wow. I can see why it freaked you out. I'd have left the city and sought witness protection."

"Yeh right! Witness protection from what?"

"You know what I'm saying."

That she understood why Ruth had been scared, that she didn't blame her. It made Ruth smile. It was great to have a friend like Lucy around.

"Yeh," she said, "I do, and thanks."

"They're very pale," said Lucy. Yes they were. As if they'd been living under a rock all their lives. So pale that when Ruth screwed her eyes up a little they almost appeared to be light green. "Like vampires."

"Yeh. OK Luce! Don't feed my warped fantasies; they scare me enough on their own."

Oops, Lucy, who was only trying to make a joke, now wore a worried frown. Time to lighten things up, "I'll be sure to keep up my garlic intake."

They were wearing sunglasses, like the one who had followed her, except they were merely frightening, a little bit creepy perhaps? The other one had been in a class of his own, the sheer malevolence of him had been almost physical.

He was still out there somewhere. Searching for his 'Chosen One'.

What if he'd sent them to follow her? What if she actually was? That was a bad thought. Time to stop thinking. She kept staring straight ahead, but glanced back as she turned the corner of the street and saw with relief that they were continuing to walk in the opposite direction.

Chapter 44

The Mervinettes spent three months planning their greatest – and in The Pan's view, dumbest – bank heist. Gradually and meticulously they pieced together the information required over the course of the days and weeks – even that which the old man had already provided (except when it was unobtainable anywhere else) because they didn't trust him and, as Big Merv said, you can never be too careful. The other robberies stopped except for when the Mervinettes needed more information, or the cash with which to buy it. The Pan had been practising his driving alone, usually by baiting traffic cops, until Gerry the Work Experience Creature from Snurd had arrived a week previously to collect his wheels and his spare keys.

Now here he was, driving Big Merv's midnight blue MK II into the heart of Grongolia's capital city, which, with characteristic Grongolian lack of originality, was also called Grongolia.

"What in The Prophet's name am I doing here?" he asked himself.

If he could have arranged to have been anywhere else, even being closely questioned by the Resistance, a process often involving pain, inflicted with surgical precision, by experts, he would have done. One hand on the wheel, he ran the gearstick hand through his hair.

"How did I get myself into this?"

"By being an idiot and not paying attention." Oh no! He didn't have the time or will for an argument with his Virtual Father right now.

"I know Dad, you don't need to tell me. I'm wondering if I should have called the old gimmer's bluff." His voice tailed off as he remembered how the old man had been able to quote a private conversation between himself and the other three Mervinettes. He was probably listening.

"And as for you, you conniving old git. It's bad enough you putting us up to this but you'd better not be tuning in right now. A little privacy if you please."

The Bank of Grongolia was the most heavily guarded public building in the city. Grongolia was the army's garrison town, home to the Grongolian High Leader and chock-full of Grongles. Non-Grongles were only allowed into the city with special passes, and were most definitely barred from the country's national bank. Big Merv and his colleagues had got round this technicality by wearing dark glasses and realistic green rubber faces made by a contact in Ning Dang Po's film studios. They were wearing Grongolian army uniforms and carrying replica weapons, also made by the film studio contact, Grongolian military hardware being unavailable to civilians, let alone non-Grongles. Their false IDs were constructed by an expert forger named Derek and well ... they were all tall enough to pass for small Grongles and built the right way; that is, extensively. Derek had also produced the prerequisite special NGLF (Non-Grongolian Life Form) pass to allow The Pan to gain entry into the city, so he had no need for a disguise other than the one he usually wore.

The bank was in a large square and The Pan dropped his bosses off on the dot of midday, as planned, and drove round the block. Big Merv, Frank and Harry were to go into the vaults under the pretence of opening their 'own' safety deposit box, or at least the box belonging to the Grongles on their fake IDs. Once in the vaults they were to open a different box with a stolen key which Big Merv had been given and which he had secreted in the heel of his shoe. They were to remove the contents and walk back out. There were to be no heroics and no other boxes were to be touched, this was a high-class bespoke job. If they succeeded, the heist would take three minutes, if they failed, they wouldn't come out again.

From behind the protection of the MK II's bullet-proof, tinted glass, The Pan watched the inhabitants of the city going about their business in the midday sun. It was hot and the heat reflected off the pavements made it doubly warm. His palms were clammy and he was sweating. He had a bad feeling about this job and felt more nervous today than he had ever previously felt before a robbery. This was the Bank of Grongolia, he kept telling himself. His nerves were natural and only to be expected, but despite the gang's best efforts, it had been planned with the cooperation of too many outsiders for his liking. The old man hadn't struck him as the type to grass, but these days you could never be sure and the preparations had required input from many 'suppliers' outside Big Merv's routine sphere of influence and trust.

Then there was the actual heist. The Pan knew nobody could waltz into the Bank of Grongolia to carry out a major theft without inside help and he kept asking himself, with growing disquiet, who that inside contact would be. The bank didn't employ non-Grongolian staff, so the informant would have to be a Grongle. As Grongolia was a police state, most of the proper criminals were part of the Government, working in information retrieval for the secret police. Surely any other criminals would be political. They would be working against the state, for a resistance movement, if there was one. The point was, no-one with a similar background to the Mervinettes, or at least, no-one on their side, would work in the state bank.

Members of the political underworld had no scruples and considered themselves above real, honourable bank robbers like the Mervinettes. They would see Big Merv and his gang as expendable scum. What better way to deflect attention away from recovering the loot than handing over K'Barth's most wanted gang of robbers?

He was marginally reassured by the fact he had the thimble with him, although there were so many checkpoints that he had hidden it in his boot, tucked under his instep, in case he was asked to get out of the MK II and searched. That was another worry. He'd driven through all those checkpoints without being stopped. That was enough to make The Pan nervous, on its own. It wasn't natural. There was the timing too; midday, high noon, the perfect time for a gunfight if you wanted to stage a theatrical show-down, pocket the loot and pretend nothing had gone missing. Too many omens and too much theatre. It had to be a trap. The only question was exactly when it was going to be sprung. He turned up the air conditioning.

The Grongles, for some strange reason best known to themselves, drove on the wrong side of the road, measured their distances in some archaic unit long since abandoned by everyone else, and had a different highway code to the rest of the world. The Pan had spent several days learning to convert distances from Grongolian to K'Barthan units of measure, and reading and re-reading their highway code from cover to cover.

However, he was still nervous and he felt out of place driving on a different side of the street. He hadn't seen anyone behind them but he was sure they were being shadowed as soon as they entered the city. He realised that his paranoia about being followed had mushroomed since his encounters with the old man. Maybe it was nerves, or perhaps it was normal to tail foreigners in Grongolia – after all, they were driving a snurd from K'Barth which, though not unusual, was distinctive. K'Barthan snurds were considered the best available and the MK II was the type of snurd the flasher, higher-ranking officers in the Grongolian army might bring back from a tour of duty there. A class staff vehicle to suitably impress the Grongolian ladies.

"Not that there appear to be any," said The Pan, to himself. His visual radar was always finely tuned but the Grongolian streets were depressingly devoid of any form of female distraction. He supposed they were all kept locked away somewhere. He wondered if that was why the Grongles were all so bad tempered and prone to violence.

The three minutes were up and he was turning back into the square. Big Merv, Frank and Harry, still disguised as Grongolian army officers, were waiting for him. No klaxons were sounding, no shots being fired, no notice being taken. Nothing had gone wrong. Something always went wrong. Usually the Mervinettes spilled out onto the street in a hail of bullets and wailing alarms and leapt dashingly into the snurd with Big Merv shouting 'Drive!' just as the Grongolian police arrived. It was all part and parcel of the glamour.

"The public loves a snurd chase," Big Merv would say.

It wasn't natural. Once they were safe inside, The Pan scrutinised his passengers carefully. Yes, they were definitely Big Merv, Harry and Frank. As the snurd left the suburbs of the city they pulled their rubber Grongle faces over their heads and relaxed but The Pan didn't. This had been too easy. He smelt a rat. He checked behind him, there was still no visual evidence but his belief that they were being followed hadn't abated.

They soon left the city behind as – choosing small, less-frequented roads – The Pan headed to the coast. He'd memorised the relevant sections of a Grongolian road atlas and now, as he drove, he could picture the map in his mind's eye and imagine the MK II as a small red dot moving slowly across the page, towards the sea.

Every mile he put between himself and the Bank of Grongolia was a head start.

In The Pan's view, that meant the closer they got to the coast, the more relaxed he should have been.

"Hmm, so why isn't that happening?" he muttered. Instead of relaxing he was experiencing an unaccountable feeling of foreboding and it was getting worse, not better.

"What's wrong?" growled Merv, next to him. "You're mooning away like a great girl."

"Nothing."

"Don't lie to me you moron. Talk, or shut it!"

"Nothing yet," The Pan corrected himself, "I'm still thinking it through."

161

"I ain't comfortable with you doing any of that thinking malarkey unless you're gonna share it with us, right boys?"

"Yeh," said Frank and Harry in unison from the back.

"I appreciate that," said The Pan.

"Then get a move on."

No pressure then. Was this a hunch? It was certainly a strange sensation. Almost supernatural in that he couldn't explain it properly. His spine tingled, the little hairs were standing up on the back of his neck and though the air in the snurd was warm enough, goose bumps were rising on his arms. As if he'd walked into somewhere very cold – like a meat safe.

He was experiencing the same sense of foreboding that comes of watching too many horror movies, late into the night. The feeling you get when that logical, sensible part of your brain, the bit which guides you in moments of abject fear, has been bypassed.

He scanned the horizon behind him. No, nothing unusual there.

In front? No, still nothing, but the feeling persisted. It was a long way from the city of Grongolia to the coast, a good six hours drive on the roads, and they were using the roads rather than flying, to keep a low profile. They were being watched, The Pan was sure, the Grongles were anticipating their every move and waiting for the best, most effective moment to trap them.

A premonition then? Possibly. The Pan wasn't superstitious.

He racked his brains to try and think of anything he might have seen, anything, no matter how innocuous or tiny, which might help him make sense of the way he felt. No, he was doing this wrong. The *why* was academic, the most important question was *how* to react.

Easy. Stop trying to be intelligent about this. Stop trying to blend in; just panic, floor the accelerator and take off. Then again, what if there was nothing to fear? He would draw attention to the MK II for nothing, or worse, make both himself and the other Mervinettes look stupid. The Pan knew he would rather be alive and uncool than dead with cred, but he also knew he was at variance with all three of his colleagues in this respect.

On a number of occasions, Big Merv had made The Pan painfully – physically painfully – aware of the fact he didn't like to look an idiot.

"Arnold's snot!" He was going to have to say something.

"Done yer thinking then?" asked Big Merv acerbically.

"Yes and no. OK. Perhaps it's my nerves but something isn't right—" he began.

"What ain't right?" demanded Big Merv impatiently.

162

"Nothing I can be sure of," said The Pan, "that's the trouble," he took a deep breath, "but I know this is all wrong."

"Why?"

"Not sure," he shrugged, "but nothing fits."

"You great mincing wuss," snapped Frank in the back putting on a high-pitched voice. "Help me, help me, Big Merv! This is all wrong but I don't know why! Nothing fits! Holy Arnold!" he exclaimed, reverting to type, "how can that make sense? Either something IS wrong and you know what and why, or it isn't?" Frank was uncomplicated.

"It's nothing concrete, it's a gut feeling," began The Pan.

"Aw, don't listen to this namby-pamby nonsense Boss," said Harry

"Shut it! All of you," shouted Big Merv.

"No. I'm doing my best to explain here. If you won't listen then fine! When we die it's your fault."

Big Merv turned sideways and leaned towards The Pan.

"No," he corrected, "if we die, it's your fault and if there is life after death, you can bet that wherever it is we go, I'll find you and make you pay. Do you want to take that chance?"

The Pan coughed delicately.

"Nope. But if you're entrusting your safety to me, shouldn't you take my advice?" he replied, hoping Big Merv wouldn't thump him.

"It depends what your advice is," said Big Merv, "you're not the only one who's shaky about this job. We all knew it could be a setup, eh boys?" He nodded at Frank and Harry in the back.

"Yeh," they agreed in unison.

They had almost reached the ocean. There were two ways to cross it; the first was to go over it, in aviator mode, which Big Merv disliked intensely. The second, The Pan's preferred method, was to go under it, in submersible mode, which Big Merv loathed and detested. The submersible mode was slow and uncomfortable, and if they were discovered, escape would be far more difficult, although, of course its lack of practicality meant that the Grongles were unlikely to consider it a viable escape option. If the Grongles had found out about the robbery, their eyes would turn to the skies, for who would travel under water at a few miles an hour when they could travel through the sky at a few hundred?

"We could travel all the way up the Dang without being noticed," said The Pan as he expounded his theory to Big Merv. "We would drive up the bank in the Goojan Quarter. Nobody would see us." As he got to the end of his argument they had reached the brow of a hill. Below them the ground fell away to the coast. It was low tide and mile upon mile of shining wet sand reflected the pink of the sunset sky. Driving across the sand would be idiotic – snurds were as susceptible to quicksand as anything else. He would have to fly to the water first and then submerge – Big Merv would never buy that; once they were up in the air, that would be that. He shrugged his shoulders.

"Mmm," he said, "perhaps we'll have to fly."

"Yeh," growled Frank from the back, "maybe we will."

The Pan glanced at Big Merv and although expected, his nod of assent was still a disappointment.

"Fair enough."

He revved the MK II and took off.

Chapter 45

The Pan flew the MK II low, a few feet above the sand, partly to avoid detection and partly because he hoped to persuade Big Merv to change his view on underwater travel. As they left the land behind them, the sky gradually faded from pink to purple, the last rays of daylight disappeared altogether, the first stars came out and, to The Pan's alarm, the moon rose. A few feet below them its reflection glistened off the dark waters of the ocean.

To his right, The Pan could make out the shape of a ship, presumably a Grongolian trawler fishing for the large boring fish the Grongles ate – they would throw away the interesting ones, like the Angler Fish and the Octopus. Being Hamgeean The Pan preferred crustaceans, or things that were covered in tentacles or hideously ugly. He watched as the ship moved towards them. It was going quickly for a trawler. He glanced idly left and saw another one; it was nearer and also closing on them.

"Er, Merv?" he said.

"Shut up, you! I'm trying to sleep!"

"I know, I'm very sorry but I think this might be urgent."

Big Merv grunted.

"I think this is a trap."

"Get a grip you pansy! This isn't a trap. Not this far out! If they're waiting for us, they'll be waiting at home where they can humiliate us in front of our whole nation."

"Mmm, good point," said The Pan, "but those trawlers—I don't think they're there by coincidence."

"In the name of The Prophet you paranoid girl," began Big Merv but he was interrupted by an insistent beeping from the dash. It was getting louder and the beeps were getting closer together. The Pan's stomach turned over.

"If they're so innocuous, how come they've fired a missile at us?"

"Arnold's armpits! How long before it hits us?" asked Big Merv.

"Ooooh," The Pan looked at the read-out on the dash, "about thirty seconds." Thank The Prophet he'd spoken to Snurd after their experience with the Interceptor; the MK II was now equipped with anti-missile chaff. But he couldn't remember where the button was. He accelerated and the missile sped harmlessly past them. He gave it an appraising glance as it disappeared upwards into the sky. It was ground-to-snurd, they would have another thirty seconds before it made a second pass. He pointed the nose of the MK II downwards, straight into the sea. The MK II hit the surface of the water at high speed, throwing a huge column of water up into the air, the missile hit it and exploded. Below the surface, the water leaking in had risen to their knees before The Pan had the presence of mind to press the submariner button and turn on the bilge pump. As they sank lower, the water swishing around their ankles began to disappear, the oxygen conversion unit kicked in, and The Pan risked turning the headlights on briefly.

Of course! How could he have been so utterly dumb? They were trawlers. There was bound to be a net and here it was.

The Pan winced at the volume when the other Mervinettes screamed "Aaaaaaarrrrrgh!" as he hauled on the wheel and the nose of the snurd turned upwards again. He pressed the nitrous oxide boost button. The MK II rocketed out of the water at high speed, transmogrifying itself back into aviator mode as it went.

"What the smeck are you doing?" bellowed Big Merv, more out of fear than anything.

"Saving you, as usual!" snapped The Pan.

"And knackering my snurd! I'll bet you've invalidated the warranty doing that you snivelling little scrote!"

"Yeh, there's a stern warning about that in the handbook," said Frank and everyone took a few moments out to turn and stare at him.

"I suppose thanks would be out of the question," retorted The Pan.

"Too right you little git," snapped Big Merv, "your friend got us into this!"

"For the last time, he is not my friend! I don't know where he came from and I'd never met him until about 24 hours before you did. I don't hang out with old people," he said, pretending for a moment that Gladys and Ada didn't exist. "Most especially old people who are trying to blackmail me."

"And succeeding," said Big Merv.

"Yeh, don't rub it in. He blackmailed you, too, remember."

"Yeh, and remember what happened? If you want another nosebleed, you carry on talking you big nonce."

"If you thump me I won't be able to drive, will I, you stupid K'Barthan halfwit, so don't hit me while I'm driving if you want to live!" retorted The

Pan, putting his arm up to fend off any blows.

"Don't worry I won't touch you now but I'LL PUNCH YOUR BLEEDIN' LIGHTS OUT WHEN WE GET BACK, YOU BRAINLESS HAMGEEAN PUFF!" shouted Merv angrily.

The two trawlers were far behind them now but a small pin-prick of light flashed from one of them as it fired a second missile.

"Incoming," said Harry, helpfully.

"Thanks," said The Pan, who had already seen it but believed, firmly, that it pays to be polite to everyone, especially, to big scary people.

He wasn't worried this time – he'd remembered the position of the chaff button. When the missile was close to impact, he'd press it and a cloud of aluminium tinsel would be released, causing the warhead's guidance system to think it had reached its target and explode. For a second time, the insistent beep which heralded the missile's approach could be heard from the dash. The nearer it came, the closer together the beeps became until eventually, when it was ten seconds away from impact, the beeps changed to one long, continuous tone. The Pan waited for the tone, reached out with all the affected nonchalance he could muster and pressed the button. Nothing happened. He stifled the inevitable scream but a small mouse-like squeak escaped him as he flipped the snurd into a dive with the missile in hot pursuit.

"Oh great," he whimpered as they plummeted downwards, "we're going to die." He couldn't risk submerging again, there was bound to be more than one net and this time they might not be so lucky. The snurd wove from left to right as The Pan tried to think of a way to throw the missile off their tail. He swung the snurd sharply left and the missile drifted to the right long enough for the tone to become a beep again. The Pan looped the loop and found himself flying towards it in a game of deadly chicken. If only the MK II had been armed it could have blown the missile apart but the four All Purpose Torpedo tubes behind the lights were empty. Even Big Merv's contacts couldn't get hold of APTs, these days. Anyway, as he had explained to The Pan, while threatening bank tellers with what Frank insisted on calling a 'shootah' was one thing, killing them, or police officers – even Grongolian ones – was public relations anathema.

"Don't hurt *nobody* unless it's him or you, and *never* shoot to kill. I mean it. The minute anyone gets hurt, we've lost the respect of the bloke in the street, and if you lose the bloke in the street's respect, the little bleeder will grass you up in no time," was how Big Merv had actually put it. "They love us because we succeed and there's no harm done. This isn't serious to them, it's a comedy turn and the Grongles are the butt of the joke. Don't you ever forget that."

Big Merv was right, of course but he had never envisaged an emergency such as this one, even if The Pan had. Anyway, procuring missiles was a dangerous business, so The Pan could hardly blame him when he hadn't made an enormous amount of effort. In the absence of any alternative he fired a red distress flare. They heard the metallic clunk as it bounced off the warhead and then the snurd was catapulted upwards by the force of the explosion.

"Arnold's ear wax! That was close! Any damage?" asked Big Merv.

"Hmm," said The Pan as he checked the telemetry system, "nothing I can see." According to the screen on the dash all sectors were functioning normally but his instinct told him otherwise. Either that or he wasn't functioning normally. That wasn't beyond the realms of possibility; he had been very shaken up by the explosion and the telemetry system would be significantly more reliable than his off-the-wall hunches. All the same, he wished it was easier to be honest with Big Merv.

He pressed the telemetry button again. Still no faults reported and yet the MK II wasn't handling the way it had before the explosion; something somewhere was vibrating and the steering wasn't so – he had no idea of the technical term – pointy. It's nothing, he thought, but deep down in the bottom of his stomach he felt a little knot of fear, one which wasn't going to go away until Gerry the Work Experience Creature had performed his post-robbery check and given the MK II the all clear.

The beeping resumed. Ah yes, The Pan remembered, the other trawler. He checked the status of the red distress flares, none left. They had been flying 40 minutes since the first missile attack, they were two minutes from land and he was willing to bet that when they hit the coast they'd hit another ambush. Things were not good.

"Arnold," he muttered as the time between each beep began to shorten. There were no more flares, no APTs and no chaff. The Pan realised the only thing standing between himself and an early bath was one very bad plan.

"OK," he said. "Unless you want to die I need everything metal you can lay your hands on."

"Why?" asked Frank, a hint of belligerence creeping into his voice.

"Because there's another missile coming and we're out of flares, APTs, chaff and therefore, other options. So. Here's my suggestion. You find all the metal things you can, then we stuff them in a bag, we chuck it out of the window and the missile hits that instead of us."

"This weren't the usual robbery, we done this by stealth," wailed Harry, "there's detectors at the bank—I even left me knuckledusters at home."

"Yeh," said Frank, "'S why I ain't got no knife either, same reason."

"The lads are right. There isn't anything metal," snapped Big Merv, "except the snurd and this," he held up the safety deposit box containing the loot and something rattled from one end to the other, "and if you think I'm going to let you throw that out of the window you've lost your mind."

"I'm going to lose more than my mind, I'm going to be vaporised if you don't find something, anything metal, within the next forty seconds, and so are you!" said The Pan.

"It was long odds but we've pulled off the biggest heist of all time—I was gonna retire on what your mate agreed to pay me."

"I think we've agreed, whoever he was he is *not* my mate," said The Pan, "and if you want to live to retire you're going to have to bung that," he gestured to the safety deposit box in Merv's hands, "out of the window." The beeps were getting closer together now. "According to this we've now less than forty seconds before the missile hits us and we'll be over the coast soon; you can bet there'll be a reception party waiting on the mainland. By The Prophet, you're a master criminal! Can't you pick the lock, stick the loot in your pocket and chuck the box out?"

"The box stays where it is," said Big Merv, "don't open the box was part of the deal."

"Well it wasn't part of the deal I made," said The Pan.

"No, but it was part of the deal I made," said Big Merv shoving the box into his leather trench coat and holding it there.

"Look, does it matter about the deal?" said The Pan. "If we ditch the safety deposit box at least the old guy gets the loot."

"If I open the box, I've broken my word," said Big Merv, "where does that leave me?"

"Exactly where you would have been, the only difference being, the loot is in your pocket and we don't get blown up with the box," said The Pan. The beep from the dash changed to one long continuous tone. "Come on!" He took both hands off the wheel and waved them outwards expansively. "At least my way *someone's* happy."

"Ah shove 'em both," said Merv. He pulled the box out of his coat and turned it on its end. Whatever had been rattling about inside had stopped.

"Nothing's worth dying for," he said, wound down the window and pitched it out. The Mervinettes heard it bang off the front of the pursuing missile and braced themselves for the explosion but nothing happened.

"Holy Arnold, it's a dud!" whispered The Pan as he yanked on the wheel in an effort to dodge the missile. They had been so close, he could see the coast ahead, if they could have just made it to the river Dang. Even if they had been ambushed, it would have been the usual chase, twenty or thirty police snurds all competing to bag their quarry, all on top of each other, getting in each other's way. He could have submerged in the river in the confusion and slipped out of sight. Instead they'd lost the loot and they were still going to die. Which seemed highly unfair.

In a last desperate effort to avoid the inevitable he put the MK II into a dive, only to find himself directly in the path of the black snurd which had pursued them so relentlessly over the recent months. It, too, went into a dive in order to head them off. The Pan almost laughed.

"Brilliant! Two in one!" As he flew under the rapidly descending Interceptor the missile flew into it, exploding on impact.

"Blimey!" said Harry.

"Mmm," said The Pan. The black snurd had better armour than the MK II but it was still damaged. It headed downwards, belching plumes of rancid brown smoke. The Mervinettes watched with satisfaction as it made an emergency landing among the waves.

"So now it's the ambush," said The Pan. "Them and me, but not him."

"Yeh," said Merv, "I reckon you're right; unless he changes snurds."

"Mmm, don't go giving him subliminal ideas," muttered The Pan. In the driver's mirror he watched the lights of the Interceptor diminishing in size as they left it behind.

"Shut up and drive you ponce," retorted Merv, from force of habit rather than necessity as they sped off into the night.

Chapter 46

They were over land now and The Pan scanned the moonlit countryside around him for signs of an ambush. Nothing so far. He took a second glance at the lights of the Interceptor. They were fading remarkably slowly. He checked the speedometer. Nope, he was still driving flat out. His misgivings about the MK II were increasing. Would it survive a chase? The outskirts of Ning Dang Po were only minutes away but it was still several miles on foot if they crashed and The Pan was beginning to worry. If there wasn't an ambush, there would be something unimaginably worse; a squad of Grongles or the black snurd, miraculously unscathed, waiting for them all at the lock-up. Ahead of them the night sky glowed orange from the street lamps of the city. In the mirror, the headlights behind them hadn't got any smaller. In fact they were getting closer.

By The Prophet's pants! It must be missile-proof.

As the all too familiar shape of the Interceptor appeared behind them again The Pan accelerated. The engine sputtered, the rev counter fell to zero and then climbed back up again. He looked at the fuel gauge; no, that wasn't the problem, there was plenty of water in the tank, far more than he would have expected. Far more than would have been remotely possible, in light of the fact that the MK II had travelled between the two continents without a break. The engine missed again and with a sinking stomach The Pan tapped the glass on the fuel gauge. The needle dropped to empty.

"Oh Arnold," he muttered.

"What NOW?" demanded Big Merv. The Pan gestured to the fuel gauge.

"We're out of water," he said.

"What?" he fumed. "Do I employ you to make elementary errors? Why haven't you switched to the reserve tank?"

"What d'you think I am? A dork? This *is* the reserve tank," said The Pan, "there should have been ample."

"Then maybe somebody forgot to fill the reserve tank," said Merv venomously.

"Get a grip! D'you think I want to die that much?" snapped The Pan. "There isn't a feature on this thing the lads at Snurd and I didn't double check. Anyway, I switched to the reserve miles back. It must have been the missile, the one we hit with the distress flare. It exploded too close and ruptured the tank."

There was a massive crash as the Interceptor rammed them. The MK II shuddered and a red warning light came on. In the rear view mirror the vehicle behind them was obscured by a plume of flame billowing out of the exhaust pipe.

"Arnold in Paradise!" shouted Harry in alarm. "We're on fire."

"That's right boys," said The Pan. He glanced at his boss sitting next to him.

"We should land," said Big Merv grimly.

"Yeh right, with that thing behind us," said The Pan, jerking his head backwards towards the Interceptor.

"We can take him down," said Big Merv.

"No you can't, not if he's who I think he is. Anyway, he won't even get out, he'll just fire his machine guns and turn us to vapour." Big Merv growled and his antennae twisted themselves together in irritation but he said nothing. "I'll take us as far as I can—we may make it to the suburbs—there'll be more cover there," said The Pan. There would be more things to hit, too, but he was happy to take his chances on the streets rather than in an empty field with no-one for company but three angry Mervinettes and whoever was driving the Interceptor.

He took the snurd lower. The damage was almost helping, as the Interceptor couldn't endanger itself by coming too close while the MK II was ablaze. It pulled back and launched a missile. The Pan yanked the MK II sideways and it sped past. There was no chance of outrunning it and no chance of outrunning the Interceptor either. He racked his brains trying to think of a way to even the odds. If only he could get to the suburbs. Once they hit town it would be easier to throw off their pursuer and the missile, weaving across the city until one by one the pursuing police snurds hit the lamp posts, or traffic lights, or each other. But Ning Dang Po was three miles away. Any minute now the missile would be coming back for its second pass. He gazed down at a copse a few hundred feet below. It stretched over a couple of miles, to the outskirts of the city. If only he could get there. He looked at the copse again and thought about the trees.

"What are you doing now!" shouted Big Merv as the MK II headed towards the woods as fast as The Pan could make it to go.

"Trying not to die," he yelled back. They were travelling at half their normal speed with the missile approaching fast. The Interceptor was hanging back, keeping out of the way of the flames. They hit the edge of the trees at about a hundred miles an hour. As The Pan flipped the flaming MK II onto its side and flew into the woods, the missile hit a nearby tree and blew up.

The Pan was glad they were beech trees, tall old beech trees with nice big gaps in between. He could tell that Big Merv, on the other hand, wasn't certain he wouldn't rather have taken his chances with the Interceptor and the missile. Their pursuer hadn't followed them and The Pan assumed it was hovering somewhere above, waiting for them to emerge. He fought to control the snurd as they flew on, only a short distance to go now and they would be coming out into the suburbs. If the MK II could stay in one piece that long. The engine started to whine and the snurd bucked and dipped as it lost power. All three Mervinettes remained silent, praying that they weren't about to have a close encounter of the woody kind. The Pan felt sorry for them; he was feeling sick, and he was the one driving. A momentary glance at Big Merv next to him was enough to tell him he wasn't the only one. Big Merv had gone an orangey-green.

The cockpit began to fill with smoke. The Pan wound the window down in an effort to let the smoke out or the air in, he wasn't sure which. All four of them began to cough as the acrid fumes filled their lungs. Flames began to lick around the front of the bonnet and windscreen and the engine was making a metallic grinding noise which told them, more eloquently than any of the dire warnings emanating from the telemetry system, that it was ripping itself apart from the inside.

"I can't control it much longer!" he shouted over the din and they came out of the trees. Still flying sideways they shot between two houses and turned left down a leafy suburban street. "I think now would be a good time to land."

There was black gunk all over the windscreen which the burning wipers were merely serving to smear into an impenetrable fog. The snurd lurched and swayed and, as he tried to hold it steady there was a whining sound as the mechanism to lower the wheels tried to engage and stuck.

"No!" he shouted, thumping the dash and jabbing at the button. It whined again but the wheels remained where they were. Never mind, they'd probably melted.

"Hold on," he said, "this is going to be rough." The MK II fell like a stone to the road and skidded sideways along the tarmac in a shower of sparks, making a high-pitched screeching noise, like somebody running their fingernails down a blackboard. The Pan could see pieces of charred and twisted metal flying off in all directions; he managed to straighten out and engaged the reverse thrusters. The MK II hit the kerb and bounced into the air for one last time as the road bent sharply to the left. In spite of The Pan's frantic efforts to steer, the snurd went straight on, over a small wall and into somebody's garden pond, where it stopped abruptly, its nose against an ornamental heron. Coughing and wheezing, the Mervinettes leapt out and ran for their lives. Once they had crossed to the other side of the street and jumped over another garden wall they threw themselves to the ground and waited for the MK II to explode.

A minute passed and nothing happened, so they stood up. The MK II was bent and crumpled out of all recognition. For a few moments the polymorphic metal attempted to resume its normal shape, giving the impression of a machine writhing in its mechanical death throes, before it, too, failed and became still. The impact, or the pond, had put the flames out and all that could be heard was a low hissing and the ticking sound of hot metal cooling down. It wasn't going to last though, curtains were twitching and lights were coming on. It was time to go, quickly, before the police or the black snurd arrived. Big Merv looked sadly at the wreckage.

"That was a good motor that," he said, "been through a lot together, right boys?"

The Pan, Frank and Harry nodded mutely. Big Merv opened the garden gate and ushered them all back out onto the street.

"Let's get moving," he said and he began to walk away. He reached one hand over his shoulder. "Map?"

It was in the snurd. The Pan cleared his throat.

"Hang on a minute," and he turned to run back towards the MK II, but as he did so, it exploded. He was thrown backwards into the arms of Harry, who smartly plonked him upright. There was a moment of silence as the four of them watched, in awe. Was that a tear running down Big Merv's cheek or damp from where he'd been lying face down on the lawn?

"No map, no loot, no MK II," said Harry sullenly, "how much worse can it get?"

"We could be dead," said The Pan before he could stop himself.

"Any more out of you and you will be," growled Big Merv as he turned and began to trudge off into the darkness.

"Stop right there!" said a voice. "If any one of you moves, I'll kill you all."

There was a rustling sound as camouflaged guerrillas climbed out of hedges, dropped down from trees and stepped out from behind walls. They were disciplined, armed to the teeth, and more importantly, a lot of them were under three feet tall. Their uniforms were also very clean. Not Grongles, then. The Resistance. The lesser of two evils ... possibly.

Chapter 47

Farringdon, late at night. The station was empty and for the first time in months, Ruth had been out after work with friends and was waiting for the last tube home. Since being followed she'd been so afraid she had always taken taxis.

Now she'd had enough.

Tonight it was time to reclaim the city for her own. She would not live in fear. She would use the streets at night and she would use the tube. She was not Chosen and Mr Scary Sniff-the-air Creepy Man was not going to stop her from enjoying the freedoms of a normal human being. The train was empty and as it pulled into the deserted station, the driver leaned out of the cab.

"Get in behind me, luv!" he called. "Any trouble, bang on the door an' you can lock yourself in here with me."

Great start. He was trying to be kind and reassuring but his words had the opposite effect.

"Thanks," she said, climbed in and sat at the end of the first carriage where the driver had said. If the driver's cab wasn't safe, there was no way out and if that bloke came after her, she didn't believe a couple of inches of London Underground Formica would stop him.

"Will you listen to yourself?" she whispered.

This was the twenty-first century goddammit! It was London and it wasn't like that. Since she'd seen the scary sci-fi guys on her street, she'd kept imagining she saw them wherever she went. It was usually a glimpse, in the distance, out of the corner of her eye. In other words, never a certain enough sighting for her to be sure they were real. Somebody was either following her very badly or trying to send her mad. Nigel? Who knew? She had to get a grip and start doing the things she used to do again. Using the tube late at night, for example.

The train was the last one and Ruth would have to change to the Jubilee line at Finchley Road to get to Kilburn. That was OK, as all it entailed was a casual saunter from one side of the platform to another. Total journey time home from here, half an hour, tops. Five, six songs, she thought as she plugged in her earphones. She glanced up at the map above the window. She liked to mentally tick off the stations as the journey progressed. The Metropolitan Line train began to move.

King's Cross, empty. Next, Euston Square.

"You alright in there?" said a disembodied voice from behind the driver's door as they slowed to go through Euston Square.

"Fine thanks!" said Ruth with a cheerfulness she didn't feel. The driver had asked her where she wanted to stop and since she was the only one on the train, unless the signal was red or somebody was waiting at the station he wasn't actually bringing the train to a halt, merely slowing down. Probably against the rules, Ruth thought, but if it would get both of them home earlier it was OK with her.

From where she sat, she could see right down the train to the other end through the windows between the carriages. She liked the way their outlines receded into the distance; all half glassed, all the same, each one appearing to be a tiny bit smaller than the other. They moved to and fro or up and down as the track curved, creating geometric patterns and playing with the laws of perspective. She liked that, too.

Great Portland Street.

As the train crashed into the station, she caught a glimpse of two figures waiting at the end of the platform. The opposite end from her. It stopped, they got on and it continued on its way. She watched the long line of empty carriages moving.

Oooh. The door at the end opened and closed. The two figures moved from one carriage to another. Not surprising; people did that when they wanted to go to whichever carriage would be nearest to the exit at their station. Not so much in the day, but at night when they were less inhibited and there was more room. Londoners are like that. She took no further notice. They'd be at Baker Street in a moment anyway. Then the door of her carriage banged and she looked up.

Two of them. Dark glasses, uniforms, the military-style belts with the swords, walking down the carriage. The train hurtled into the station. There was somebody waiting here, too. Good. If she got out and ran up the platform she would be able to get into the driver's cab. It might not be so obvious as banging on the connecting door; they might not even notice. She leapt up and made for the exit as they strode purposefully towards her.

The train slowed. Stop dammit. Stop! Now! And came to a halt.

They reached her exit and she backed away until she was pressed up against the glass partition between the door and the seats. They were right next to her, closing in.

The doors slid open with a squish and Ruth nearly collided with the passenger who was boarding the train.

"Oh I say! What a splendid surprise!" said a familiar voice. Sir Robin, complete with the ubiquitous shopping bags. The scary sci-fi dudes stopped where they were. "Oh! Are these friends of yours?" he asked her – or at least – half her and half them. It seemed he expected her to say they were not. He expected them to understand this, too and to leave her alone. Blimey! Was he going to take them on? Yeh right. Ninja pensioner.

"I've seen them about, I think they live near me but we don't know each other," she told him.

"My mistake. I thought they were going to talk to you," his voice changed, he seemed to grow a little and he fixed them with a steely gaze. "Perhaps they are?" he added authoritatively. They stayed still. It made Ruth relieved he was on her side.

The strangers turned abruptly and their cloaks swished as, to her surprise, the two of them walked over to the nearest seats and sat down.

Ruth shuddered. What was going on? Sir Robin, on a train, in almost the small hours, at a completely different station from the one where he usually got on, in a situation where he might have saved her bacon. No! She was turning into Ms Paranoid. It was a straightforward coincidence. It had to be. She gestured to the bags in his hands. "Do you want a hand with those?" she said in order to give her brain a little time.

"Why yes, thank you very much."

Nope. Still not computing.

The bag he handed over was lighter than it looked, lighter than usual. She peered in and saw it contained an old jumper, a pair of shoes and some rolled-up newspapers. It was the kind of thing you'd find in prop shopping bags for a play, or if somebody who needed to have a bag with them had stuffed whatever they found to hand into one as they left their house in a rush. She glanced up at him quizzically.

"Where have you been shopping today, the bins on Embankment?"

"My dear, I promised I'd take these to the charity shop tomorrow for a friend. Said I'd had a clear-out and before you know it he's given me much of the junk in his wardrobe to take along as well."

She glanced over at the two large gentlemen opposite. They had swords and guns! It wasn't as if an old dodderer like Sir Robin was going to be a match for them. If they were going to kidnap her they'd have dealt with him and gone right ahead, except that one comment from him when he'd boarded the train, only half directed at them, and they had backed off.

They weren't doing anything, just sitting there opposite her like a couple of clones with their legs crossed in the same direction, staring straight ahead, each one holding the sword with his left hand, the right hand resting on his holster. They weren't as scary as the first evil, sniffing-out-prey one. Sir Robin and Ruth travelled to Finchley Road in companionable silence. She smiled and did a thumbs-up at the kindly driver as they walked across the platform to the Jubilee line and clambered onto a waiting train. The two sci-fi men followed but stayed in the carriage when she and Sir Robin got out at Kilburn. She watched, with relief, as the doors closed and the train carried them away to Willesden Green.

Her mind was racing. Had she imagined it or had Sir Robin rescued her from a mugging? Possibly. The two strangers had been heading straight for her so, at the very least, he'd saved her from having to have a conversation. He interrupted her thoughts.

"How's work?" he asked her, congenially, as they walked down Kilburn High Road.

"Pretty good." Small talk, but Ruth had the impression his mind was on greater things. He slowed down and turned towards her.

"My dear, are you happy in your job?" He stopped, and as she was about to say she was he added, "Are you committed, do you feel it's what you were put on this Earth to do?"

"Oh c'mon. Nobody does what they were put on Earth to do. Well ... maybe people with vocational careers do, but I don't. No calling for me."

"And yet you enjoy your work?"

"Oh yes, a great deal."

"You believe what you are doing has a purpose?"

Blimey! This was all a bit deep.

"Er, I love my job, that makes me pretty jammy—most people don't, after all." She tried to lighten things up, "Most people do their jobs to earn money so they can do the stuff they want to do, but they end up never doing it because they're working all the time." Sir Robin adopted a disapproving expression. Hmm, he must be expecting a serious answer, then. "OK. Honestly?"

"If you please."

"I get to help people sell themselves or what they do. If that means they can give up some dead-end career they hate and be happy doing something they enjoy it must be a good thing. In the grand scheme it's probably not that important, but it feels," she shrugged, "warm and fuzzy."

He chuckled and started to walk again.

"Do you think, you will be in the same line of work in ten years' time?" he asked.

"I hope not. For starters I'd like to be promoted and secondly it'd be very boring to do the same thing forever. Who knows what I'll be doing by then?" She gave him her best appraising stare, "Are you interviewing me?"

As he smiled his gold tooth flashed in the sodium lights.

"Not exactly."

"Not exactly. Partially then?"

"No. I was merely curious. I must apologise, I didn't wish to be over inquisitive. I am interested," he waved one arm casually, "you wouldn't mind then, if your life changed?"

"It'd be a bit annoying right now, because I'm learning so much—not only my trade but, you know, about dealing with people, being tactful and diplomatic that kind of thing. If I lost my job tomorrow, I'd be gutted, but I'd get over it, I expect. Changes are always interesting, even scary ones, although I prefer to initiate them myself!"

"Yeeees." He sounded a little doubtful, as if he was the bearer of bad news.

"You think my life's about to change, don't you?"

"All things are possible," he said.

She eyed him with her best pointy-brained expression.

"You believe it though," a statement of fact since he obviously did, "are you psychic?"

"No. I'm not." Emphasis on the 'I'm' though, as if somebody else was. Strange. Who? "Fate can be an odd creature."

"Yeh. I tried and tried to get my career started and nothing happened until I gave up on it. I guess the trick is not so much coping with things changing as not worrying," she thought for a moment, "and being happy with what you have, too, I guess."

Why was she telling him all this?

"Wise words," said Sir Robin.

"Not really. Sensible, more like." Ruth was tired, her nerves were pretty much shot and the old boy was so easy to talk to. "Those blokes on the train."

"Yes?"

"You asked if I know them."

"Yes."

"I don't—but would it sound mad if I told you I'm beginning to think they're following me?"

A sharp intake of breath which surprised her. She glanced at him. He was concerned.

"You've noticed them before?" he asked her.

"Loads of times."

"I see," he said in that patient manner, like a doctor listening to a long-winded patient. Had he seen them too, or more to the point had they seen him somewhere else, somewhere a long time ago, perhaps, before Ruth had met him and before he had grown old? What would he have been, a general? No, unlikely. A captain of industry, a politician? Somebody important enough to command their respect, even scare them? Maybe.

"Is that a bad thing?"

He cocked his head on one side and looked at her quizzically.

"Perhaps."

"Who ...?" No. Start again, "What are they?"

He seemed almost proud of her.

"Now that's an astute question. It's a long story," he said.

"I have time."

"Hmm." A nod.

"Are they from this planet?"

"Oh yes," a pause, "in a roundabout way." They had reached the door of her flat and he stopped, even though officially she was carrying a bag for him and his flat was down at the end of the street. He took it from her. "Please allow me to walk *you* home tonight, Ruth. These bags are very light and you look tired; you need to get some sleep." She nearly giggled, partly because she was mightily relieved, on this particular evening, not to have to walk back up the street on her own and partly because sometimes, he behaved as if he was her dad. Or would that be her granddad?

181

"Sir Robin, can I tell you something in confidence?"

"My dear girl, of course you can."

"Three months ago one of them followed me, a different one, not those two," she shuddered, "I think he wanted to kidnap me. He was grim." Unconsciously she hugged her arms across her chest, as if to comfort herself. It was the way he watched her that made her realise what she was doing. "He was tall, and even though it was about, well ... about this time of night, he was wearing sunglasses, and he had this evil voice. Most of the time, I think they're watching me, following me, making sure they know where I am, but I don't know why. I wondered if they were here to protect me from him."

She told him how she had hidden in the bushes from the first one and how he had searched for her.

"He called me 'Chosen One'," she explained. "He said," and she did an impression of the stranger's voice, "you will not evade me forever, Chosen One. I will find you." So I know it can't be me he's looking for, because if I were Chosen, I'd realise wouldn't I? Somebody would tell me. But I keep seeing them, and on the one hand I'm too frightened to go up to them and explain, on the other, I'm afraid that if I don't, he—Mr Darcy's Evil Twin—may find me." She felt on the brink of tears. "I know I should ignore it all and eventually they'll either go away or tell me what they want, but it's so hard to keep it together, to carry on being normal. I'm scared I'm cracking up."

"Quite the contrary, I'd say, you seem perfectly in control of your faculties in the face of a great deal of provocation. You realise, don't you, that if you would like to have a chat I am always ready to listen?"

The authoritative I-have-people-who-will-fix-this tone again.

She nodded.

"I would." Her voice sounded small.

"Capital!" He looked at his watch, "but now is not the place or the time," he said kindly. "First, a decent night's sleep will do you the power of good. Would you do me the honour of dropping round for tea tomorrow? Say, six o'clock?"

"I can't—I'm managing an event, a concert at the Barbican."

"Oh dear. Are you happy to wait a day before we sort this out?" He spoke with total confidence as if a simple conversation between the two of them would fix everything. Whether or not it would, Ruth felt considerably happier. Perhaps her life wasn't out of control after all. Yes. It would be OK. Sir Robin would be able to help. She rallied.

"Would you like a ticket? I can get you a freebie if you like, Lucy and Nigel are coming."

"Please, not Nigel," said Sir Robin, "when will she stop seeing him? He is quite insufferable."

"I know, but Lucy's lovely and at the moment he sort of comes with the territory."

"Yes, I appreciate that."

"If I got two tickets you could bring a friend."

"You are kind—and I thank you—but no."

"Could I come round the night after?"

"Why of course. Splendid! Let's make it a date." He made to go and then stopped, "Ruth, don't worry yourself, you have nothing to fear." Again a reassuring aura of absolute confidence. He smiled, waved and strode off down the street. She watched until he had gone into his flat on the corner and waited until the light went on and she saw him silhouetted in the window as he drew the curtains, before she closed the door and went to bed.

Chapter 48

The Resistance searched the Mervinettes for weapons, even though they knew none of them were armed. The Pan was glad he'd slipped the thimble into his boot. Then they were taken straight back to the woods The Pan had flown through originally, but via a circuitous route through other people's gardens. Due to the number of Grongles searching for them, it took them most of the night to make the two or three mile journey. On several occasions they had to lie low for what felt like hours, while Grongle patrols passed.

In theory, he and the Resistance were on the same side, inasmuch as they both wanted to see the fall of the current regime in K'Barth. However, The Pan doubted this would make the end results of being captured by them any different to being captured by the Grongles. Indeed, if anything, he suspected the Resistance would be more thorough with their questioning. They were similarly disciplined, well trained and fanatically devoted to their cause, and while neither party showed any evidence of a sense of humour, the Resistance appeared to be even less prepared to relax and enjoy themselves than the Grongles. The Pan, who regarded humour as evidence of sensitivity, intelligence and all round civilisation, considered this a bad thing.

The odds were there wouldn't be much reasoning with the Resistance. He'd also heard they were more than able to match the Grongles when it came to beating or even killing their own to punish disobedience or failure. If they were prepared to kill their own troops, The Pan held little hope for his chances. He'd never had an easy relationship with authority and he knew the type of blind obedience demanded by the Resistance, even as a put-on act for a day or two, was beyond him.

Then there was their thoroughness. They were as violent as the Grongles towards their prisoners but more calculated in their intent. Most likely they'd administer the same kind of beating as the Grongles, but ignore him when he first pretended to crack. Then, when they were sure he wasn't faking, they'd write down what he said and when they thumped him the next day they'd write that down too and compare notes. They'd keep doing that for a week or two and only stop when he produced the same story for several days in a row. To be able to convince the Resistance he was spilling his guts without actually doing so would take every ounce of The Pan's powers of concentration and mental energy. Levels of energy and concentration he couldn't hope to command if he was concussed, drugged or confused. Then there were the other three Mervinettes. What would they say? The four of them had to tell the same story and it had to be credible.

By the time The Pan's party arrived back in the woods it was getting light and the thimble in his boot pressing against his instep was making his whole foot ache. Their armed escorts took them to a clearing, just out of sight of the road, where they were met by a high-ranking Resistance leader. She was the type of tall, leggy blonde The Pan usually went for, but she would have to be psychotic to have joined the Resistance. She ordered them to line up, took four scarves from her pocket and blindfolded her prisoners.

"I am Lieutenant Deirdre Arbuthnot. I am fighting for the freedom of this country and I don't have time for games or tricks. Move, and you die."

"Is this not a firing squad then?" asked The Pan.

"That includes moving your mouth," she snapped.

"Sorry, sweetie, my colleague ain't that smart," said Big Merv.

"That goes for you too, swamp guy," she shouted. "Don't make me ask you to shut up again unless you want a bullet in your brain. Which one of you is the driver?"

Nobody replied.

"Answer me!" she yelled.

Another long silence. The Pan assumed that, like him, neither Frank, Harry or Big Merv felt like cooperating. After all, she hadn't asked nicely and she'd told them to stay quiet. No-one would want to risk speaking and getting a bullet in the brain.

"If nobody answers my question by the time I count to five, I'll kill one of you every fifteen seconds until somebody does!" she bellowed.

A minute of carnage and then oblivion. Oh dear.

"One."

"Blimey, she's got a set of lungs on 'er," whispered Big Merv.

"Shut up! She'll kill us," whispered The Pan.

"Looks like she's gonna do that anyway."

"Well, don't encourage her to kill us more quickly."

"What did you say?" boomed the officer.

"For heaven's sake keep it down," said The Pan standing up and taking off his blindfold. "If you go on yelling like that, we're all going to get shot! There are Grongle patrols all over the place and they can probably hear you in Hamgee!"

"Yeh, and while you're at it darlin', make up your mind!" said Big Merv standing up and taking his blindfold off, too. Frank and Harry followed suit. "Are you going to kill us if we talk or if we don't talk? It'd be good to know."

"See, at the moment it ain't clear," said Frank.

"Yeh," said Big Merv, "you've a thing or two to learn, girl. In a 'situation' it's important your victims are crystal clear what you wanna know. Otherwise you might kill 'em before they've told you everything and miss something important, see?"

"Yeh. 'S right," said Harry.

"Will you shut UP!" she yelled. "And you," she shouted at her colleagues, "how come you just stood there and let them move?" There was a general mumbling and shuffling of feet which stopped abruptly when she felled the nearest guard by hitting him around the side of the head with the butt of her sub-machine gun. "Idiots!" she grumbled as the guard climbed unsteadily to his feet and she reverted her attention to the Mervinettes. "You prisoners are allowed to answer any questions I ask but you are not allowed to talk spontaneously to me or each other, do you understand?" Big Merv, Frank, Harry and The Pan nodded. "AND it's Deirdre. Not 'love', 'honey', 'sweetie' or 'darling', got it?"

"Well, um, Deirdre—" began The Pan.

"That's *Ms* Deirdre to you, scumbag or *Lieutenant* Arbuthnot."

"But you said—" Deirdre gave The Pan a withering glare. *Go ahead!* it said. The Pan cleared his throat nervously and started again.

"Right, er, sorry, Ms Deirdre. Well, er, you might want to keep your voice down a bit," he said.

She strode over to him and put her nose to his. The Pan noted that allowing people their personal space clearly wasn't her thing.

"Alright, wise guy," she said through gritted teeth and she stuck the muzzle of her sub-machine gun under his chin. As she did so one of the other Resistance fighters grabbed his arms and pinned them behind his back. Why did this always happen to him? He wasn't the leader, or the largest or the bravest – in fact he was totally insignificant compared to the others, so subjugating him shouldn't prove anything. Why was he always the

186

psycho magnet? Size? Could be. He was small enough to thump, tall enough for it to look impressive. Whatever it was, they always picked on him.

"I'm going to aerate your brain if you don't answer this question," she told him. "Which one of you is the driver?"

The Pan made eye contact; her eyes were blue, light blue, and they were staring into his with the zealous intensity of extremists everywhere. She was true, dyed-in-the-wool Resistance. Making eye contact with a human so apparently devoid of any humanity was not something The Pan had spine enough to do for long. Her icy gaze held his, contemptuous and uncompromising. He managed to stare back at her long enough to say, "I am," before his gaze slid away from her face. Noooo! Not that way! He was looking at her chest. Her vest top was stretched tightly across what Big Merv would have called, 'a well-stacked rack'. Mmm, they were nice; rounded and firm – the perfect size to take one in each hand – with the kind of cleavage a man could dive into and drown in. She was sweating, not much, but just enough to make them glisten. "Holy Arnold," said The Pan. That was some of the Creator's best work, right there. He was half hypnotised by the movement as they rose and fell with her breathing and his mind was wandering in absolutely the wrong direction. Arnold's pants, what was he doing? Now she'd realise he was ogling her bosoms and thump him for being a pervert. Yeh and he'd deserve it, too.

She made no move to take the gun away. The Pan tried to avoid looking into those scary eyes, or that scary cleavage, again. After a few seconds of indecision he decided to look at her right ear.

"Well, Ms Deirdre, I've owned up now, so you can remove your gun from in my face," he said. Oh no no no! What was he thinking? Why did his mouth always go into action so far ahead of his brain. He knew she was going to thump him now. Mentally, he prepared himself for the pain when her fist, or worse, the butt of her gun, made contact with his head. Perhaps that was why it was such a shock, and hurt so much, when she punched him in the stomach, instead. The unseen accomplice holding his arms let go, and he sank to the ground, winded. He felt sick. She had known exactly where to punch for maximum effect, but then she was Resistance trained, so he supposed she would. Somebody was making a noise like an asthmatic duck and he had a nasty feeling it was him.

Two more guards ran forward, swept the earth and leaves away from a hidden trap door and opened it.

Deirdre hauled The Pan to his feet by the scruff of his neck and gestured with the gun.

"In," she said.

The Pan peered into the hole. There were steps disappearing into complete darkness. His knees were shaking far too much to do dark stairs without light.

"What? In there?"

"Yes."

"First?" he asked weakly, "without a torch? What do you think I am, an owl?"

She turned to Big Merv.

"You! Swamp boy! Are you the leader?"

Big Merv drew himself up to his full height.

"Yeh, that's right. I'm Big Merv, not 'you there', 'swamp boy', 'swamp guy', 'swampy' or—if you wanna live to see tomorrow—'slimy'. In fact to most people it's 'Sir' but I'll allow you to call me 'Mr Merv'," he said, exuding a palpable aura of menace which made everyone take a step backwards except Deirdre, who didn't appear to notice.

"Is this little smecker always so annoying?" she asked, gesturing to The Pan.

"Yeh."

"Arnold! I'm going to end up killing him before we get anywhere near Denarghi," she sighed petulantly. "Well if you're the leader, you can make him shut up, can't you? If he annoys me any more I kill you instead, understand?"

Big Merv glared at The Pan.

"You may as well top me now then, Mrs Deirdre. I can't stop him wittering on any more than you can."

"It's pronounced MIZZ, as in Ms Deirdre."

Big Merv folded his arms and gave her the kind of measured look The Pan had seen him giving some of the Big M dance troupe when they were having a strop on what the male staff of the cartel euphemistically referred to as 'a red letter day'.

"MIZZ Deirdre," Big Merv corrected himself.

With another sigh of annoyance she turned her attentions to a small pack attached to her cartridge belt and after a brief moment of rummaging about, took out a torch.

"Here," she told The Pan, "since you're that much of a drip you'll have to have this flashlight. You can thank Mister Merv for that," she shoved it into his hand. "Now get in before I push you. There are a lot of stairs and you don't want to fall down them, do you?"

"No I don't, do I? which might be why I didn't want to lead off without a torch."

The Pan got the impression she would like nothing more than to see him fall down the stairs. Then again, that was probably why he'd had to go to such lengths to get a torch out of her. Stupid woman, he couldn't see in the dark, even if she could. This minor piece of insubordination was not what The Pan would call a victory but it was definitely a result.

"Do you know, Deirdre, if you weren't a psychopath, you'd be very attractive," he said as he stepped into the darkness. It wasn't his best, but it was the most annoying thing he could think of to say on the spur of the moment and it made him feel better.

"If she really was a psychopath, she'd chuck you down those blinking stairs. And the way you're going on I'd be happy to give 'er a hand," growled Big Merv from somewhere behind him. The passage was dark, full of cobwebs, and The Pan was unimpressed. Perhaps Big Merv was right; this was not the time for a hissy fit, but the Resistance had finally got to him, and behaving like a spoiled child took his mind off the fear.

Chapter 49

At the bottom of the stairs they came to a small room with a door at one end.

"Out of my way," said Deirdre as she barged past them all and unlocked it. Once on the other side, things were entirely different: the passage beyond was spotless. Lamp brackets hung on the walls, but as it was getting light outside, the lamps were extinguished and the lighting was provided by daylight, reflected via a series of mirrors, hidden in tubes drilled in the trunks of the trees in the forest above. They were taken down what looked like an underground main street to a large room where, assisted by her troops, Deirdre locked a ball and chain round one of each of their ankles. Once finished, she left them there with four armed guards. They listened in silence to the sound of low voices outside the door, before it opened again and Denarghi walked in with his usual burly gun-toting escorts, except this time there were four of them.

"Finally, the Mervinettes," he said smugly, "I believe you have robbed the Bank of Grongolia."

"Believe what yer like," said Big Merv. Denarghi nodded and one of the heavies flanking him pulled out a sawn-off shotgun.

The Pan wondered if they ever put the weapons down and had a normal conversation. Judging by how strung-out Deirdre was he guessed not. They probably ate with one hand only so they could still keep a loaded gun in the other. He could imagine Deirdre at supper time hefting a rifle at the guy opposite and shouting, "You! Pass me the ketchup NOW if you want to live to have grandchildren." Either that or she would taste her food, decide it wasn't properly seasoned, run hot-foot to the kitchen and blow the brains out of the cook.

"Are you paying attention to me?" asked Denarghi.

"Yes!" said The Pan smartly. Arnold! Had the rest of him missed anything important while his mind had been wandering? He hoped not.

"Good. Because you have a simple choice. Give us the loot or we'll hand you over to the Grongles."

"You'll do that anyway," said Big Merv, "I know you people."

The heavy levelled his sawn-off shotgun at The Pan.

"Insults will do nothing for your cause," said Denarghi.

"But we can't help you," said Frank sullenly.

"Yeh, Big Merv chucked the loot out of the window about a mile out to sea," said Harry.

"You WHAT?" shouted Denarghi. The Pan shut his eyes and waited for the impact as one of them was shot. Nothing happened, so he opened them again. He watched as Denarghi took a deep breath and pulled himself together with a visible effort, before starting again, calmly. "Let's start with you!" He walked over to The Pan, jumped up and ripped off his false moustache. Arnold's Y fronts! That smarted.

"As I thought. Nice disguise from a distance but close up, my friend, it doesn't cut the mustard." He took a standard Grongolian issue, static-powered, personal organiser from his belt. Unlike the Grongles, Denarghi had plenty of fur to charge it up with. He looked The Pan up and down. "I will start with the obvious facts; five nine, blue eyes, shifty," he tapped at the keyboard and everyone waited in silence. Denarghi didn't share the results of his search, instead he laughed and said, "This simplifies things a great deal."

"Yeh. I know about the triple star," said The Pan.

"Obstructing the course of justice?" asked Denarghi.

"A long story."

"One you do not wish to share?"

"Not with you." Not with anyone. It was too stupid.

"Five years is a long time," said Denarghi. Was that admiration or jealousy in his tone? Hard to tell.

"You're not wrong there, Your Majesty," said The Pan, with more feeling than intended.

A pause. There must be a reward for a blacklisted person with stars, a big one if Denarghi's expression was anything to go by. He gave The Pan a measuring look. The wrong kind of measuring look. The type of evaluating look a butcher might give livestock.

"Let us revert to the robbery," said the blurpon, changing the subject abruptly, "do you expect me to believe you were involved in a robbery at the Bank of Grongolia—the world's most impregnable bank—and then threw away the things you stole? Explain."

"Why are you asking me? I'm the getaway man, I don't think. I drive,"

The Pan began. There was the click of a safety catch being removed.

"I don't usually waste resources," said Denarghi, "but for you I am prepared to make an exception. Oh I know you're the driver, and I know you're good. No." He laughed mirthlessly. "You're more than good, you're untouchable —none of my people come close —but you are worth a lot of reward money for who you really are, before I even factor in that you are one of the most wanted gangsters in the world."

"I'm not a gangster."

"You are one of the Mervinettes. What else are you if you are not a gangster? And you are also a risk. My Lieutenant, Deirdre, tells me you are high maintenance and untrustworthy. What is more, she says you're incapable of doing what you're told. I don't need free thinkers here, I need people who are prepared to follow the orders they have been given, even if it means laying down their lives for the cause. Are you prepared to follow orders?"

The Pan glanced at Big Merv. Big Merv's orders could be tall but they were usually very general, things like 'Drive!' or 'Let's get out of here!' Even The Pan could obey common sense commands like those, and when he couldn't, he argued. But Big Merv had never given orders in the manner Denarghi was referring to, or the way Deirdre did.

The Mervinettes followed a plan. The Resistance did what they were told. The Mervinettes did whatever it was they needed to do to make the plan work even if, sometimes, that meant binning the plan altogether and doing something else.

Each gang member had a clearly delineated area of responsibility and for that, he was the acknowledged 'expert'. That meant their heists could be more flexible and their group dynamic was more informal. The Pan might have been scared of Big Merv, but broadly speaking, he trusted his judgement and his abilities as a leader. Sure, Big Merv made all the decisions, but he listened to the others and took what they said into account first.

"I asked you a question," said Denarghi, "are you prepared to follow orders?"

"Not if they're downright stupid, no."

"Ha! I thought as much. I don't need people who think they know better than their superiors. I am looking for obedience."

"If you're looking for people like Deirdre then we're clearly too clever for you," said The Pan sullenly, "that woman is an idiot! She was shouting her

192

head off in forest full of Grongles so I suggested, very politely, that she keep her voice down and she had a complete meltdown. She can die for your cause if she wants, but going out of her way to get martyred is just stupid—especially when it means we have to die with her."

"That is exactly the kind of behaviour I am talking about," growled Denarghi, "you are walking very close to the edge my friend."

The Pan rolled his eyes.

"By contradicting a moron? Deirdre may be a magnificent soldier for all I know but laying down her life is one thing, wasting it—and the lives of the others around her—that's a different matter entirely." No! What was he doing? Not again! He'd already got himself thumped once today. Why didn't his big mouth have an off switch? Why did he always have to argue with everyone about everything? What was it about people like Deirdre and Denarghi, people who always had to win, that so badly wound him up? There was no debate with people like this, they were always right! Even if they contradicted themselves in back-to-back sentences, they were still always right because they believed they were and they had big men with guns to deal with anyone who disagreed.

"Deirdre is a brave and honourable freedom fighter," said Denarghi.

In The Pan's view she was only brave because she was too stupid and unimaginative to be frightened. Never mind, now was not the time to point it out; now was the time to make amends, before Denarghi had him shot.

"Look, I'm sorry, I didn't put that very well. What I am trying to say is that I've been on the blacklist for five whole years and in that time I have learned a few things about not getting caught and one of those things is not to go yelling my head off when there are Grongles around. I guess Deirdre's braver than me. I was scared we'd be caught, that's all." Even to The Pan's own ears his words sounded hollow and insincere. Maybe the aggressive line was best after all. No, the best thing would have been to shut up completely or ideally, to not have shot his mouth off in the first place. But it was too late for that now.

"Did you not think that Deirdre might be a highly trained and disciplined soldier with more battle experience than you?"

"Nope," said The Pan, "I'm sure she is, but my frame of reference wasn't soldiering, it was running away. I'm an escape man, that's what I do."

"You admit you let your fear sway you?"

"Of course I did! I have a strong survival instinct. It comes with the territory."

"And you are proud of this? You are proud to be a coward?" asked Denarghi incredulously.

A tricky one.

"I'm not exactly proud to be a coward, no," said The Pan, "but I am proud that I can do something well. If being yellow gives me a useful skill then I can live with it." He wondered if he should point out that being a coward made him good enough at what he did for Denarghi to call him 'untouchable'. No, probably not. He would only take it the wrong way. He wasn't making any headway, but the idiot in him still made the mistake of a further attempt at explanation.

"Running away is what cowards do best, right?" he said, "so if I wasn't a coward I wouldn't be any good at making an escape, would I?"

"If you are so afraid, how can I rely on you not to turn tail and run at the slightest sign of danger. How can I be assured you will wait until the right time before you run?" said Denarghi.

"I've no idea," said The Pan, flatly, "I've never thought about it. I'd guess there's a clue in the fact I haven't up until now. Perhaps I have some principles, after all." If Denarghi noticed his sarcasm he made no sign.

"There is no room for fear in this organisation," he said, "cowardice makes people selfish."

The Pan was exasperated. It was like talking to a robot.

"But I'm not 'people' I'm me and it makes ME good. You're not listening are you? What am I supposed to do? What do you want me to say? Everything I've said has gone straight over your head hasn't it?"

There was a sudden silence. The Pan had mentioned size to a blurpon. It was oblique and he hadn't meant to, but it was done. It was the worst thing he could have said. Great. Who was the moron now, he thought dourly?

194

Chapter 50

Denarghi's scarlet fur bristled with anger.

"Are you making reference to my size?" he asked.

"Not on purpose!" The Pan looked helplessly at Big Merv.

"Your Majesty. I understand that my stupid, mincing puff of a driver is rambling on like a great girl in a way that might make you kill us all," growled The Big Thing, his voice rising to a bellow by the end of the sentence and glaring at The Pan all the while. "Arnold knows, I wouldn't blame you if you topped the little Herbert! But for all his pink, girly wussiness he knows a thing or two about escaping and he can handle a snurd better than anyone alive. That's how come he has been blacklisted for five years and survived, see? Because he doesn't wanna die. He doesn't wanna die so bad he's good. That's why, even though he talks cobblers and behaves like some high maintenance bird with PMT," The Pan winced, "I listen to what he tells me."

A back-handed compliment. Pity about the PMT bit though. Never mind, Big Merv seemed to have got Denarghi's attention, and at last he appeared to be listening.

"Go on," said the blurpon, coolly.

"So he weren't too smart with Deirdre—" began Big Merv.

"Not you!" said Denarghi. "You," he pointed to The Pan. "Before you speak, bear in mind I don't have to keep you here. The reward on your head is worth far more than I'd get out of using you. So you can carry on being a wise guy if you like, changing the subject, insulting my organisation and me. If you do, I can hand you over to the Grongles with a clear conscience. Or, you can tell me the truth, and I might change my mind and let you stay here and work for us. I have a simple question for you, my friend, and I would like you to answer it. Where's the loot?"

Bugger! Bugger, bugger, bugger! Now what? The Pan glanced over at Big Merv with a questioning look. Almost imperceptibly, he nodded.

"I'm afraid Harry was telling the truth, Your Majesty," said The Pan, deciding full adherence to royal protocol might increase his chances of survival, or at least sugar the bitter pill of truth. "We lobbed—" no, that wasn't the right word. This called for tact and diplomacy. He started again, "We'd run out of anti-missile chaff, so we needed something metal to act as a decoy."

"You threw the priceless items you were contracted to steal out of the snurd window while you were over the ocean, to save your pathetic skins?" Denarghi asked. His attention still focussed on The Pan, clearly he'd decided he was spokesman. Arnold! Why did they always do that? Whatever he said he was bound to get thumped by one of the henchmen, but if he got the story wrong he'd probably get punched by Big Merv, too. He really, really must learn to be less conspicuous.

"Er, that's about the size of it, yes," he said. Denarghi signalled to the heavy with the shotgun and he pulled the trigger. There was a massive explosion as the shot hit the ground in front of The Pan's feet and blew a hole in the floor. He leapt backwards straight into the waiting clutches of the guards behind him who held him still, despite his efforts to scrabble as far away as his chained ankle would allow. He noticed the others had grabbed Big Merv, Frank and Harry to stop them trying to come to his aid.

"Where is your dedication to the cause?" hissed Denarghi.

What cause? There was no cause, not Denarghi's at any rate. The Mervinettes were bank robbers. For all of them, including The Pan, this was about self-preservation – and money of course. The Pan didn't think it was wise to be truthful about the gang's motives. A direct answer was definitely best avoided.

"Er, Your Majesty, Mr Denarghi, sir, we had no choice," he said. "It was a case of keep the loot and die or bin the loot and live. Anyway, it's no big deal, I know roughly where it is. We can go back and get it for you, but only on condition you let the four of us go alone." Oops, stupid to add that last bit. Good to ingratiate his fellow Mervinettes but bad to do so with such a glaring lack of subtlety.

"Let the four of you retrieve my loot and do a runner? Don't insult my intelligence!"

"It ain't your loot," said Big Merv, "we didn't steal it for you. Even if we still had it, it's not yours to take."

Thank you Big Merv, thought The Pan as Denarghi hit him. He was expecting it after the scare tactics with the shotgun, but the shock to his system was still substantial. Denarghi might have been just over three feet tall but he could still jump high enough to deliver a hefty punch in the jaw,

196

just at the point when The Pan had been bracing himself for being head-butted in the stomach.

He bent double for a few moments, his hands to his face, while he waited for the smarting to go away. Oh well. At least he wasn't bleeding mutant blue blood all over the place. There was usually an upside to everything.

"That's right, punch me," he said as soon as he'd straightened up. "What did I do? He's the one who rattled your cage," he flung one arm outwards, gesturing in Big Merv's direction, "why don't you go and punch him?" And on Denarghi's signal one of the guards replied with a second punch to The Pan, in his ribs this time.

His jellied legs didn't take much persuading to dump him on his knees again. He had to think straight. Denarghi yanked his head up by the hair and looked into his eyes. Yep, he definitely had to think straight! He had to persuade Denarghi to let go, otherwise his secret eyes were in danger of being discovered, and then Arnold in heaven knew what they'd do.

"Have you any idea how much that hurt?" he gasped, "and this is unnecessary." He rolled his eyes upwards to indicate the tuft of hair Denarghi was clutching, "You haven't knocked me out yet, I can still hold my head up on my own."

"I am making a point," said Denarghi, shaking The Pan by the hair to accentuate each word. He did let go when he'd finished, though, and The Pan heaved a sigh of relief. The temptation to look down for a moment was almost overwhelming but he didn't dare in case it precipitated another bout of hair-grabbing.

"Alright, you and me then, Denarghi, sir, we can go and get the loot," he said wearily. There was a cough from somewhere behind him, "with Big Merv," he added hastily.

"Even if that were possible and we could mount a search, it would be like looking for a needle in a haystack," said Denarghi. "As it is, the entire area is cordoned off with half the Grongolian army crawling all over it."

Ah. Whatever that stuff was, it must have mattered then. Oh dear.

"So the artefact is lost to us," said Denarghi. "No matter, it is also lost to the Grongles and now we must make the best of our situation. The bounty on your heads will more than compensate us for our time and trouble, not to mention your carelessness."

"You're not really gonna to hand us over to the Grongles are you?" asked Big Merv incredulously.

"I might, it's up to you," said Denarghi smugly, "if you are lying, now is the time to admit it. There are winners and losers in this world and you, my friend, are a loser. We have won."

"Why you snivelling, cheating—" Big Merv snatched up the weight chained to his ankle and ran at Denarghi. Three of the four guards attempted to restrain him with little effect until the other heavy stepped into his path and put the muzzle of his shotgun to his chest. He stopped struggling abruptly.

"That's right. I'd give some thought to my actions if I were you," said Denarghi, "you are Big Merv and these are the Mervinettes. The famous gang, identified beyond doubt; signed, sealed and delivered. Do you know how badly Lord Vernon wants you, how much you're worth? More than we could ever earn if we set you to work for us. Without the loot you have nothing to contribute to my organisation. None of you have skills enough to outweigh the bounty on your heads," he glanced at The Pan, "not even your driver. I have little to gain from keeping you here, so if I was in your place, I would show some more respect. It's up to you to convince me you are worth keeping."

Two of the guards were still holding Big Merv's arms. He shrugged them off but made no move to brave the sawn-off shotgun and continue his attack. His antennae were sticking straight up, as if they were statically charged, a sure sign his anger levels were at the dangerous red-alert-coloured end of the dial.

"We'll see who's a winner you rat-faced little runt! Gimme the name," he growled, "I ain't stupid, I know when I've been sold down the river and you're gonna tell me who squealed."

"I don't think so."

"Yeh?"

"What's the problem? Can't see the *grass* for the trees?" sneered Denarghi.

"I have standards in my organisation and the way I keep those standards is by making sure that people who grass me up pay," said Big Merv.

"Ha! The honour of thieves! I have heard so much about this supposed code yet, if it exists, why have I never seen any evidence?"

"Maybe you're too stupid to notice it," said The Pan quietly.

"Silence! You and your kind are the same scum whether it's us in power or the Grongles," said Denarghi. He seemed to be waiting for a reaction, but despite his obvious rage Big Merv stayed silent. "Big Merv," Denarghi spat, "not so big now are you? Perhaps somebody in your organisation is smarter than you and knows who the winners are in this world, because we are the winners around here. Trained, committed freedom fighters—not some bunch of chancers robbing banks for kicks." He waved an imperious arm at Frank and Harry. "Bring them," he told the guards and they were dragged away. When he reached the door, he stopped.

"I'll deal with you two later. I may sell you or, if you can convince me you are worth my time and effort, I may keep you here. I don't think you'll be going anywhere in the meantime." With that, he turned on his heel and left. The guards closed the door behind him and locked it, leaving The Pan and Big Merv on their own.

Chapter 51

There was a thud as Big Merv angrily threw his ankle weight to the ground. The Pan couldn't help noticing how easily he had done it; he could hardly lift his.

"Pompous little twot! The small ones are always the worst," Big Merv muttered, before turning slowly towards The Pan. "It's your friend who grassed us up. It has to be," an ominous pause, "or was it you?"

"Get a grip Merv," said The Pan heavily, "if it was me I wouldn't be stuck in a cell with you, would I? I'd be home free, with the loot, the reward and everyone else's cash."

"Listen, sonny. It's you what got us into this mess. What's to stop me taking this ball and chain and smashing your head open with it?"

Clearly, Big Merv felt like thumping somebody. The Pan could hardly blame him, but Arnold's armpits! Why did he have to be the only thing around to hit? "Not much."

"Well?"

"Well, what, Big Merv?" said The Pan. It was difficult to speak, his jaw ached where he'd been punched and his mouth had gone dry. "Go ahead! Be my guest. The way I feel it would be a blessed release. I told you we shouldn't do this job."

"Yeh, I hear you, mate, I weren't happy about it neither. But your old gimmer's paying us good money."

"If we live long enough to receive it."

"Yeh. Sell us, an' he gets his job done free, don't he?"

"That's a horrible thought," one The Pan had been trying, expressly, not to have.

"Yeh, ain't it?" The conversation lapsed for a moment. "You know what, I reckon that fluffy-arsed nonce wants me to smash your face in. 'S why they've left us alone, so you ain't gonna be able to escape—on account yer injuries—before they hand you over to the Grongles."

"Very possible. Or they want us to talk so they can listen," said The Pan, "I expect they want to double check we really bunged the loot," he winked at Big Merv and realised, with surprise, that his boss was looking a little shifty. "They're probably hoping you hid it in the MK II or somewhere near the crash site and that you're going to tell me," he added.

Big Merv looked even more uncomfortable and The Pan began to suspect he might have inadvertently hit on the truth. However tough The Big Thing was, he was a rubbish liar and earlier, in the MK II, when he'd first showed them the box, something had been rattling about inside. The second time he had held it up, moments before pitching it out of the window, it hadn't made a sound. So. What if he had palmed the loot? He wasn't the type to betray his colleagues but then, he hadn't had a chance to tell them what was going on and he was even less the type to go to all the trouble of robbing a target as heavily defended as the Bank of Grongolia, only to chuck his prize into the sea. If he suspected The Pan or the old man had betrayed him, he might have held it up so the others would know it was empty and realise what he'd done. True, the Resistance had searched the Mervinettes but only a quick pat down for weapons. They hadn't found The Pan's thimble so if the loot was similarly small and easy to conceal, there was a chance Big Merv had managed to keep it hidden.

"Yeh. 'S a shame. I wish I had hidden it in the MK II," said Big Merv resignedly.

"Not that it would change anything," said The Pan.

"Nah, it'd have been blown up instead, so we'd still be up the creek."

There was a long silence during which The Pan thought he heard a resigned sigh and a squeak, the type of squeak a small metal plate makes when it's being slid into position – over a spy hole for example. He wondered if Big Merv had heard it too and gave him a quizzical look.

"Nice to stick a spanner in their plans, eh?" said Big Merv. As he spoke, he passed his hand over his face and down across his chest. The Pan thought he caught sight of something glinting in his palm for a moment, even though when he held both arms out in front of him immediately afterwards, his hands were empty. He sat down on the floor and settled back against the wall.

"We're in for a rough ride mate," he told The Pan, "you should have a lie down, get some shut eye. A fresh mind—"

"Is a nimble one. Yeh, thanks Merv, you sound like my dad. Unfortunately, abject terror isn't conducive to sleep."

"Suit yerself," said Big Merv. "'S no point being afraid though, it's a waste of energy."

201

"Yes, I appreciate that but I can't seem to get it through to my brain, it will keep dwelling on the doo-doo we're in and my stomach, it will keep churning and my knees, they will keep knocking."

"Will you shut it, you daft tart?" said Big Merv, not unkindly.

Yep. He had the loot alright; there was no way he could be that relaxed unless he was confident of his bargaining power. The question was, did Frank and Harry know and more to the point would they crack? The Pan wiggled his foot and felt the reassuring, if painful, presence of the thimble in his boot; he didn't want to lose it. He thought about the old man, who didn't seem the type to grass people up. In fact, The Pan was sure he hadn't; all he knew about the old man was that he was in league with Gladys and Ada, and to The Pan, that counted for something. Anyway, the old boy looked so much like Their Trev he had to be a relative – or worse an old flame. Big Merv obviously hadn't grassed them up. If he had, he wouldn't be hanging onto the loot. The Pan knew he hadn't blabbed to anyone, so that left Frank and Harry, which didn't make sense either.

The Pan remembered how the old man had known pretty much everything about the gang, mostly things he couldn't have known without physically being with them at the time the events had taken place. He thought about what the old man had said to him when he'd asked how he knew. So had the old man used his thimble to watch the Mervinettes the way The Pan had used his to watch the girl? And if The Pan, a novice, could get a picture, was it possible that the old man, a seasoned pro, could get sound? If there were more than two thimbles, could somebody else be watching them, too? What if the Resistance had one, or worse, the Grongles? Even if the Resistance hadn't a thimble up to now, The Pan thought morosely, they soon would have because they would search him more thoroughly and find his. He looked across at Big Merv. They'd find the loot, too.

That couldn't happen. It would be proof they'd lied to Denarghi and make the outlook even bleaker than it was now. For Big Merv to strike a deal, the loot would have to be somewhere else.

"Merv, we have to get out of here."

"Yeh, well you're a slippery little bleeder, but if you can get us out of this I'm a big pink skipping rope," said Big Merv.

The Pan couldn't blame him for being cynical, but he had hatched a plan. He took off his boot.

"What are you doing now?" asked Big Merv.

"Sore foot," said The Pan, "I think I got a stone in my shoe during all that trudging about. Either that or there's a nail sticking up somewhere."

"And you've gotta fix that now?"

The Pan gave him what he hoped was a look of subtle meaning and said, "Yes, Merv, I have to fix it now." He held up his boot and put his hand inside, slipping the thimble into his palm as he did so. "Nope," he held the boot right up to his face and peered in, "nothing there." Thimble still in hand, he put the boot back on.

Now he was ready. He thought about the Parrot and Screwdriver; more specifically, he thought about his stash of loot in the cellar, and under the guise of ostentatiously rubbing his eyes, he looked into the thimble. He couldn't see much – it was dark in the cellar, but with the tiny cheam of light spilling through from The Pan's surroundings – he could make out a couple of gold sovereigns and the box which had once contained the ring worn by forty generations of Architraves.

By The Prophet! He must stop thinking about the ring. He'd sold it and nothing could alter that now. It was merely another item on the list of things he regretted having done, but he wasn't going to let the thimble go the same way. It was his only link with the girl, reason enough to hold onto it, but he suspected it was also important, just as the ring had been. It was his only link with the old man, too, which might be another reason he should keep it – even if, right now that seemed like a good reason to let it go. He rubbed his temples.

"What?" demanded Big Merv.

"If we'd managed to keep the loot, would you have trusted me enough to let me stash it?" asked The Pan.

"Where?"

"Where I keep my own."

"Depends where that is."

"Nowhere anyone's ever found it."

OK, so that was a lie, but nobody had *admitted* finding The Pan's loot. It was just that he knew Gladys dusted it once in a while, when she spring cleaned behind the barrels in the cellar. Gladys was a cleanest-front-step-in-the-street kind of woman, and so was Ada.

"How are we gonna get from here to the loot and from there to stashing it?" asked Big Merv.

"By combining a little imagination with the wonders of quantum physics," said The Pan smugly.

"You're cracking up aren't yer?"

"But if I could do it, shift the loot somewhere safe, would you trust me?"

"Maybe," said Big Merv.

"Shake on it?" said The Pan, giving his boss what he hoped was a meaningful look.

Big Merv stood up, picked up his ball and chain and sauntered over to where The Pan was sitting.

"Yeh. OK," he said, sticking out his hand. The Pan shook it and felt the pressure of something cool and metallic in his palm, he turned his hand over to hide it and Big Merv sat down next to him. In his hand he could feel a small box. The loot. In his other hand was the thimble. All he had to do was combine the two, put the box through the thimble into his stash in the Parrot's cellar. Gladys would find it eventually and when she did, she could hand it on to the old man. Box, thimble, stash – easy as one, two, three. Except it wasn't. The Pan was so nervous he thought he was going to be sick. His hands were clammy and shaking. Big Merv was watching him intently which was making it worse. No, forget Big Merv, he must concentrate on what he was doing and be careful not to drop anything.

"It'll be fine," he muttered and taking a deep breath he jammed the box in his right hand into the thimble in his left. There was a loud sucking sound and lots of pressure, he could feel it trying to draw his hand in, as well as the box, before he remembered to let go. Then there was a pop, like a champagne cork, and it had gone. The Pan just had time to raise his left hand to his eye and check that the loot, their loot, was in the cellar of the Parrot and Screwdriver before the door opened and Denarghi walked in flanked by the ubiquitous sawn-off shotgun-toting guards. Big Merv was visibly paler but he collected himself admirably. The Pan wished he could explain – he hadn't thought about the noise, he hadn't thought about the fact that Big Merv was unlikely to have seen anything that bizarre before. He showed him his other hand, the empty one and hoped he would understand.

"Holy Arnold! What in The Prophet's name was that?" said Big Merv.

"On your feet," barked Denarghi, "now!"

"Don't worry, long story," said The Pan as they stood up.

"Oh, but we have plenty of time," said Denarghi, who had heard. "Guards!" There was a loud click as the four guards aimed their sawn-off shotguns in perfect precision. "You may begin, Hamgeean scum."

Chapter 52

The Pan wondered where to start. There was no way he was going to flannel his way out of this one, he was going to have to tell them the truth, although maybe not all of it. He didn't think Big Merv would like it or that Denarghi would believe him. The silence lengthened.

"Any time this decade will suit me fine," said Denarghi, "I would advise you to speak up soon though. I have had enough of recalcitrant criminals today. Your mute friends have met with the fate they deserved and you will go the same way if you don't start talking."

"You shot Frank and Harry?" asked Big Merv, his natural colour all but disappearing. He was now beige, if he was any colour at all. "That's worse than the bleedin' Grongles. They ain't done nothing to you."

"They crossed me," said Denarghi flatly, "they had a choice; they could join us, be sold to the Grongles or choose an honourable death—they chose death."

"Merv," muttered The Pan, "they're the Resistance, they're doing what they do; you chuck people into the river Dang all the time, it's the same deal."

"It smeckin' ain't, on account of the fact I don't hardly ever chuck 'em in."

"You mean Frank and Harry do it, er sorry, did it."

"No! I mean it don't get that far. It's all about applying pressure innit? A little bit of pressure and they crack like you did, you great puff! Why would I waste blokes; deprive a family of a father or a mother of a son when with a little bit of nous," he tapped the side of his head, "I can use 'em instead? I'm a civilised businessman, not an animal! Arnold knows the Grongles do enough killing."

"But all the stories—"

"Are stories! Spin! Nothing more! By the eyeballs of The Prophet! No wonder you're so scared of me! Whaddaya think I am? A monster? Lord Vernon? I have morals as good as the next man. Nobody wants a war, training ain't that quick and lives ain't that cheap. Where I come from, nobody dies unless they have to." He glared belligerently at Denarghi. "We could have sorted this out between us. We're men of the world! You didn't have to top Frank and Harry!"

"But I did, my friend, in order to have your full attention," said Denarghi. "This is not some light altercation between cartels, this is a holy war, our holy war against the Grongles and we will not rest until it is won. We must move fast to ensure the Candidate becomes Architrave and rightful ruler of K'Barth."

"You've found the Candidate?" asked Big Merv.

"Yes."

The Pan was exasperated.

"Denarghi, everyone thinks they've found the Candidate, Lord Vernon is even trying to set himself up as a false Candidate. You think you've found one, the person who paid us to rob the Bank of Grongolia, I'm pretty sure he thinks he's found one ..." He stopped, he was going to say he thought his father might have found one.

"There is only one true candidate," said Denarghi acidly, "it is Deirdre."

"Oh get a grip! She's a psychopath!" said The Pan with a vehemence that surprised him. What was he doing? It was as if he suddenly felt strongly about all this. The Pan made a point of never feeling strongly about politics. It was a waste of energy, and since the Grongles took power it was often a waste of life. But Deirdre! Denarghi must have a screw loose.

"Look, I'm sorry, I shouldn't have said that about Deirdre. But if you're so sure she's the Candidate, why are we here, why do you need the loot? If it's for the Looking and you need it badly enough to murder Frank and Harry it means you're no surer Deirdre's the Candidate than I am!"

"She is the Candidate," said Denarghi firmly.

"Isn't the Architrave supposed to be smart, though?" countered The Pan. He tried to remember what the old man had said. "Somebody who can think for themself? Deirdre is an insane nutter who blindly follows orders; that rubs her out for starters." Oh dear. That wasn't what he'd meant to say at all, he'd wanted to make his point in a calm and adult way. Pants.

"Deirdre is brave and dedicated to the cause," retorted Denarghi, "she will not rest until the Grongle nation is wiped from the face of the earth."

"And when, in all history, has the Architrave ever sanctioned wiping out an entire race?" asked The Pan. "Never. Not even if they are Grongles." Anyway, he remembered, he'd checked the genocide question the night the old man came to see him. If the old boy considered it unethical to change reality to a version where the Grongles never existed, how much more unethical would it be to murder each and every last one of them? Although he had to admit that from where he was standing, the notion had a definite appeal.

"You can't just wipe out a whole nation—life doesn't work like that," said The Pan.

"We can and we will," said Denarghi.

"You can't! Look, if there is a real Candidate surely they must be chosen by the priests," he held his arms out sideways in a why-don't-you-get-it gesture and let them drop to his sides. "That's how it's done. That's how we've done it for the last forty generations. You can't just pick someone at random because it suits you—there have to be signs, they have to be found by the Looking—and genocidal tendencies aren't going to impress."

Silence.

"Can't you see? Murdering the Grongles is wrong, it's doing what they do! Being like them! It's not the answer."

"And who are you to judge right and wrong?" asked Denarghi venomously.

"Someone who clearly has a better grasp of what they are than you do!" snapped The Pan. There was a long uncomfortable silence during which, to his surprise, nobody shot him.

"Don't play games with me, I will not be goaded by your taunts. You have a choice, my friend, you can play your part, you can join us."

"I'd rather die," said The Pan, before he could stop himself. Arnold in heaven! Where had that come from?

"That can be arranged," said Denarghi, "I'll give a count of five for you to change your mind and explain the origin of that sound we just heard. Meanwhile, your mutant Swamp Monster friend had better think long and hard about whether or not he intends to hand over the loot. I know you've stashed it somewhere. Where is it?"

The Pan berated himself, why did he have to be so touchy about this Candidate thing all of a sudden? Was it something to do with his father? He was going to have to backtrack now, apologise and support the odious Deirdre. That was always assuming Big Merv could see past being called a Swamp Monster, of course, and a mutant one at that, which, on the face of it, seemed pretty unlikely.

"One."

OK, so it was simple. All he had to do was say Deirdre was the Candidate and begin at the beginning about being blacklisted; the Mervinettes and the old man and everything would be fine. No, he couldn't.

How could he have been so stupid? Why hadn't he thought ahead and seen this moment coming? Nothing and no-one was ever worth dying for! But he couldn't save his own neck by betraying his friends. The old man was a 'friend' of Gladys and Ada; to betray him was as good as to betray them. They were like a second family.

"No. Not again," he said angrily to no-one in particular, "this is not going to happen again!"

"What are you talking about?" said Denarghi, "You may be the best escape man in K'Barth but you only have one life. Now I will ask you once more. What did you steal and where is it? Two."

The Pan turned to Big Merv who was glaring at him with murderous intent, antennae sticking straight upwards in rage position again. He was going to get himself shot and Big Merv too. Bang on cue, his life started to flash before his eyes: his childhood, his parents, the Grongles, Big Merv, the visit from the old man, the robbery, back to the visit from the old man. He felt the thimble in his hand and he had an idea.

"Merv. Hold my hand."

"No! Die like a man, you nerk."

"I'm not a man, I'm Hamgeean and neither of us has to die! Hold my hand."

"Save yourself, Big Merv," said Denarghi. "Hand over the loot and I'll spare you. Three."

"OK, OK. You win. I didn't bung the loot," said Big Merv, "it ain't here though, we stashed it, so we'd have to go get it."

"You didn't have time to stash it."

"Did. Search us and see!"

"So you LIED to me," said Denarghi.

"Yeh, we lied, coz we didn't nick it for you, so it ain't yours to take."

"It wasn't yours either."

"Well it sure as hell ain't yours, Denarghi! You people make me sick! I'm a bank robber and I ain't ashamed to admit it. You? You make out you're so effin' noble, like you're above us, and then you let us do your dirty work, kill two of my lads and now, you're trying to rob me! Honour like that'd get you sliced in my part of town."

"Nobody in your part of town would dare touch me."

The Pan had never seen his boss so angry.

"Wanna give it a try, Big Man?" asked Big Merv quietly. Why did he have to go and say 'big'? At this rate, The Pan thought, Denarghi wouldn't finish the count before he had them shot.

"Four." There was a new sense of anticipation emanating from the Resistance leader now, as if he was looking forward to pulling the trigger.

"Merv, you don't understand, HOLD MY HAND!" said The Pan.

"Shut up you big ponce! I'm talking.

"You wanna know about the loot, Denarghi?" asked Big Merv, except he said the word 'Denarghi' the way he might say the 'punk' at the end of 'make my day'.

"Let me tell you about the loot. We took the risk, we stole it an' that means, since I'm in charge, that it's mine to do what I like with. If you want it, you'll have to ask the bloke what paid me and my gang to steal it in the first place! You never know, if you're lucky he might let you have it for the right price. I 'spect he'll be a bit short of cash after what he's promised us—but that's the thing, see? You have to talk to HIM because unlike you, Denarghi, I am HONOURABLE and I blummin' mean it when I tell someone I've made a deal."

"You're a dying breed Big Merv and when we take power we will cleanse society of scum like you, the way I'm about to do now," said Denarghi.

"Don't bet on it you snotty little twonk! We'll kick your jumped-up behind back down the sewers where you belong."

"Merv, please, this is not gratuitous touchy-feeliness, think about the interesting noise, Mr Denarghi has asked me to explain! Remember what happened? HOLD MY HAND YOU BONEHEADED SLIMEBAG!" said The Pan. He was going to get punched for the 'slimebag' bit but it was the only way he could think of to get Big Merv's attention.

Glowering at The Pan, Big Merv took his hand.

"There, you big wuss. That better?" he growled.

"Five. Well?"

"I swear on my life we don't have the loot," said The Pan.

"Don't think your life is worth that much!" said Denarghi. "The Grongles will pay the same reward for your carcass, regardless of whether or not it's breathing, and I am confident I will find the loot on one of your bodies."

The Pan tutted. He knew he was being cocky but he couldn't help himself.

"Shouldn't you check? Pride before a fall," he said lightly. He had a plan! Tra-la-laaa!

"Yeh, I told you! We don't have the loot here!" said Big Merv.

"But we do have this," said The Pan, holding up the thimble in his left hand and curling his thumb into the open end.

There was a loud sucking sound as the power of the forces began to build and he held onto Big Merv's hand tightly as they were dragged in. From somewhere far away he could hear Denarghi's voice shouting.

"Don't just stand there! Open fire! Kill them!" before he and Big Merv were crashing onto the floor of the cellar in the Parrot and Screwdriver, bottles, packets of crisps and the odd maturing cheese scattering in all directions. There was a final crash as a pot of Gladys' home-made pickle fell off a shelf and smashed on the ground, a short hissing noise as the contents ate its way into the stone flags, and then silence.

Chapter 53

"Arnold's Y fronts!" yelled The Pan leaping to his feet. "It worked!" He started to run forwards but was brought up short. Ah yes, the ball and chain. As he reached the end of the chain, his feet stopped where they were and the rest of him blundered forwards onto a beer barrel.

"You mean you didn't KNOW it would?" asked Big Merv incredulously. "Why you little scrote! AND you insulted me! I'll show you who's a boneheaded slimebag, you snotty little Herbert! I'm gonna knock your block off!"

The cellar resonated with the sounds of bottles tumbling over and yet another loud crash as Big Merv got to his feet, launched himself at the place where he'd heard The Pan's voice and bumped into the same barrel.

Hiding behind a pillar, The Pan waited while his eyes acclimatised to the gloom. The cellar wasn't in complete darkness; a faint phosphorescence emanating from Gladys' stock of home-made preserves illuminated the scene. Outlined against the glow, fourteen stones of angry Swamp Thing rose to its feet, ball and chain in one hand.

"Merv, don't kill me, it was the only chance we had," said The Pan, ducking swiftly as, with another crash, Big Merv made towards the sound of his voice. A moment later the light came on and Gladys and Ada appeared in the doorway with a large shotgun. Humbert careened past them and circled the room, squawking and swearing vociferously.

"Humbert! Come here this minute!" shouted Ada, as the parrot flew past her head. On the dimly lit stairwell beyond, Gladys' son Trev ducked out of the way as Humbert made his way to his second favourite perch on the coat stand in the hall.

"Don't anybody move or I'll shoot!" Ada ordered them, waving the gun in the air. There was an almighty bang and a large chunk of ceiling fell onto The Pan who was lying over the lid of the freezer, where Big Merv had him in a headlock. "Oh dear! Did I do that?" she trilled.

"Put that down or you'll do someone an injury," said Gladys.

"No," said Big Merv belligerently.

"I weren't talking to you, young man," said Gladys, "but since that's my lodger you is manhandling I'll thank you to put 'im down, anyway." Big

Merv let go of The Pan's neck. "Thank you," said Gladys, with a nod and a 'hmph' of satisfaction. She turned to her friend. "Ada?"

"Oh. Yes. Here you are, dear," said Ada, handing the gun to Gladys, who immediately rounded on The Pan.

"Where has you been? We was sat here worried to death about you."

The Pan glanced at Big Merv and shrugged. There was no point in carrying on the pretence, if they hadn't realised what his 'job' entailed before, they would now he'd brought his boss home with him. There wasn't any official evidence to support Big Merv's connection with the Mervinettes, but even so, there was enough speculation for him to enjoy a certain notoriety.

"Robbing the Bank of Grongolia," he mumbled.

"You was what?" asked Gladys.

"Robbing the Bank of Grongolia," he spoke a little louder this time, adding bullishly, "for YOUR friend."

"I does not consort with crim'nals," said Gladys archly.

"Yes you do, even if he pays others to do his robbing for him. Old bloke, looks not unlike your Trev," said The Pan. He knew that was a cheap shot, and when she coloured in a deep blush, his sense of guilt was overwhelming.

"Never you mind who he looks like, young man," said Ada, coming to Gladys' rescue, "and we know what you've done, we weren't born yesterday. But the Bank of Grongolia was robbed over 24 hours ago! We were expecting you back last night."

"We ran into a spot of bother," said The Pan.

"We suspected as much. The Grongles are looking everywhere for you; they've been here twice already and searched the place from top to bottom."

"Yer," said Gladys. "Only just gone. They ain't got nothin' on us but we had to move yer stash," she pulled a red freezer bag from the pocket of her apron. "Catch!" She threw it across the room to him.

"Thanks," he said, sheepishly.

"Well, what do you think you're doing crashing about down here?" asked Ada. She picked up a cheese which had come to rest at the bottom of the cellar steps and put it back on a nearby shelf. "How long have you been here, anyway?"

"A few seconds."

Gladys pulled a fob watch from the pocket of her moth-eaten cardigan.

"'S opening time in an hour. I reckons you is dressed too con—con—I reckons you oughter ditch the fancy dress. 'Specially you," she nodded at Big

Merv, "I 'spect Our Trev's got something you'll fit into."

"We do have one small problem," said The Pan and to illustrate their predicament, Big Merv held his ball and chain aloft. With a heavy sigh, Gladys' Trev made his way past her and Ada into the cellar while the sound of somebody pummelling thunderously at the front door could be heard upstairs.

"Oh dear, that'll be the Grongles again," said Ada. "My! They are keen today!"

"Yer," said Gladys, "I wonder why." She glowered meaningfully at The Pan who felt put upon. The least she could have done was glare at Big Merv, too. "Over to you, son, we'll stall 'em as long as we can," she told Trev and, gun in hand, she followed after Ada.

The Pan knew that unless Ada and Gladys could persuade them to take a drink of specially laced fruit smoothie, the Grongles would not be delayed for long. They had a minute or so, at the outside. Not enough time to get rid of the shackles. Then there was the fact that Big Merv was dressed as a major in the Grongolian army. Impersonating a member of the Grongolian armed forces was a capital offence on its own, let alone when coupled with a bank robbery – their supposedly thief-proof state bank. It was a long shot but he thought he might have hit upon an escape plan.

"Lads, we are short of time here," he said in what he hoped was an authoritative voice – it was vital both Trev and Big Merv did what he said, before they had time to think about who was saying it and argue. "Trev, you don't have time to free both of us and Big Merv, you're dressed as a major in the Grongolian Army; they're going to string you up if they find you like that. Do you still have your rubber face?"

"Yeh."

"Then put it on! Trev, if you can, get the ball and chain off him and then we can pretend that he's one of them and he's captured me."

While Big Merv struggled with the rubber mask, Trev went at the shackle round his ankle with a lumphammer and chisel.

"It ain't working," he wailed after a brief spate of concerted effort.

"Here, give it me," said Big Merv. He spent a few seconds examining the metal before carefully positioning the chisel and splitting the chain with one well-aimed blow, and hiding it under one of the barrels. "You wanna find the weak spot," he told the astonished Trev by way of explanation.

They could hear heavy footsteps above moving towards the cellar. Big Merv stood up and put his sunglasses on.

"Here," said The Pan, handing him the bag of loot Gladys had given him. "There's no time to stash this so we'll have to pretend you caught me red-handed."

Ning Dang Po's premier gangland boss gave him a curt nod, straightened his jacket, and almost pulling The Pan off his feet as he did so, picked the remaining ball and chain up and strode up the stairs to the door.

"I am most grateful, underling," he told Trev loftily over his shoulder as he flung it open. Outside, two Grongles stopped in surprise. "You! What are you doing?" asked Big Merv, seizing the initiative. The Pan had to give it to him; he was good.

"We've been ordered to search these premises—" one began.

"Then you are wasting your time. My squad and I have already done so successfully, as you can see." He yanked at The Pan's chain causing him to trip up the stairs, "On your feet, scum!"

"Alright, alright. Keep your hair on," muttered The Pan. Big Merv was taking his role a little too seriously for his liking. As he stomped up the stairs in his wake, he didn't have to act to appear sullen.

When they reached the bar where the rest of the search party had gathered, The Pan was relieved to see that the highest ranking among them was a corporal.

"What are you doing here?" demanded Big Merv. "My squad has already searched these premises and as you can see," he grabbed The Pan by the scruff of the neck and threw him to the floor in front of him, "we have been successful."

"Yessir! Congratulationssir!" said the corporal, saluting smartly.

"This is the driver. I doubt the others are far away," said Big Merv. "They have been captured already, I presume," he added, almost as an afterthought.

"Nossir, we're unable to make clear identifications but we believe the leader is a local businessman, Big Merv. The snurd used in the robberies is the same model as his and there is evidence it may belong to him, even though it's registered in another name."

"How so?" asked Big Merv.

"Wellsir," the corporal was gabbling excitedly, "that would be on account of the fact that the vehicle was leased through a complicated succession of companies in a clear attempt to obscure the identity of the owner. But the Forensic Business Investigation Team is in the process of untangling them to find out who it is. My brother-in-law is a member and it's only a matter of time.

"You are sure of this?" asked Big Merv.

The Corporal hesitated. The Pan had to hand it to him, he made an uncomfortably realistic Grongle. Big Merv, who had seemed the antithesis of a natural actor was, quite clearly, brilliant. He assumed just the right level of arrogance, spoke with a near-perfect Grongolian accent, and he was the right height of course. The Pan wondered why he had bothered with a career as a gangland boss when he could have been truly great on the stage. Then he remembered that there were limited roles available to a Swamp Thing, especially one the wrong colour. Even so, his acting put a new, intriguing inflection on what he had said, to Denarghi, about stories, spin, puff and not throwing people in the Dang unless he had to. Clearly the Big Merv The Pan knew wasn't necessarily the real one.

"Wellsir, they can't be sure at this stage, but initial evidence points to Big Merv."

"Interesting," said Big Merv showing no apparent sign of anxiety.

"Yessir. The investigating team is awaiting a warrant to search his property and they have been examining his assets closely. Under questioning, members of his staff have identified the snurd the police brought down as his." The Pan winced at the words 'brought down' but no-one noticed. "Big Merv has no alibi for the time of the robbery and in his continued absence there is speculation that he owned the snurd which was destroyed yesterday."

This was bad news. The Pan knew that Big Merv had kept the identity of the MK II's owner suitably obscure – on paper, at any rate. Pity it hadn't worked.

"This Big Merv," said Big Merv, his authoritative tone faltering noticeably for the first time, "what of him?"

"It seems that he has done a bunk, sir, suggesting guilt. If he is not the leader of the gang, he must have realised how his snurd was being used. He has been blacklisted, accordingly, so it's only a matter of time before he is taken."

Big Merv nodded.

"Would you like us to take your prisoner back with us?" asked the corporal, helpfully.

"What and claim *my* reward? I don't think so!" sneered Big Merv. "My squad will be here in a minute and when they arrive I will send him with them. Now get on your way and stop wasting time or I will have you on report before you can say, 'Lord Vernon Kicks Arse!'"

"Yessir," said the corporal and with that, the Grongles left.

"Arnold above," Big Merv sank down onto the nearest stool, pulling the rubber face off as he did so and flinging it onto the table in disgust. "That was a close one! You think fast for a slippery little bleeder."

"That's why I am a slippery little bleeder," said The Pan, adding as an afterthought, "thank you, I think."

"'S nothing," he handed over The Pan's loot bag, "here. 'S yours."

"Not all of it," said The Pan rummaging around for the box. He paused before handing it over. It was similar to his thimble. Had it been made by the same person? He turned it over, looking for a mark. Stuff this good was usually signed somewhere.

Nope. Nothing.

Hmm, maybe inside? He opened it.

"Oi!" shouted Big Merv. "Don't open that effing box! We made a deal!"

Oops! He tried to close it at once, nipping a carelessly placed finger.

"Ouch! Sorry." To his immense surprise, Big Merv laughed.

"'S OK. Most likely he was talkin' about the safety deposit box so I've broke my word when I chucked that outta the window."

A short silence. They were both wondering if it would affect their payment.

"I suspect we still have the important bit," said The Pan, with a smile.

A shrug from Big Merv.

"Yeh."

The Pan held up the box, still open. He didn't want to give it up. It went with the thimble. And he liked it; and he had an idea. He rummaged in his pockets and took out a stub of pencil and a piece of paper. It was the one which had been inside the thimble, originally – which was gradually disintegrating – so if the thimble and the box were a pair, and he believed they were, the paper probably belonged there anyway, where it would be safe.

"What you doin'?" asked Big Merv.

"Nothing major, just larking about," said The Pan.

"Well don't."

"Oh come on." He held up the paper for Big Merv to read. On the blank side, it now bore the inscription: 'Stolen by the Mervinettes in return for amnesty for all misdemeanours.' With the date of the robbery underlined.

216

Big Merv was sceptical. "No-one's gonna fall for that."

"You never can tell," said The Pan, "someone might." He folded up the paper, dropped it inside the box and closed the lid.

"An' what's gonna happen when your old geezer checks I've kept to the deal?"

"You've just said the deal concerned opening the safety deposit box."

"Maybe but—you great plank! Give it me." Big Merv took it from The Pan's outstretched hand and failed to open it.

"What've you done, you muppet? 'S stuck." He handed it back.

"No it isn't." The Pan took the box from Big Merv and opened it to demonstrate, "See?"

They were interrupted by a polite cough from the bar behind them, which caused The Pan to close the box rapidly. It was Ada.

"We open in a minute or two, and when that happens, you two should be out of sight. But first, a little something for the shock, dear?" she asked. The Pan nodded. He glanced down at his feet. Ah yes.

"Something for the ball and chain would be good too," he added.

Trev went and found the lumphammer and chisel from earlier and handed them to The Pan who handed them straight to Big Merv.

"You seem to have a knack for this," he gestured to the shackle, "would you help me with mine?"

"You spanner," muttered Big Merv removing it with the same swift ease as he'd removed his own.

Ada glided over to them with a tray. It contained two rounds of cheese sandwiches, with – for The Pan – and without – for Big Merv – Gladys' home-made pickle and two pints of special extra-strength beer. There was also a packet of crisps to keep Humbert away from their sandwiches if required.

"Perhaps you should come upstairs to the flat now, dears," said Ada. "You are both," she stressed the 'both', "far too conspicuous to stay out here."

"Yer," said Gladys from behind the bar, "I reckons it would be best if you two wasn't 'ere. Go an' finish yer sandwiches and Our Trev'll be along with some normal togs for Mister Merv." The Pan was impressed to hear her use Big Merv's proper underworld title. "Go on, now! Away with you!" she said, and, sandwiches and beers in hand, Big Merv and The Pan allowed themselves to be shooed upstairs to the kitchen in Gladys, Ada and Trev's first-floor apartment.

Chapter 54

In the warmth of Gladys, Ada and Their Trev's kitchen, The Pan and Big Merv munched their sandwiches in silence. Big Merv's rubber face lay mutely on the table between them. For all of the size and scariness of his ex-boss, The Pan was, for the moment, relaxed and at ease, although appearances suggested Big Merv was not.

"You OK?" The Pan asked him.

A dejected shrug.

"Nah mate, not really. That scrote Denarghi killed two of my best men and now I get home and find I'm a GBI, so I can't do nothin' about it. I've been insulted an' I don't like that. When people insult me, they pay. Except that what with the blummin' state lifting everything I own, making him pay's gonna be hard. That little smecker'll get away with this scot free coz I can't afford the info I'd need to top him myself, let alone take a contract out on him," he thumped his fist on the table. "Arnold's conkers! If I had my way I'd find his weak spot quick smart and then, I swear to The Prophet, we'd see who's an effin' winner."

"I thought you said it was all an act and you didn't really kill people!"

"I said I don't kill 'em unless I have to. That ain't the same!"

"Well, I wouldn't advise going after Denarghi—although, I can understand why you're tempted," said The Pan. He knew a part of him would thank Big Merv if he did, on the grounds that anyone offering to shorten the list of people who wanted to kill him could go right ahead; the same part which was almost relieved, in many respects, that Frank and Harry would no longer be featuring in his life. On the other hand, it was a very small part of him which had these thoughts and one the rest of him didn't listen to very often.

For all their obvious animosity towards him, The Pan didn't like Frank and Harry's departure any more than his boss, but Big Merv seemed to think being on the wrong side of the law was an automatic guarantee of moral fibre. It must have been a substantial culture shock to him to discover the modern truth.

"I ain't tempted, I'm gonna do it. I'll have to bide my time coz the

218

scumbag's ruined me, but I'm gonna get that little scrote. D'you know how long it takes to build up a business like mine?"

The Pan had a good idea but merely shook his head.

"Years. That's how long. And when I get the satisfaction of icing Denarghi then—and only then—all this palaver might be worth it. One day, mate, you wait and see."

"Well, look on the bright side, you'll have one million Grongolian," said The Pan. "The old man hasn't paid us yet. When he has and you have that behind you, maybe you can think about going after Denarghi. I'd still consider it carefully, though, if I was you, unless you're going to do it yourself. Even one million Grongolian won't get you far against the kind of resources the Resistance has to play with. Anyway, most of the contract killers work for them now."

"Yeh. Fair point. Fanciful one, and all, believing your old gimmer's gonna come through with that kinda money. I haven't built up one of the biggest businesses in Ning Dang Po on dreams and promises. I deal with reality and facts. Always have done. And the dosh ain't gonna be much use to me anyhow is it? I'm blacklisted. Everything I own belongs to the blummin' state."

"You'll get used to it. You'll be amazed how much you can own without them finding out. Who's to know who a few hundred grand in used notes belongs to. You can buy a new identity."

"I ain't the type for hiding my dough in a tin under the bed. Money's for spending or investing. And I'll be lucky to last long enough to buy a new moniker. There's a lot of people in this town'd like to see me go down. 'S trouble with being the boss. A lot of jealous men wanna fill your shoes. Comes with the territory."

The Pan felt sorry for Big Merv. He knew what it was like to be an outcast and he knew how it felt to be unique, not that it would be safe to admit why. He felt a sense of comradeship, even grudging loyalty towards him. He would never know if the episode on the edge of the River Dang that night had been an act, like Big Merv had told Denarghi, but Arnold knew it had felt real enough at the time, real enough to give him flashbacks. But perhaps the moment had come to forgive and forget. Big Merv had given him a chance then, spared his life and subsequently, for the most part, listened when it mattered.

The old man had been right, Big Merv was straightforward and honest and he had principles. He would be a good man, well, Thing, in a tight spot. The Pan gestured to the rubber face on the table.

"You have a disguise and it's pretty convincing. I'm beginning to understand why it was so easy for you and the lads to get into the bank."

"Yeh and without it I'm one of the best-known faces in Ning Dang Po. I ain't gonna blend in, son."

"C'mon Merv, this isn't like you, you're a ..." Should he mention genus? No, "Man of action. Where's your get up and go?" The Swamp Thing glowered at him.

"Looks like it got up and went don'it?" he said sourly. "What's the point? It's my own fault! I've brought it on myself. Stiffed by my own vanity. That's what I am! I could have made it clear I weren't connected with the gang, very clear. I left it cloudy coz I liked the attention. There's plenty of women out there who like a bank robber and not many who like a Swamp Thing, even a Swamp Thing who's a powerful businessman."

"I hear you, Merv," said The Pan, "you're only human, or at least ..." he stopped, unsure as to how he should finish the sentence. Big Merv glared at him a little harder. He was going to have to find a way of getting the Swamp Thing issue out into the open. "Look, what I mean is, I'm in a similar situation, women don't find any of my disguises very appealing and unless I want to practise my evasive skills, it's tricky to leave home without them."

Big Merv nodded.

"What about some of my girls?"

"The Big Ms?"

"Yeh. I reckon they liked the bloke with the shades and the cigar, although the pin-striped suit geezer made 'em nervous. Too establishment for girls like that."

"Too establishment! He was pure gangster. I modelled him on you without the ..." Probably best not to mention antennae yet, "On you."

"Nah, you were too understated, mate! That suit was the wrong type of classy! I look like a gangster, you looked like a politician. I can tell you for nothin', a girl like that ain't gonna trust a politician. With yer first look though, you coulda had any of 'em."

The Pan was slightly taken aback.

"Well, um, they are very friendly and helpful with advice but one, you can't mix business and pleasure, and two," The Pan blushed, it was difficult to find a tactful way to say that some of them were old enough to be his mother and the ones that weren't, his grandmother, "they're not my type."

Big Merv grinned.

"Fair enough. So what now? Do we sit tight and wait for the old fella to come through with the dough?"

"I guess."

"You think he's gonna?"

"We have his loot."

"How long'll it take?"

"Search me. I'll have to ask Gladys or Ada when the pub closes."

"It's gonna be tough if he takes his time. No-one normal lasts more than a month on the blacklist without a lotta cash," said Big Merv.

"I have. Five years and counting—and you've seen how much cash I have."

"Yeh," and to The Pan's surprise, he laughed, "sweet eff all. 'S my point though! You ain't normal."

"No?" said The Pan.

"Nah."

"Neither are you." Oops that had come out sounding far more belligerent than intended.

"You talkin' about my colour?" asked Big Merv, menacingly.

Time to grasp the nettle. The Pan concentrated on the tone of his voice, keeping it neutral.

"Yes," he said with a calm he didn't feel, "I am talking about your colour. Not out of disrespect, but because it makes you conspicuous, and you're right, that makes you vulnerable. Since we're stuck with each other until the old man pays us, it's an issue we're going to have to address."

Life on the blacklist was harsh. They both knew Big Merv was going to need help finding his feet and The Pan was the only person who could give him that help. To make sure, he checked the antennae. Yep, they were waving backwards and forwards in thought. Good. He said nothing more, leaving his erstwhile boss room to think. Eventually, The Big Thing nodded.

"Fair enough."

"You'll be OK here, for now. Gladys and Ada are the height of discretion. They won't be asking you any questions or talking about you either. They like a quiet life. They're not ones for attracting attention."

Another nod.

"Did you make any plans for this?" The Pan hoped Big Merv had some cash, otherwise, if the old man didn't come through with the money, they'd be picking pockets or scamming tourists by the end of the week, both of them.

"A couple, not enough though."

The conversations lapsed and they carried on eating their sandwiches. The Pan needed to think. Big Merv needed somebody to help him and he'd offered because it made sense that person should be him. However, as a long-term arrangement, helping Big Merv get by could be tricky. Yes, having a comrade-in-arms would make a pleasant change, but that implied friendship between them. The Pan had a great deal of respect for Big Merv but he wasn't an actual friend exactly, not even so much of an acquaintance, more someone he was very scared of who was stuck in his life. Then there was the day-to-day business of combining GBI status and well ... living. It was complicated enough on his own, let alone as a pair.

The Pan sighed. Naturally, the heist had provoked a security clamp-down across the Grongolian world. It would be sensible to have an ally until the heat died down, even one he was really scared of, especially if the Grongles had realised he was the Mervinettes' getaway man. And it stood to reason that if The Pan was really scared of Big Merv, other people would be, too; the kinds of people who would usually have tried to beat him up would now take one look at Big Merv and leave him alone. It depended if Big Merv could be persuaded to trust him, of course.

The job hadn't been watertight, the Resistance had known about it in advance or how would Denarghi have known that the loot played an integral part in the Looking? The Grongles, they had been waiting hadn't they? They must have known, too. "I can't get your empire back but I can help you keep out of trouble until we find the old man, or until he finds us," he said, "two brains are better than one."

"Yeh, 'specially your brain," said Big Merv. "There's something I wanna know first though." Had he drawn the obvious conclusion? Was he going to accuse The Pan of being a grass? "You saved my life. Why? You didn't have to." Ah. That was an even more difficult question. The Pan scratched his head.

"I dunno. Habit? I've saved your life often enough in the last year."

"Nah, that was work, an' anyway, you did it because I made you. This was your chance to get me off your back."

The Pan was taken by surprise. What Big Merv said was true and he'd

222

had no concrete idea why he was rescuing him at the time. He'd acted entirely on instinct. He decided to tell the truth, or at least a tactfully presented variant.

"I didn't know you were a GBI, did I? And since *I'm* blacklisted and *you* are the only being alive prepared to give me a job," even if it was a difficult job fraught with opportunities to make potentially lethal mistakes, "I would be an idiot to leave you behind and go back to living hand to mouth."

"Yeh, well Denarghi would have got a lot of cash for me. Enough to make him forget about you, maybe."

"I doubt it. I'm worth more than you, remember?"

"Yeh? Then p'raps you need the cash. Maybe you're thinking of claiming the reward for yourself," added Big Merv, a hint of menace creeping into his voice.

"If they want me more than you, how would I be able to claim it?"

"You could disguise yerself."

"Look, Merv, we both know somebody squealed, but it wasn't me and I'm as confident as I can be it wasn't you—otherwise, neither of us would be here, would we? I didn't think, I acted on instinct and if you have to know the truth, you scare the, um, you frighten me. I'm a coward. I didn't dare leave you behind in case you caught up with me later." Big Merv raised his eyebrows. "Yes, I'm that yellow," said The Pan, flatly.

"Second, I would have been leaving you there to die! That's not the same as giving you the slip and falling off the grid so you never, ever find me. You know what I'm like, I don't have it in me to kill anyone, even indirectly. I wouldn't want it on my conscience—couldn't have it on my conscience."

"What about now?" asked Big Merv. "Now that I'm blacklisted like you are? Does that change anything?"

He asked the question with an ominous do-you-want-to-make-something-of-it edge although, whether out of habit or intent The Pan couldn't be sure. Without Big Merv they would never have escaped the clutches of the Grongle corporal and his search squad. He was wily, he had to be – you didn't build an empire the size of his from nothing – but it helped that he was also big and intimidating. The Pan looked over at him. Very intimidating.

"Well, we wouldn't be here if you hadn't given the performance of your life back there in the role of Nutter Grongle Major. Arnold! Even I began to believe you were a Grongle. You also have things I don't have, like size and presence. That's enough to justify letting you tag along! You're six foot three, built like a wall and nobody messes with you. In case you hadn't realised, I'm five foot nine and I'm a psycho magnet. You saw the way Deirdre picked on me, the way Denarghi wanted me to explain everything, even though it's obvious you're the leader. Come to think of it, that's pretty much how I got blacklisted, I bumped into the biggest psycho of them all in the street—Lord Vernon—and he didn't like me any more than Denarghi does! Surely it's obvious why I'd want to keep you around now, I need you to take them down before they get to me."

"And ...?" said Big Merv.

"What d'you mean? And ...?"

"There's more," Big fixed him with a steely green glare and The Pan was glad he had told the truth so far, there was no way he could have disguised a lie.

"OK *and* because I know how it feels alright? I'm sorry for you because in your own way, you're as much of an outcast as me."

Eventually Big Merv nodded thoughtfully.

"Yeh. Now I believe yer," he eyed The Pan appraisingly, "coz of the bit about being a big scaredy wuss."

There was an uncomfortable pause in the conversation. Fighting words, but there was a hint of a smile on Big Merv. The Pan, still unsure as to whether it truly was a smile or just wind, remained serious in case Big Merv took a reciprocal grin as barefaced cheek and smacked him one. Eventually, Big Merv said. "You coulda left me there though. 'Specially when I wouldn't hold hands, you great mincing girl."

"No Merv. I couldn't and I just explained why!"

"You've got principles mate."

"No Merv, trust me, I have none of those."

"You've a conscience then."

"Nope. Where do you get all this stuff from? I'm merely hedging my bets in case there's an afterlife."

The Big Thing put out a large hand.

"Yeh, well I reckon I owe you one. Shake on it."

"I don't think you do," said The Pan with a smile, but he did as he was asked.

Chapter 55

Later, after the pub had closed, Gladys sent Ada up to the kitchen to see how The Pan and Big Merv were doing, while she and Trev put away the last of the glasses and locked up. By this time they were washed and changed and a great deal more relaxed. Big Merv, ever the gangster, wore a pair of dark blue silk pyjamas with white piping round the collars and cuffs, which Trev had found somewhere, and The Pan of Hamgee, a pair of blue and white striped pyjama bottoms with a white T shirt. As a man who still tended to regard a night in a bed as a luxury he was feeling pleasantly drowsy and looking forward to a good sleep.

Gladys, Trev and Ada often had a cup of cocoa to wind down after a busy night on duty, so he had made a pot. The slightly smarmy, do-goody feeling this small gesture had given him contributed to the lightening of his spirits. They'd pulled off the biggest heist of all time. They had the loot and they had evaded the Grongles. He felt bad about Frank and Harry, but in a callous way it merely increased his thankfulness to still be alive; alive and on the brink of buying a new identity, leaving the twilight behind and becoming human. He would make it up to them, pay for a memorial, buy some flowers. Perhaps he and Big Merv could get their money out of the old man and give it to their families. Hmm, well, some of it. OK, most of it, minus commission.

Despite his doubts about the old man, The Pan was confident that, though unscrupulous enough to commit blackmail, he was honourable enough to come through with the cash. The fact that his only post was a receipt from the Great Snurd (of K'Barth) Company Ltd, confirming that Gerry the Work Experience Creature had taken delivery of his wheels and spare keys, raised his hopes further, until he saw the expression on Ada's face when she joined them after closing. Humbert – there was no getting away from Humbert – flew in behind her and settled himself high up on the top corner of one of the wall-mounted cupboards.

"Something up?" The Pan asked her as he handed her a cup of cocoa and proffered a plate of Gladys' home-made biscuits.

"Oh dear, yes, a dreadful thing has happened," she told him. In Ada's world 'dreadful' was a flexible adjective and described events which could range from burning the toast to the death of a close relative.

"Bite my winky!" said Humbert. There was a short silence while everyone waited to see if he would say anything else. The Pan could feel the parrot's beady eye boring into him but in the presence of Ada, Humbert behaved and stayed where he was. Good.

Ada continued, "Remember the gentleman who came to see you that time, the one who gave you such a fright that you fell out of the window?" She stifled a nervous giggle and Big Merv looked sharply at The Pan.

"I remember," he said quickly before any mention could be made of smelly bin bags and humiliated Hamgeeans, "I'm hardly likely to forget it. Especially since it's his job we've just done."

"Yeh," Big Merv gave him an I-get-you nod.

The Pan nodded back at him before returning his attention to Ada with his best serious grown-up expression in place. Ada squirmed.

"He's been arrested."

"Arnold's pants!" said Big Merv. "Flamin' typical."

"It had to happen eventually," said The Pan. "He's the most obvious Nimmist I've ever met, so obvious I reckon they could even get a religion charge to stick. Presumably that's what's happened, is it?"

"Oh no dear," said Ada, "they've no idea who he is."

"That makes two of us," muttered The Pan.

"Shush dear. He's quite safe; he's only been arrested for jaywalking, but it means he won't be able to meet you this evening. He'd intended to come round after closing."

Idiot, thought The Pan's brain, privately, to itself. "I'm sorry to hear that," said his mouth, publicly to Big Merv and Ada.

"He asked me to look after these. He planned to give them to you so I may as well, even though he's not going to be joining us." Ada rummaged in the cupboard under the sink and produced two canvas holdalls, one each for Big Merv and The Pan.

OK. Generous idiot, thought The Pan as he looked into the bag. It wasn't a fraction of the money they were owed, but there must have been a few thousand Grongolian dollars there – naturally in used, small denomination notes. Enough to make a statement of intent or good will. Enough to live on for a couple of months, but not enough to pay for a new empire for Big Merv or a new identity for The Pan. He and The Big Thing looked up from their bags at the same time and exchanged glances.

"Not bad," said Big Merv.

"But not enough," said The Pan. Bye-bye sleep, bye-bye bed, hello cold night rescuing the moronic old giffer from prison. Most likely the Grongles would simply leave the old man in gaol until morning to teach him a lesson. Most likely – but, with all this high-security alert going on, they might charge him or check to see if he had a record and if they did that they would fingerprint him. If they found a match, The Pan could imagine there might be all sorts of interesting information on file which, at best, would cause them to put the old boy in prison and throw away the key. At worst they might even realise they could lay the blame for their current heightened state of security at his door, then Arnold alone knew what they'd do. The only way for The Pan and Big Merv to be sure of their anonymity, not to mention their money, was to go and get him out. With a sigh, The Pan turned to Ada.

"Does your friend have a criminal record on file?" he asked.

"There is that possibility, dear," said Ada, warily, "but of course, they have no idea who he is. He has an alias."

"Until now." He explained about the fingerprinting, "For people like me and ..." Ada glared at him and he realised she considered the old man to be a better class of criminal than the one she was talking to, "metaphorically speaking," he added quickly, to demonstrate his awareness of the distinction between them, "...him, the trick, when you're arrested, is not to be charged. Just supposing they did take his fingerprints, um, might there be a match?"

There was a pause while the gravity of these words sank around them, like a wet blanket. Of course the old man's fingerprints would appear all over the kinds of activities the Grongles considered treasonable. After all, he had clearly been a friend or a colleague of The Pan's father, and look what had happened to him.

"There might be," said Ada.

"Mmm, I am assuming, from the job we've just done for him, that he's been in plenty of trouble before."

"Yer," said Gladys, who had arrived in the doorway, the vast hulking silhouette of Her Trev looming in the shadows behind her.

Oh blummin' brilliant!

As the two of them came in and sat down, The Pan poured them each a cocoa and pushed the plate of biscuits across the table to them. He raised his eyebrows at Big Merv whose antennae tied themselves into a reef knot and then untied slowly.

"I'm sure they'll let him out, dear," said Ada, "they usually do."

"Usually, yes," said The Pan, "on the other hand, somebody's just committed a major heist at their impregnable national bank. They might be feeling a little vulnerable at the moment and if they do write him up on a charge, well, he's not just any old man is he?" He hesitated; what he knew about the old boy could be written on the back of a teaspoon, but it was more than Big Merv knew. Never mind, Denarghi was right, Big Merv was a creature of principle, anyway there was no alternative, he'd have to trust him. "I know he was involved in the Looking with my father. I'm guessing that's enough to put him in deep doo-doo if they find out who he really is—which reminds me, Gladys, who is he?"

"You doesn't need to know who he is," said Gladys, "'S for your own protection."

"He's an old friend of ours," Ada chipped in.

"I can see that," said The Pan with an involuntary glance at Trev.

"Then that should be enough for you to take him on trust," said Ada.

The Pan thought about it.

"Despite what's happened with the job we've done for him, I think we've decided we sort of do," he said. Big Merv nodded. "It'd be nice to know who we're dealing with though." Trev, Gladys and Ada stared back mutely. Nothing doing there, clearly. "Look, if he is charged and he has a history on file, it could put us all in danger. Not just us, you too. Frank and Harry died in this robbery and if they make the connection, if they come here after us, then I have to say that Big Merv and I, um, we've had an interesting couple of days and we're a little ... how can I put it? ...twitchy about lining ourselves up for a second helping?"

"I is sorry," said Gladys.

"Yeh. We are an' all," said Big Merv in a way that suggested he was not feeling overly pleased, either.

"If they finds out who he is, we is lookin' at the end of civilisation as we knows it," said Gladys ominously.

"Really?" said The Pan drily.

"'S true! More's the point, as you well knows, you won't get yer money neither."

Yes, The Pan realised that, but Arnold's ear wax! She knew how to push the buttons of a criminal mind. He glanced across at Big Merv who raised his eyebrows. Yep, there was only one thing for it. He stood up.

"Excuse me Trev," he made a slight bow, "ladies. Merv, sir, you got a moment?" he asked. The Swamp Thing nodded, left the table and followed The Pan into the hall.

"You thinkin' what I'm thinkin'?" asked Big Merv.

"Yep. We're going to have to spring the old gimmer from gaol or we can say goodbye to our reward and I, for one, am not going to let a cool one million Grongolian and a pot-shot at normality slip away."

"Yeh," said Big Merv. He smiled, a slow, easy smile revealing wall-to-wall white teeth. Blimey! That was a first. The Pan had never seen Big Merv smiling, ever. His surprise was soon overwhelmed with worry as to why he should suddenly be doing so now.

"What are you looking so confident about?"

"'S not a problem with that gadget of yours. We can slip in, grab 'im and be out in two ticks."

No they couldn't. The Pan was sure.

"I seriously doubt that. This isn't the Resistance. We're talking about a Grongolian gaol here, they may know about my thimble and what it does. The old man told me it wouldn't work everywhere."

"Works most places tho' don'it and we ain't talking about public enemy numero uno."

"Actually, I think we may be."

"Cobblers! I'm public enemy numero uno!" said Big Merv, pointing proudly at his chest with both thumbs.

"Don't get fussy, you know exactly what I mean," said The Pan.

"Yeh but even if he is, they don't know that coz he's in disguise you twonk. So he won't be in high security will he?"

"Not yet."

"So?"

The Pan hated being beaten in an argument, especially by the sheer force of logic.

"Alright, alright." He went to collect the thimble from his bedroom. When he returned he pictured the old man in his imagination and held it up to his eye. "Well, well. You're right. I can see him." It was the usual palatial suite: dark, dank dungeon, bucket in one corner, straw on the floor and not forgetting a big and violent-looking cell mate, although this one was slumbering on the wooden pallet which passed for a bed. The old man was sitting on the floor reading a book. "I don't think I've ever been in that particular cell but it looks like the Central Police Station to me," he held out the thimble, "want a squint?"

Big Merv peered in.

"Piece of cake then," he said. "You hop in, grab 'im and hop out again?"

"In theory." Would it be that simple? No. He hesitated.

"Go on then. What's the problem you big pink skipping rope?" Big Merv asked.

The Pan held the thimble up and regarded it thoughtfully.

"This thimble was loot. Our loot, the first share you ever gave me, the stuff that was supposed to have come from Lord Vernon's safety deposit box."

"Nah, it never did, they told you that to scare you."

"Absolutely, but it was a Grongle's safety deposit box wasn't it? That was the point of the robbery, we only stole the stuff put in the bank by Grongles."

Big Merv sucked the air through his teeth like a plumber about to deliver expensive news.

"Yeh but my bloke on the inside was a geezer called Bent Tony. He's good, but everyone knows there's no such thing as a hundred per cent right when your information's coming from an informer—even the best stuff it up sometimes and I reckon he did. I reckon the box that bit of stuff came from were K'Barthan."

"What if it wasn't? What if the owner was a Grongle? What if they knew what it was? What if the cell has some sort of portal proofing?"

"'S a lot of what ifs," said Big Merv, "only one way to find out."

"Mmm, but what if the portal proofing proves fatal?"

"We ain't gonna know much about it. An' it won't, they'll want you alive, they'll want that." He gestured to the thimble.

The Pan heaved another sigh.

"Mmm. I suppose it's better than letting him sit there. He'll only get questioned and squeal, unless ..."

Big Merv looked at him quizzically.

"Unless we play safe and use your rubber face. You can do your impressive act and pretend he's being transferred and that you've come to collect him."

"'S not playing safe, 's a lot more dangerous."

"You think so?"

"Yeh."

The Pan looked at the thimble in his hands and back up at Big Merv.

"Don't bank on it."

"Yeh? Well if I'm gonna have to schlepp out there at this time of night, you're coming too, you lily-livered scrote. I'll need a cover an' I'll need someone with me who knows their way around. No point in asking what cell the old git's in if I ain't got no clue where it is when they tell me."

"You don't have to know, you make them go and get him."

"And if they won't? I'll need a bloke with me who knows their way round."

"What makes you think I'll have any more idea than you do, you great lummock?"

"Coz you practically lived there till I stepped in, that's why, and we 'ave to get him back. I ain't waving goodbye to one million Grongolian any more than you mate, 'specially if it's all because some silly old tool-bit can't cross a road. And you heard what the lady said. We're skint and blacklisted, and chances are, it stays like that forever unless we spring 'im, and that's a short forever an' all."

The Pan felt disappointed. Big Merv was right, they had no option, which was galling enough, but he was also correct in asserting that he couldn't go alone. He shrugged.

"Yeh," said The Big Thing, "I knew you'd see reason. Now let's get in there and tell 'em we're gonna go get the dippy old twonk."

Chapter 56

A short time later, The Pan of Hamgee and Big Merv were standing, with an air of grudging resignation, in front of the Central Police Station. It was opposite the Security Headquarters, the ominous building where the secret police were based. The Pan had been in there, too, of course, but only once and he doubted he'd ever get out a second time. Big Merv wore his Grongolian major's uniform complete with rubber face while The Pan was dressed as himself, complete with hat and cloak. It was against all of his better instincts but on Big Merv's insistence. He also happened to be wearing a ball and chain – again, at Big Merv's insistence – though to give The Big Thing his due it wasn't locked and he'd carried it the whole way there because The Pan couldn't.

The Grongolian sergeant at the desk greeted Big Merv with a distinct lack of enthusiasm. No surprise. It was nearly three o'clock in the morning. If he was on split shifts he'd be due to go home in a moment or two. Good. All the more chance he'd hand over the old man without any fuss, or more importantly, paper work.

"What do you want?" he asked.

"I've come to pick up a prisoner—an individual who was jaywalking shamelessly this afternoon."

"Oh yeh, I know the one. Old bloke, well annoying," said the desk sergeant, thawing a little. "You got a chitty?"

Smeck.

"No, I'm a major in the Grongolian Army and you're a policeman, I don't need a chitty," snapped Big Merv, settling into his bolshy Grongolian persona.

"On the contrary, Major, sir," said the desk sergeant, "that is exactly why you do need a chitty."

"Can't I just—" began Big Merv.

"No. Not without a chitty, sir; too much paper work. It's three am. I'm going off duty in a minute."

"Well, I don't have a chitty," said Big Merv striding towards the desk. He grabbed the sergeant by the lapels and pulled him across the scratched wooden surface. "I'll tell you what I do have though," he growled, "I have a direct order from Lord Vernon, in person, to fetch that old man and deliver him over the square." He jerked his head in the vague direction of the Security Headquarters opposite. "So we can do this the easy way or the hard way. I could go back over there and explain your stance. I'm sure our Lord Protector will be most understanding when I ask him to sign a chitty for you." The Pan noted, with approval, how rather than outlining the consequences of angering Lord Vernon, Big Merv left the sentence unfinished and allowed the sergeant's imagination do the explaining. "Or," Big Merv carried on, "we can stuff the paperwork and you can go get him right now."

Wow he was good! The desk sergeant's green face paled visibly.

"Alright, alright! If you would like to put me down now, sir. I need to check which cell we put him in." The Swamp Thing dropped him and he started tapping away at his computer. Almost immediately, he stopped and scratched his head. Something wasn't right by the look of it.

"I can't," he said. Big Merv took a deep breath and hauled him back over the desk towards him, "Nooo, I really can't," said the desk sergeant, holding his hands up in the universal sign language for 'calm down'. The Big Thing tensed and The Pan wondered if he was about to start shaking the guy.

"Why not?"

"One of your colleagues collected him an hour ago."

"You certain?" asked Big Merv. With difficulty the desk sergeant nodded, "You're not just telling me that so I leave you alone and you get to knock off when you're s'posed to?" The desk sergeant shook his head.

"No, it must have been while I was on my break. Bert was covering for me—he's out back—you can check with him if you don't believe me," he gabbled.

"'S OK. You can leave Bert where he is. I believe you," said Big Merv, letting go of the sergeant's lapels.

"It's not like you boys to slip up," said the sergeant as he smoothed down his tunic with shaking hands.

"No," said Big Merv, "d'you know what they wanted him for?"

"It's this security alert. Right pain in the arse if you ask me. He's a repeat offender so they took him over there for questioning—you know, fingerprinting, usual routine stuff. Can't see why we couldn't do it here."

The Big Thing glanced at The Pan.

233

"Me neither. I guess I'll have to take this one on his own then."

Oh brilliant.

"Night." He gave a desultory salute, jerked The Pan's chain and ushered him out into the street. For most of the walk over to the Security HQ they would be visible from the desk at the Central Police Station. Stopping and having a heated debate as to what to do next would arouse suspicion so The Pan and Big Merv began to walk slowly towards it.

Unlike the Central Police Station, the Security HQ was less of a headquarters, and more of a castle. It had thick walls, a drawbridge complete with portcullis and a moat of murky water, below the surface of which, so rumour went, there were spikes. Nobody knew if the spikes were really there or just made up to stop prisoners trying to leap from the battlements and swim to freedom. The Pan had only escaped by a fluke himself. An administrative error on the part of his captors which had classed him, correctly, as the petty thief he was, but incorrectly, as a non-blacklisted one – and saved his life. They'd never even allocated him a cell, merely turned him around and marched him straight back over to the Central Police Station. He'd not found anyone else since, who had been inside the building as a prisoner and lived to come out again.

"What now?" asked Big Merv. "We're not gonna go in there are we?"

"It depends. Do you want to be blacklisted forever?" asked The Pan.

"Do I look stupid to you?"

"Exactly. I don't want to go in there either but I can't see an alternative, can you?"

Big Merv shrugged.

"Nah. You got your whatchacallit?"

The Pan assumed he meant the thimble.

"Portal."

"Yeh. Portal with you?"

"Yes. And you're suggesting we use it to get in there are you? I don't think so!" He paused, an idea was forming. Not a plan exactly but a viable starting point. "We may be able to use it once we get in, though."

"Yeh?"

"Think about it. The place is impregnable. Even if a prisoner could slip their guards, where could they escape to? Nowhere. Why would the Grongles worry about stopping people moving about inside? No-one's going to try because there'd be no point. Once we get past the squad on the gate you won't have to ask anybody anything! All we need is to find a quiet corridor somewhere and then we step through into his cell, grab him and step back out again. As long as we come back to the same spot inside the building, so we can find our way back to the entrance, everything will be fine—we get to spring the old idiot without getting lost or asking too many revealing questions."

"Gettin' in ain't that easy. I gotta be a pukka Grongle. All you've gotta do is stand there and look scared."

The Pan had to agree that was his default setting, and decided it would do no harm to give Big Merv some encouragement. Anyway, if Big Merv thought getting in would be difficult, it was probably best to distract him from any thoughts about getting out.

"Trust me. You play Grongolian psychopath like a natural. You're not mixed species are you?" No, no, The Pan hadn't meant to say the second bit out loud. Arnold. Too late.

"That's rich comin' from you, you mongrel Hamgeean half-breed!" said Big Merv but he was laughing. "Blimey, you've a cheek. Go on like that an' I'll leave you in there."

"You can't, you'll need me if we get out."

"Not if I have the old man! I'll have yer money an' all."

Oh dear.

"You didn't mean that did you?" said The Pan, nervously.

"Course not, you big nonce. Learn to take it, mate, or don't dish it out. And watch it, I'm gonna add realism."

"You're wha—" The Pan began as Big Merv yanked the chain attached to his ankle, almost pulling him over. Ah yes. The Security Headquarters was only a few hundred yards away now and relations between the two of them were supposed to be hostile.

Big Merv and The Pan stopped a short distance from the barrier in front of the drawbridge. Close up, the Security HQ was even more daunting.

"A good scrub up would improve it," said Big Merv following The Pan's gaze up the dingy walls. Before the Grongles it had been the centre of government and, as castles go, it might, once have been a reasonably welcoming building – in a forbidding, medieval kind of way – but not since somebody had elected to paint it black. Now, it was never going to look like anything other than the final resting place of hundreds of tortured political prisoners, which it was. The moat had that grey-yet-whitish tinge that indicates the water is polluted beyond repair and any fish found would soon be dead or were already floating lifeless on the surface. The tiny slit windows – all barred – and the building's fearsome reputation didn't help either. The only way in or out was across the drawbridge, which was bristling with exactly the wrong type of Grongolian guards; or, The Pan supposed, you could take a leap off the top of the battlements, though, judging by the look of the moat, it would most likely be fatal. Even if there weren't the fabled spikes in the bottom, there was probably cholera.

"That reminds me. How are we gonna get out?" asked Big Merv, bringing The Pan sharply back from his reverie.

"Mmm?"

"You heard."

"Same way we got in," Big Merv gave him a cynical look, "only more difficult. Well, for you. All the old man and I have to do is look relieved and ecstatic."

"Ha blummin' ha."

They approached the gate and waited. An officious guard stepped smartly out of the sentry post and saluted Big Merv; he was flanked by two others who pointed semi-automatic laser cannon at them. Big Merv saluted casually back.

"You!" He pointed to one of the accompanying guards before the sentry could say anything. "What's the password?"

"Apple Six," said the guard smartly.

How did he do that? The Pan wondered, the sheer brass neck of it all was amazing. And people always did what Big Merv said; they never argued or tried to thump him or did any of the things that would routinely have happened to him if he'd tried the same thing. Maybe it stemmed from an inexhaustible supply of self-belief. Whatever it was, The Pan was becoming gladder and gladder that The Big Thing was on his side. It was an unusual sensation after such a long time of feeling the exact reverse.

"Good!" said Big Merv. "Pleased to see you are on your toes. I have a prisoner to deliver."

The sentry looked The Pan up and down.

"Him?" he asked doubtfully. He was wearing a helmet and a flak jacket, The Pan noticed. They all were.

"Yes, him," said Big Merv, a hint of petulance creeping into his voice.

"He doesn't look very high security to me, sir," said the sentry doubtfully.

"Well I've been told he is. So are you going to let us in or do I have to put you on a charge for insubordination?" snapped Big Merv.

"Sorry, sir," said the sentry, saluting again. The armed flankers lowered their weapons with a snap.

"Thank you," they raised the barrier, "at ease," said Big Merv, casually, as they passed.

As he made his way to the next checkpoint The Pan wondered why it's so often the dumb and officious people who get put on sentry duty. They were so much easier to fool. Then again, he remembered Big Merv's doormen at his nightclub – people with no imagination are difficult to reason with. Once over the drawbridge they breezed through the other checkpoints using the password Big Merv had so generously been given at the first, finally arriving at a large central quadrangle. The scene which met their eyes was entirely unexpected.

Chapter 57

No black walls or dingy concrete courtyard, but a lawn with colourful flower borders glowing in the dawn light. Even at this ungodly hour the Grongles were up and about in pristine uniforms, marching here and there with a sense of purpose, and in many cases, a clipboard. It was the garrison headquarters of the Grongolian armed forces in K'Barth but looked more like the quadrangles of the University of Hamgee. It had always been a special treat to be allowed to visit his father at the Department of Random Mathematics, even though The Pan usually got into trouble and ruined it. What with all those provoking signs sternly warning him not to, he could never resist the urge to walk on the grass, to his father's initial delight – he'd said it showed independent thought in a youngster – and later embarrassment.

"Place is overstaffed," said Big Merv, quietly.

"How can you tell?"

"Nobody looks that busy or purposeful unless they're pretending, and the clipboards give 'em away. Take a shufty next time you've a chance, half's got nothing on them." A Grongolian private scuttled past with a sheet of paper and a serious expression.

"See?" The sheet of paper he'd been carrying was blank.

"It might be written in invisible ink," said The Pan.

"Don't make me laugh."

They crossed the courtyard, being careful to follow the path and not to walk on the grass or the flowerbeds.

"Where next?" asked Big Merv.

"Search me. The furthest I've been was the special area for admissions, and by the looks of it, we've missed a turn. I've never seen this bit before." He took the thimble from his pocket. "Shall we find an out-of-the-way corner and get on with this?"

They found a door which led into a service corridor which, in turn, led to an airing cupboard full of table linen.

"This'll do," said The Pan. He thought about the old man and put the open end of the thimble to his eye. Yep, there he was in a similar cell with a similar cell mate, but both were different to where he'd been before. Good, he was probably somewhere downstairs then. He took off the shackle round his ankle and Big Merv hid it on the top shelf, where hopefully it wouldn't be found, before taking a good look round the airing cupboard. It would be a pity if he imagined the wrong place when they made their way back. "Hold my hand." Big Merv gave him a sideways look but complied as, with a flourish, The Pan held up the thimble and put his thumb in.

Everything happened as it should; there was a loud sucking sound, a pop and the pair of them rolled onto the floor of the old man's cell and came to rest in an unruly pile against one wall.

"Sorry, I think I'll have to practise my landing technique," said The Pan as they disentangled themselves from each other and stood up.

"Not 'alf," said Big Merv as he brushed the rank straw off his uniform. "I'm s'posed to look pukka tidy you great spanner! How am I gonna do that covered in this crud?"

"I've every faith you'll find a way," said The Pan.

The old man stood up and was waiting with an expectant expression while they finished bickering.

"Well, well, well, my boy. I wondered when you'd turn up."

When. Not if. A touching display of faith in humanity. Flattering, if misguided.

"Had you known how to cross a road we wouldn't have needed to," said The Pan acidly.

"Ah but a little rebellion is an essential tonic to the soul," said the old boy with a mischievous smile, "not to mention society. I don't need to be told when it's safe to cross a road, when the simple answer is patently, when it is clear of traffic."

The Pan counted to ten in his head so that he wouldn't say anything he'd regret. He could sympathise with the old man on this one but there was a time and a place for everything, and the middle of a high-security alert was not it. He could see the old boy was the type of person who strolled through life turning other people's worlds upside down without the faintest notion of the ramifications of his actions. Then again, he was a religious leader so presumably that sort of behaviour was all part and parcel of his job.

"I appreciate your viewpoint but if you don't mind me saying, your timing sucks. You might have held back on the soul tonic until you'd picked up your loot—which we have, by the way—and paid up for the robbery.

Frank and Harry are dead and to be brutally honest, we were quite chuffed to have survived until we discovered that, to top it all, we'd have to come here looking for you. In case you haven't noticed, nobody's ever come out of here alive before."

"You did," said the old boy.

"Oh come on! I hardly count. They kicked me out again, pretty much at the gate, certainly before I got this far in."

"Oh, well, of course I have. Before the Grongolian invasion I used to come here a lot. Did you see the quadrangle?" asked the old boy. "It's rather splendid. Very historic."

"Yes, it's wonderful," The Pan cut in, hoping to hurry him up. This was all very interesting but now wasn't the moment for historical reminiscences.

"Lord Vernon lives in the Architrave's old apartments up at the far end."

"Oh, marvellous," said The Pan. Except it was more of a croak. Fear taking its usual effect. Lord Vernon was bound to be an early riser. What if he'd looked out of his window and seen them coming in, or what if he decided to leave his apartments for a bit of fresh air at the precise moment they were walking out again? No, it didn't bear thinking about.

There was a loud snort from the bed as the old man's cell mate turned over in his sleep. He might wake up. That didn't bear thinking about either. The Pan and Big Merv exchanged glances. Yep, time to move.

"Look, if you don't mind, I think we'd better hurry this along," he told the old man. He paused. He had to explain about them all holding hands and for some reason it was embarrassing. There was bound to be a simple, straightforward way of using the portal which was less awkward and he was going to end up looking like an idiot again, just for a change. Oh well, here went nothing then. He held up the thimble.

"Ah yes," said the old man making to take Big Merv's hand without demur, "you didn't use that to get in did you?" he added. His voice was flat and neutral but the anxiety behind it was obvious.

"From outside? No," said The Pan, "I'm not a complete idiot."

"Quite, of course not." The usual tone with its underlying 'yes you are'. The old boy nodded at Big Merv. "Is this one of your men on the inside?"

"No. It's Merv."

"Big Merv." Big Merv corrected him.

"Er yes, Big Merv."

"But he's Grongolian."

"Nah. 'S a disguise," said Big Merv, "from the bank heist."

"Good heavens! It's absolutely capital! Really. First class. No wonder you did such a splendid job! I'd love to learn how you do that. When we get out, will you show me?"

The Big Thing nodded. "Yeh, if you like, *if* we get out."

The old boy turned to The Pan. "I hope you've the sense not to try and get us out using that either." He waved a hand at the thimble.

"Well, yes. I thought we would. I really want to die tonight and I thought it'd be nice to take you all with me." By The Prophet The Pan wished his mouth would wait for his brain sometimes. That wasn't the right thing to say even if he felt better for saying it. How did the old man manage to be so irritating and so likeable at the same time? He reminded The Pan so much of his father. Maybe it was just a personality clash. No, the guard at the Central Police Station had called him 'well annoying', so it wasn't just The Pan he irritated, it was everyone.

"Sorry, forget I said that. We're only going to use it to get near the door because neither of us knows the way from here. Then we'll go out the same way we came in. Big Merv will escort us. He's going to pretend to be setting you free and taking me back to one of the suburban police stations."

"Why not have him set both of us free?" asked the old man.

"Because they won't buy that, not with the excuse we're making."

"Which is?"

"Dodgy paperwork."

"Yeh, administrative error," said Big Merv.

"I see." A pause for thought. "Will that work?"

"As you appear to know, it's happened before."

The old man gave The Pan a long, appraising stare which he wasn't able to return for more than a few seconds. He sighed, partly in annoyance and partly in resignation, as his head turned away first, contravening the stern, direct orders from his brain to glare the old boy down.

"Didn't you ever wonder about that?" asked the old man.

The Pan bit his lip. Of course he had, he wasn't that dumb. He would let this one go, though. He couldn't be bothered to spend the entire conversation explaining, repeatedly, that he wasn't completely stupid. Especially when the old gimmer so patently refused to take it in.

"Yes I did," he said. At the time he'd thought it might be a rescue, but

241

no-one had owned up to it afterwards and anyway, why would anyone bother with a small-timer like him?

"And?"

"And what? I escaped and nothing happened. I have an anonymous benefactor or I'm drop-dead lucky; either way the only thing to do is be thankful and get on with it. Which reminds me," he held up the thimble.

"Ah yes, of course." The old man held up his hand, still clutching Big Merv's. The Pan, in turn, took his hand, while Big Merv picked up the old boy's ball and chain. He imagined the inside of the linen cupboard, and after a brief glance to check it was there, put his finger in the thimble. With a gentle rustle they tumbled into a pile of dirty table cloths.

Phew! Once they had scrambled up, the old man pointed to the thimble.

"Are you likely to be using that again?" he asked.

"Not in here," said The Pan. The old boy nodded.

"Good. You never know who might pick up on it."

That was ominous.

"I thought it was marginally safer than our having to ask the way to your cell."

"Are you saying you didn't know where I was?"

"We hadn't a clue. Or rather, we knew you were in a cell and once we'd been to the Central Police Station we knew it was here, but not your exact location. That was the whole point. I'd never use this thing otherwise."

"So you found me by ...?"

"Imagining you and using this," he gestured with the thimble, "how d'you think we did it?"

A beat.

"Not like that—it would be unusual, to say the least."

Uh?

"Well, how else would I find you?" A longer pause and that look again, the appraising one with the dash of pleased surprise, or was it pride? Who knew? As usual The Pan cracked first. "Oh come on. You do it, at least, I assume that's how you knew so much about me, either that or ..." No, Gladys and Ada wouldn't blab.

"I watched you, my boy, and that makes running into you perfectly straightforward—a simple matter of listening and ensuring I wait in the place mentioned at the time stated. Transporting oneself to the proximity of a person one knows without any visual idea of the place they are in is fiendishly complicated and not to be undertaken lightly."

"But I'd looked at you in there, once I'd found you, I looked at your palatial accommodation and imagined myself in there with you."

"But even if all the cells are the same, how did you know to imagine the right one?"

"Because you were in it."

"Exactly my point. You didn't imagine the cell, you imagined me. A place is still and fixed, a person is moving."

"You were only moving a little bit and lots of other things move; trees, the sea ...?"

"That is not the same. What you have just done is most remarkable."

"I bet you've done it, though, haven't you?"

The old boy seemed taken aback.

"Only with the help of several other pieces of specialised equipment and I am not an ordinary person, while you, my boy—"

"While I am."

"Indeed," the old man smiled benignly, "except that it would seem, perhaps, that you are not." Loaded with unspoken meaning, the words hung in an uncomfortable – but mercifully short – silence. "Well then, shall we crack on?" He'd chickened out of something there, or had he decided there wasn't time for it? Never mind. Maybe he'd open up later. If they all survived that long.

It was time they left the relative safety of the airing cupboard and put their escape plan into action. The Pan glanced down at the old man's ball and chain. "Big Merv is officially releasing you, so we should open that before we leave. They normally unlock it and kick you out of the door, but we don't have a key. If Big Merv marches you out of sight so he can get his chisel out it'll look a tad suspicious."

Big Merv took Trev's chisel from a pouch on his belt, turned the shackle on the old man's ankle this way and that until he found a suitable point to position it and then, using the ball as a hammer he broke the lock with his usual speed and aplomb. The three of them were so engrossed in what they were doing, they didn't notice the sound of footsteps until the door handle began to turn. Luckily, whoever was outside wasn't alone and they paused with the door ajar to finish a protracted conversation in Grongolian.

"Quick!" whispered The Pan. He put out his hand, the one with the thimble in it and in his haste rapped his knuckles on one of the shelves, knocking the thimble from his grasp. It arced into the air, as if in slow motion, and landed in a plastic hopper full of dirty linen table-napkins.

Arnold's pants!

"Hide!" he told them as he leapt after it. It had disappeared down to the bottom and after what seemed like minutes of impotent fumbling he got it and stood up, just in time to see that the Grongle outside had finished talking and was pushing the door open. Where to hide? Big Merv and the old man had climbed up to the top shelves and moved to the back. From the ground they couldn't be seen. Big Merv leaned his arm down and beckoned to The Pan but there was no time to join them now. He glanced round for another place to conceal himself. The only thing large enough was a trolley with a cloth over it. Good. That would do. He barely had time to climb underneath before a Grongolian kitchen porter came into the room. The trolley had a shelf on the bottom and The Pan crouched there, praying the porter would finish up quickly and leave. He did, which was good news, but he took the trolley with him out into the corridor, which was not.

Never mind, he would have to make his escape when it stopped. The Mervinettes had a rule for this type of thing, wait ten minutes and go. It should be long enough for him to sneak away. Or perhaps he should risk using the thimble.

No.

Not after the old man had warned him like that. He shifted carefully so he was kneeling rather than crouching. It would be harder to run away but it was more stable; easier to stay still and avoid discovery.

Chapter 58

The trolley trundled down the corridor and into a busy kitchen. Through a thin patch in the fabric The Pan could see there was no chance to leave his hiding place yet without being discovered. He could hear the gentle scrapes and taps as the porter laid things on the surface above his head. A place setting, perhaps? Breakfast for somebody? Maybe.

Another Grongle arrived and began to complain at length about how fussy Lord Vernon was about his scrambled eggs and bacon.

"Relax," said the one laying up the trolley cheerfully, "you won't be getting it wrong."

"I hope not," said the complainant, "I don't want my head kicked in like the last bloke he sacked."

"Yeh well," said the first, "that sort of thing's more to do with his mood than your eggs."

This worrying conversation finished, The Pan felt the trolley being wheeled into a service lift, which ascended a few floors before they were on the move again, this time out into an upper cloister, where it stopped.

He peeped out from under the cloth. Good. No-one around except the Grongle who had originally collected it, and he was standing with his back turned, knocking on a door. There was no time to lose. Breakfast with Lord Vernon was a no-no!

The Pan slid out from his hiding place and tiptoed silently back to the lift. Through the arches of the cloister he could see Big Merv leading the old man across the quad. No! They couldn't leave him here! He wanted to shout for them to wait but he knew it was impossible. He had to get down there and join them. Please Arnold let the lift still be there. He might be able to open the door and get in without being seen, but if he had to wait, he was dead.

The door was open. Thank the Prophet! He crept in, closed it and pressed the down button. Big Merv and the old man were walking slowly, they wouldn't have gone far. If he ran and was lucky with the human – or at least, Grongolian – traffic in the quadrangle, there might still be time to catch them up. The double-crossing scummers! That had never been ten minutes, had it? He consulted his wristwatch. Oh. It'd been twenty.

With a gentle hum the lift came to a standstill. Before he could open it the door was wrenched open from the other side and The Pan was face to face with one of the largest Grongles he'd ever seen. A general. Using the service lift. Why? Why would a member of the Grongolian Imperial Guard have to decide the service lift was the way upstairs this morning, of all mornings? His luck had run out, disastrously. The Pan reacted first, slamming the door shut again and leaning all his weight on the up button while the general was still standing pointing, with his mouth open. The lift began to ascend again.

What next? No using the thimble, that's for sure. Something must have brought such a high ranking officer to the kitchen area; could it have been over-enthusiastic portal use? Almost certainly. Arnold's pants! What now? More to the point, where? The lift was still ascending. There was no way out unless he could get far enough away from the building to use the thimble in safety, but there was only one gate and it was heavily guarded. He needed to think of another way across the moat.

"Wait a second!" whispered The Pan in the empty lift.

There was a plan!

Yes! Like all The Pan's plans, it was, at best, hit and miss and at worst ... hmm. It was the most rubbish plan of all time, almost certainly.

As soon as the lift came to a halt he opened the door and leapt out. There was no-one around, but to his right was a flight of stairs. The sound of shouts and running footsteps rose up from below. He peeped over the banisters to see if he could find out where his pursuers were.

"I see him! He's on the stairs!" shouted a voice. There was a pinging sound and a volley of laser gun fire hit the wall behind him, melting the plaster. Eek!

"Hold your fire!" bellowed someone else, "Lord Vernon wants him alive."

Oh no. No way. He'd met Lord Vernon once, and that was enough for anybody. The Pan could feel his legs start to shake as a huge burst of adrenaline pumped into his system. Right then. Better start running it off. He hurtled up the stairs two at a time. Three more flights up and he found himself on a landing at the bottom of a ladder. His pursuers were getting closer as, heart pounding, The Pan began to climb. He wasn't moving fast enough; they would catch up with him soon and then they'd start shooting. Not to kill, of course, just to wing him so he'd fall. Lord Vernon might have wanted him alive, but that wouldn't exclude 'wounded' and presumably any subsequent questioning would involve further injury. His breath came in gasps and he swore as he struggled to climb faster. At the top, a trapdoor. He fumbled with the latch, held onto the ladder with one hand, and thumped it with his free fist. Finally it opened.

"There he is!" came a shout from below and a volley of laser fire melted the brickwork near him but he was already on the roof. A large, flat lead roof surrounded by a two-foot red brick crenellated wall, high above the city.

"After him!" shouted somebody below, and The Pan kicked the trapdoor closed, casting about him for something heavy to drag over the top of it. Nothing there. Never mind. He was ahead of them now. Far enough ahead. He ran to the edge and peered over. Below him the walls of the building dropped sheer into the moat.

This was it. The last thing he did. The end, or, if he was lucky, the beginning. A new identity, a real life, a fresh start. He walked calmly back to the far wall, checked he had a firm grip on the thimble and thought about his bedroom at the Parrot. He peered in. There it was, most specifically, that lovely soft bed. Yep, this might work. Arnold knew, nothing else would. He removed his hat with the other hand – he didn't want it to fly off – took three deep breaths and ran. The trapdoor began to open as he passed, but it was too late now, they weren't going to catch him. He leapt up onto the wall, and with all his strength, dived off into the void. For a moment he was flying, arms and legs kicking as if to propel him further. Everything depended on how far he could get over the moat. The world slowed down and his thoughts came with calm, cool precision. He was as far out from the wall as he was going to get and was plunging rapidly downwards.

Was it safe to use the portal now? Who knew? But the ground was getting closer very quickly.

Time to choose. Take a gamble that his plan had worked or wait another millisecond and end it. No. He could never end it. He had always wanted to live. That was the trouble.

He concentrated his mind on the Parrot, his room and the bed and squeezed the thimble over his thumb.

There was a loud sucking sound and the three fittest members of the pursuing Grongle squad reached the edge of the roof just in time to hear a loud pop and see The Pan of Hamgee vanish into thin air.

Chapter 59

Far below The Pan stood two figures, looking up.

"Blimey!" said Big Merv as he watched his remaining colleague launch himself out over the battlements.

"Blimey indeed," said the old man as The Pan disappeared. "He's a resourceful lad, your driver. If that came off it was pure genius."

Big Merv shrugged. He agreed and he was surprised to find it made him feel proud, almost paternal. "Yeh. He's a good man. 'S a fine line between genius and madness, though, mate. You really reckon he's gonna be waiting for us at the Parrot?"

"I sincerely hope so. If he isn't we'll have to find him, and fast." Big Merv subjected him to his best felt-tip green stare. What was this 'we' all of a sudden? "And you are far too conspicuous to stay here. Once we get back, we will have to think about how we can hide you."

"Hide me? I ain't hiding," snapped Big Merv, the 'we' thing forgotten for the moment. Hiding was for big puffs, people like The Pan. Big Merv might be a lot of things but he wasn't one of them.

"Yes you are! Lord Vernon's after your head on a pole! You're one of the most wanted felons in the nation."

"So? I ain't the hiding type."

"My dear man! You can't stay knocking about here or you won't be the living type—Arnold's prophecies, book seven verse sixty three: 'He who turns and runs away, lives to fight a better way.'"

That was wrong, even Big Merv knew that and he was a creature who occasionally, even if it was only very occasionally and only when all other avenues had been exhausted, chucked people into the River Dang, with concrete boots on. So, not a good Nimmist, then. Not really.

"'S not right. It's fight another day."

"Quite so, old chap but my version is nearer to the truth. You're a jolly useful type in a tight spot and that means we need your services."

Oi, oi? What services? Big Merv was an old hand at this kind of stuff and knew when to proceed with caution.

"It'll cost yer," he told the old boy. That should dampen his enthusiasm.

Big Merv wasn't a political animal. Politics was for shysters as far as he was concerned, devious people, people with no principles. He was an honest, upstanding gangster.

"That won't be a problem," said the old man smoothly.

Arnold's trollies, he was as up for it as ever. Never mind. It wasn't as if the old gimmer hadn't promised to pay well. Big Merv was nothing if not pragmatic. He'd wait until he knew what they wanted him to do, then he could tell them, with proper conviction, where to get off.

"Now, we should be getting back. Gladys and Ada will be worried about us." Big Merv didn't move. "We'll want to see if your young friend's escape plan worked," he hesitated, "and you'll have to stick with me if you want to see a penny more of your one million," the old boy added, with a knowing smile.

By The Prophet's Y-fronts!

The Pan had been right. He was a manipulative old toad. In this case, though, he was a manipulative old toad with lots of money. Big Merv's money.

Bummer.

Anyway, he thought about the face he was wearing. A cheap movie prop. It was good, but before long it would wear out and then, as The Pan had tactfully explained to him, he would be a tad distinctive. Now he was a GBI Big Merv didn't give much for his shelf life without help and this old git, he looked like he'd been a GBI even longer than The Pan. Probably best to stick with him then, for now.

"Needs must," he muttered to himself and with a sigh, The Big Thing followed the old man down the dawn streets.

****

The Pan landed with a thud. That was the first wrong thing, the second was the absence of a bed and then the third, of course, was the pain. He rolled several times and crashed into a wall.

"Ouch," he said. This didn't feel right, quite apart from the fact he was in an office and very definitely not in his bedroom. He stood up, or at least, half up. Then something cold and metallic touched his neck, a jolt of white hot pain shot through him and everything went dark.

Chapter 60

Later, The Pan awoke. He was where he'd landed except he had the mother of all headaches. Slowly he stood up and looked around.

He was in a penthouse suite, set back from the castle walls and high enough above them for the windows along one side to afford a panoramic view over the roof to the city. He realised, from the view, that he was still in the Security Headquarters. Oh dear. He also realised he must have been unconscious for most of the day because it was dark and through the windows he could see the night sky and the lights of Ning Dang Po as they twinkled and shone. If he hadn't been so frightened he would have thought it was beautiful. The room was lit by spotlights throwing pools of bright, white light which dramatically contrasted with the surrounding darkness. Set in the wall furthest away from him was a medieval-style inglenook fireplace and to one side of it, facing outwards into the room, was a desk. The Pan could make out a number of items laid out neatly across the blotter, including his hat and the keys to his snurd which must have been taken from him earlier while he was out cold. To his dismay, he realised the thimble had gone.

Arnold's pants.

He would never see that girl again.

Right. Like it mattered. He was still inside the Security HQ and unless he rectified that he was never going to see anyone again who wasn't a Grongle.

He looked around him. This suite was more than penthouse. Judging by the books and the general decor it was the best. Top class. All of it.

Marvellous. That would be Lord Vernon's then, wouldn't it? So these were probably the last moments of his life. His worst fears were confirmed when the door opened and the owner walked in flanked by two guards.

"At last, The Pan of Hamgee." Lord Vernon had the kind of soft, quiet-yet-carrying voice which can only be achieved through a lifetime's indulgence in unspeakable evil – and lots of practice. "I have been waiting for this day." He strolled towards his prisoner, smoothing his black suede gloves over his hands as he went.

The guards grabbed The Pan and he felt them tighten their grip as his nemesis approached.

His fear engulfed him like a tidal wave. He had to escape! He tried to break free. One of them punched him in the ribs but that only made him struggle harder. As he thrashed and writhed in blind panic he heard the soft voice cut through the sounds of his cries and the shouting of the guards.

"Not like that, you imbeciles," said Lord Vernon. The Pan felt a hand lock round his throat and he was flung forcefully against the side of a filing cabinet and held there. He noticed the volume of the sound as he made contact more than the pain of the impact and, luckily, it brought him to his senses.

This was not the time to panic. It wouldn't help. Arnold knew if he had ever needed every last one of his wits about him, it was now. Wriggling about like an idiot wasn't going to achieve anything; it would only waste energy, energy which might be far more profitably used staying alive or even better, running away, if there was a chance.

Lord Vernon was breathless, although whether from anger or the excitement of catching up with his quarry after all those years of pursuit it was difficult to tell.

"My preference, would be to slit your throat, now, and watch you die," he said. Hmm. Not a good start, "Although naturally, I had envisaged something a little more ..." he paused as he sought the right word, "interesting for us both than that. For the moment, at least, it seems you are more useful to me alive however, so..." A theatrical sigh, "I must deny myself my sybaritic pleasures. I have some questions to ask, and when I am done, if I am satisfied you have answered me truthfully, I may spare you."

No. Not likely, unless The Pan was going to be indispensable. Hmm, how to arrange that?

"I find it hard to believe you'd ever spare me," said The Pan's mouth, taking the rest of him by surprise.

"Really? Why? Do tell."

The Pan tried to shrug his shoulders but being held against the side of a filing cabinet by the neck made it difficult.

"You've spent years trying to catch up with me. After all that trouble, I can't see you letting me walk away."

How to play this? Probably not like that. It had been years though, thought The Pan.

"That is true, and yet, I assure you, if it transpires that you will serve me better alive, you will live ... Unless I give in to temptation and decide that the cost of maintaining you is disproportionately high, in which case, I will kill you, slowly and painfully, now."

"What if I don't want to serve you?" Arnold no! Why couldn't he ever shut up? Even for him that was stupid. He was talking tall, of course, because he was utterly, comprehensively petrified, but even so, he wished his mouth wouldn't run off like that without waiting for his brain. He could always let himself turn into a gibbering wreck, he supposed. There was a strong argument to suggest a bit of gibbering might be preferable at this point.

Lord Vernon smiled, without any hint of warmth.

"What you want is immaterial. By one means or another, you will cooperate fully, if I require it." He stopped for a moment, to let The Pan's imagination provide its own explanation for the meaning of 'one means or another'. "Incidentally, I would advise against flippancy if you wish to keep your levels of maintenance ... tenable. Perhaps you do not fully understand your situation. Allow me to make it clear. Not only is your very existence treason but you have further flouted the authority of the state by joining a criminal gang."

Oh marvellous. Just marvellous. It was inevitable, but The Pan was still disappointed that Lord Vernon knew about the bank robbing. And he'd taken the Mervinettes way too personally to let any of them go free. No. He either thought The Pan knew something or was about to ask him to do something unspeakable.

"It's not my fault, what could I do? It was join or be thrown in the river. And I'm not the one to blame if your people can't keep up!"

Uh-oh. That might have been a bad thing to say.

"If that is so," murmured Lord Vernon menacingly, "then how is it that you are here now?"

The Pan felt the pressure on his windpipe increasing, but the idiot in him was still firmly in control of his centre of speech.

"Nothing to do with my driving. I jumped off a roof," it said, before the rest of him could knock it out, drag it away from the wheel and tie it up in a corner. Oh Arnold! What in the name of The Prophet was he saying?

Lord Vernon breathed in and out, slowly and then laughed. A spine-chilling, humourless laugh which made the little hairs on The Pan's neck stand to attention.

"I think you would prefer me to kill you now," he said, "and yet, this merely underlines my suspicion, that you have knowledge that would be of benefit to me, which you are endeavouring to take to your grave. The Resistance may have bungled your capture—and they shall pay—but you and your master's snurd were outclassed, by me, in mine. Now, your life is in my hands, a concept which, I appreciate, you may not be comfortable with, and you have a choice. You can listen to what I have to say, answer my questions and if I see a further use for you, I may spare your life. Or you can continue as you are and I will kill you in a way that will bring me immense pleasure, but which you will not enjoy. Which is it to be?"

It would do no harm to listen first, The Pan decided, who could tell what interesting information he might pick up and it would give him time to think of a plan. "I don't want to die," he said.

"And so?" asked Lord Vernon, squeezing his neck even harder.

"So, I'm listening," he croaked. He hoped the Lord Protector would let go now because his grip was so tight there wasn't enough oxygen. Big green blobs were beginning to appear round the edges of his field of vision.

"Excellent. I am glad we understand each other," said Lord Vernon, taking off his sunglasses with his free hand. The Pan's gaze travelled along the Lord Protector's arm and into his face. The mesmerising grey eyes locked onto his blue ones and he tried to conceal his fear as the grip on his neck tightened some more, not much, but enough to make it obvious who was in control of the conversation. With difficulty, he swallowed.

Chances of keeping up eye contact? Zero. It was impossible to fully turn his head away with Lord Vernon's hand round his throat, but his eyes slid sideways.

Having made the identity of the alpha male in the room abundantly clear, Lord Vernon let go and walked casually over to the window, where he gazed out over the city below.

The Pan slid to his knees and then flopped forward onto all fours where he spent a few moments concentrating on getting his breath back without audibly wheezing. A glance at the window confirmed that Lord Vernon was still ignoring him, standing with his back turned, ostensibly enjoying the panorama of Ning Dang Po. Gingerly, to avoid passing out, The Pan stood up. The guards watched him, warily.

He had to play this carefully, and to do that he had to be intelligent and adult. But Arnold in the Skies, how to do that?

Chapter 61

In the absence of a better plan, The Pan took a deep breath and seized the initiative.

"I'd like to ask you something, Lord Vernon." It was difficult to keep the frightened wobble out of his voice. Lord Vernon didn't turn round but raised one arm a little, as stopping traffic and said,

"Speak."

So condescending. So irritating. No, that's what he was aiming to achieve. The Pan knew he had to stay calm and think rationally. He took another deep breath and tried to steady his voice.

"Why am I here?"

"Because your existence is treason," said Lord Vernon, casually.

"But it doesn't have to be, does it? I do what I do because it's the only thing I can. You killed my family and blacklisted me. If you hadn't, I'd just be an ordinary kid."

"Unfortunately, Hamgeean, you will never be ordinary, as your presence here after five years on the blacklist should attest. I would have thought even you could understand this."

"Why does everyone think I'm so special? Believe me, I just want to be normal and blend in, and if you left me alone that's what I'd do."

"At the risk of repeating myself—"

"But why bother?"

Lord Vernon turned round slowly.

"Because I can."

OK. Not too much progress there then. Never mind. Press on. The Pan continued.

"What's in it for you, though? I'm a pushover. It's not as if I'm a worthy opponent."

"And yet, at the wheel of a snurd, perhaps you are."

That was some concession from a Grongle like Lord Vernon. The Pan managed to feel smug AND scared; now there was a new emotional combination.

"I thank you," said The Pan, "but I still don't understand any of this."

"You pretend you do not know?" Sneering but intrigued. Good.

"I'm not pretending."

"Perhaps, you are telling the truth. Anyone attempting to escape from here the way you did is either very ill-informed or very foolish."

The Pan shrugged, "I'm probably both, but it might have worked."

"No, it would not," said Lord Vernon. "Since you have asked, I shall answer your question." He flicked one wrist and the gold thimble appeared in the palm of his hand; a neat trick, which The Pan grudgingly admired. He had always been rubbish at sleight of hand at school, unlike pretty much everyone else, which meant he had felt it keenly. He wondered how it was done. "This is mine now," said Lord Vernon.

In spite of his efforts to remain calm, The Pan was angry.

"I don't think so. You just happen to have it."

Arnold's snot, what was he doing? A good answer, but maybe a touch on the forceful side. This was a wimp versus psychopathic nutter situation. Inflaming the nutter was not a smart move. A touch more diplomacy – or maturity – was called for.

"Possession is nine tenths of the law."

"But I have the moral high ground with my one tenth."

"I think not. It belongs to the individual you stole it from. Perhaps you are thinking of trying to take it back," he put the thimble in his pocket and faced The Pan, "please do, you will give me the perfect excuse." He stood still, waiting, seemingly relaxed and yet radiating an aura of pent-up violence.

Hmm, scores on the doors? Lord Vernon, well off the mark, The Pan of Hamgee? Nope. Nothing yet.

"Let us continue," said Lord Vernon, "originally you obstructed the course of justice." The Pan bit back the urge to repeat the retort which had originally got him blacklisted.

"You tripped over me in the street, it was hardly obstruction."

"Whether or not it was deliberate, it was obstruction and you further compounded it when you insulted me."

"You nearly killed me; my father had to beg for my life."

At the mention of The Pan's father Lord Vernon advanced towards him. Even though there was nowhere to go, it took every ounce of self-control not to run. That had been an impressive reaction. The Pan made a mental note not to mention his father again.

"And here we come to the point! Your father," Lord Vernon snarled angrily into his face, "was a renegade and a fool. He dared to stand in my way and now here are you, his son."

Whoa there! Where had that come from? The Pan had spent five years avoiding the authorities and running away from Lord Vernon, how could that remotely be classed as standing in his way? Then again, it did answer one question; this wasn't about him. Clearly, it was about his dad.

"Trust me, I would never knowingly stand in your way," he said. Was it so difficult to understand how cowards worked, he wondered? "I'm not a mind reader; you'll have to give me a steer. Tell me what I have to do to keep out of your way."

"Ideally, you would die, but alas, as I have explained, at this present moment you are too useful," he looked The Pan up and down, "if I were your masters, I would not have left you so unprepared. Perhaps it is time for you to discover who your father really was." The Pan said nothing and listened. "You have encountered the Resistance?"

"Yeh, we've met," said The Pan, "as you seem to know."

"The Resistance view their conflict with my government as a clash of worthy adversaries; titans of the battlefield, who, though forced to differ, respect one another. And of course, they give the people hope—hope that somewhere, others are rebelling, thus allowing the average, apathetic K'Barthan to believe that until the situation reaches a tipping point, he or she, need not. Naturally, the Resistance are under my control, so I can offset every victory they achieve with enough set-backs to ensure our apathetic K'Barthan's idea of the tipping point is never reached." Interesting, thought The Pan, and not surprising, either. "So as you may appreciate, they pose no threat to me. Indeed, they perform a useful function, in that, if I arrange to have them informed correctly, they can be manipulated to intervene where the state cannot."

The Pan couldn't imagine a situation where the state Lord Vernon ran couldn't intervene. And surely the average K'Barthan was better than that.

"What if we K'Barthans aren't as apathetic as you think?" he said.

"What if we K'Barthans aren't as apathetic as you think?" said Lord Vernon, in mocking imitation. "What if you are?" Touché. Lord Vernon paused to let this sink home, "Perhaps you are partially correct, there is another group of K'Barthans, although I flatter myself there aren't many left, whose ways are more secretive. Their subtlety makes them difficult to trace and yet when captured, they often have insurances that make them harder, even for us, to convict. They are the Underground."

The Pan remembered that Gladys and Ada had talked about subtle resistance. Oh Arnold, was that what they had meant? And the 'we' the old man kept referring to? He could feel himself going pale.

"I see you are beginning to appreciate the gravity of my words," said Lord Vernon. "Your father brought you up a Nimmist, I assume."

"It was banned—" The Pan began.

"Nevertheless, your parents brought you up as a Nimmist."

There was no point arguing and since his family were dead anyway, it wasn't as if it could do any harm to answer the question.

"I suppose they did."

"So." A long pause after the so. "You will know what the Looking is."

"Am I meant to?"

"Your mere existence is treason, surely you appreciate that anything you do is illegal," Lord Vernon raised his eyebrows, "on this rare occasion, you can be honest with me without fear—it will bring you no further trouble." Obviously, because, as The Pan knew, he was in about as much trouble as it was possible to be in. Lord Vernon continued, "The Looking is a treasonable offence, which in this case was organised and conducted by the Underground. They set up the Council of the Choosing which was led by two of their most respected leaders: your father..."

Arnold. The Pan could feel the colour draining from his face.

"...and an old man."

The old man! Of course, that was why he looked familiar. The startling resemblance he bore to Trev was a red herring and it had thrown The Pan, but the old boy's face should have been etched on his memory for all time. That morning on the main street in Hamgee, an old man had run past, surprisingly quickly, followed by Lord Vernon, while he was still a sergeant, with whom The Pan had his sidestepping incident.

"The old man you were chasing."

"Yes," said Lord Vernon. "The old man who escaped and evaded me until his death."

His death? The Pan tried not to look surprised. Arnold! It hadn't worked. Not if the way Lord Vernon guffawed was anything to go by.

Could this interview get any worse The Pan wondered? How could he be such an idiot? He'd blown the old boy's cover and now the Grongles would come looking for him again, worse, there'd be no-one to warn him. He had to do something.

"Excellent," Lord Vernon rubbed his suede-clad hands together, "I suspected he was still alive. And since you have confirmed this for me, now you will tell me where to find him."

"How can I? I haven't seen him in years."

A fine effort but even to his own ears, unconvincing.

"But I disagree, you have not inherited your father's emotional control. Such an expressive face, so eloquent of your surprise and now, of your fear for those you might betray. Oh, how I am going to enjoy this. All that is necessary is that I ask you the right questions; you will give me your friends without uttering a word."

The Pan was angry and scared, a horrible combination. He couldn't control his fear but he had to control his anger. He must keep a clear head if he stood any chance of surviving this interview, and now he had betrayed the old man, he had to. It wasn't only the old man, it was Ada and Gladys and Their Trev. He was as determined as ever that his unofficial family should avoid the fate of his real one.

"That's a very interesting story but you still haven't told me why I'm here," he said through gritted teeth, or was that chattering teeth, "or why you might let me go."

"On the contrary, as I have stated, you are here to give me information, and whether or not I free you afterwards depends how much information you are able to give."

"Well then, you can see I don't have the nerve to talk in circles with you," doubtless, the exact reason why he was drawing it out, "so shall we cut to the chase and get on with it?"

Honesty. Probably not the best move.

"Habitually, I reward levels of impertinence greatly inferior to yours with torture and death. However, since I am feeling magnanimous today, I shall indulge you." Magnanimous? Never! This was confirmation that Lord Vernon needed him. The Pan stayed silent while his nemesis kept talking. "As we have already agreed, your father was embroiled in an outlawed organisation and in the conduct of a treasonable activity, the Looking. I believe you knew this before I told you."

The Pan took a breath, to speak.

"I would advise you to think before you repudiate my claim," Lord

Vernon cut in, "you were of the age to be questioned, presumably by your father, himself." The Pan shrugged. Now he thought about it – and Arnold knew he'd done a lot of thinking about it since his first conversation with the old man – he was certain that was true, especially coupled with what he had just heard. His father had questioned him, subtly, over a number of days. He couldn't vouch that he was given the standard one-hour interview, but he had definitely been interviewed. It was just that, for some reason, his father had wanted to make sure he had never known. Why? No time to think about that now.

"At that time I did not enjoy the same influence as I do today," said Lord Vernon, "and the legal system still afforded me certain constraints. So, though numerous witnesses were ready to denounce the activities of your father and his colleagues, I required evidence to make my case. When I found it, your father aided and abetted their escape. Every single one slipped through my fingers," he held out his hand and slowly clenched his fist while he spoke, "I had one chance of capturing their leader, and you got in my way. An uncanny coincidence, is it not?"

"Uncanny, yes, but a coincidence is all it is," said The Pan as evenly as he could.

"Really? Then how is it, that when I seek to capture the Mervinettes, you are the reason that they evade me?"

"I'm the getaway man, it's my job to escape."

"Exactly, you are their driver and you kept them from justice."

"That's not—" began The Pan, but Lord Vernon cut him off.

"I seek an artefact used in the Looking, and when it finally comes to light, who is at the centre of the gang stealing it?"

"Steady on! I don't rob, I drive. And believe me, my colleagues view me as scum."

"Yet you stole it for the old man."

Once again, The Pan felt his face giving him away.

The corners of Lord Vernon's mouth curled upwards in a sinister smile.

"I see you did!" His tone changed, reverting abruptly to menacing, "I know you have been in contact with him recently. Do you understand what this means?"

Obviously nothing good. The Pan shook his head.

"You are the one consistent link in the activities of these dissidents over the last five years."

"Oh no, I—"

"Do not deny it. Do not take me for a fool."

Arnold's Y-fronts! This was going very badly.

"OK, so yes, I am linked with them, but socially, that's all. I'm not like my father. I don't do rebellion—not intentionally. I'm a coward. All I want is a quiet life!" He thought of the girl in the thimble and her parallel world, "I could—I *would* disappear, if you'd let me."

"As I may have previously stated, and you have now proved—twice—the typical K'Barthan is at best apathetic and at worst ..." Lord Vernon looked The Pan up and down.

"I thought I wasn't typical," said The Pan, "I thought that was your point."

"You are, unusual, Hamgeean, but you display the same racial deficiencies as your peers. A man, or a Hamgeean—even one as lacking in fibre as you—will be who they must be. 'Quiet' is not your destiny, my friend, and you can thank your father for that," he added.

He gestured to the guards and put on his sunglasses again. His tone changed – brusque, businesslike, "And now, I am going to ask you some more questions." A nod from their master and one guard strode over to The Pan, wrenched his arms behind his back and held him still. The other guard, who had brought over a tray containing a syringe of mauve liquid, walked over to Lord Vernon and stood at his side.

"Unfortunately for you, no matter how genuine your desire to cooperate, I must ensure beyond doubt that your answers are factual," Lord Vernon took the syringe from the tray, held it up to the light and pressed the plunger so a small jet of the contents squirted out of the end. "You have heard about the Truth Serum, I assume?"

The Truth Serum. A rumour, a figment of the imagination, like monsters under the bed, a story about a nightmare that didn't exist. That was what The Pan had heard.

"Perhaps you did not believe," Lord Vernon said, apparently reading his prisoner's mind, "and yet, every legend holds a grain of truth."

Holy Book of Arnold 5, chapter 53, not sure which verse. Lord Vernon was quoting The Prophet, a part of The Pan's mind realised, with strange detachment, while the rest of it was busy panicking.

Chapter 62

Again The Pan's fear gripped him: he couldn't tell the truth, he had already betrayed the old man and now he would grass up Big Merv.

Worse, Gladys, Ada and Their Trev were surely as deeply involved in the Underground as the old man. They were all in danger and somebody had to warn them, and who else was there? The Pan knew that if he told the truth, he would betray everyone and everything he cared for. Even worse, there would be no more reason for Lord Vernon to keep him alive.

His only chance of survival was to keep schtum. His only way of saving the others was to keep schtum and the only chance of actually keeping schtum was not to be around to do any talking. He must escape. Now. He struggled half-heartedly, enough to confirm he could not wriggle free of the guard's grip. OK, let's call that plan A. Time to think of a plan B.

"Hold him still," said Lord Vernon as he approached. "The serum may be injected into any part of the victim's body, but I find it concentrates the minds of my interviewees so much more closely when it is delivered just—below—the—eye." He spoke these last words slowly, giving The Pan plenty of time to appreciate what was about to happen. Lord Vernon put his hand over The Pan's face, pushing his head back so he couldn't move it. "I would not like you to miss this," he said, and as The Pan's eye instinctively tried to close, he used his thumb and first finger to force it open, forcing him to watch as the needle approached. He was shaking, he couldn't help it; he knew his teeth were chattering, too.

"You are frightened?"

"Well, duh," said The Pan. He couldn't keep the sarcasm out of his tone. For someone devious, smart, evil and out-and-out vicious enough to beat all other Grongolian comers to the position of Lord Protector of K'Barth, Lord Vernon was being remarkably thick.

"You're about to stick a needle in my eye! Of course I'm scared." But the thing that was frightening him most was not the needle, it was that he was about to tell the truth.

"Just below your eye; like this," said Lord Vernon as he injected half a syringe full of Truth Serum into The Pan's face. Arnold in the Skies that smarted! He screamed in a manner that Big Merv would undoubtedly have termed 'girlie', but at least, on the up side, it stopped him from crying.

The pain passed, though, and was quickly replaced by numbness. It spread across his face, round the back of his neck, up over his head and down his back. His chest felt numb, as if his heart had stopped. Pins and needles pulsed down his arms and legs to his feet and hands and then back to his body on an endless cycle, like breathing. Lord Vernon was waving in and out of focus. He tried to concentrate.

Where was he? What was he doing? Not talking, that's right, he mustn't talk. What was he doing again, he'd forgotten? Oh yes. He had to stay silent but he knew he couldn't. Maybe he could sing. Yes, that was it! Get something lodged in his head, a repetitive, annoying song which would drive out everything else. Something to block the honesty, an irritating song. By The Prophet's eyeballs! Why couldn't he think of an irritating song when he needed one?

After a few minutes, the pins and needles abated and he was able to focus. Not that he wanted to, since the only thing in his immediate field of vision was Lord Vernon. On the upside, he had finally remembered an annoying nursery rhyme and it was buzzing around his brain like a bluebottle in a jar. He took several deep breaths and waited for the questioning to begin.

"Let us start with something simple," said Lord Vernon. "What is your name?"

"I'm The Pan of Hamgee," said The Pan's mouth before his brain could do anything to shut it up. Oh dear, this was going to be ugly. Concentrate on the rhyme, concentrate on the rhyme.

"Occupation?"

The Pan could feel his mouth forming the words but with an immense effort of self control, he managed to say nothing. He felt wobbly, as if he was using somebody else's legs or at the least, borrowed knees.

"Resistance," murmured Lord Vernon, "from you? I am surprised. Perhaps you are your father's son after all." He took the syringe, grabbed The Pan by the face and injected the rest of the liquid just below his other eye.

"What did you do that for?" The Pan tried to say, but since his tongue felt like a large rubber brick, all that came out was incoherent mumbling.

"I'm sorry? I didn't catch that," said Lord Vernon. He stood back to admire his handiwork and The Pan watched him muzzily. He was looking

262

at his watch, presumably waiting for the effects of the second dose of Truth Serum to kick in. The Pan concentrated on the nursery rhyme. He could only remember the first line. Never mind, it was annoying enough and it was stuck in his head alright.

After a suitable interval, Lord Vernon started his questioning again, but at the deep end this time.

"You stole to order for an old man who is, undoubtedly, very much alive. You may, or may not, know his name, Robin Get, Sir Robin Get—although naturally, as a GBI, his title is revoked and illegal."

In spite of, or perhaps because of, the gallons of Truth Serum coursing through his veins, The Pan wanted to laugh. What a great name! It should have been Big Merv's, since he was far more of a robbin' get than the old man. With a monumental effort he managed not to smile. Ha, poker face was in position! Or was it merely palsied by too much Truth Serum? Who cared? The issue, now, was to keep it there.

"He shares your inability to conform." This was not intended as a compliment, but The Pan was flattered. In his view people who refused to conform were the people with enough brains to think about what they were asked to do. "He comes from an old banking family but he rejected their morals and became a Nimmist priest, the High Priest, by the time we purged this nation of religion."

Interesting. It hadn't occurred to The Pan that he would learn anything like this from Lord Vernon and he made a mental note to try and remember the old man's name, at least. If he was really the High Priest, then perhaps The Pan should be a bit more deferential in future, too. If he had one, of course.

"So," Lord Vernon continued, "your landladies—oh yes, I know about them, too—introduced you to Sir Robin, and he hired the Mervinettes to conduct a robbery. You took a safety deposit box containing the one definitive tool used in the Looking from the world's most impregnable bank, I must congratulate you on your achievement. What was in that box? What was it that you stole?"

Once again The Pan's mouth went straight into action. This wasn't good. He was going to ruin everything. What was it Gladys and the old man had called it? 'Civilisation as we know it' – yeh, that was a goner. Then The Pan's ears, which had been concentrating on other things, caught the tail end of what he'd been saying.

"I asked you what you stole," said Lord Vernon, his voice soft with evil intent. "I will not do so, politely, again."

"A box," said The Pan's brain, "I'm a little teapot!" said his mouth. It was working! Result! On the downside, he could see it was not the result Lord Vernon was looking for, and in that respect it might be, well ... if not dangerous, then uncomfortable.

He watched as, slowly and deliberately, the Lord High Protector of K'Barth removed his sunglasses, folded them carefully and put them in a pouch on his belt. Then, in a blur of lightning-fast movement, he punched The Pan in the face, the force making his head snap sideways. More pain, more pins and needles, but very little time to acclimatise before an equally hard punch in the stomach. The guard must have let go of him, because he was on the floor now. He felt his body lift with the impact as Lord Vernon kicked him and he rolled himself into a ball, gasping and wheezing.

"I'm a little teapot!" he said. Instead of 'ouch'.

"Do not play games with me," shouted Lord Vernon, savagely kicking The Pan again, "you may be a fool, but whatever you told the Resistance, I know you have wits enough not to have thrown the items you stole out of the snurd window! Where is Sir Robin Get? Where are the things you took?"

"I don't know! In the basement of the Parrot and Screwdriver!" said The Pan's brain, "I'm a little teapot!" said his mouth. Lord Vernon picked him up by the scruff of the neck and threw him sideways. He was almost winded by the impact as he hit the front of the desk; never mind, at least it was flat – a single leg would have done a lot more damage. He rolled over and tried to get to his feet, but Lord Vernon was too quick. Grabbing him again he hauled him over the top, the blotter and its contents scattering in all directions as he did so, and flung him into the chair.

"Tie him down," he ordered one guard, and to the other: "Get me more Truth Serum! His resistance is astounding."

While the guards did as they were told he glared at The Pan, his anger almost tangible, dripping across the space between them like molten lead.

"Clearly, I have underestimated you," he hissed, "but no-one can resist the Truth Serum for long. One way or another, you will tell me everything I wish to know."

Nope. Oh ho ho.

"I'm a little teapot?"

Three more syringes-full later, The Pan could say nothing else. He hoped Truth Serum wore off as he didn't want to spend the rest of his life with a four-word vocabulary. Not that it wasn't convenient right now, or that the rest of his life was likely to extend long enough for it to matter. He had been kicked and beaten – he suspected Denarghi had already broken his nose – and now he also had a black eye, judging by the way it was smarting. Lord Vernon could certainly pack a punch and the ring worn by 40 generations of architraves hadn't helped. The Pan wished, even more keenly than before, that he had never sold the wretched thing.

Chapter 63

Lord Vernon took a knife from his belt. Not a penknife, a great big hunting affair, with a blade about six inches long. Marvellous, thought The Pan; thumped, kicked and now cut. Smiling nastily, Lord Vernon waited long enough for the sweat to appear on The Pan's face, before viciously spinning the swivel chair round and cutting the ropes binding him into it. He spun the chair back, a little more slowly and stepped away.

"Stand up," he said.

The Pan, borrowed knees aside, managed, by concentrating very hard, to do as he was told. It was a bit like trying to stand after one too many of Gladys' home-made Calvados or high-alcohol beers. Difficult, but not impossible if you swayed backwards and forwards with the right momentum.

"It would seem you are impervious to the Truth Serum. That is," Lord Vernon waved the knife in an expansive gesture, "inconvenient—not to mention unusual—but not insurmountable." He spoke to the guards.

"You may leave us, gentlemen," he said without taking his eyes off The Pan. "If you cannot tell me the information I require, then you will have to show me."

What in the name of The Prophet was he on about?

"Perhaps you think I am stupid?"

The Pan realised he must have been looking quizzical, and tried to rearrange his bruised face into a noncommittal expression. He would have liked to have said that the idea of Lord Vernon being a fool would be the last thing he thought, but he feared another 'I'm a little teapot' might provoke the Lord Protector to do more with the knife than wave it about. At all costs he must survive this interview and warn his friends of the danger they were in. He shook his head.

"Good."

The Pan watched as, for a second time, Lord Vernon turned his back and walked away across the room. His neck ached, and since he could do so unobserved, he rolled his shoulders, rolled his head from side to side and then backwards, looking up. He was standing almost in the great inglenook fireplace and far away in the distance, high up the chimney, he could see a patch of sky. It was a big opening, you could climb up there, possibly right to the top where a well-built Grongle, no matter how prone to violence, might not be able to follow. He'd have a gun, of course, or he'd throw the knife, so it wouldn't make any difference unless ... there were darker patches which might have been other chimneys; if it was a main flue and others joined it, that would add the option of a passage into another room. It would be a gamble, a dangerous gamble but then, being trapped in Lord Vernon's office with Lord Vernon was a fairly life-threatening situation. The Pan realised, with alarm, that the Lord Protector had turned round without his noticing.

"Perhaps you are thinking of trying to escape?"

Was it so obvious? The Pan shook his head.

"I see you do not understand the hopelessness of your situation. Your efforts to withstand the Truth Serum for which," the casual wave of the hand again, "I must grudgingly admit my admiration, will not save your friends. Incidentally, if I believed you were able to tell me I would be interested in knowing your method. However," he twirled the knife from one hand to the other, "I fear I will lose control and do something I may subsequently regret if you inform me, once again, that you are a little teapot."

The Pan wanted to reply but in light of Lord Vernon's threat, he kept quiet. Anyway, if he listened, he might learn something he could use.

"I must say this in your favour, Hamgeean, you are full of surprises. Once you had shared your knowledge with me I had anticipated ending you, here, now. However, since you have verbally inconvenienced yourself in this intriguing manner, I must alter my plan. Unwittingly, I believe you may have presented me with a greater opportunity. You see, since you are unable to tell me the whereabouts of Sir Robin, I have no choice but to spare your life in order that you may lead me to him."

The Pan couldn't believe his luck. He'd disappear and make sure the Grongles never found him again; it'd be a piece of cake. He would warn Gladys and Ada, he would find the old man and warn him and then he would step through his thimble into the girl's world and live there. He might not know how it worked but he would soon learn, and it had to be a better version of the universe than the one in which he currently resided.

"Don't think I would set you free if there was any chance of escape. I know what you are thinking but even there, I will find you."

Did he though? Did he know about the girl's world?

The Pan shifted from one foot to the other and trod on something. Of course, strewn about the floor, mostly round his feet, were the things which had been neatly set out on the desk, until he had been dragged bodily across the top of it, that was. Carefully, because the Truth Serum had given him even more of a monster headache, he bent down and began to pick them up, setting them out across the blotter again in a wonky row. It was good to do something small and mundane, it helped to balance his mind, or at least to focus it on a more normal and useful train of thought than the current one, which was firmly centred around his fear.

There was the usual stuff, pen, ruler, pencil, blotter and of course, the keys to his snurd. Should he? No. Tempting though it was to slip them into his pocket, he placed them on the blotter. Lord Vernon was too sharp, he would notice they were missing. But, as The Pan picked them up, he was able to press the homing button without being seen. He had no real hope. Apart from the receipt, there'd been no word from Snurd so it probably wasn't finished, in which case the homing function wouldn't work, and even if it came to his aid, what could it do, outside, with him indoors?

Apart from his hat, which he put on, there were some strange items which reminded him of the loot Sir Robin had taken from him when he came to visit him that night at the Parrot. The first was a thing that looked like a gyroscope, only not, because it had a stand with a dial and a pointer. The second was a fountain pen and a round gold ... was that a powder compact? Yep. Interesting. The pen and compact were replicas, by the looks of things. There was a box, exactly like the one he and the Mervinettes had stolen from the Bank of Grongolia. For a moment he thought it was the same one, and felt as if his heart had stopped. Closer examination showed it to be different, though. The carving wasn't as good quality, for starters and it was newer. Another replica? He opened it. Yep. Definitely modern. Too badly finished inside for the real deal and no piece of paper. There was also a thimble, like his own.

He turned it over. Lord Vernon was watching him, so he didn't dare put it to his eye, but he was able to catch a glimpse of something white in the bottom, daylight? Yes, it must be, the thimble was, after all, very similar to The Pan's but silver like the old man's – or platinum, perhaps? He placed it on the blotter with the rest.

"You understand what that is." More of a statement than a question.

"I'm a little tea—" he began, before noticing the way the blade of Lord Vernon's knife reflected the light, and stopped abruptly. He nodded.

"Good."

After successfully resisting the Truth Serum The Pan felt different. Brave would be an exaggeration but something in him felt better. Without appreciating what he was doing, he looked up at Lord Vernon's face. Still no sunglasses. The icy eyes bored into his, but to his surprise he was able to meet their gaze. Indeed, it was Lord Vernon who looked away first. A brief millisecond glance at the desk before continuing to glare at The Pan but still a minute concession. There were advantages to being tanked up with Truth Serum, then. Pity about the headache.

"And by that knowledge, you will also understand that you have no secrets from me."

The Pan shrugged. Clearly everyone in the entire world had a thimble through which they were watching him the way he had watched the girl – presumably, bearing in mind what Sir Robin had said about listening being an easy enough skill, with full sensurround sound. Gits.

"An artefact with as much power as this," Lord Vernon held up The Pan's thimble again before placing it on the desk next to the other one, "is clearly wasted on you. Rest assured I will use it to its full capacity."

"Oh yeh? I'd like to see you work out how to use it for yourself—" began The Pan's brain angrily. He was annoyed; it wasn't as if he'd been given any tuition. "I'm a little tea—" he heard himself say but again, he stopped talking as soon as he caught Lord Vernon's expression.

"Do that once more and I will be involuntarily compelled to act in a way you may find painful," said the Grongle coolly. "Sir Robin and your father, as members of the Underground and the Council of the Choosing, conducted the Looking and found a Candidate. Despite the escape of their colleagues initially, I soon apprehended all the members of the Council except Sir Robin. Of course, as you know, those captured included your father ..."

A long, long pause to let the gravity of what he was saying sink in.

"Unfortunately, despite my best persuasive entreaties, none of them were kind enough to share the Candidate's identity with me before they died."

Oh Arnold no. Not that.

The Pan's legs felt distinctly wobbly. It wasn't only the Truth Serum, it was that phrase: 'persuasive entreaties'.

It meant Lord Vernon must have beaten and tortured them to try and make them confess. It meant his father had been in this very situation, only probably worse. It meant he was going to keel over unless he concentrated very hard on standing upright.

The Pan's mind was foggy, he felt sick and angry, but for the first time since he was eight years old, he also felt he shared a common bond with his father. He didn't know whether to be elated at the idea or to cry for what he must have suffered.

"Doubtless even a creature as lacking in drive as you, can appreciate that I am ambitious. I was no more content then with being a sergeant, than I am with being Lord Protector of K'Barth, now. If I am Architrave though, the people will accept my rule as law."

A horrible thought which made The Pan wince.

"You think I can never be Architrave because I am not the Candidate? You are correct, for the moment, but I am a great believer in the maxim 'knowledge is power'. I have studied Nimmism. You see these objects here?" He gestured to the stuff on the desk. Even with a brief glance, The Pan could see him checking them, and was glad he hadn't palmed his keys. "These are not ordinary things, these are the tools used in the Looking."

Not all of them, thought The Pan. He reckoned two of them were fake and he knew for sure that wasn't the real box.

"Long ago," Lord Vernon continued, "there was a constitutional crisis when the Architrave was killed in an accident before his time and a Candidate was not found. In order to ensure continuity, the Nimmist priests were able to establish a false Candidate, one who showed some, though not all, of the signs. This woman was Head of State for twenty years until a real Candidate was found and the true order of things restored. I believe you may know this."

The Pan remembered the old man telling him the same story. Oh dear, Lord Vernon was remarkably well-informed.

"Here we are, a few short years after the untimely death of the last Architrave with a Candidate who, if he does exist—and I believe he does—is unknown to his people and dare not come forward. And here am I, with the information and the skill to establish myself artificially as Candidate in his place. The situation is quite simple: if he challenges my authority, I will kill him. If he does not challenge me soon, I will be established in his stead and the thread will be broken forever. There will be no more Candidates. I will be Architrave and I will choose my successor."

The Pan shook his head.

"You disagree?"

Mutely, The Pan nodded.

"Because you think the thread will never be broken? Because you think the people will never believe? Oh they may hate me, but they are malleable enough and they have no stomach for a fight, if they see the right signs, they will convince themselves."

Surely not; The Pan was ready to admit that people in groups are often dim, but believing Lord Vernon was the Candidate would be a step too far for the lobotomised – or would it? The Pan remembered another part of his conversation with the old man, about how conservative people are, how they tend to prefer the world they are used to even when offered the prospect of a better one. But Lord Vernon as Candidate? No-one would buy that.

"I'm a little—" Lord Vernon glanced sharply at him. The Pan stopped himself and shook his head.

"I think you underestimate the passivity of this nation's populace. The people *will* believe and, if you are alive to witness it, you will see them elect me Architrave and obey my word. In time, my remarkable success will be noted in Grongolia, and having proved myself here, my rise to power, there, shall be inevitable. I will own this planet and everything on it."

World domination. It figured. Lord Vernon was, after all, a power-hungry psychopath, everyone knew that.

Even so, thought The Pan, surely people would have to realise. In forty generations the Architraves had sometimes been eccentric – there was that one with the thing about chickens – but none of them had ever been evil. The Pan glanced up at the Lord Protector's grey eyes, the colour of lead and cold as marble. Human eyes yet lacking any shred of humanity.

"You seem unconvinced," there was an underlying hint of glee to Lord Vernon's tone, "true, while any bona fide Candidate lives, even after my installation as Architrave, there is a negligible risk he could lead a revolt," he snorted, "why, there is an even smaller risk that it might be successful. But as I have explained to you, even now the thread is weak; when I have found and killed him it will be broken," that casual wave of the hand again, "the people will believe, and K'Barth will belong to me."

271

Had Lord Vernon told his father this? The Pan wondered.

"Sir Robin is the last person alive who knows the identity of the Candidate. So, you will return to his side and you will ingratiate yourself with him."

The Pan raised a sceptical eyebrow. The old boy was smarter than that.

"If he is here in K'Barth then he will, doubtless, need a chauffeur. Your skills in that direction are undeniably impressive and he will not pass up the chance to utilise them. Thus, when you have won his trust—which you will—and discovered the whereabouts of the Candidate, you will inform me; I will remove this impediment from my path and assume my rightful place."

The Pan shook his head.

"Perhaps you misunderstand me. You do not have a choice. You know what this is?" He picked up The Pan's thimble and looked into it for a moment. Then he placed it on the table and made a complicated set of hand movements over it. The Pan took a careful note, he might find them useful in future. Yeh right, what future? This was Lord Vernon ...

Once finished Lord Vernon held it up again.

"This is a portal. A very useful item, it can be used for travel or viewing pleasure." He pointed the open end towards The Pan, more or less at eye level. "It is a quantum mechanical device powered by the imagination or desires of the owner. By holding it, you establish a connection to your mind. Thus, by imagining the place to which you are travelling or the items you wish to see, you allow the portal to reveal them. Insert your thumb to travel, and if required you can be transported many thousands of miles, immediately. This you understand, yes?"

The Pan nodded.

"Then, look and see for yourself. Do not touch it or you will interfere with the connection and see what you wish to see rather than the view I have prepared for you."

The Pan squinted in, he was very afraid he knew the scene that would greet him, but it was still a shock when the girl's face appeared. She was on her own, walking down a street and he would have thought that he'd accidentally touched the thimble or affected it somehow, were it not for the fact that there was sound. Not from the girl, herself, she was alone, after all, but she was surrounded by traffic, birdsong and the voices of a couple who passed her, deep in conversation. Her clothes were smarter than usual and he wondered where she was going. It appeared to be getting dark, so wherever it was, she was probably going there after work. He hoped, hopelessly, it wasn't a date.

"There is a girl?" asked Lord Vernon. The Pan nodded. "A very particular girl?" The Pan didn't nod his head but clearly his expression was eloquent enough.

"Good," Lord Vernon chuckled ominously as he put the portal down on the desk beside the other one, "then perhaps you are beginning to understand your situation fully. Do you know what this is?" he asked as he began to set up the thing that was like a gyroscope, only not.

The Pan shook his head.

"Among other functions this denotes the significance of people. For want of better words let us call it ... an Importance Detector. Most people score one or two out of ten because in the eyes of Arnold, The Prophet, everyone is of some importance." The scorn in his voice made it clear that he was at variance with The Prophet in this view. "No-one scores more than eight, except the Candidate who will usually score nine or a maximum ten. I say, usually, because some Candidates have only attained a high score of eight." He set it up with the dial pointing towards The Pan and pulled a lever which set it spinning. Flecks of blue light flew across it and it hummed quietly. The needle flipped to the top of the dial, sank slowly to zero and after remaining there for a few seconds began to flip wildly from zero to ten.

"Interesting," said Lord Vernon slowly. "It is unable to determine your significance. Perhaps that is because you are about to perform an important act—the betrayal of your precious Candidate. No matter, let us see if we can achieve a reading for her." He gestured to the thimble, turned the Importance Detector round and performed some more complicated hand movements over both it and the thimble before pulling the lever again. The needle flipped straight round to seven and stayed there.

"She is not the Candidate," said Lord Vernon, answering The Pan's immediate thought. "As I explained, she must score eight or over; seven is not enough. Even so, she is Chosen. Her name is Ruth. She does not live here; hers is a parallel universe, different and yet the same. Naturally, as a civilised being, her first language is Grongolian.

"Her fate is inextricably linked with that of the future Architrave—I believe love may enter the equation—perhaps she is going to give me an heir." He laughed; a distinctly lascivious laugh.

The Pan was repulsed and wished he was brave enough to thump him, not to mention strong enough for it to be worth bothering. Lord Vernon laughed even more.

"You are angry."

Arnold in the Skies! Was he that transparent?

"You are fond of her? Oh that's priceless," he sneered, in a way that demonstrated he regarded affection as a weakness. "Then you will be all the more willing as my accomplice. Your situation is simple: you will find out where the true Candidate is and you will bring him to me or," he clicked his knuckles, "I am afraid I will be compelled to hurt this girl."

Chapter 64

The Pan felt as if the world was collapsing round him. Logic dictated that his feelings for the girl, Ruth, could be nothing more than a crush. After all, he hadn't even known her name until Lord Vernon told him. Then again, he'd never been one to listen to logic. There was something about her which had taken hold of him. She haunted his dreams and most of his waking thoughts. He realised how little he knew about her or her world, how completely powerless he was to help her.

"Do not waste your time fantasising! She will never love you," said Lord Vernon spitefully, "good taste aside, her destiny will not allow it. She will have eyes only for the Candidate, or when He is gone, His replacement—for He has chosen her."

It wasn't just the Candidate who had chosen her, The Pan thought, sadly. Lord Vernon went on.

"I should warn you she is also under my protection, so if you try to reach her I will ensure my guards intercept her first. Now, it is time for you to leave. Remember," he gestured to the two thimbles, standing side by side on the desk, "I will be watching your every move. Your *every* move, do you understand?"

The Pan stood defeated, crushed and in despair; Lord Vernon had outwitted him on all levels – and then as the Grongle turned his back and walked to the door to summon the guards, The Pan was distracted by something outside.

"APT tubes engaged, please stand clear," said an electronic female voice. A voice which, in his view, was a very sexy one.

Oh yes.

With an almighty crash, the window at the other end of the room blew in. The snurd, his snurd, was, well ... if not finished then armed and angry. He wasted no time. Remembering to grab his keys and both thimbles from the desk, he ran towards the window, jumped onto the sill and as Lord Vernon made to grab him, leapt out into the darkness. He landed on the bonnet of the SE2 which was waiting for him, top conveniently down so he could jump straight in. If he hadn't known it was an inanimate object and unable to think for itself, he would have sworn it flipped him up so he landed in the seat. The automatic getaway option engaged and it accelerated at high speed, while The Pan wrestled to get into position at the controls to stop it smashing into the buildings opposite. Yanking at the wheel he careened upwards, the undercarriage almost clipping the mortar.

The snurd's shadow skipped over the windows and brickwork as it flew and sparks showered past it as both guards fired at him with machine guns and Lord Vernon with a laser pistol. Once at the top, he flipped it over the roof of the building and sped off into the night.

****

Lord Vernon stood at the remains of his office window and looked out over the city. That was a surprise.

Plus points to this situation? The Pan of Hamgee was gone with the most prized of all the portals, but he had no idea how powerful it was or how easy it would make him to follow if he used it. He had a certain spirit and his ability to resist the Truth Serum was unique, but he was a snivelling coward and not his father's son. Sooner or later, he would use the portal and when he did, he would be traced. Meanwhile, the boffins were making good progress reverse engineering the bronze thimble, and he had the copper one. A temporary setback then, most likely.

The barrel of the laser gun was still warm from firing but had cooled enough to put back in the holster now. He rubbed it on his jacket, to replace the charge, before doing so. The sudden movement made one of the guards next to him step nervously backwards. Time to sort out the logistics.

"You! Wait where you are," he ordered. He took out his mobile phone and again, rubbed it on his jacket to give the power a boost before pressing the speed dial button for General Moteurs. He strode across the room, phone clamped to his ear and the general answered after one ring. "Tell your troops to apprehend the Chosen One and bring her to me," he said shortly, and without giving the general time to say anything, pressed the red button. Now ...

He turned to the two guards, flipping his phone closed and dropping it into his pocket as he did so. They had allowed the Pan of Hamgee to escape. He would have to punish them for their failure. He smiled. That would be a treat. Yes, it was important to see the positives in a situation.

They stood, mutely, waiting for orders. He smoothed the suede gloves over his hands and adjusted the rings to maximise their impact. All the while he kept his eyes on them. He allowed his anger to build, gradually revealing it in his face and his expression. They reflected it back, in their fear. Could he be bothered to walk over there and hit them? No.

"Come here," he said, "both of you."

They did as they were told.

****

When he was flying straight, with no immediate sign of pursuers, The Pan of Hamgee took a few moments to check his options. No sliding dash any more, just machined and polished metal with rows of buttons and switches, all neatly labelled, many with options The Pan had never encountered. A large green arrow, pointing to a small hole, flashed on and off. Beside the hole was a button.

Well aware that he would be wise to read the instruction manual first, he pressed it.

"Transference drive cannot be engaged, insert portal device into portal plug and try again." The plastic lip round the hole illuminated blue. It looked thimble-shaped and both the old man and Lord Vernon had called the thimble a portal. What the heck? If he could get to the girl with wheels he would have a much better chance of whisking her away from her Grongolian guards. He put the first of the two thimbles, Lord Vernon's, into ... yes, he supposed that was the portal plug. It fitted remarkably well.

"Transference drive engaged," said the female electronic voice. What in the name of The Prophet was a transference drive?

Mmm. Only one way to find out, he thought to himself and imagined the girl – Ruth as he now knew she was called. A small image of her was projected onto the windscreen. She was standing at the top of a staircase in what looked like some kind of public space although what it was for he couldn't tell. She was talking to another woman who, The Pan noted with relief, wasn't Grongolian. However, two very tall gentlemen were making their way along the landing behind her about a hundred yards to the right. They were almost but not quite human-coloured; pinkish but pale with a hint of green. Colour aside, the Grongolian army uniforms they wore were a bit of a giveaway.

"To transfer to your chosen destination, press the red button," said the voice. For all his anxiety The Pan still found the time to notice it sounded sexy.

"Yeh baby!" said his brain, "I'm a little teapot," said his mouth. He sighed, rolled his eyes and did as the sexy voice instructed. There was a loud sucking sound, receding bathwater style, and a pop, followed by the sound of breaking glass. Oh dear, there had been a window. It wasn't there now of course, since The Pan had flown straight through it. He landed at the bottom of the stairs, skidding sideways to a halt with a loud squealing of tyres, in a shower of broken glass which continued to fall for some seconds after the snurd had stopped. Hmm. Less of a window, more the front of the building by the look of it. Ah. It wasn't only the girl who froze at his sudden arrival. Everyone did. She was halfway down the stairs by this time, out at the front of a crowd which was flowing out of – mmm what was that, a temple, a concert hall? Something big, anyway. The two Grongles he had seen were still to her right, pushing their way towards her through the throng of people.

"Ruth!" he stood up in the driver's seat and shouted. Brilliant! Maybe the Truth Serum had worn off, "I'm a little teapot." Or not. "Ruth! Look behind you!" shouted his brain, "Ruth! I'm a little teapot!" shouted his mouth. He reckoned she got the Ruth the second time, but stared at him, nonplussed. Of course! She spoke a different language!

"Ruth! I'm a little teapot!" he shouted, in Grongolian this time, the 'I'm-here-to-rescue-you' part getting lost in the fog of Truth Serum somewhere between his thoughts and his speech. Maybe it was the urgency in his voice, maybe it was the way he was gesticulating to the Grongles but something made her turn round. They started to jog purposefully in her direction and as they did The Pan leapt out of the snurd, flipping his cloak over one shoulder so it didn't trip him as he ran up the stairs towards her.

He had to make her understand. The two Grongles behind her were unhooking their guns. He stopped on the step below hers.

"Ruth." He wanted to explain that she was in danger; that she had to come with him. "I'm a little ..." he began.

By The Prophet's bogies.

Speaking wasn't going to work. He patted his pockets.

Arnold's pants! No pen.

He moved his hands backwards and forwards in front of him in the classic no-no gesture and pointed to the Grongles again. "They're going to